C[...]

"Genu[...]

"Many of these stories dance across the high wire, knowing there's no net below to catch them, but never looking down or faltering."

—Jonathan Carroll

"Peter Crowther's a remarkable writer."

—*Locus*

"Peter Crowther writes chilling, profoundly human stories. His best stories call to mind an honor roll of mid-twentieth-century dark fantasists: Ray Bradbury, Charles Beaumont, Richard Matheson, Rod Serling. A delicious collection."

—Michael Bishop

"In our minds there's a curtain which we generally prefer to leave in place. It's a modern thing, and a very old thing. Peter Crowther has a cunning craft of twitching the curtain. He draws it only partially aside. We glimpse only part of the horror. The rest is left to miscegenate with our own private horrors, behind our own curtains. 'Cankerman' is a classic story in this respect."

—Brian W. Aldiss

"'Cleaning Up' by Peter Crowther is an object lesson on writing a story about a haunting. Gruesome, disturbing, unsettling, and very good."

—*Interzone*

"Peter Crowther is not only a great storyteller, he's also a first-rate guide through the darkest regions of the human soul. His work is always exciting and original. He's one of the best writers we have."

—Ed Gorman

"Amid a genre strewn with dim exertions, Peter Crowther's work pirouettes. His sly grace disturbs invisibly; blueblood voodoo."

—Richard Christian Matheson

"Peter Crowther's 'Too Short a Death' is a cracker of a vampire tale."

—*All Hallows, The Journal of the Ghost Story Society*

PETER CROWTHER

THE LONGEST
SINGLE NOTE

LEISURE BOOKS   NEW YORK CITY

A LEISURE BOOK®

April 2003

Published by

Dorchester Publishing Co., Inc.
276 Fifth Avenue
New York, NY 10001

ISBN 0-8439-5078-1

Visit us on the web at www.dorchesterpub.com.

Affectionately dedicated to all practitioners of the short story form . . . and to all those readers who support them. Small is beautiful—spread the word!

CONTENTS

THE LONGEST
SINGLE NOTE

All We Know of Heaven

Adam sat with the rest of the fifth grade on the grass out-side Forest Plains School. The greensward ran down from the school entrance to Sycamore Drive, where a high, metal fence separated the children from the sidewalk. Momentarily oblivious of the other children and squinting his eyes at the sun's glare, reflected off the windows of the Forest Plains General Hospital diagonally opposite, he looked up the street to the corner of Sycamore and Main.

Still squinting, and now holding his hand above his eyes as though he were saluting, Adam watched a man cross by the intersection and jog the last few steps to get out of the way of a car, which had slowed down anyway to turn from Main onto Sycamore. The man waved to the car, smiling. The man in the car waved back, also smiling.

Adam felt the warmth of the smiles. It was as strong as the May sunshine. Even stronger. Thinking about it, maybe that was the warmth he most missed at home: smiles.

He turned back to see Mrs. Stewart come out of the school holding a book. A movement by his side caused him to turn in time to see Jimmy Jorgensson finger a thick booger out of his left nostril and casually wipe his hand on

1

Peter Crowther

the grass. "Save some for lunch, Jimmy," Mrs. Stewart trilled as she moved her chair around so that it faced the group. The assembled children tittered. She missed nothing.

Chrissie Clemmons, sitting cross-legged in front of them, leaned back and whispered, "That's another piece of brain you'll never use, JJ."

Adam smiled.

Jimmy gave Chrissie a Bronx cheer, just like Adam had seen his father do at the ball game, only without the volume. Chrissie stuck out a tongue reddened by eating raspberry candies and leaned forward again.

"Okay, class," Mrs. Stewart announced, "let's settle down now." She took her seat and smoothed out her skirt.

Brian Macready had once told a small group of wide-eyed would-be playboys that he'd seen up that skirt once, all the way to Mrs. Stewart's pubes. "I tell you," he'd said conspiratorially, "the lady wears no pants." They'd been in fourth grade then and Adam had taken every opportunity to check out the facts.

Face it: It was his duty.

He had dropped pencils, math books, erasers and all manner of other objects just to get a glimpse of the fabled thatch. But no luck. Just a missed recess for continued clumsiness—he'd been trying for almost an entire week. It had been a timely reminder of the benefits of subtlety and, although he remained vigilant, Adam learned to pick his opportunities only when they actually presented themselves.

But since then, whenever Mrs. Stewart crossed her legs or lifted one leg as she bent down to pick up something from the floor, Adam turned away.

The reason was that Mrs. Stewart was a mother. Okay, so Barnaby Stewart was only six years old—"That's just one step up from an erection," the worldly Chrissie Clemmons had confided to Adam and several others one day behind the gym—but some things just weren't done. And Adam sure wouldn't like anybody trying to get a flash of his mother's private parts. No sir! Particularly with his mom in the hospital and all defenseless. In fact, he might just have to haul off and smack them in the face it he ever caught somebody doing it. Which is just the way he always felt when he went with his father to visit her and they were interrupted by some doctor who wanted to check her over.

Check her over.

It always sounded so ominous. And, hand-in-hand with his sad-faced father, Adam would schlep out of his mother's room while the doctor pulled the screens around the bed and went to work. But doing *what*?

Adam felt his cheeks go red as he imagined the doctor lifting his mother's white gown. *"Hmm, nice bush, Mrs. Showell. Now, if you have no objections, I'd just like to—"*

Adam shook the thought out of his head. The comment would have been a waste of time, anyway. His mother never objected to anything anymore.

In fact, she never *did* anything anymore.

Adam reached out and pulled a few blades of grass, scrunched them up in his hand and looked up. Mrs. Stewart was holding up a book for everyone to see.

"... of our finest writers," she was saying.

He read the book's title. Boy, was it long. *The Acts of King Arthur and His Noble Knights: From the Winchester Manuscripts of Thomas Mallory.*

"That's not a title, it's a sentence—a life one!" Felipe Stroymaur hissed behind his hand with a snigger. Felipe kind of had the image of himself as a comedian and there was no doubt that, at least to the ten-going-on-eleven-year-old inmates of Forest Plains School's fifth grade, he'd be following in the footsteps of Eddie Murphy and Steve Martin. Even Mrs. Stewart had to laugh at him sometimes, though she usually tried to do it without anyone noticing. Everyone did, of course.

"Felipe, you are *so* precocious," Mrs. Stewart droned.

"Thank you, ma'am," he replied, and there was another around of sniggers.

Life sentence.

Those were the words that the doctor had used to Adam's father last week when they had made their usual weekend visit to the hospital. Adam only went down there on Saturday and Sunday afternoons. His father would have him wear his best pants and a shirt and they would drive down to the hospital and sit by his mom for an hour or so.

3

During the entire visit, John Showell would hold his wife's hand and just stare at her. Or he would stare at the stack of screens and dials on the table by her side, watching the little green lines and digital displays give out an occasional blip every few seconds.

Adam had not been with his mom and dad when the delivery truck had sideswiped their car, but there were times—dark times when the lights were out and he could hear his father walking the night floors, drinking coffee and smoking cigarettes—that he almost wished that he had. He would get out of bed every now and again and go into his father's room and watch him sitting on his mom's side of the bed, whispering to her photograph.

"John Steinbeck was born in Salinas, California, in nineteen hundred and two," Mrs. Stewart said, in a tone designed to create amazement. "And he was awarded the Nobel Prize for Literature in 1962. Anyone know what that is?"

Nobody did, apparently.

"The Nobel Prize . . ."

As Mrs. Stewart explained, Adam stared at the book's cover.

It showed a gray, armor-suited knight on horseback, reining back and waving his sword. His horse wore what looked like a green-and-brown patchwork quilt, all the way from the tip of its tail to the point of its nose. The lines on the knight's helmet made him look brave—even the horse looked brave. Adam wondered what it must have been like to be a knight in the days of King Arthur.

He glanced around at the other children and saw that they were settling down, becoming engrossed. Mrs. Stewart was reading from the book.

" '. . . a great block of marble, and in the marble was set a steel anvil in which a sword was driven. In letters of gold was written: WHOEVER PULLS THIS SWORD FROM THIS STONE AND ANVIL IS KING OF ALL ENGLAND BY RIGHT OF BIRTH.' " Her voice had assumed a booming resonance as she read from the inscription. Now she lowered the volume again and, with a slight breeze blowing through her hair, she leaned forward to the children.

" 'The people were amazed,' " Mrs. Stewart continued, " 'and carried the news of the miracle to the Archbishop, who said, *Go back into the church and pray to God. And let no man touch the sword until High Mass is sung*. And this they did, but when the service was over, all the lords went to look at the stone and the sword, and some tried to draw out the blade, but no one could move it.

" '*The man is not here who will draw this sword*, said the Archbishop, *but do not doubt that God will make him known*.' "

Mrs. Stewart paused while she pulled back a piece of hair that had blown over her eyes. Adam watched her, open-mouthed. The words from the book had triggered off a memory.

No one could move it.

When Mrs. Stewart resumed her place in the tale of King Arthur and the sword, Excalibur, Adam was not listening. Instead, he was thinking back to the first time that he and his father had visited the hospital. It was something he had replayed in his mind many times over the months that he and his father had been living alone.

John Showell had still been limping badly, even though it was already a month since the accident. And he wore a bandage and a large pad over his right eye, where his face had collided with the back of Angela Showell's head. Then she had rebounded into the window on her own side of the car just in time to take the impact as the truck's back end smashed into them. The Showell family car, an eleven-year-old Dodge sedan, had mounted the curb halfway along Beech Street and taken down the telephone pole. The Dodge's wheel arch had pushed back through the engine block, snaking the pedal-stems off the floor like gunshots. At the time, John Showell's feet had been pressing on those pedals and, even now, almost eight months since the accident, he walked with difficulty.

But John Showell had got off lightly compared with his wife.

Adam's dad hadn't allowed Adam to visit the hospital at first because Angela Showell's face had been so badly hurt. But finally the day came and Adam dressed his best, taking particular care with his appearance. He even bought a small bunch of bluebonnets—with his own allowance—from Wild Things over on High Street. The owner, Geoff Macavoy, whose son, Danny, was also in fifth grade, knew all about the accident and he didn't want to take Adam's money. But Adam had insisted.

Sitting on the grass, with Mrs. Stewart's voice droning pleasantly in the background, Adam remembered Mr. Macavoy's eyes and how they looked so shiny.

Later that first afternoon, Adam had walked into Forest Plains General Hospital with his silent father, listening to the sound of their shoes clacking on the polished floors. They had gone through the large, automatic glass doors, past a large, circular reception desk and along a long corridor to the elevators. His father, who now seemed to carry a fog of cigarette smoke with him wherever he went, had pressed the button and waited, hands in his pants pockets. Adam had been surprised that his father had taken no flowers himself, nor even any candies.

The elevator had arrived with a *ting* and they got in. Adam's father had pressed "4" and leaned against the back of the elevator car. The doors had closed with a *shusssh*, and Adam had felt the initial jerking movement of the car as it started up. But then there had seemed not to be any motion at all. He had supposed it was so they could carry really sick people around in there without spilling things.

The *ting* of the elevator arriving on the fourth floor had seemed much quieter than when Adam had been standing waiting for it to arrive. The doors had slid open to reveal a tin sign tacked to the wall corner. The sign read:

WARD 14
INTENSIVE CARE

In an increasingly rare show of contact, John Showell had placed his arm around Adam's shoulder and, with a couple of pats, guided him out of the elevator, through a small wooden-slatted swing gate to the Ward 14 reception desk. A young nurse, who actually seemed to be not much older than the girls in his year, had smiled warmly at Adam and made a big deal out of admiring his bluebonnets. Adam had remained silent throughout the ordeal.

He had watched his father sign his name in a book on the counter and then followed him through two full-length swinging doors, which actually overlapped at the middle.

Halfway along the small corridor on the other side of the doors, Adam's father had stopped, just in front of an open door, and visibly straightened himself up. Then he had said, "Come on, Adam, let's see how your mom's doing today, huh!" And they had walked into the room.

What had he been expecting?

Throughout many of the lonely nights that followed that first visit, Adam tried to picture what he had been expecting—hoping?—to find. Whatever it had been, it was not what he discovered when he walked into the small room that Sunday afternoon, when the first fall of leaves from the trees was already making the sidewalks along Main Street slushy and the winter snows were building up across the Canadian border.

An imposter.

Someone was trying to plant an imposter in his family.

There, stretched out on a metal cot, its frail arms attached by wires and tubes to a host of blinking and dripping objects, was an emaciated husk of humankind. He had blinked, first at the absurdity of anyone trying to make him believe that this was his mom . . . and then he had blinked again, wetly this time, at the realization that it was.

The figure's mouth was slightly open, its cheekbones drawn and languid. The eyes were closed tightly, sleeping perhaps, though there was no movement beneath them. Adam realized that whatever dreams his mother dreamed now—if indeed she dreamed at all—were lonely landscapes of fractured memories, missed opportunities and failed intentions.

On her cheek was a long Band-Aid. On her head was a taped wire which led to a stacked bank of what looked like hi-fi equipment, each box showing digital displays and traveling bliplines: a second wire, attached to a pad on Angela Showell's left forearm, also ran into the equipment. Adam watched them blip, thinking that this was the only way his mom could talk to him now.

But the biggest, meanest-looking wire of all was a large-diameter tube that ran from a separate machine standing beside the bed into his mom's throat. Adam reached toward it, unthinking, and heard a voice say, "No!" sharply. He turned to his side and suddenly saw that they were not alone as he had first presumed. There was a woman in here. She rose to her feet from a chair at the side of the room, a folded copy of *Life* magazine in her hand, and smiled at him. It was a practiced smile.

"No one can move that, young man," she said.

He looked around and saw his father's glassy eyes watching him. Then he dropped the neat bundle of bluebonnets onto his mother's unmoving feet and ran to him. They cried together.

No one can move that.

"Adam?"

He blinked and looked around. The other kids were watching him. He cleared his throat and tried to smile. "Yes, ma'am," he said, recovering his composure.

"Are you with us, Adam? You wanting your lunch, is that it?"

"No . . . I mean, yes. Yes, ma'am, I'm with you."

"Good. I'm pleased to hear it." And in that split second when the rest of the class were turning their faces away from him, Mrs. Stewart slipped Adam a gentle smile—*"It's okay, Adam, I know what you're going through"*—and then spoke to the whole group. "So—anybody—what is the message we get from the story of King Arthur and Excalibur?"

A hand went up near the front.

"Yes, Sally," Mrs. Stewart said.

"Does it mean that it's good to be strong?"

Mrs. Stewart smiled and nodded. "Well, yes, it does, Sally. But the strength it talks about isn't simply physical strength like Arnold Schwarzenegger—" She held up her right arm and flexed the muscle, scowled at it and shrugged. Everyone laughed as she returned the arm to her lap. "It means a strength of purpose, too," she added. "It means . . ." She searched for the words. "It means that if your cause is good, then you will prevail."

" 'Prevail?' "

Mrs. Stewart leaned forward and rubbed a tousled blond head. "I'm sorry, Andy. 'Prevail' means 'to win' . . . 'to succeed' . . . 'to be—' "

The lunch bell sounded its clamor across the grass, and a ripple of movement began at the edges of the gathering, working its way to the middle. Within what seemed to be only a few seconds, the grass cleared of bodies and books and a tide of color swept noisily toward the school buildings and the waiting cafeteria.

Only Adam and a smiling Mrs. Stewart remained.

Adam gathered his books and walked over to her and she smiled at him warmly. "Hi, Adam."

He nodded.

"You like that story?"

He nodded again.

"Yeah, me too. It's a doozy." Mrs. Stewart ran a hand through her hair, the way Adam's mother used to do, and picked up her file of papers from the grass. "You going in to eat lunch?"

"I guess," Adam said.

"Mmm-hmm," said Mrs. Stewart, nodding. "Something you wanted to ask me maybe?"

Adam shifted his weight from foot to foot. "What were you going to say?"

"Pardon me?"

"At the end, there. You were going to say something. 'To be something,' you started to say." He took a breath. "To be *what?*"

The teacher frowned and tried to think, then shrugged. "Oh, to be something . . . yes! I think I was going to say, 'to be victorious.' "

Adam nodded.

"Is that what you meant?"

"I guess so, but just 'To be' is enough."

And he ran to the buildings leaving behind Mrs. Stewart with a puzzled expression on her face.

* * *

9

That night, after he had returned from his regular evening visit to the hospital, Adam's father sat with Bob Wissan, a friend from around the block, and talked. Bob was a doctor.

Adam had been sent upstairs to get ready for bed, but he sat cross-legged in the shadows of the upstairs landing, leaning against the banisters, listening.

"What can I tell you?" Bob said, his voice sounding sad.

"Don't speak too loud," Adam's father said.

"Oh, yes, sorry!"

Adam could hear coffee percolating. The sound was so much a part of his mother's home, her own activities, that, just for a second, Adam thought that maybe it had all been a big joke . . . a dream or something. That he could stand up and walk downstairs for his mom to pick him up and spin him around, while the smell of fresh coffee wafted through the house with the sound of her laughter and all of their collective happiness. But he knew that that wasn't to be. He listened.

"Just give it to me straight is all I ask, Bob."

"I've given it to you straight." Bob Wissan paused. "Angela isn't going to be coming home, Jack," he said. "Not tomorrow, not next week, not even next year."

"You're saying there's no chance at all?"

There was no response to that, or none that Adam could hear.

"But she's still breathing! And they told me—"

"Well, okay, yeah . . . there's a chance. One chance in a million that Angela will recover. But, I'm telling you—*me, I'm* telling you—it won't happen.

"It's the machine that breathes for her . . . through the endotracheal tube that they inserted; it's not Angela breathing, it's the machine. The tube goes all the way down her throat and into her lung. It inflates and deflates her lung—which is what you and I do by ourselves—and monitors the gases in her body. It's a mechanical procedure, nothing more."

Adam heard glasses clink and then a muffled "No thanks, Jack.

"And that's not all, Jack," Bob Wissan continued. "She

has muscle relaxants, which are designed to keep her from fighting the breathing apparatus; analgesics to keep her free from pain; hypnotics to keep her sedated—"

"Jesus Chr—"

"No, hear me out, Jack. She has drips to her subclavian vein, which take samples and provide parenteral feeding; a monitor stuck into her main artery to measure the oxygen and carbon dioxide content of the blood and to make sure the mixture of gases is correct; and an ECG to check on her heart."

Another clink.

"She's gone, Jack. Let her rest."

Adam heard a sob.

"Let her rest."

"I—I can't. God help me, I can't." John Showell sobbed. "That's like . . . that's like asking me to mourn her while she's still alive!"

Adam crept along the floor to his bedroom.

Much later, in the security of his bed, in the confines of his room, Adam clasped his hands behind his head and stared into the nighttime sky through his window. His heart was beating fast. It was now or never.

He slipped from the bed and pulled on his clothes.

As the library clock struck midnight, Adam was running through darkened back gardens, heading for Main Street. He felt like a knight on horseback, riding to rescue the fair maiden.

Adam figured that there seemed to be so many patron saints for so many things, maybe there might be one for ten-year-old boys with a mission. And, sure enough, things seemed to be going his way.

The people on the main reception desk were busy talking as he casually walked by.

The corridor to the elevators was deserted.

And, when he reached them, both of the elevators were standing open-doored . . . just like they were waiting for him. He stepped inside the one on the right and pressed the button for the fourth floor. The elevator doors closed, hissing ominously.

When the doors opened again, Adam half expected to see

11

a doctor waiting for him . . . or his father, his pajama pants on underneath his topcoat, drumming his fingers against his leg. But there was nobody. Silence reigned.

He tiptoed out onto the corridor and stepped over the swing gate. Just as he was preparing to move forward, a nurse walked out of his mom's room, stood for a second and checked her watch. She was facing a blank wall. If she turned to her left, she would walk farther down the corridor to more rooms and a group of desks. If she turned to her right, she would come face-to-face with Adam. He waited. Which way would she choose?

The nurse rubbed her face with both hands and turned left. Adam opened his mouth wide, so that his sigh of relief would be silent, and moved forward . . . into his mom's room.

The light was on but muted. It came from two wall lights, one on the wall facing the bed and the other above the chair to the right of where he stood. On the chair was a copy of *Time* magazine. It had Clint Eastwood on the cover.

The figure on the bed looked the same as it had always looked, and Adam felt a pang of guilt that he could ever have doubted that it was his mother. Her face was the same, if thinner, and her hair was just as golden and tousled. Adam wanted to speak to her, but he knew that he did not have time. He pushed the door closed behind him so that they could be alone, him and his mother.

With the steady drone of daytime hospital noises finished for the day, Adam could hear his mother breathing. But no, the sound was not coming from the bed—although his mother's frail chest moved gently up and down, up and down—but from the stack of hi-fi equipment at its side. Something in one of the boxes creaked and sighed . . . *creak* . . . *sigh* . . . *creak* . . .

He dropped to his knees and scuffled along the floor to the array of wires that led from one piece of equipment to another. It was darker down here, and he had trouble finding where everything was. But soon he saw the wall socket.

He lay down on the floor so that he was in a position to see the digital displays and the bliplines, and reached his hand out until it touched the plug. He looked up at the displays and pressed the switch.

The displays disappeared.

Adam waited to hear alarms.

There was nothing.

He shuffled back, taking great care not to disturb anything that might fall over, and stood up.

Creak . . . sigh . . . creak . . . sigh . . .

Adam's blood ran cold, as though someone had poured icy water down his back.

He looked in horror at the equipment. The displays were still out. What had gone wrong?

He knelt down beside the boxes and listened.

It was the one on the floor, the big one, that the creaking and sighing noises were coming from. He moved back and stared at the box. Switches and tiny panels covered the face.

He lay down on his stomach and looked around the back of the box. There was no wire coming from it. No wire leading to the wall socket.

Creak . . . sigh . . . creak . . . sigh. . . . Outside in the corridor footsteps sounded.

Adam rolled over soundlessly beneath his mother's bed.

The footsteps grew louder until they were right outside the door. And then they started to fade. Adam waited until he could no longer hear them and then pulled himself out from under the bed. As he reached his hand up, he touched his mom's arm. He pulled his hand back, staring at his fingers, twitching them as though he had just inadvertently dipped them into a jar of acid. He shuffled out into the light and got to his feet.

Looking down at his mother, Adam watched the almost imperceptible movements of her chest beneath the bedclothes. It matched the sounds of the machine beside her.

He moved over to the bed and sat on its side, next to her. This time, he took her hand from where it lay on her stomach, and held it in his own. It felt warm. He bent over and sniffed. It smelled of hospital . . . of drugs and medications, of machinery and wiring. It smelled of many things, but it did not smell of his mother.

He turned and glanced at the door, biting his lip nervously, then looked back at her face. It was just the same as it had always been, and yet . . . and yet it was different.

Peter Crowther

She was there but not there. It was the face of the woman who had looked after him all of his life . . . and the face of a woman he didn't know at all.

"*She's gone, Jack. Let her rest.*"

The words of Bob Wissan echoed through his head. He saw them like words on a class board, shimmering, fading. And then Mrs. Stewart's face appeared.

"*The strength isn't simple physical strength—like Arnold Schwarzenegger . . .*"

He leaned closer and whispered, "Mom? Mom . . . are you there, Mom?"

"*. . . asking me to mourn her while she's still alive.*"

Adam moved one of his hands away from his mother's hand and looked at it. It was shaking.

"*If your cause is good, then you will prevail.*"

Still holding his mother's hand tightly in his left hand, Adam reached out his right hand toward her throat. His hand was no longer shaking. Then he took hold of the thick tube, staring wide-eyed at his fingers as they folded around the wide cuff just above the thick patch on Angela Showell's neck.

" '*And Arthur grasped the sword by its handle,*' " he heard Mrs. Stewart say, " '*and easily and fiercely drew it from the anvil and the stone . . .*' "

He braced himself and pulled.

The tube offered no resistance and withdrew itself from his mother's neck with an ease that almost made Adam fall from the bed, his foot narrowly missing a small, white pan of strange instruments. Adam checked the door for any sign that somebody heard and then turned back to the bed.

The end of the tube had not come free.

"*The tube goes all the way down her throat and into her lung,*" Bob Wissan had said.

Adam moved away from the bed, now holding the tube with both hands.

He closed his eyes and kept pulling.

Arm over arm he seemed to pull until, at last, the tube came free, squirming across the floor, its end wet and shiny. As he watched, it came to a rest and blew a small bubble, which suddenly popped.

Creak . . . sigh . . . creak . . . sigh . . .

The machine was still breathing.

Adam dropped the tube and walked carefully to the bed. His mom's chest no longer moved. Now she was truly still.

He sat beside her again and held her hand for a minute or so. Then he held it to his face before resting it gently across her stomach.

As he looked at her face, Adam thought he saw the faintest ripple of movement . . . a shadow, passing across her features and drifting away.

Although she did not look any different from the way she had looked only minutes earlier, there was now a peace about Adam's mother. And as he made to leave the room, Adam realized that what he was looking at on the narrow hospital cot was little more than a photograph. An image of something that had once been . . . the briefest record of a moment passed. But memories—*real* memories—were the priceless and insubstantial things that you carried in your head, not disposable bits of card containing chemical magic and mystical likenesses.

Creak . . . sigh . . . creak . . . sigh . . . said the machine, only now its voice sounded lonely.

Adam rose to his feet and left the room, satisfied that it was now completely empty.

Minutes later, he was running through the early-morning darkness, the bravest of all the knights of old, resplendent in tunic and color, strong of will and truth, and accomplished of purpose . . . breathing in the faint perfume of night-scented stocks and the promise of summer.

Going home.

Parting is all we know of heaven,
And all we need of hell.

—Emily Dickinson (1830–1886)

Cleaning Up

Mostly it was only in his room when Chris woke up or as he waited for sleep, but just now and again, particularly on dry nights when he wasn't dodging puddles, he would think of Susie when he went to the park for his evening toiletries.

It was then, walking by the hospice, humming, that he would occasionally see the waxen-pale statuettes, hanging stiltedly from the arm of an orderly or nurse as they passed from one brightly lit room to another. Sometimes he would hear them calling. It seemed that whenever he went by, his proximity caused a degree of excitement to the inmates. It seemed as though they were calling to *him*, sending messages from his mum.

Shortly after he had received the news about his parents one old woman actually waved to him. She looked shrunken and mummified, leaning on the glass and shielding her eyes from the reflected light. Chris had stopped and watched as the woman stared out into the uncomplicated darkness.

'Your mother says not to drink the water,' she had seemed to mouth to him as he watched her wave one hand limply in the artificial light of the hospice room. Her other

16

hand, flattened against the pane, had left greasy prints as she shifted from side to side. Strange, considering the undoubted warmth of the hospice, that there seemed to be such a lot of moisture on the windows.

Tonight, alone in the winter gloom of his kitchenette, listening to a handful of records, he was thinking of the old woman again. And of Susie. It was the records that did it. Huge musty piles of scratchy 45s still in their original sleeves and each with their individual memories of the way things used to be.

In the early years the memories had been good. But as time went by, after Chris's mum and dad died in the boating accident in Greece, they had become soured.

Someone's mother, someone's daughter, someone's wife, he thought now, remembering the old woman's vacant expression. She hadn't smiled at him but had simply repeated her feeble wave. Slowly and seemingly without any effort, her scrawny arm had moved from side to side like a frail fleshy beacon in the gloom. Without thinking, Chris had waved back, safe on the outside, away from the condensation, heart aching.

The woman had been dying. He had known that even then because she was obviously close to his mother. Hadn't she given him a message from her? Not that she needed to, of course. He hadn't had a drink of any kind for almost a year. He had stopped drinking water almost straight away but, at least at first, it had seemed safe to drink bottled drinks. Now he made do with fruit.

He had stopped washing a few months later and now he even avoided using toilets. Instead, he went to the park or, if it was raining, he peed into freezer bags which he tied up tightly and disposed of later.

Chris couldn't shake the old woman's face from his mind. She had had a proud and yet lost look, with perhaps just a hint of madness. 'Freedom from reason,' was how Susie called it.

Chris realized now that Susie had had that same look, though he hadn't recognized it back then. It was a look he now saw every day, staring from his shiny table top or from the kettle, all warped and twisted like a funhouse mirror.

He looked over at the worktop and stared hard at the kettle, so long left idle: he must throw it out. Things were in there, he was sure. Now and again he had heard them scurrying.

Down the hall he could hear one of the bathroom taps straining, trying to make noises to drown out his records. It seemed they conspired to make a tune, though what it was he could never quite grasp. It seemed like a simple song, one he knew from long ago. 'I know it's him but he can't get at me,' he whispered to the room, while at the same time humming discordantly. The music and his accompaniment fought briefly with the hiss of the fire and then faded, mingling with the shadows thrown off by the single shadeless bulb. 'He hates his independence,' he added sadly.

If Susie was here now she'd say, Chris was sure, that she was never really independent. 'We're all prisoners of morals, codes and ethics,' she would say. 'You play the game. It's expected.'

Everything you do is expected, Chris thought. Down the hall the tap had stopped making noises although there were now occasional creaking sounds from the pipes that he knew ran through the walls and beneath the floorboards. He tried not to think about how vulnerable he was.

Susie's time had been the 60s, a decade during which she became 14 and 24 and all the years in between. She also became stoned, drunk and sick more times than she would have probably cared to remember. And she got pregnant, too. Once. She also died.

She was socially conscious, and politically and sexually aware. Her enjoyment of sex was legendary within his circle of friends. She did it anywhere and she always did it well.

A breeze entered the kitchenette from somewhere and set the bulb to swinging. It cast strange elongated shadows which dipped and swirled and then moved in a lumbering fashion, sliding around the greasy green and beige walls and ducking behind the cooker when he looked at them.

It seemed that he only ever thought about sex and death. 'What else is there?' he said to a small and seemingly deformed shadow as it made to pull itself from the boarded-over sink. It stopped and slid back out of sight with another fresh gust of wind. Where *was* that wind coming from?

Richard, one of Chris's friends, had once told him that the only difference between suicide and masturbation is that you don't need to clean up your own suicide. 'Both are merely performances,' he had told Chris.

After telling him that, Richard went onto drink most of a large can of lighter fluid. And the funny part was he didn't even smoke.

Down below, a pipe shuddered. Chris stamped his feet hard on the floor. 'Be quiet!' he shouted. The noise stopped. He started humming again.

He tried to remember what it was like to drink. It had been so long he couldn't even recall the action. He swallowed hard, as though swigging a cold beer. The noise sounded completely alien. There was a soft rustling from the kettle that sounded like someone sniggering.

Scratching at an irritation in his beard, Chris got to his feet and walked over to the filthy worktop by the sink. He lifted the kettle and shook it angrily. Then he turned and shuffled out of the kitchenette into the dark hallway. It must be the strange shape of the kettle that seemed to make it so unbalanced in his hand, as though something was shifting around inside it.

Seeing the railed boards across the bathroom door made him realize he needed to pee. That meant walking down to the park or sneaking into one of the adjoining gardens to use their drains. He was out of freezer bags.

He moved quickly to the front door and opened it, staring out into the night. He pulled the door closed behind him.

Susie had thought that masturbation relieved the pressures of existing. Suicide, too, must achieve this, Chris thought. And that was what Susie must have thought, in the end.

When she had decided not to sing to him anymore.

As he passed the driveway to the big house at the end of the street, Chris thought he saw a figure lurking at the side of the garage. Stepping back, he saw that it was only a clothes dryer, one of those rotational things that look like

19

a pyramid upended on a pole sticking out of the grass. How could he possibly have thought that it looked like a woman with her head tilted heavily to one side?

The hospice windows were all covered so Chris was spared the sight of all those pale faces watching him as he sneaked by. In the park he dumped the kettle in the litter bin and crept stealthily down by the train tracks.

On the way back he thought again about why Susie had done it. He went over, again, Richard telling him that she was dead. He still hated him for breaking the news, but not enough to have had him drink lighter fluid. He often wondered if it had been finding Susie that had made him do that.

He walked by the hospice again, humming louder now, refusing to look up at the windows and acknowledge the silhouette of the woman that seemed to have a long straight aerial growing out of her head, which was pulled down to one side.

Somewhere off to his right a door closed quietly and he heard the clanking of dustbins but, when he turned to look, the house in question was in darkness.

When he had first heard about Susie he had walked off into the fields. They had often walked together in the fields. And it had only been then, out there amidst the grass and the trees, with the sun setting on the horizon, that he had actually given any thought to the baby.

He hadn't seen Susie for ages. It had been her idea. She had said he should sort himself out and then let her know what he wanted to do. But he didn't get back in touch with her. The days became weeks and the weeks turned into two or even three months. She must have sat there in her flat, feeling the baby growing inside her, thinking about what a rough deal she had been given. He had forced the thoughts from his mind and had concentrated on the positive aspects. He had been free again. But then, over the following days, he had got to thinking about death.

He remembered going with his father to visit someone from the office. John, his name had been. Chris had been about eight. They had gone to John's house and there was an air about the place, as if it were deep summer. The whole place was lazy, still and solemn. John had sat at the piano all the time, plonking on the keys in no particular tune while he talked.

Chris remembered his father's attitude, so relaxed, and remembered the little boy playing on the floor with his toy cars but doing it halfheartedly. As if he was waiting to go off somewhere. When they had left, Chris's father didn't speak all the way to the bus stop. It was a Saturday and the following Tuesday his father came in and told his mum that John was dead.

In a garden to his left he heard a dog bark and then whine as though it was suddenly frightened. A lonely, lost sound. He was suddenly very pleased that he was nearly home. He knew how the dog felt.

Without even realizing he was doing it, he looked back the way he had come, noting with some discomfort the strangely distorted figure down by the park. It was hard to make out, protected as it was beneath a cloak of darkness which only minutes before had been illuminated by street-lamps.

He shuddered and turned back to face across the street. It was then he noticed his front door was open. What bit of moonlight there was disappeared as a huge gray cloud drifted across the sky.

Did he leave it open in his rush to get rid of the kettle? Or did he only manage to pull it half-closed, the wind pushing it open again?

He rubbed a shaking hand through his beard, started a jaunty-sounding whistle which he didn't recognize and pulled his jacket more tightly around his body, looking first left and then right. As he stepped off the pavement he realized he wanted a shit. There was a cheesy-smelling plastic container in one of the cupboards. First thing in the morning, he could go to the supermarket and buy some more freezer bags. He was oblivious to the looks he received from the shelf-stackers and checkout girls, mindless of the pinched noses and temple-twirling fingers behind his back.

He was at the door now. The hallway looked somehow longer in the darkness. But hadn't he left the light on when he came out? Maybe the bulb had gone. He reached his hand in along the wall and flicked the switch. Nothing. The bulb *had* gone. Something made a noise behind him like a wet sack of rubbish being pulled along the ground. He braced himself. A wind had risen, only a gentle breeze, but he was surprised at how warm it was on his neck, like breath. Without looking round, he stepped forward into the flat and slammed the door, trapping the wind outside.

He checked the bathroom and the kitchenette, finding an old metal torch in one of the drawers in the cabinet. Its faltering beam was sufficient to show him that the hall was empty. He hadn't realized it had been raining outside until he came back into the hallway from the kitchenette and shone the torch on the damp slurred footprints he had brought in with him. He wished he had been able to see along the floor while he was still outside, before he had actually walked on it. And he was annoyed to see that he had slammed the door so hard it had failed to sneck and had drifted open. Outside it was raining again, the fine spray bouncing off the front step and into the hallway.

Once in bed he began to feel a little easier. The flat was pleasantly silent. Even the pipes were quiet. As it was now, in the stillness of the night and the solitude of his bedroom, Chris's thoughts turned again to death. His own death. It was often the way when, curled on his bed, with the breeze ruffling the curtains, he would stare at the clock on the shelf and watch it removing seconds, then minutes and then hours from his life, bringing his final moment closer. On rare pulse-quickening moments of perverse, almost sexual excitement, he would think of bringing that moment forward.

How must they have felt? Susie and Richard, dazed and confused on the wine of leaving, lost and alone in the maze of life, proud and victorious in their last decision, their final endeavor . . . and maybe just a little bit scared. And then he realized what the song was . . . the song he had half-heard for so many years. Thinking of it woke the pain in his stomach and he remembered that he hadn't had a shit. Too late now, he thought. He was warm in bed and couldn't face unblocking the bedroom door and going down the windy hall—just listen to that wind blow down there: it sounded like torrents of air rushing past his door. And in the wind were the unmistakable strains of a lullaby—the song. He listened hard. It was as though a thousand tiny whispered voices were swirling along like a river.

Despite the warmth of the blanket he felt suddenly cold. That was when he heard the noise, loud and splintering, like a door bursting open or porcelain cracking. The song was still there, as if the house were tearing itself apart, planks and plaster pulling themselves up in some perverse rhythm of destruction.

Maybe tonight was the night to bring the moment forward. He had had enough. But he did not have the heart for it. Or the strength. He could not bring himself to drink lighter fluid or hang himself like a lonely Christmas decoration from an attic rafter. That's what Susie had done.

The baby was a boy, big as a large potato and wrinkled and wizened like an empty orange skin, floating endlessly around and around in the toilet, Richard had told him.

He ignored the racket the wind was making outside his door. Ignored the way it sounded as though the toilet cistern was filling up. All he could think of was the baby. For a few years he had been unable to understand why she hadn't flushed it away, but when at last he had had the courage to visit her flat he wondered how he could think that. It was simply that she hadn't wanted him to go it alone. You could see into the toilet from where Susie was swinging. And, if you climbed up the steps to where her head must have been, cocked on one side like that of a playful mother, you could actually see into the toilet bowl.

When the bedroom door started to edge open, pushing the chair and trunk before it, Chris was almost relieved. The noise of the house had subsided now. All was quiet. He wanted, suddenly, to hum . . . to sing a reassuring little song. That's what Susie had done, he realized, reaching for the old meat knife he kept by his bed.

The door was straining wider now and there was a smell of old wetness coming into the room, of foul sewage, of tea bags, shit and piss, potato peelings, cabbage leaves, vomit, the sweet cloying aroma of garden refuse.

He listened to the song, strangely guttural now, devoid

23

of any softness or warmth. It was the song *she* had taught it as it had swum around the tiny pond of the toilet bowl. Chris's eyes widened, anticipating the first glimpse of what he knew was coming through his bedroom door.

The trunk was out of the way now, scattering his precious seven-inch memories in shiny black piles across the floor, and, relieved of most of the pressure mounted against it, the door toppled the old chair easily to the floor. As the door drifted open, Chris laid the old knife carefully on the blanket covering his stomach and waited, squinting into the gloom. He only hoped that his son's clumsy excitement would be short-lasting.

'Rock-a-bye, baby,' he sang softly, as the shape entered the room and the moment drew nearer.

Gallagher's Arm

I believe it is customary in literary records of this nature to begin with a likely date on which the matters one is about to relate actually commenced.

If that is, indeed, the case, then I am faced with three possible choices:

Chronologically, and in the increasingly customary reverse order of favor, the first of these must be the time when a deranged eighteenth century doctor, one Leopold Vaschimone, produced the infamous grimoire *Cyclical Cantata and Rhymic Stigmata*. This I have rejected simply because, save hearsay, I know little of the gentleman concerned nor—despite having seen it, albeit briefly, on one occasion—of his reputedly arcane tome.

The second—or runner up, if you will—would be the fateful day on which my story's hapless protagonist elected to further his studies through a prolonged stay in the obscure University of Secola, whose ivy-clad walls of learning reside in the small New England town of Mennen.

My third and preferred alternative is a late spring evening in 1954, in the once influential Quaglino's restaurant, a stylish brasserie situated in the St. James's area of London, whose opulence—even during those now long-ago pre-baby boom years—was a far cry from the troubled township of Mennen, with its brooding, gargoyle-festooned rooftops and seemingly constant sea frets which, between them, conspire to maintain an almost constant air of wintry solitude and even, dare I say, hopelessness.

I had first met William Gerold Gallagher some years earlier when we studied together amidst the verdant greenswards and the sleepy spires of Cambridge's King's College.

We had been something of an odd couple even then, with Gerold opting to forego the customary frivolous pastimes of university life for the austerity of a cloistered existence in the College library, lost in hulking great volumes of handwritten lore and obscurely scribbled illustrations.

I had come up to King's from Blenheim, a small village near Wisbech in the fenlands of East Anglia.

Unlike many of my contemporaries, the path of learning had, for me, been one fraught with potholes that, more than once, threatened to unseat me and land me securely and forlornly on the ground. Not for me the almost brazen casualness of drifting into vivors and tutorials without even lifting a book, though that did not stop me from enjoying the myriad distractions that invariably present themselves when one should be doing something else.

Rather, my sixth form life was one plagued by late-night cramming and numerous parrot-like learning sessions (one could hardly have referred to my singularly non-intellectual binges of committing vast chunks of note-taking to memory as *studying*) aided by my mother, perhaps the least scholarly person—save myself—it has ever been my great pleasure to meet.

Nevertheless, one should always pay heed to the old adage *The end justifies the means* and, indeed, my travails were successful and I obtained satisfactory passes in all of my subjects (more by good luck than by good management, it falls to me to point out). And so it was that I embarked upon this additional foray into the attainment of knowledge with something less than the salivating enthusiasm for information that is so common in the great thinkers of yore. (I should say here that I considered—and, indeed, still do consider—Gerold Gallagher to be an exemplar of this latter group.)

My young grandson, Thomas, asked me only a few days ago what I had done at university. My answer was a simple and truthful one—though, I suspect, it did not meet with my son Stephen's approval. I told him, by way of reply, that I had enjoyed myself. The bewildered boy merely frowned and countered, "But surely that was not what you were supposed to do, Granddad"—much to his father's agreement, I might add. (Thomas is a remarkably precocious child for whom I have little affection, a sad but entirely true summation of my half of our relationship and one which I am sure relates equally to his own.)

Gerold Gallagher, on the other hand, was a born student. He thirsted for knowledge as a man lost for years in the most arid and depleted of deserts might thirst for sustenance of a far less cerebral nature. Gerold had come up to King's (one always comes 'up' to the Oxbridge colleges, just as one always comes up to the Capital, irrespective of one's original point of departure on the map) from Egton, a lonely hamlet, some six miles from Whitby on the north eastern coast.

It occurs to me now, with the unquestionable benefit of hindsight—that most accurate but most useless of perceptions—that Egton is not dissimilar to Mennen itself, not only by virtue of its geographical setting (a close proximity to the sea) and meteorological excesses but also through its troubled history . . . though Egton's tainted past is a merely fictional one, the nearby town of Whitby having been used by the novelist Bram Stoker as the arrival point on these shores of his infamous vampiric count, Dracula. Mennen's reputation is, I fear, more grounded in reality.

However, I must press on.

Blighted with a succession of hills and hedgerows, along and beside which Gerold had bicycled daily to attend his classes, Egton had little to distinguish it save a seemingly ever-present fog, which hung, rarely moving, over the fields like a dewy gossamer veil, and—at least, at that time—the most awesomely plain young ladies it has been my misfortune to behold. (I hasten to add—particularly for those who either now reside in the village or who know personally a modern-day Egton resident—that the situation has changed dramatically.)

I met Gerold during the early days of my first term, when the impending demise of the decade (the 1940s) hung tiredly in the air with a mixture of anticipation and trepidation, at a lecture on the poet Polermus, a man whose marked lack of any grasp of stanza construction and meter must surely qualify him for some kind of prize. But I digress.

I noticed him immediately upon entering the room. He was an imposing youth as, indeed, he developed into an imposing adult. His hair was unfashionably long, certainly for those simpler days, swept back from a high forehead in thick, blond waves which tumbled over each ear and nestled on the collar of his jacket. His jaw was square and strong, bearing the faintest trace of stubble (being so fair, Gerold was late in starting to shave). His nose was thick without being bulbous and carried a gentle curve below the bridge.

But it was his eyes that so entranced me.

I confess here, in the intimacy of this memoir and at an age—both my own and that of the planet—where such revelations hold little if any significance, that I found him to be a singularly attractive man. This feeling was to give cause for great confusion and an almost indescribable sense of loss when I bade him farewell in Southampton, scant hours before his ocean-bound departure for the United States and, ultimately, for the University of Secola.

But, again, I go too fast.

Gerold's parents made no secret of their intention to ensure that their son was suitably educated.

They were what is euphemistically referred to as 'well-heeled', the father being something-or-other in local Government and the mother, a shy and withdrawn woman whose appearance and general behavior resembled more that of a squirrel or some other rodent than that of a human being, was very active in voluntary work (long before it became fashionable—perhaps even *de rigeur*—to be so overtly committed to do-goodery) and coffee circles (though it must be said that, then as now, that part of the country—like my own homeland of the fens—was thankfully bereft of the poseurs and prima-donas who seem to populate the more gentrified areas of these sceptered isles).

Gervais Gallagher was a blustering, red-faced tower of a man and something of an archetypal country gent. He was an Oxbridge man through and through while Constance, his wife, had boarded in some Scottish school whose name now escapes me but whose reputation—at least in those days—was quite formidable. And the pair had already established leanings toward America by virtue of extended stays during their own formative years.

Mrs. Gallagher had then gone on to finish at Emma Willard, formerly the Troy Female Seminary, a classic example of the American girls' school by virtue of its remoteness, intimacy, social exclusivity and nonsectarian attitude, while Gervais had spent many happy years at Roundhill, the very first New England boarding school, founded in 1823 by Joseph Green Cogswell and George Bancroft Harvard.

And so it was that, one hot and humid August at the Gallaghers' rambling but strangely inhospitable country retreat at Egton, where I had been invited (if not virtually press-ganged) to spend the seemingly endless days and hours awaiting our finals results, Gerold proudly announced he would be seeking to further his education at Secola.

I can still recall his father's puzzled frown, squinting eyes and bristling mustache as he chewed the word repeatedly in some vain attempt to gain a familiarity with it.

"Secola, dear? Wherever is that?" his mother inquired from the chaise longue, the *Times*, neatly folded upon her lap, bearing the giveaway swirled letters denoting anagram detection.

"In New England, Mother," my friend replied boldly. "I am to follow your and father's footsteps to—as Grandfather was wont to say—'the Colonies.'"

I wondered if perhaps Gerold should wait until his results were in, and said as much.

"Whatever for?" he asked, assuming the time-honored stance of one arm on the mantelpiece and the other crooked by his side, its hand firmly enveloped in jacket pocket. "First, Honors. We both know that that will be the outcome."

I could not disagree with him, although I did blanch inwardly at his apparent conceit.

Gerold, as I have already said, was a singularly gifted and hardworking student, though his brazen and even pompous high self-esteem and total lack of anything even resembling a self-effacing character was vaguely unpleasant. But, if I had remarked on his need to embrace perhaps a little more modesty, Gerold would have been genuinely puzzled. For him, such words merely reflected the truth of the situation as he saw it. His parents, like so many of the more successful classes—both then and now—were equally unafflicted with the common niceties and sensibilities expected by the great majority of polite people within our society, though I am tempted to believe that the resulting confirmation from them was geared more to one-upmanship than, as in their son's case and to use the vernacular of today, simply 'telling it like it is'.

"Quite so, my boy," Gervais Gallagher announced, thrusting his own right hand into the unfathomable depths of his twill trousers and looking for all the world like Nigel Bruce's celluloid version of the eternal Doctor Watson. "Quite so."

"What will you read?" I asked.

Gerold turned to me and, just for a moment, I caught a glimpse of an expression which was marked not only by its speed in moving across his features (such infinitesimal brevity . . .) but also by some kind of wide-eyed . . . I can only think of the word 'malevolence'. And then it was gone, and my friend said, "Why, everything of course." And, at that, everyone laughed pleasantly and correctly, though in my own case the undisguised merriment was more with a sense of relief at seeing my friend's expression resume its usual intellectual innocence.

And that was that.

The dog days of August did, indeed, bring Gerold his expected First (Honors) while I received the less thrilling (but no less anticipated) workmanlike Second. And, to give

Gerold's parents their due, they were equally congratulatory at my relatively humble achievement as they were on hearing of their own son's success.

Thus, as I prepared to take up a position with an accountancy firm in the City, Gerold packed his bags to embark on the next part of what we all believed would be a lifelong adventure.

When I walked with him along a country lane on the outskirts of Southampton, in the early part of September 1952, and with an uncharacteristically early fall of leaves imbuing our impending separation with even greater sadness than perhaps it truly warranted, he pleaded with me not to accompany him to the docks the following day. I must say that I was somewhat taken aback and even touched by this apparently fierce and uncharacteristic show of regret and, dare I say, humanity. Of course, I acceded to his request, though with the appropriate measure of reluctance, and, when we parted early that evening so that I could catch the train back to town, I was not surprised to see his demeanor had returned and he was as noncommittal and stoic as ever.

Life goes on, they say, and, safely ensconced in the daily financial and judicial comings and goings of the accountancy profession, it proved to be as true or even truer than most of those comfortable old homilies can ever be. Indeed, with the double challenge of full-time employment and meeting new people, I soon lost the strange feeling of emptiness which had accompanied me back to London on the evening following my last day with Gerold, as my train sped through the darkening countryside.

Thus it was that, the following March, 1953, with the buds barely out on the trees, I received a letter from Gerold suggesting that I go to spend my summer holiday (I was surprised and not a little amused to note that he now referred to this as 'vacation') with him in Mennen. Enclosed with the letter was a generous check drawn, thankfully, on a British bank. Clearly, the time and the distance had not diminished my friend's spirit of generosity.

Although flying, essentially still a rich man's mode of travel in those days, was somewhat slower than it is now, the trip from London to New York, and on, by Greyhound bus, to Boston and then, by means of a local coach service, on through Dunwich and its moody neighbor, Arkham, across to Mennen, was not in the least arduous. And so, only some twenty-seven hours after lifting off from Heathrow Airport, I finally arrived—disheveled and weary of the endless wooden-frame houses and barren scrubland which littered the roadside that flashed mercilessly by the bus windows—at Mennen, home of Secola University, the enigmatic seat of learning favored by my dear friend.

Without any further delay I made directly for the campus, suddenly aware of a growing apprehension whose seeds and, indeed, continuing growth, I could neither fathom nor credit.

I drifted slowly along winding Saltonstall Street, past tall houses whose gambrel roofs leaned low to the pavement ('sidewalk', Gerold would have undoubtedly called it) as if in the throes of imparting some fabulous and forbidden secrets, until I came to the University grounds.

At first, the surroundings seemed no different to any other campus—I must confess here to that opinion being based solely on the questionably limited experience of my own college, though I was and still am given to understand that they are all much the same in general appearance. But I was quickly able to discern some small but marked differences from what I understood to be the norm. The most obvious of these was the simple lack of noise . . . of conversation.

And, at first, the students looked the same as any students but then I noticed—in addition to the fact that they seemed not to need verbal stimulation of any kind, walking silently along the paths and in and out of buildings in the customary twos and threes but without even the most casual exchange of views—that they seemed to carry with them an air of what I first identified as superiority. This was quickly dispelled, however, when, in order to ascertain from which building I might discover my friend's whereabouts, I stopped one young fellow outside a building bescrolled with some huge Latin motto and received the most pleasant and attentive response. My surprise became even greater when it became obvious that the man was of European stock—French, I believe—and his concise directions and the warmth with which they were given soon dispelled my concerns.

I walked to the building that the young man had indicated and inquired at the counter. An equally friendly young woman informed me, after looking through a musty-looking volume which, for all the world, resembled an aged family bible or the kind of financial record that Bob Cratchett probably used in Charles Dickens's *A Christmas Carol*.

It has always interested me how so many Americans seem to phrase the information they give as a question, lifting the tail of the sentence up against itself as though needing some kind of confirmation. Perhaps that in itself is an indication of the great warmth of the American people in that, even with so simple an act as the passing of information, they invite some involvement, albeit small, from the receiving party.

"Go out of the door?" the girl said, pointing back the way that I had come, "And turn to the left. Go ahead—let me see . . . go ahead two blocks? And you'll see an old brownstone?"

"Brownstone?"

She smiled and tutted at herself. "An old, three-story house set back from the sidewalk?"

I nodded and smiled my understanding, and the girl continued with the directions.

I thanked her for her trouble and, as I walked back to the door, she shouted after me that I was welcome.

On the journey to Gerold's rooms I was able to study the students' demeanor more closely. It was then that I began to recognize what it was that so marked it different to the attitude and bearing of the students in my own college: concern. These were worried people. The strange fact was that I am sure they did not realize that they *were* worried.

I found the house the girl had described and pressed the bell-button, wincing at the hollow sound of its ring echoing inside the house.

Seemingly only moments later, as the door opened, I gave my biggest smile and stretched my arms wide in a 'Here I am!' gesture. But the smile froze and then faltered and, finally, dissipated completely.

Gerold held the door tightly, so that only his right hand side was completely visible—though his arm was propped against the inside of the jamb, up and out of sight—and squinted at me, checking to either side of me . . . though what he was looking for I have no idea.

"Yes?" he said.

I was taken aback and undoubtedly showed as much on my face. "Gerold?" I countered. "It's me."

His eyes narrowed still further while he considered my greeting. Then, "What do you want?"

"What do I *want*? Gerold, you wrote to me and asked me to come over. For the summer hol—vacation. Don't you remember?"

"Of course I remember," he snapped.

I waited.

"I'm afraid you've come a long way for nothing," he said at last. "I suggest you go back home immediately." And he began to close the door.

Without even realizing that I was doing it, I shot out my hand and stopped the door in its tracks. "Go home?" I said. "Immediately?" I added. "Whatever for?"

"It's . . . it's not convenient."

I held the door and shook my head in amazement and disbelief.

"I'm sorry," he said.

For a second I relaxed my arm and the door once more began to close, albeit more slowly this time. Sensing a softening of my friend's resolve, I halted the door again and Gerold's face reappeared, and his expression did now seem to have lightened.

"Can I not at least come in and rest awhile?" I inquired. "It has been an extremely long journey, you know."

He studied my face and then, with a loud sigh, he opened the door wide. "Very well," he said, softly, "if you must."

I lifted my suitcase and stepped into a dimly lit hallway. It was as I turned to face Gerold that I first noticed he had hurt his right hand, which was encased—sloppily—in a swathe of bandages so thick that it gave the impression of being some two or three times its normal size.

When I inquired as to the nature of his injury Gerold shook his head and shrugged, apparently hiding the hand behind his back. "Trapped it in a door," he said, and, just for a second, a thin and somehow ironic smile played across his mouth. And then it was gone. "Here," he said, reaching for my bag with his left hand, "let me help you with that."

He took the suitcase and bade me follow him.

We trudged up three flights of stairs until we reached what I considered to be the attic rooms of the house whereupon Gerold set down my bag and, for the first time since my arrival on his doorstep, smiled. "Would you . . ." He paused as he looked around and, as though suddenly realizing his predicament, he grimaced. "Can I get you something to drink? Coffee? The tea over here is absolutely abominable."

I nodded. "A cup of coffee would be marvelous," I said.

For a moment he seemed confused as to what to do next. "Right, coffee," he said at last. And he turned sharply around and left the room.

As I looked around at the piles of books and papers littering the expansive room, Gerold's voice rang out. "Make yourself at home."

"I certainly will," I shouted back. "As soon as I can find somewhere to sit down."

I have to say here that I was not exaggerating.

Cabinets stood against every piece of visible wall and each one contained thick, black, dingey-looking books, either standing side by side or piled one on top of another. It was in one of those cabinets—one bedecked with vertical metal bars behind the glass and secured at the handles by thick chain and padlock—that I espied the fabled *Cyclical Cantata and Rhymic Stigmata*, though I confess that, save for its unwieldy size—at least equal to its cumbersome title—and the fact that it was covered in a distinctive bottle-green binding which looked like some kind of material, it was a singularly unimpressive volume to behold.

Elsewhere, every single surface—including the floor, from which a thick carpet (of apparent Persian origin) had been rolled back to expose bare floorboards, long ago painted in the most frightful shade of brown—had been covered ('festooned' might be a more appropriate word) with reading and writing materials. Bending to shuffle through one or two of the piles, I noted that even the floor itself seemed to have been enlisted to the task for there were clear signs of partially erased chalk marks dotted here and there on the boards. Their appearance reminded me of the distant days (even then) of my youth, when the girls would mark up the school playground for games of hopscotch.

I smiled at the memory and glanced at the books in my hand.

Their spines gave little clue as to their contents, bearing words I could scarcely articulate let alone explain. I returned them to the floor, noting the tiny explosions of dust mushrooming around them, and moved to a sofa whose arm bore sufficient space for me to rest my bones.

Gerold returned momentarily, carrying two mugs of steaming coffee in his left hand. I jumped up and took one of the cups from him.

"Only instant, I'm afraid," he said.

"Instant?"

"Maxwell House," he said, as though that explained everything.

I nodded and took a sip. It was hot but refreshing, and I said as much to Gerold.

We sat in silence for a minute or so and then my attention was drawn again to his injured hand. Studying it as it rested on his lap, I noted that there seemed to be something other than merely his hand beneath the bandage. Indeed, it looked as though he were holding a small plate or a saucer . . . or even that he had inadvertently trapped his hand in a goldfish bowl and then, unable to free it, had simply swathed the thing and dismissed it. I asked him what exactly was wrong with it.

"Oh, just bruised," he said.

Recognising his reluctance to discuss it further, I didn't press for more.

Eventually, conversation did blossom between the two of us and Gerold seemed visibly to relax. He even started enquiring about the weather, a staple stand-by in times of extended silences, and he was anxious to be brought up to date on things back home. In fact, it was at this point that he seemed to grow less distant and even, or so it appeared, deeply wistful.

" 'England! My England! can the surging sea

That lies between us tear my heart from thee?' "

Finishing the lines, he turned to me and gave a sad smile. "I think not, my friend," he said. "I think never."

"A poem?"

He nodded.

"By whom?" I asked.

"Howard Lovecraft," came the reply. "He came from near here—well, New England anyway . . . Providence."

"So he wasn't British then?"

Gerold went on to speak about Lovecraft for some time, reciting the entire *An American to Mother England* poem, and, during that conversation at least, there seemed to be a return of sorts to the Gerold I had always known. However, his softened spirits did not prevent him from reminding me that it was still inconvenient for me to stay, though he did sound more apologetic. And so it was, barely one hour after I had arrived, that I was saying goodbye to him and was once more faced with the trial of crossing the Atlantic. The prospect was simply too much even to contemplate.

Accordingly, I returned to the campus building and asked the very same girl whether local accommodation was possible and, more importantly, if it was reasonably priced. She seemed to think that it simply was not available—"Nobody comes to Mennen unless they're going to study," she said. Then, suddenly clicking her fingers, she asked if I had considered getting a bus to the coast. "Wells or Ogunguit?" she added, once again twisting her sentence into a question. "It's not too far and you're bound to be able to find something there."

I thanked her once more and was on my way.

I was not due back at my office for a week and a half and I was determined not to miss the oportunity for some relaxation. The following six days in a small town called Wells were blissful: beautiful scenery, friendly people and the most wonderful food—mostly fish—I had ever experienced. And the portions! On more than one occasion, when I visited one of the local restaurants, it seemed as though there had been some kind of contest in the kitchen to see just how much food could be accommodated on a single plate.

Wells itself was little more than a bend in the road, the type of small, self-sufficient community which is so typical of the United States, though I'm sure it had the most generous display of old-book shops *per capita* that I have ever encountered. And so it was that I spent the days reading old paperback crime novels and copies of the *Saturday Evening Post* magazine, while gorging myself on a steady if unimpressive diet of doughnuts (or 'donuts', as the Americans would have it) and *Coca Cola* while soaking up the sunshine and the wonderful Atlantic coastline of Maine.

It was with a heavy heart indeed that, my meager funds virtually exhausted, I set off again for England just six days later, though I had made up my mind to call once more on Gerold to see if his situation had improved.

This time it was late evening with the sun already setting when I arrived in Mennen, and I made my way to Gerold's house with a somewhat lighter heart, confident in the belief that my friend could surely not turn me away so late in the day.

The street on which his house stood was dim and somehow forbidding, the light cast by the occasional streetlamp far too weak to provide anything but the barest of illuminations.

After two wrong turns, I finally arrived at the correct house and rang the doorbell. This time, however, there was no sound of the thing ringing. I pressed again but it was no use. The bell was clearly broken.

Leaving my suitcase on the porch, I stepped back along the path and looked up at the house.

Everywhere save the top floor was in darkness, while on the top floor itself a faint light shone. While I watched, a figure passed in front of the curtained window and it was all I could do to restrain myself from calling Gerold's name, as though I were a clandestine suitor come to carry my true love away.

I walked back to the porch and tried the bell once more but it was no use. Finally, just as I had resolved to leave (having discounted throwing pebbles at the top floor window), I tried the door handle in desperation. The gesture, though I had thought it to be futile or, at best, ridiculously optimistic, paid a handsome dividend when, to my surprise, the handle turned and the door opened.

Just for a second—no more—I considered what I was about to do: what if Gerold were entertaining someone? What if he were about to retire for the night? But the second passed and I stepped inside, closing the door gently behind me.

The smell hit me straightaway.

Clearly someone had been cooking something, though I was immediately delighted and relieved to have missed any meal at which whatever had caused that dubious aroma may be served. Sprouts, I thought, or cabbage. Perhaps a mixture of the two . . . with parsnips and swede thrown in for good measure, and Parmesan cheese scattered on top for even further culinary insurance.

As I mounted the stairs, the smell grew stronger and, by the time I had reached the middle floor, it was so intense it was causing my eyes to water and my throat to retch.

As I reached Gerold's floor, despite being out of breath from the climb and the need to carry my suitcase (now weighted down still further with gaudily-covered paperbacked books), I had to hold what breath I still possessed lest I crumble to my knees and expel six days' worth of partially-digested doughnuts onto the landing.

Covering my mouth and nose with my handkerchief, I rapped loudly on the door. The distant muttering that I had heard upon reaching the floor stopped immediately, to be replaced initially by an empty silence and then by a fevered shuffling. Inside the room something fell over and clattered loudly causing Gerold (for who else could it be?) to cry out as if in pain.

I thought of calling out to see if he was hurt but I thought it might disturb him still further. Presently, I sensed rather than heard his presence behind the door. It was as though there was a slight change in the air between us, a shifting of the particles perhaps. But I could sense it.

And then he spoke.

"Who's there?" His voice sounded tired and hoarse, and the words formed with apparently great effort.

I told him that it was me and that if he were ill or hurt he should let me in so that I might help him.

After a brief pause, he said, "You can't help me. Nobody can help me. Go away."

"Gerold," I began but his voice barked beyond the door and there was an accompanying thump against the wood.

"Please! Go away!"

I waited for a minute or so and then heard a further shuffling as, I presumed, Gerold moved away from behind the door. I glanced down at my suitcase and then back at the door to Gerold's rooms. And then my gaze fell to the keyhole. Without so much as a second thought, I crouched down and peered through the keyhole.

At first, it was difficult to make out what was happening but then I saw Gerold moving back to a space on the floor.

The room was in even greater disarray than it had been on my previous visit but this increased chaos had been caused by the fact that all furniture and other items—namely huge piles of books and papers—had been cleared (no, not cleared: their state of complete jumble suggested rather that they had been thrown and discarded) from the center of the room. Even stranger was the fact that, all over everything—books, furniture and even the floor itself (though only that part outside of the area now occupied by my friend)—were what appeared to be lumps of mud, of varying sizes.

I frowned and suddenly realized that I had quite forgotten the revolting smell that hung over the entire house. I shook my handkerchief and replaced it across my mouth and nose before returning to my spy-hole.

I saw that someone (presumably Gerold) had chalked some kind of diagram on the floorboards and, as I watched, I saw my friend shamble through into the cleared space and then stoop down to pick up something from the floor.

When he turned around I felt my heart skip several beats.

He looked a complete wreck of a man. His hair was long and lank and, even from my restricted vantage point, I could see that it had not been washed for some time. His clothes were creased and stained and hanging in general dishevellment from his body. But it was his arm—or what was left of it—that most dismayed me.

Gerold's right arm ended just below the elbow. At the point where it ended was what appeared to be a black disk. I blinked and moved even closer to the keyhole.

Gerold had now crouched down and was busy drawing— or reconnecting, as I quickly realized—the chalk-lines of his diagram. Just behind him was a crumpled cloth which he had clearly used to open a way through the diagram in order to respond to my knocking. When he had finished drawing, he wrapped the piece of chalk within the cloth and set it down in the center of the floor. Then, as he moved back, I saw two things: the first was a book, previously obscured from my vision, which lay open near the edge of the farthest chalklines; the other was the stump of Gerold's apparently diseased arm.

I had never seen nor even heard of such a thing.

When he had had his back to me, and I was looking down his arm toward his hand, it appeared that his arm was thrust into some kind of hole whose blackness was impenetrable but whose circumference was several inches greater than that of Gerold's arm. But when he moved the arm in any direction, the hole remained in exactly the same relative position to it.

It was as though the thing was actually attached to him.

But now that Gerold was facing the door, and, of course, me beyond it, I could see from the opposite angle. Now, I was nearest the hand—although there was no trace of that appendage—and looking toward Gerold himself. The strangest part of it all was that there was also no trace of the black disk.

I moved back and rubbed at my eyes. Perhaps it was simply fatigue that was preventing me from seeing things as they truly were. I leaned closer again.

No, that was the simple truth of it. The hand was missing; indeed, the entire forearm was missing. All that was visible was the stump of his arm just below his elbow. Suddenly, he shuffled around again and reached for the book.

Now that he had turned, I could again see the disk. Clearly, the thing was positioned at exactly the same point at which, when viewed from the other direction, the stump ended . . . apparently in thin air.

It all defied logic and reason. I was about to shout out, in the fervent hope that so doing might arouse me from the troubled sleep that I was undoubtedly experiencing at the rooming house in Wells or even (I silently wished) in my own rooms back home in Wimbledon, when Gerold began to rock back and forth within his chalked diagram . . . and he started to moan some kind of incoherent babble which I took to be an intonation of some obscure chant or incantation.

My God, I thought, the man had become quite mad. I could bear to watch no more. And, anyway, the damned smell about the place was beginning to make me feel quite unwell. It was, I am sure, the sudden realization of that fact—that I was about either to pass out or to become violently ill—that I got to my feet, retrieved my suitcase and lurched, like some inebriate ruffian, down the stairs and outside to the sanity of the evening air.

The restoration of my health—or a return to simply feeling myself—was almost immediate when I reached the street. Without so much as a look back, I sped with renewed energy to the small bus depot and, less than an hour later, I was traveling through the beautifully mysterious countryside of night-time New England attempting to rid my mind of my friend's disgusting and quite demented situation.

It was only on the airplane back to England the following day, as I stared out of the window at small pockets of cloud shaped like the candyfloss my mother used to buy me at the circus, that the image of Gerold's mud-piles returned. Lost in the recollections of the simpler times of my youth, I had been thinking of the different and varied attractions that the circus offered. When my mind recalled the inevitable troupe of performing elephants, I suddenly realized what those mud-piles really were. They were excreta. And all the rest of the way home, I could not dispel the lingering smell of the house in Mennen. Surely now, with the clear proof that Gerold was defecating over his own belongings, there could be no doubt that my friend had quite lost his mind.

There is an undeniable recuperative power in the simple passing of time and, once home and back at work, it was not long before the events of my trip to America had faded from memory.

Nineteen fifty three drifted into an absolute beast of a winter, during which the streets of London seemed to be either shrouded by the most abysmal fog or ankle-deep in snow.

The new year dawned and, with it came a promotion to the hallowed rank of Senior Accounts Supervisor. The weather improved along with my spirits and, although I managed to keep contact with a few of my old chums from King's, I never heard from Gerold Gallagher.

That is, until that fateful evening in early May, 1954, when a cabbie all but burst into Quaglino's restaurant and inquired for me by name with the head waiter. Somewhat taken aback, I sat in a virtual trance-like state while the fellow, a hearty cockney chap who had failed to remove a tweed cap sitting askance on his head, explained the situation as he saw it. He had been flagged down by the landlady of a rooming house in Clapham at the request of one of her lodgers, a Mr. Gerold Gallagher. The cabbie had gone to my place of work—where there is always someone scribbling well into the late hours—and obtained the address of my lodgings. He had then visited my address and discovered from Mrs. O'Hanlon, my wonderful landlady, that I was actually out entertaining a young lady.

At this point in his story, we both turned to the young lady in question (whose presence, I confess, I had all but forgotten) so as to verify that part of the tale. The cabbie went onto say how he had asked Mrs. O'Hanlon if she knew which restaurant or theater I might be visiting— "bein' as 'ow it's a matter of great urigency, an' all," he said—and Mrs. O'Hanlon (bless her floral apron) recalled my saying something about Quaglino's.

Breathless, but clearly pleased with this discourse, the cabbie stepped back and nodded.

There seemed little else for me to do but accompany the fellow to Gerold's lodgings and discover exactly what all this was about.

My companion for the evening was most understanding and wouldn't hear of my waiting to see her home. I paid the bill immediately and joined the cabbie out in the street.

At the end of a hair-raising drive from St. James's all the way to Clapham, the cabbie showed me the house concerned and made ready to drive off. When I inquired about payment, he explained that the gentleman had instructed his landlady to pay—with a broad grin, he waved a five-pound note—and so that was that. Nevertheless, I gave him an additional five shillings for his trouble and the speed with which he had undertaken his assignment (not mentioning that I was simply relieved to be still alive at the end of it). He was grateful, to say the least.

Watching his taillights disappear around a bend in the road I was suddenly aware of my situation: alone, at night, in a distinctly less than salubrious part of London. With a couple of quick, furtive glances around me, I rapped loudly on the door. A woman's voice shouted that she was coming and there began a succession of loud tramping noises as the landlady descended the stairs.

As soon as she opened the door, I could tell that she was less than happy with the situation. She directed me to my friend's room advising me that, if it had been 'up' to her, she would have called an ambulance or, at least, a doctor. "But 'e wouldn't 'ave none of it," she added.

"Whatever is the matter with him?" I inquired.

The lady shrugged. "Don't know . . .'e keeps 'imself all wrapped up like a bleedin' whatchacallit—"

"A mummy?" I offered.

She slapped the side of my arm. "A mummy," she agreed. "Won't let me in to tend to 'im or nothin'. Just got to 'is room—paid for a week in advance, 'e did—*and* it took him a full 'alf-hour to climb the stairs!—and then slipped a five-pound note under the door and told me to—"

I told her that the cabbie had explained the rest and asked which was my friend's room.

As I mounted the stairs, she shouted up to me. "And watch out for that smell. It's as though he's opened a bleedin' sewer up there."

The woman had not exaggerated. The smell was just as I remembered from the house in Mennen, though perhaps even worse—which puzzled me: hadn't Gerold only just arrived this very day? Surely insufficient time to recreate the conditions that prevailed at the end of several days . . .

I pressed on with growing apprehension.

At the door to Gerold's room I feared I would pass out, so bad was the odor which leaked out into the hallway. I rapped loudly and announced myself. There then came a feeble groaning and a lazy shuffling noise which culminated with the sound of a key being turned in the lock. I took a further guttural groan to be an invitation to enter, turned the handle and stepped forward.

It was like stepping through the portals of Hell.

The room was dimly lit, a single electric lamp glowing from the far corner. Gerold's suitcase lay open and strewn with books. Here and there, on both carpet and bare floorboards, sat huge lumps of excrement (though the color, quantity and general shape of the stools would surely have given cause for grave concern for the owner of the bowels which created them), while, on the carpet itself, was another chalked diagram whose lines looked considerably more shakily-drawn than those of the earlier example I had seen in Mennen. Of Gerold there was no sign.

Suddenly, I heard the door close behind me and the sound of the key being turned again in the lock.

I turned around.

"Oh, my God . . . Gerold!" My voice came out as barely a whisper. Before I could say anything more, the thing behind the door waved its arm at me and made to shuffle to the sofa against the wall, upon which lay more books, all opened.

It is hard, even now, to try to describe my friend's condition.

All of his right side—though of his right arm, there was no trace—was now encased in the same type of black hole that I had seen in Mennen.

It now sat against his mouth and his nose, covered his right shoulder and part of his torso, and extended down to enclose most of the top of his right leg and all the way down to the floor. It was as though he was a drawing of which the artist responsible had seen fit to erase large sections of his right hand side—half of his face, his right arm and shoulder, and parts of his rib cage, stomach, pelvic area and leg. What bits were visible were emaciated and filthy, and covered in sores. I was frankly amazed that the landlady had allowed him to enter, let alone rent him a room . . . though money can often quash even the most earnest of principles.

Gerold plopped onto the sofa and regarded me with an ironic smile. He motioned for me to move closer to him. I pulled a high-backed dining chair over to the sofa and sat beside him, whereupon he began to speak.

Almost immediately upon his arrival at Secola, Gerold explained, in a voice that resembled the creak of old floorboards, he had immersed himself in readings and studies which continued on from those he had undertaken at King's. But there was so much more information available—and he was so anxious—that he had failed to observe, or so he believed, certain cautionary preparations.

He had, he pointed out—and the confession was news to me—subscribed to the theory that there had been civilizations on Earth long before our own, but that, while humankind had disposed of these other civilizations, they were still there . . . existing in some other dimension beyond our own. Further, he believed, as many would have it, that there were means and methods to contact these other dimensions—perhaps even to visit them or allow them entry to our own.

Thus he had thrown himself into the studying of various metaphysical and cabalistic texts—the aforementioned Vaschimone tome, plus von Junzt's *Unaussprechlichen Kulten*

The Longest Single Note

and Remigius's *Daemonolaetria*, and many others whose names and contents were completely beyond my comprehension—until such time as he made a breakthrough of singular importance. Namely, he produced a tiny window, little bigger than a large coin, which offered passage to this other world.

Had my friend's condition been any less shocking than it was or his conviction any less fervent, I might have adopted the stance that any normal person would adopt: namely one of skepticism. But there was an undeniable truth and, indeed, hopelessness in Gerold's words that completely carried me forward and suppressed my disbelief.

This entrance appeared in Gerold's rooms in Mennen as the result of a long session of incantations and preparations. Its tiny size, however, offered more in the way of frustration than of revelation: the thing was entirely dark and he could make nothing out beyond the first inch or two—though he told me of the noises he heard . . . of large shuffling and grunting noises that quite belied the prospect of anything vaguely human being able to make them.

Then, one fateful evening, Gerold decided that he would try to extend the dimensions of this 'peephole', and, without further ado, he inserted the index finger of his right hand into the hole in an attempt to widen its circumference.

The consequence was immediate.

Something on the other side took a firm hold of Gerold's finger and began to pull. Or not so much *pull*, he explained: the damned thing merely began to work its way forward toward him. Early experiments proved that this hole was not anchored in any way, so Gerold could exert no pressure against it. He ran and he jumped and, God help him—his words, not mine—he even tried to surprise the thing, by pretending to move one way and then, suddenly, moving in quite the opposite direction. But it was all to no avail.

The hole moved inexorably forward, eating away at his flesh and bone, until it was at the advanced state I could now see before me.

This was all that—and, indeed, more than—any man could bear to hear. I asked if he had considered hospital, at which point he gave a sarcastic laugh and shook his head.

"Can you, you know . . . can you feel your arm? In there?" I asked him.

"No." He changed his position awkwardly and then thumped his chest. "But I can feel it in here," he said. "I think . . . I think something is coming inside me . . . something out of that other world, worming its way through the gateway and into our world, using me as its vessel." At this point, he pulled aside his shirt to unveil an emaciated and bruised chest beneath which one could clearly discern movement which, for all the world, resembled the passage of large worms moving beneath a loamy soil.

I looked away, partly in revulsion and partly for some kind of inspiration, and then, having quite forgotten them, spied the ominous lumps.

Gerold thankfully re-covered his torso and explained. Those, it transpired, were, in fact, the objects I had presumed them to be though they were not of human origin. As part of his attempts to resolve his situation, Gerold had called upon other 'help', by means of the hellish volumes to be found in abundance at Secola, but there was no hope along that avenue, either. Moreso, the things that he had called upon, recognizing his weakened circumstances, had now taken it upon themselves as a result of, Gerold presumed, an oversight during an earlier summoning—to visit him unannounced. It was merely a matter, he finished off by saying, of which got to him first: the things in the hole or the things from which he had sought some kind of assistance or advice.

I shook my head and asked him whatever did he expect of me.

It was at that point that my blood, already somewhat chilled by the events my friend had described, turned completely icy.

"I want you to kill me," he said simply.

There is absolutely nothing in life's experiences that can in any way prepare a fellow for such a request.

Of course, I refused. I got to my feet and called him all the names under the sun, suggesting medication, rest, surgery . . . But it was of no use: Gerold's mind was set. There was but one course of action and, to him, but one person on whom he could call to administer it.

From his pocket, he produced a pistol, which, he said, he had smuggled from America having bought it in a shady deal with a young gentleman in Dunwich, a town not far from Mennen. This he handed to me, and then reposed himself upon the sofa and closed his eyes.

I have no idea how long I considered what he had said—and what he had called upon me to do—nor have I any real idea what it was that finally convinced me. Perhaps it was the light, which was dim at best in that damnable room, but it did seem that the blackness which engulfed so much of my friend was now making visible progress to complete its task. There was clearly no medical expertise in this world—then or, indeed, now—that could have repaired him. Further, even with his shirt replaced across his body, there were unmistakable signs of movement beneath it as he lay there.

And so, without even considering the consequences, I moved across the room and turned on an old wireless set to unleash a barrage of the dance-band music then so popular into the room. I then returned to Gerold, knelt beside him, with my eyes closed and my thoughts on happier times, and holding a cushion against the far side of his head I placed the pistol's muzzle against his temple.

There was surprisingly less noise in its report than I had imagined—or feared. Gerold twitched once and then lay still. I got to my feet and, even as I considered my actions, there came the most distressing howl from somewhere just to my friend's side, his right hand side . . . from within the doorway to that other world.

And, as I watched, Gerold seemed to crumple and, like a sheet of paper pulled through a knothole in a wooden fence, he was gathered together and pulled through, amidst a volley of cracking and crunching sounds which I took to be the sound of his bones breaking.

Though I am no student of the human anatomy, there were fewer of those sounds than one might imagine and my friend's body folded and disappeared easier than one might expect: my only conclusion was that the inside of his body had been changed even more drastically than he or I had first thought.

At the end, as his shoe-clad left foot vanished from the head of the sofa, the hole shrank in size. But it remained there, hovering in the air . . . and, just for one second, I thought I could discern a hint of movement within the blackness, as though some thing had moved closer to take a look through. And I felt its eyes fall on me.

Shaking off the feeling as pure conjecture, I pulled Gerold's belongings together. There was little mess caused by my actions, which, in itself, is another puzzling factor to be taken into account. Perhaps his normal bodily fluids had also been changed or, at least, taken up by whatever lived on the other side of that hole. Looking back I am amazed at just how calm I was, tidying up the books and clothes in a workmanlike manner and placing them neatly into his case.

When I was ready to leave, I threw a cloth over the hole and was not at all surprised to see the material hanging in mid air like some avenging ghost from a cheap mystery novel. This I then added to the contents of Gerold's suitcase and, ensuring that nothing had been left, I went downstairs.

The landlady stood in the downstairs hallway, undoubtedly warned of my impending departure by the sound of my feet on the stairs. I explained, in a surprisingly lucid and entirely believable manner, that Gerold was, indeed, very ill and that I would be taking him with me this very evening. Then, leaning forward conspiratorially, I mentioned his grave embarrassment at his condition and asked if she would be so kind to remain out of sight while he left. She obliged without question, particularly when I passed her two neatly folded pound notes to assist in her decision.

A simple piece of acting, clumping on the stairs and false dialogue followed and I was pleased to note that the landlady stayed true to her word. I left the house, with Gerold's suitcase in my hand, a little before midnight.

It was a pleasant night and, before long, I had quite forgotten myself and my situation and grown so used to the weight of the suitcase that it caused me no hardship at all to carry it.

I have no idea for how long I walked until I came to find what I was looking for but find it I did, across from a thankfully unlit public house called *The Friendly Lion*: a disused and derelict area of torn-down terraced housing awaiting some property developer to erect new accommodation.

When I found it, I opened Gerold's case in time to see the cloth with which I had covered the hole disappearing. Then I saw why the suitcase had seemed so comfortable to carry: there was nothing inside it at all . . . neither clothes nor any of those hellish volumes from which my friend had sought some kind of solution to his plight. In a moment of panic, I slammed the lid firmly closed and carried the thing across the rubble until I spied a shaft—probably the remains of a cellar staircase at some time—over to my left. I shuffled across to the shaft and pitched the suitcase down, waiting until I heard the distant clatter of it reaching the ground below. Then I threw after it several large pieces of masonry and cemented brick fascias until the shaft was quite filled in.

I waited for some time, watching the point where the shaft had been, though I am not sure what I was expecting or fearing might happen. I do not like to think.

A good night's sleep, despite some tossing and turning, and a bright morning sun seemed to dispel the gloominess with which I had gone to bed. Gerold, I reasoned, was better off now: there had been no realistic alternative to what I had done. Gerold knew that and I am sure he was pleased that he was able to persuade me so readily of the fact.

Time went on after that quite peacefully.

It is not necessary nor even germaine at this stage of the tale to go into the events of my own life from that point save to say that it was no less happy nor, at some points, any less traumatic than any other person's existence. It was, to put it plainly, a life.

The months, the years, and even the decades came and, amazingly, went, increasingly faster with each one. And, with them, I grew more and more accepting of my life's winding down.

That is, until recently when some aspiring investigative journalist ran a series of reports from all parts of the country in one of the weekend color magazines.

The series was the usual sort of thing—bumps in the night and objects moving of their own accord—save for one item which caught my eye. It told of a number of reports over the years featuring a particularly troubled area of London.

This, in itself, meant nothing and I confess that I have no idea of why I read the damned thing but, at this stage of one's life, there is little else to do but read the newspapers.

"Noises, strange shaking in the walls of the houses and even reports of disappearances have plagued the Tremaine Street area of London's bustling Clapham district for over forty years," the report went. "And the health services have frequently been called in to attend to an obnoxious smell believed to be a ruptured underground drainage pipe or sewer, though none has ever been discovered.

"According to Councillor James Sheridan, the next step will be the demolition of the houses in the area, most of which have been standing empty because of the various well-documented problems for some twenty years. 'We're taking these reports very seriously indeed,' Mr. Sheridan recently told BBC Television's local reporters. 'Knocking everything down and starting again is the only way we'll ever be able to get to the bottom of it,' he said."

It was only as I got to the point at the very end where, in an attempt to get some controversy brewing over potential loss of business, the journalist sought comments from the local public house landlord that my blood, for all of its age-induced thinness, ran so perilously cold that, despite the early hour, I had to call to my daughter-in-law to pour me a small whiskey.

The name of the public house concerned was *The Friendly Lion*. And the Tremaine area—particularly Tremaine Street itself—was a development on which building had commenced in the summer of 1954.

Perhaps there are some doors which, once opened, may never again be closed.

> I am the Law
> Older than you
> And your bidders proud.
> I am deaf
> In all days
> Whether you
> Say "Yes" or "No."
> I am the crumbler:
> Tomorrow.

(from *Under* by Carl Sandburg)

Stains on the Ether

Everybody is ignorant, only on different subjects.
　　　　　　　　　　　—Will Rogers

　If a little knowledge is dangerous, where is the man
who has so much as to be out of danger?
　　　　　　　　　　　—Thomas Henry Huxley

"Well, can you figure that!"
　The words, followed by an equally unexpected burst of
false laughter, rang out sharply and filled the bar with an
appropriately heady mixture of disdain and feigned amusement.
　Tad Shellick turned in the direction of the noise, unable
to disguise a scowl at the intrusion on his thoughts. It
wasn't so much that his thinking had been interrupted . . .
more that the sudden exclamation had served to make him
aware. *Aware of what?* Shellick thought.
　A man two stools away was shaking his head and folding
his newspaper with one hand. With the other, he swished
the contents of a highball glass before raising it to his

mouth and draining it. Then he slammed the glass onto the bar top and continued to shake his head. He caught sight of Shellick looking at him and turned to face him. "I mean, can you *figure* that!" he said again, this time tapping the newspaper with his finger.

"Figure what?" Shellick asked, anxious to regain his concentration. What *had* he been thinking by coming to this bar! And when had this guy come in? Shellick couldn't for the life of him remember.

"Says here," the man said, still jabbing the newspaper, "how some judge put a guy away for six months for killing a rat. I mean a *rat*. Now can *you* figure that?"

Shellick shook his head and turned back to face his own drink and his own thoughts. "Nope," he said. What exactly am I doing here? he thought.

"I mean," the man continued, "I mean, you know, you got child molesters and . . . what was it Arlo Guthrie said?"

"Pardon me?"

"You know, Arlo Guthrie, the folk singer. Woody's son. He did this song about . . . about some restaurant."

" 'Alice's Restaurant,' " Shellick was amazed to realize he knew the song. Popular music had never been . . . *Popular music*. The term seemed suddenly alien to him.

"Hey, yeah, that's right. 'Alice's Restaurant.' Good."

The man had slid the last word with a smile. It was a small one, almost reluctant, tugging at the sides of his thin-lipped mouth. Shellick frowned.

"Anyways . . ." The man paused and checked his glass before waving to the bartender for a refill. "Anyways, he sings about getting locked up with all these . . ." He chuckled and shook his head. "All these 'mother-killers' and 'father-rapers.' " He chuckled again and moved his newspaper around the bar for a second or two. "Stuff like that."

The bartender poured a generous helping of vodka and a quick splash of vermouth into the highball, swizzled it once and laid a tab next to the coaster.

The man nodded and did some swilling himself.

Shellick watched the bartender drift back up the bar where he resumed his position leaning against the beer cabinet and stared into the afternoon street. Looking back at the man, Shellick waited until he had taken a long drink and said, "And?"

The man turned around, frowning, a small dribble of liquid hanging from his bottom lip.

"You were talking about child molesters and then . . ."

"Oh hell yeah." He set his glass down and dabbed at his mouth, "Yeah, well, I was just, you know, thinking about how unfair it was. That the child molesters are out there, and all the other weirdos, walking around free as a breeze, and they put some guy away for shooting a rat."

"Oh, right." Shellick turned back to his drink.

"You read all kinds of things in newspapers."

Shellick took a sip of his beer and nodded without turning around. Where was I before I came here? he wondered.

"Yeah, like this new prison they've built near Florence. That's Florence, Colorado, not, you know . . ."

"The other one."

"Yeah, right, the other one,"

Another smile. Shellick ignored it. "What about it?"

"What *about* it?" The man picked up his drink and shuffled along the stools until he was next to Shellick. "Well, it cost forty million dollars is what about it! Forty million bucks to keep guys like John Gotti out of our hair." He took a sip of his martini and shook a cigarette out of a crumpled pack.

"John Gotti?"

"The Mafia guy."

"Oh, right."

The man lit his cigarette and blew out a thick column of smoke, watching it swirl among the bottles on the shelf behind the bar. "They could've got the guy that shot the rat and had the job done for the price of a bullet." The man held out his hand in a gun-shape and made an explosion noise with his mouth. "Hell, he probably wouldn't have charged for the bullet!" He pronounced the word *probably* as *probberly*.

Shellick poured a little more beer into his glass and shifted on his stool. Why did it have to be him? He looked up at the large mirror in front of him and saw the answer reflected in the cracked and smoke-stained glass: Aside from himself and the newspaper reader, there was only one other customer, an old woman snuggled into one of the booths along the back wall.

"Never make concessions."

Shellick shifted his eyes from the old woman—who was slouched low in the plastic seat, like she was asleep—and looked at the man's face reflected in the mirror. The man was looking right at him. "What?" Shellick asked the man's reflection, unable to keep the first note of irritation from his voice.

" 'Never make concessions.' That was one of Gertrude Stein's favorite sayings. And, you know, she never did. Even at Harvard she refused to learn the approved style of essay writing." He laughed out a cloud of smoke and shook his head side to side, slowly, as though he were trying to make himself see through the haze. "When she'd said all she had to say, she'd finish off her essays with 'Well, goodbye, gentlemen.' "

Shellick smiled bravely and made to turn his head away, but the man grabbed his arm so that he looked back into the mirror. The man's face smiled down at him almost conspiratorially.

"You ever hear of Gertrude Stein?"

"Sure . . . sure I've heard of her." Shellick racked his brain until he came up with an image of a short-haired, almost mannish-looking woman whose prose, he suddenly remembered (*remembered?*), Wyndham Lewis had once described as "a cold suet-roll of fabulous reptilian length." He thought about telling the man, impressing him with his knowledge, but he was speaking again.

"And when she sat her psychology finals," he was saying, "she wrote a note on her question paper to explain that she didn't feel in the mood for exams that day—it was a real nice day. Anyways, the examiner gave her the top mark. Can you figure that?"

Shellick shook his head to show that he couldn't and, gently pulling his arm free, he took a sip of beer. Against Shellick's better judgment, the man was beginning to fascinate him. He sipped and watched. Did he have to be somewhere else? He frowned as he tried to remember and watched as the man finished his highball, stubbed out his cigarette and knocked loudly on the bar top. When the bartender turned around from staring out of the window, the man shouted, "Hit me again, Joe."

Shellick drained his own glass and pushed it forward as the bartender waddled down with the vodka and the vermouth bottles.

"Name ain't Joe," the bartender said as he poured the drink.

The man shrugged. "What is it?"

"What's it to you?"

Another shrug. "Hey, you don't want to tell me your name, it's just fine and dandy with me."

The bartender turned to face Shellick. "Same?"

Shellick nodded, threw a five dollar bill onto the counter as the bottle of Michelob seemingly appeared from nowhere and slid into his hand.

The newspaper man shook out another cigarette and lit it, blew more smoke into the air above him, and swizzled the plastic stick around his martini a couple of times. He turned to Shellick and said, "You hear 'bout Albert Einstein's eyes?"

"I guess not."

"You know Albert Einstein, though?"

"Yes, I know—well, I never *knew* him as such. He's dead."

The man studied Shellick for a second and then started to chuckle. "Good," he said, drawing on his cigarette. " 'I never knew him 'cause he's dead!' I like that." Another chuckle. "I like that."

"Thanks."

"Yeah. No problem. Anyways, his eyes. Well, they're kept in this glass jar in a bank vault in New Jersey." He took another sip and nodded, raising his eyebrows. "No fooling," he added as he swallowed.

Shellick raised his own eyes in genuine amazement. Maybe the guy was the reincarnation of Ripley . . . Ripley? The answer to Shellick's unspoken question flooded into his head amid a sea of bizarre images which included people turning their heads all the way around, a woman with incredibly long fingernails, animals smoking cigarettes and pipes, animals with heart- or Indian-shaped markings, and a man named Jack Frost who sold refrigerators in Washington in the 1930s.

"Robert LeRoy Ripley," Shellick said. "Born Christmas Day, 1891. Died May 27, 1949."

"Pardon me?"

Shellick shook his head. "Oh, nothing." Where had *that* come from?

The man's smile now seemed a little sad and he looked down at his cigarette, turning it around in his fingers. "Yep," he went on, looking back at Shellick, the thick shine of pride coloring his words like he'd done something himself rather than simply passed on information about what somebody else had done. "And his brain," he went on, "that's kept in for . . . formm . . ."

"Formaldehyde?" Shellick offered. It was as though a secret voice had whispered to him.

> **Formaldehyde:** aldehyde of formic acid—HCHO—
> used as a disinfectant and preservative and in
> manufacture of synthetic resins.

And, just for a moment, Shellick glanced up at the mirror, almost expecting to see someone reading entries from some fabulous encyclopedia. But there was only the old woman, still sitting slouched in her booth . . . and she seemed to be watching him. Shellick looked back at the man.

"Right," he said. "That's kept in formaldehyde in an apartment in Kansas. It's in pieces," he added. "Now, can you figure *that*?" The man suddenly leaned forward and said, in a Mickey Mouse voice, "Hey, Pluto, this don't look like Kansas anymore." His head slipped forward, wavering side to side, as he chortled to himself.

Shellick shook his head. "Toto," he said.

The man closed one eye as he looked at Shellick. "How say?"

"Toto. Dorothy's dog."

"What's Dorothy's dog?"

"Dorothy, in *The Wizard of Oz*. Her dog's name was Toto, not Pluto. Pluto (it's from the Greek *Plouton*, the god of the underworld), aside from being the farthest known planet of the solar system, was Mickey Mouse's dog." He turned around on his own chair and said, in a falsetto voice, "Hey, Pluto!"

The man frowned and then sniggered. "Hey, that's good!" he said, pointing at Shellick. He turned around and shouted to the bartender. "He's good, this guy. Regular Walt Dizzy."

The bartender nodded.

"Disney," Shellick corrected.

The man turned back and smiled and winked before lifting his cigarette to his mouth. "Good," he said again, and he took a long draw on the cigarette.

"Thanks," Shellick said. He watched the man close his eyes as he took a final drag on the cigarette and then stubbed it out in the ashtray.

"Yeah, Walt Disney." The man laughed with undisguised admiration. "Now *there* was a man."

Shellick nodded.

"And . . . and even all these years after his death, he's still going strong."

"How . . . how do you mean, 'going strong'!"

"Hell, Disneyland, Disneyworld, EuroDisney and now . . ." He paused and pretended to play an invisible trumpet. "Ta rarrr! His own damned *town*. The one that just opened—got its own schools, fire service, police force. I mean, that's some going."

Shellick racked his brain for almost a full minute, a slight frown pulling across his forehead. Then, out of the blue, it appeared. "Of course, *Celebration*," he said at last, feeling a curious sense of relief whose origin or cause he could not quite place. "Near Kissimmee, Florida."

The man slapped his knee with his hand. "Celebration! That's right. I forgot its damned name."

Shellick smiled *never mind*.

"You been?"

"To Celebration?"

The man nodded.

Shellick shook his head, both in response and in an attempt to dispel a sudden gnawing anxiety he could feel in the pit of his stomach.

"Hey . . ." The men leaned forward again, taking Shellick's arm in his hand, and jerked his head for Shellick to move closer to him.

Oh, Christ, Shellick thought. He moved closer anyway.

"You know a lot of stuff, right?"

Shellick shrugged. Right now, he knew diddly-squat. He didn't even know what he was doing in this goddam bar talking to Jack Lemmon in *The Days Of Wine And Roses.* "I know a little," he said.

The man swayed and gripped his arm tighter. "You know a *lot.*"

"Okay," Shellick said, pulling his arm free. "Okay, I know a lot. Lots and lots."

"Right." The man nodded and kept nodding. When he stopped, Shellick thought he might be so dizzy he'd fall right off his stool. But he didn't. Instead he moved real close, so close that Shellick could smell the liquor and stale cigarettes on his breath. "But . . . but do you know anything about faeries?" the man asked, his eyes suddenly seeming much brighter.

Shellick frowned. Just for a second, there had seemed to be something about the man's state of drunkenness, something not quite right. But it had gone as soon as it had appeared and Shellick shook the thought from his mind. "Fairies?" he asked.

The man nodded once, smiling, and then his face grew serious. "Hey, how you spelling that?"

"What!"

The man waved a pointed finger at Shellick. "Faeries."

Shellick laughed and glanced up at the bartender, who was busy watching something out in the street. Maybe he was just busy watching the street itself. Hell, he must have seen everything he could want to see in this bar, Shellick thought.

"Hey, I'm serious," the man slurred, seemingly hurt by Shellick's indifference.

"Look, maybe you've had . . ."

"Don't tell me I had too much to drink." The man wobbled back on his seat and Shellick almost reached out to stop him from falling backward. "Don . . . Don't tell me that, okay?"

Shellick nodded and raised his hands so that the palms were flat out and facing the man. "Okay."

"So?"

Shellick kept his hands up and shook his head with a mixture of confusion and exasperation. Maybe this guy was going to turn nasty. Maybe he was going to pull a knife or . . .

The man slapped the counter top with his hand and hissed, "I said, how are you spelling it?" This time, his voice was menacing and curiously sober.

Shellick blinked twice. "Er . . . F-A-I-R-I-E-S. *Fairies.* Okay?"

The man studied Shellick for a minute, neither of them speaking, until suddenly he sat back on his stool and straightened himself. He brushed cigarette ash from his suit jacket with one hand while, with the other, he reached into his inside pocket and removed what looked like a credit card holder or a small billfold. This he flipped open and showed to Shellick. Shellick frowned and looked closely.

One side of the wallet was indeed a billfold, though, in addition to a few dollar and five dollar bills, it was stuffed with currency notes whose origin was not immediately obvious; but then Shellick suddenly recognized them as Arcadian barternotes. (There seemed to be some reason why he should not know what they were, but it wasn't clear.)

On the other side of the billfold, behind a plastic guard, was a gleaming badge which, despite the dim lighting in the bar, seemed to shine with a multitude of glittering colors. Beneath the badge was a worn and dog-eared card bearing, in an ornate scroll, the words *To dance forever* and, beneath them, *Dhiobahn Boughtridder*. Finishing off the card, on a preprinted dotted line, was what appeared to be a signature of some kind. The man flipped the wallet closed and returned it to his pocket.

Shellick continued to stare at the place where the wallet

had been, gradually allowing his eyes to raise so that they came into contact with the man's face. Then he lifted his own head and shrugged, looking around like he was on *Candid Camera*.

"Hey, I . . . what's going on here?"

The man shook his head and lifted a finger to his mouth.

Shellick lowered his voice. "What's going on! What *was* that . . . that . . . I mean, *To dance forever?* What *is* that?"

"Faerie Police, Changeling Division."

"Fairy police? Changeling Division?" He laughed. "You're putting me . . ."

"It's true," the man said quietly.

"What is it that you do?"

The man smiled. "We roam the land searching for changelings so that we may free the souls of their human counterparts."

"How . . . how do . . ."

> **Changeling:** a hybrid entity of FAERIE and mortal origin; usually takes the place of a human, often at birth, and assumes its identity. Changelings imprison the soul of their human host by storing its body in a RAVAGE BAG.

" . . . you find these changelings?"

"Though I'm sure you know this," the man said, almost tiredly, "by searching the Glamour for signs of cantrip activity." He smiled. "We can see them, you know. They stand out like a fly on butter . . . like stains on the ether."

Shellick thought for a second, trying to see around the mesmerizing display of images and definition that was fast-forwarding across his synapses. In a creaky voice, he said, "And . . .

> **Glamour:** a creative energy emanating from THE DREAMING and used by CHANGELINGS to fuel their own magical abilities.

er . . .

Cantrip: spell woven by CHANGELINGS to affect the reality around them and thus protect their anonymity.

. . . your name . . .

Ether: clear sky, upper regions beyond clouds.

Dee-heye-oh-bahn Bow-tridder?

Stain: discolor, soil, sully, blemish.

That's your *name*, right?"

"Hey, come on. You know how it's pronounced. *Juh* as in *jewel, vorn* as in *porn* . . . yes!"

Shellick nodded. "Dhiobahn."

"Right. And *boff* as in *scoff* and *trider* as in . . . well, as in *trider*. Dhiobahn Boughtridder, at your service."

Shellick repeated the words.

"You know a hell of a lot of stuff, my friend," the man said, getting up from his stool. "You even know all about Celebration—which won't be completed to the degree I mentioned for another fifteen or sixteen years."

Shellick blinked. What was the guy talking about?

"And you didn't mention the notes in my pouch."

"The notes in your pouch?"

The man was now standing. He looked back over his shoulder at the door and saw that the bartender was still propped against the wall looking out of the window. "Sure," he said, turning back to face Shellick, "Arcadian barternotes."

"Yes, I saw them. So?"

The man shook his head. "You got confused, my friend. *I* confused you. You're not supposed to know anything about Arcadia. You're supposed to be a human. And you're sure as hell not supposed to know about what's going to happen fifteen . . . twenty years into the future."

Shellick started to speak but quickly clamped his mouth tightly shut. He wanted to say something . . .

Arcadia: the great kingdom of the FAE, a subcontinent of THE DREAMING, wherein all FAERIES are born and all stories live and grow from their re-telling (Greek: *Arkadia*, a mountain district in Peloponnese; an ideal rustic paradise).

. . . he wanted to say . . .

Fairy: (1) mythical small being with magical powers; (2) male homosexual.

. . . he wanted . . .

Human: of or belonging to the genus *Homo*, distinguished from animals by superior mental development, power of articulate speech, and upright posture.

. . . he . . .

Future: of time to come; pertaining to an event yet to happen.

. . . he stopped scanning and frowned at the man standing in front of him. He started to speak—"Sorr . . ."—but everything went black and blank, and he crumpled in a heap onto the floor.

"No, it is I who should be sorry," Dhiobahn Boughtridder said softly. He removed the wand from the holster attached to the inside of his jacket and turned away from the rapidly decomposing chimera, waving his free hand to dispel the fumes. He looked back at the bartender, returning the fat man's smile in all of its irony.

"That was sloppy programming," Boughtridder said.

"So sue me," the bartender said.

Boughtridder nodded down at the now empty pile of clothes still steaming thin tendrils of decomposition mist against the bar front. "Who was he?"

The bartender shrugged. "Nobody."

"*He* didn't think so," Boughtridder said.

"*He* was wrong."

Boughtridder wanted to walk over and punch out the bartender's lights but he fought the impulse. Chimera . . . there was something grossly unpleasant and unfeeling about the way changelings fashioned these androids out of their own imagination, and about the way they gave them thoughts and hopes and dreams which their creations could not ultimately sustain. He ran his tongue around his mouth, as though trying to dislodge something that tasted unpleasant, and watched the bartender for some sign of mischief. But the fat man was strangely still. Accepting of his fate, perhaps! Boughtridder did not think so. He glanced around the bar for other signs of activity, but the old woman now slumped onto her table between a collection of bottles and a glass—she was clearly oblivious to the world and all of its complications.

"What now?"

Boughtridder turned to face the bartender and motioned for him to move along the bar toward him. "I think you know," he said. "Now we free your host's soul."

"Host's soul! What are you, some kind of evangelist? What do we do? Hold hands and sing 'Yes, We'll Gather at the River'?"

Boughtridder smiled. "There's been too much taking of human identities. They want it stopped—or at least cut down."

The bartender leaned back against the wall. "They! Who's 'they'?"

"The Arcadian Council. Used to be that faeries only occasionally took over the life of a human and that was okay. It was acceptable. But back then we didn't know of the consequences."

The bartender raised his eyebrows questioningly.

"When a faerie takes a human guise, it prevents the soul of that human from escaping. The soul, as I'm sure you know, is inextricably linked to each human's individual DNA profile: you take on the physical attributes of the human and you suspend the soul. You stop it from going to the other side."

The bartender snorted cynically. "You mean like *Heaven?*"

Boughtridder shrugged. "Heaven, Valhalla, McDonalds . . . call it whatever you're comfortable with. The fact remains that each human soul that the faeries trap on earth weakens the ether, the barrier between this life and the next. Each one may only be a pin-prick but you get enough of them and pretty soon you've got a hole; you get enough holes and pretty soon you've got a chasm. Think of it like CFCs and the ozone layer. Was a time when it didn't matter diddly-squat that you sprayed deodorant or fly-killer. It didn't matter because nobody knew that it caused any damage. Now they know and now it matters," Boughtridder said as he raised his hand and pointed at the bartender. "And now you know."

The bartender glanced down at his feet.

"The Arcadian Council has created a special task force whose responsibility is to track down these weaknesses in the ether and . . ."—he paused as he tried to find the correct words—". . . resolve the situation."

The two men looked at each other in silence for what seemed like minutes until Boughtridder pointed his finger straight up in the air and said, "I tracked one of those weaknesses here."

The bartender chewed his lip and, just for a moment, seemed to appear contrite. Boughtridder felt uneasy. This was going far too easily. "Where is he?" he said.

The bartender pointed to what looked like an old freezer cabinet over by the emergency exit beside the booths.

"You lead," said Boughtridder, keeping his wand pointed at the fat man.

The bartender threw his towel over his shoulder and stepped from behind the bar, shuffling between the tables and into the aisle that went beside the booths to the emergency exit. Boughtridder followed. "There you go," he said, standing to the side of the old freezer.

Boughtridder looked and saw the rusty old padlock attaching the lid to the freezer's body. "Key," he said, holding out his hand palm up while he kept the wand trained on the bartender.

Peter Crowther

The fat man pulled an ancient-looking key from his pocket and dropped it into Boughtridder's hand.

Boughtridder unlocked the padlock and lifted the lid, grimacing at the pungent odor of death and decay. Placing his free hand across his mouth, he stepped forward and looked inside the freezer.

The child concealed beneath the thin membrane of ravagement must have been only five or six years old when it had been absorbed. It lay naked in a fetal position, its stick-like limbs, long devoid of any substance, curled up beneath its chin in a grisly semblance of peaceful rest. But Boughtridder knew there was nothing peaceful about the sleep this child now endured. He reached inside the freezer chest and gently pulled apart the gossamer binding, turning the child over toward him. Almost immediately, his eyes fell to the genital area: It was a girl's body. Boughtridder frowned. So if the bartender was not the changeling . . . He glanced up at the bartender and saw that the man was looking at something behind Boughtridder's back. He spun around in time to see the old woman stealthily creeping along the aisle toward him.

Boughtridder raised his wand to cast a holding spell, but the bartender grabbed him from behind, one thick arm entwining his neck and an equally thick hand knocking the wand from his grip.

The old woman raised herself to her full height and smiled.

"Hello," she said. "I see you spotted the inconsistency between my small friend over there and my helper at the bar. What a shame it was just too late."

As the old woman took a first step toward him, Boughtridder reached into his pocket, removed the rune-covered iron shiv from its clasp, and, in one swift movement, threw it with as much force as he could muster. The woman's eyes widened in horror and she started to feint to the side, but she was not quite fast enough and the shiv thudded into her neck, sending a thin spray of blood into the air like an aerosol.

The old woman staggered against the tables by her side, her face a mask of disbelief. She pulled the blade free, tearing a thick wedge of skin and muscle tissue free, and, with her other liver-spotted hand, attempted to stop the rush of life-fluid as it spurted from her neck.

As he watched, Boughtridder felt the bartender's hold relax as the fat man crumpled to the floor behind him. He glanced around at the chimera—two from one changeling . . . impressive by any standard, he thought—and saw, with a greater degree of satisfaction than that which he had experienced at the "death" of the other man, the first tell-tale wisps of decomposition. He turned back to the old woman, the true changeling, and watched her fall. The woman was a grump, a grown-up changeling, and, as such, the most vulnerable to the nostalgia-induced bitterness that sometimes comes with age. While most grumps went onto become wise elders of the fae, some others were inevitably less accepting of their fate. He stepped across to her and crouched down.

"You . . . you . . ." Her voice was barely a whisper.

"I did," Boughtridder said. "I killed you."

"But iron . . . is not . . . is not allowed."

Boughtridder shrugged. "I know, so sue me."

The grump's eyes grew fainter and then glazed over.

There was a noise from the freezer.

Boughtridder picked up his blade and wiped it on the old woman's coat. Then he stood up and walked to the freezer. There was a thin, almost imperceptible waft of mist rising from the makeshift coffin . . . and the faintest odor of peppermints and lavender.

"Rest well," Boughtridder said to the mist as it met the ceiling of the bar and began to fade from sight. He closed his eyes and stared into the omniscient Glamour, that shapeless barrier that enshrouded everything and anything, and he smiled.

"You're welcome," he said softly.

He retrieved his wand and walked from the bar into the tail-end of a sunny afternoon and felt the sidewalk firmly beneath his feet. He looked to the right.

A little way along, etched into the red-brick wall adjoining a delicatessen called Eats, he saw the glimmering portals of the trod, the old walking path by which he had arrived in this city. Just a few feet inside, beyond the torn line at which pavement and sidewalk abruptly ended and passersby merely passed by, Dhiobahn Boughtridder could see the tall grasses waving to the tug of an unseen breeze and, in the far distance, the familiar spires of home.

And without so much as a backward glance. . . .

I feel that I would like
to go there
and fall into those flowers
and sink into the marsh near them.

"The Widow's Lament in Springtime"
—William Carlos Williams

In Country

A strategically placed street lamp blocking the second letter of the second word made the sign say:

DRY P AINS INTERNATIONAL AIRPORT
9 MILES

It seemed appropriate, and Robinson smiled into the mirror at his wife curled up on the back seat, peering at him from under the tarp. Only she wasn't really peering at him.

The sockets—he could only see one—simply glared at the world inside Robinson's Chevy, glared around the bloodied sheets of paper that Robinson had stuffed into them. The sheets of paper that said sweet somethings. They also said *unfaithful* and *two-timing* and *dirty, stinking, no-good wetback-loving whore*. The sheets of paper that had hatched a plan, delivered through the mails. A plan that said, *Hey, let's run away together. Let's get on a plane and fly off into the blue forever.*

Delivered through the mails. He gritted his teeth at the thought of how stupid he had been.

Even the mailman had been in on it. Robinson had asked

him into the house before he left this morning and showed him Ellen. Apologized for the mess and the fact that she was leaking all over the damned carpet but, hell, it was so hard getting a home looked after these days, wasn't it? So hard, particularly when your Mexican-loving wife was busy penning sweet love-letters all the day long instead of fixing meals and keeping the place clean.

And the mailman had just looked at him. Looked at him like he was mad or something. The same look that the old woman had given him over by the side of the Song Tra Bong river when he'd cut up her husband and her two kids and thrown the pieces out, far out, into the muddy water. He'd done that for Shawaski.

Robinson shook his head and shifted his hands around the wheel. That was his biggest problem: too big-hearted, always doing things for other people. But he'd done Ellen for himself. After a while, a guy had to look after number one.

But the mailman hadn't understood. Hadn't even offered an apology. No *Hey, man, shit . . . I didn't know, okay? If I'd've known, hell, I wouldn've delivered them letters. No way, nossir. You done right, man. She had it coming.* There was nothing. He just shook, wavered from side to side like a young tree. And so Robinson had chopped him down.

Put him out in the trash.

There was a lot of fucking trash out there.

He smiled into the mirror again.

Ellen Robinson didn't return the smile, just like she refused to meet his eyes. But then Robinson didn't expect her to. That was why he had stitched her lips together. To stop her smiling anymore. To stop those *Oh, goshdarn it, Barry, you've made me all wet again, now. I guess you'd better stick the old ramrod into me one more time* smiles.

She was already dead and cooling off when he'd done it, when he'd stitched up the lips. He was taking no chances. Those lips had betrayed him, spoken softnesses—softnesses that should have been his alone—to Barry Martinez; kissed Barry Martinez's lips, big, full lips. Lips like Elvis, he'd said to Ellen when they had first met Barry. When Barry had moved into the neighborhood following his divorce. And they had laughed and sung "Don't Be Cruel" as they got ready for bed.

To a heart that's true.

Her heart. Robinson's left eye twitched and he lifted his hand to rub the eyelid. Her heart was now in the trash. Still, now, and silent. Beating for nobody at all. He'd cut the thing out, cut it clear of her body with his bayonet. Then he had used the bayonet on the mailman. Blamire's bayonet. One of many keepsakes from his time in country.

Robinson looked in the mirror at the roughly stitched-slash below Ellen's nose, thought of it sliding open, all wet-lipped, wet-lipped and ready for that dirty bastard's mouth.

He wondered idly where that mouth had been on Ellen. But it made the headache worse. He figured he knew the places anyway. He had sanded them down, removed the taint. Tainted meat, his grandmother used to say. Good for nobody, not even a dog. Which was why Robinson had rejected his initial idea of feeding the heart to Mr. Ed, the trusty family labrador. And thinking about it had made him realize that even Mr. Ed couldn't be trusted. He, too, had been an accessory. Robinson knew that Martinez had been back to his house—his own fucking house, for crissakes—and Ed had settled down in his basket with a couple of Bonios while doormat-lips Barry Martinez mounted Ellen on the sofa and rode her to a wet and sloppy oblivion.

Et tu, Mr. Ed. Now he was in the trash with the mailman.

He wondered if Martinez had felt it when Ellen died. When she had finally drawn her last ruptured breath as Robinson stood over her in the living room. The living room. Robinson started to chuckle. That was some play on words. Living room. Hell, he'd made it a dying room. Taken his sweet time and spread the pain across and around her body until it spilled out and filtered into the carpet and the walls and the ceiling and all the shelves filled with her romance books and into the telephone receiver where she whispered her plans and into the drapes that she pulled shut to keep out all the prying eyes. He wondered if Martinez had sensed the removal from the world of that single, solitary, plodding beat. A beat that he had probably started to regard as his own property.

Ka-thump, ka-thump, ka-thump, ka—

He doubted it. Martinez would be there, at the airport, waiting for her. All greasy Desi Arnez smiles and Copacabana limp wrist, like a young Xavier Cougat, decked out in one of those fucking ridiculous shirts that didn't have a collar. Made him look like he was protesting some goddamn draft. But Martinez was too young to remember that. Too young to remember the war. When Robinson was crapping in his Fruit Of The Looms because he'd just received his draft notice, old lard-ass Barry Martinez was only crapping in his diapers while he sucked on his mama's titties.

And while Robinson was crying to the wind and the rain as he scooped up Jimmy Shawaski's insides and dropped them back into the smoking hole in Shawaski's flak jacket, Barry Martinez was probably watching Rocky and Bullwinkle.

And when Robinson had come back to months of sleepless nights, when he'd wake up and see Sanchez and Termiton and Shawaski and Lunan and Blamire again, see them smiling through extra mouths and carrying their own legs and arms into his bedroom, holding whatever limbs they had left across their stomachs so's they could hold in their guts, and telling him, the way they always told him, *Get that ass off of that bed, boy, and let's go get us some gooks! . . .* when he was doing all that, where was old swivel-hips Martinez then? He was in first grade, the little slickback bastard.

Robinson had got himself some gooks now, sure enough. He'd got himself seven—counting the dog—and now he was going to get himself another.

He'd used the big, crooked needle that his grandfather used to stitch his nets with back in Ogunquit. To make sure Ellen's cheating lips didn't do it again. And her eyes had betrayed him, too, so he'd taken those out, dumped them in the trash with the two halves of Mr. Ed and all the pieces of the mailman. The fingers, too. The fingers that had stroked Barry Martinez's big, brown dick. In the trash. Along with the feet that had taken her to his house. All in the trash.

The Longest Single Note

Trash. That was what Ellen was now. Refuse.

Robinson glared through the windshield and signaled to leave the freeway, muttering to the cold-eyed god of grunts everywhere of how he was looking forward to talking to Barry Martinez.

In the back seat, Ellen Robinson communed only with a couple of flies that had followed her and Robinson into the car. The flies now buzzed and dived, dropping into the sweet, iron-smelling wetness that seeped through the tarp . . . the rich, deep red-blackness that had now run along and down the light-brown material, that had now pooled on the Chevy's old worn carpet and leaked through to floor panels rusted through by years of shot mufflers. There, it leaked out and ran along the underside of the car and dropped onto the blacktop, every few yards, in small, glistening, red-black globules.

The drips had been dripping for several miles but now, each time they hit the highway, the blobs seemed to sizzle, casting up a small puff of dusty air like bacon dropped onto a hot pan.

Robinson turned on the radio to see if there was any news about him. But it was only music. He figured that maybe they might have discovered the reason the general store at the end of Carmichael Street hadn't opened yet this morning. Actually, it *had* opened but it had closed early.

It had closed because they'd sold Ellen a pad of writing paper. They were in on it, too. He'd gone up there first thing (after the mailman), golf bag over his shoulder, and he'd asked the old woman if she remembered Ellen buying a notepad. And maybe some envelopes? Yeah, she remembered. She remembered selling her the stuff. And then he'd pulled out what he liked to think of as his driver, an M-16 gas-operated assault rifle, the one he'd brought all the way back from 'Nam and lovingly polished these past twenty years, and he'd given her a clean eight rounds in the gut and face. Then he'd given her husband two rounds in the head when he ran into the store from the back room.

Robinson had forgotten how sharp your hearing was when you'd fired your weapon. Some folks'll say how it turns you deaf but they don't know. Hell, they don't know

shit. In 'Nam you don't have no time to be deaf because
your ears are your lifeline. Your eyes are not much good,
particularly in the night, when all you got for company are
leeches and dysentery, webfoot and the shits, day in, day
out. At times like that, the sharpness of your hearing could
hear a gook's hand closing around a trigger a half a mile
along the path. Could hear the last fart of a dead grunt as
he rolled over in the brackish water.

Right then, in the general store, just after blasting the old
woman and her husband, Robinson could hear the trucks
moving along the interstate a couple of miles over by Rose-
wood Cemetery, could hear the shitty rap music pumping
out at the filling station three blocks along Main Street . . .
could hear, loud and clear, the sounds of material rubbing
against material deep amidst the stock shelves of the store's
back room. And so he'd gone through there, found the two
kids. No more than fifteen, either of them. But being only
fifteen didn't mean diddly. Over in 'Nam a fella was just
as likely to get his balls sliced off by a kid as by anyone.
So he gave the two kids he found in the back room the
remaining ten rounds, five apiece. A neat job.

Then he'd moved the *Yes, we're open!* sign around so it
said *We're sorry! We're closed! Call back soon!* and
dropped the latch lock as he went out.

Robinson saw the sign up ahead, a right turn:

DRY PLAINS INTERNATIONAL AIRPORT
PLEASE DRIVE SAFELY

He slowed down obediently and checked his mirror. Behind him he could see a heat haze drifting up from the
blacktop. He frowned. Strangest heat haze he'd ever seen.
Looked more like a mist, spiraling up in thin plumes and
then fanning out across the full breadth of the road. Must
be hot enough to fry an egg out there, he thought as he
turned the wheel and the Chevy moved onto the access
road.

The radio sputtered and squawked. A man with an an-
nouncer's voice started to say that there were unsubstan-
tiated reports coming in of problems at the airport. There

was no real news yet, he said amidst crackles and spits, but the station had sent a team out to investigate.

Robinson saw the airport in the distance now. There were no planes to be seen in the air, either taking off or coming in. He smiled to himself. This was a stroke of good fortune. If there was trouble at Dry Plains then he was surely going to be able to get in there and take care of Barry Martinez without folks paying too much attention to him.

Behind Robinson, a mist was following the Chevy.

As he turned around a dense grove of trees, Robinson saw a thick cloud of black smoke spiraling into the air on the left. The radio sputtered and then cut out. Then he heard a sound from the back seat.

Robinson looked in the mirror and saw Ellen move beneath the tarpaulin. For a second, he lost control of the Chevy and lurched over to the right, narrowly missing an old man standing by the side of the road.

Robinson pulled the car over, keeping his eyes on his wife's body, and pulled on the hand brake. He turned around and lifted the tarp. She was still dead. Must have been the movement of the car or something. But now he saw that she was leaking badly. The carpet was stained nearly black.

He looked out of the car windows to see if he had attracted any attention. But there was nothing. Except for the old man, still standing in the same place, watching him. A mist was drifting along the road so that he could hardly make out the cars behind him. There weren't many cars on the road and, for a second, Robinson thought that was mighty strange. But the radio reports had probably persuaded people to keep away. Or maybe the police had stopped people pulling onto the access road. He chuckled. He was probably one of the last cars to get through.

Robinson turned around again and pulled the tarp back over Ellen's face. He got out of the car.

"Hey, old-timer," he shouted to the man. "Like to get yourself killed standing over there. What you doing, anyhow?"

The old man raised a hand, palm flat out, like he was saying *Peace* or something. Robinson shook his head. The old guy was an Indian. He could see that now. Hell, not just an Indian . . . an American. A real, bona fide US of A American. Just like me, he thought. Not some jumped-up, drug-running, wet-backed sonofabitch like Barry Martinez. Robinson raised his hand in response and said, "How!"

"You know how," the old man shouted back to him, and then the mist seemed to envelop him. It was the damndest weather.

Somewhere overhead, Robinson heard the drone of a chopper and, way in the distance, what sounded like the familiar soft whine of incoming mail. He shook his head and crouched down beside the Chevy.

The chopper appeared over the road and drifted across to Robinson's car. He waved up at the pilot, the pilot waved back. Then, when it was just a few feet above the sloping ground over the other side of the crash barrier, two men jumped out. He recognized them immediately: Hank Blamire and Jimmy Shawaski.

Shawaski ran over to Robinson and crouched down next to him, while Blamire waved the chopper away. In addition to the standard M-16, Shawaski carried an M-79 grenade launcher. In the holster by his side, Robinson could make out the telltale bulk of a .38 caliber Smith and Wesson. Blamire, now skidding into the dust beside them, carried a Claymore anti-personnel mine and a long strip of fragmentation grenades. In his hands he carried his trusty shotgun, sawn off, with strands of the barrel folded over to scatter the load with more velocity. On his belt was a .45 caliber pistol.

"Shit, guys!" was all Robinson could think of to say.

"Yeah," said Shawaski. He pushed his hands against his stomach and Robinson heard a dim squelch, kind of like the noise a drain makes when its full of sludge and leaves. When he pulled them away from his fatigue jacket, Shawaski's hands were dripping blood.

"We gonna party or what?" Blamire announced.

Robinson rubbed his eyes. He looked back along the road, saw the blacktop shimmering, saw the way the trees seemed to crowd in on the road as though there really wasn't a road there anymore. But that was stupid. He'd just driven along there. It must just be one of those optical illusions. The curve of the trees he'd just passed, the tops sticking up just above the mist, made it look like there wasn't any road there at all. "Yeah," he said. "We're gonna party!"

Shawaski rose to his feet and pointed at something behind Robinson. "Who's the broad?" he asked. "There in the car."

Robinson turned around. Ellen was sitting up in the back seat, pulling pieces of paper out of her eye sockets with the stumps of her hands. Every now and again, she leaned forward and knocked her head against the rear window.

"My wife," he said. The words came out soft and hesitant.

"What a dog," Blamire said.

Shawaski laughed and started to howl like a coyote. He always drove the other guys nuts when he did that. Almost as if she understood what was happening, Ellen suddenly lay back down on the seat.

"We going, or what?" Blamire asked.

"Yeah," Robinson said. "We're going."

He half stood up and ran around to the driver's door, pulled it open. Blamire got into the back seat and crunched the butt of his M-16 into Ellen's face. Robinson heard her nose crack.

Shawaski got into the front passenger seat, gazing at the array of hardware that Robinson had brought. "Hey, you *are* going to party, man."

"Fucking A," said Robinson.

As the car pulled onto the highway, Robinson looked in the mirror and saw Blamire reach under the tarpaulin with a filthy hand. The hand was shaking ever so slightly. When he looked at Blamire's face, Robinson saw that the man was sweating. Outside the back window, the mist had reached the trunk of the Chevy.

There were more trees as they got nearer to the main terminal. Robinson didn't remember there being this many. They went right up to the runway at some points.

"Shit," said Shawaski, "will you look at that."

Robinson looked across the passenger seat. There was a solitary buffalo grazing beneath a sign that said:

TERMINAL THREE
TURN RIGHT

He swung the wheel. Blamire was grunting in the back seat and Robinson was aware of lots of movement, like fighting or something. But he didn't want to turn around and look.

Nor did he look in the mirror.

"Pull over," Shawaski said.

Up ahead was a Plymouth station wagon, parked up against a public telephone. Out on the road an old man wearing a Yankees baseball hat was waving frantically for them to stop. Robinson braked and pulled in behind the Plymouth. Shawaski leaned out of the window. "You havin' problems there?" he asked.

The man jogged up and leaned down. "There's something happening at the airport," he said. "Guy on the radio says there's been some kind of explosion and they're telling folks not to go in." He turned around and nodded disdainfully at the Plymouth. "And now I can't get the damned car to start."

"Yeah? Not your fuckin' day is it?" Shawaski said, smiling. He took out his .38 and planted a small hole in the man's forehead just below the brim of the hat. The man flew back and smashed against the crash rail, slid down to the ground in a sitting position looking surprised as hell. When the man slumped forward, Robinson saw that the entire back of his head, hat included, had gone.

"George?" A woman's head appeared over the other side of the Plymouth.

"I'll get her," Blamire said from the back seat. Robinson was suddenly aware of a smell he hadn't smelled since back in high school. It was the thick musky aroma of unleashed pheromones and vaginal emission. He watched Blamire get out of the car, saw him pull up the zipper on his fatigue trousers, lift the shotgun and pull the trigger. The old woman who had stepped around from the back of the

Plymouth shook as her head and right shoulder flew off in a spray of skin and bone fragments, then tumbled to the ground right where she had been standing.

"Neato," said Shawaski.

Blamire turned around and formed a circle with his thumb and forefinger. "Fucking A," he said and got back into the car.

Robinson pulled back out onto the road. In the mirror the mist gathered around the Plymouth like a pack of hungry rats.

It was another half mile to the terminal where Barry Martinez would be waiting. On the way, they saw a couple more buffalo, kind of indistinct among the paddies, grazing beneath the trees, and a few cars pulled over on the dusty side-road. They didn't see anymore people. About halfway down the road there was a crudely constructed tower of sticks and blankets over to the right. At the top, Robinson could see a pair of feet protruding from beneath a fringed shawl. Leaning against the construction was a lance with feathers blowing in the wind.

The mist now seemed to be keeping pace with the Chevy, sometimes even drifting in front of them. Up ahead, the black smoke had dropped to the building tops, covering the sunshine behind the landing tower. "Damndest weather," Robinson said to nobody in particular.

Shawaski was singing. "Somebody To Love" by Jefferson Airplane. It seemed appropriate. In more ways than one.

By the time they pulled up to the terminal parking lot area, the light was almost gone. Shawaski rolled out of the car, cursing and holding his stomach, and ran to the shelter of the building. As he ran, he dropped small clumps of what looked like raw meat along the path.

A security guard looked around at him. "Boy, am I glad to see you guys," he said.

Shawaski put a finger to his lips and the guard nodded. Shawaski pointed over to the main doors and a man lifting a young boy onto a baggage cart. The guard looked around and frowned. Shawaski waved never mind and pointed to himself. Then he pulled his gun from his holster. The first shot took out the kid, the second the guy. The guard spun around, a look of horror on his face. That was when Shawaski put a shot straight into the guard's crotch.

Robinson opened the door and grabbed his M-16, trained it on the doors. There was no movement from inside the terminal.

Robinson watched Shawaski run over and put a single shot into the kid and the guy; then he saw him walk over to the guard and crouch down beside him. As Shawaski knelt down and buried his face in the guard's uniform, Robinson looked away. The mist had drifted right up to about twenty yards from the perimeter fence. It didn't seem to be moving any closer, probably because of all the air turbulence from the planes. But, looking up above the tower, Robinson saw that there were no planes in the air. More importantly, he saw that the mist, while stopping some distance from the fence, was drifting overhead as though it were out to cocoon the entire airport. Crazy idea, he thought.

Blamire ran over to join him, his feet squelching through the mud that now covered the paving blocks. Robinson broke out of his reverie and trained his M-16, did a 360-degree sweep.

The rear door of the Chevy creaked open and Ellen fell into the slime. He started to wonder where all that had come from and then noticed a long leech attached to Ellen's face which she was trying to sweep off with the stump of her right hand. Robinson took careful aim and shot the leech off. He took her cheek, right back to her ear, off with it. Ellen rolled over and tried to sit up.

Shawaski ran over and clubbed her across the face. The impact shook her brain out onto the paving slab and Robinson and Blamire watched in fascination as the thing scurried toward the terminal doors.

"Hell, let's get that fucker," Blamire yelled from over beside the car and, hefting up his .45, he took a shot at the brain. "Eeeehah!" he yelled. The first slug missed by a country mile but the second took a long sliver of gray out of the brain and Robinson was convinced he heard it cry out in agony. The thing, which for all the world looked just like one of the walnuts that Robinson's mother used to shell come Christmas time, now spouted a milky stream against the shattered glass. It didn't move.

Ellen, too, remained in exactly the position she had fallen though Blamire was now eyeing her with a fevered gaze. Robinson ran over and pulled down her skirt to cover the bruising. He didn't remember doing some of it.

Shawaski ambled over, sliding another cartridge into his .38. "That about wraps it here," he said with a nod.

"What do we do with her?" Blamire said, looking at Ellen.

"We leave her's what we do," Robinson answered.

Over beyond the fence, the land had turned into deep bog. Robinson frowned and tried to recall seeing any rain. There was no longer any road to be seen. The sides hung with a thin curtain of rain, blowing across in sheets and foaming on the lake which had opened up on the plain and now stretched as far as the eye could see. Out in the water were small humps, like helmets floating on the surface, and each one had a circle of small red eyes that glowered in the gloom.

Above their heads they heard the sound of engines racing, screaming for release. A plane was attempting to land in the gloom. Blamire ran to the car and took out his grenade launcher. He lay across the hood, his left side pressed onto the windshield with his head over the side, and hefted the launcher onto his shoulder. "Hey, Jimmy, come load me up."

Shawaski ran over and fumbled a grenade out of Blamire's bag, dropped it into the barrel. Blamire blew it out when the plane was directly overhead, about fifty feet up, and took a piece out of the undercarriage. The machine went another sixty to seventy yards and then buckled in the middle, fire and smoke belching out. Then it seemed to lose all forward momentum and just dropped, with more explosions rippling along its full length.

"Yay!" Shawaski shouted.

Amidst the noise and the smell of burning fuel, small, curled up, fiery shapes could be seen bouncing across the runway (which now looked very neglected and overgrown with clumps of weed). One or two of them touched down and started running but Shawaski took two of them straight away: Blamire let rip with his .45 and took out another three with six rounds.

"Check the water," Robinson hissed.

The other two looked over and saw that the eye-helmets were getting nearer to the shore. They were drifting into the long grasses next to the fence, where all the smouldering peasant bodies were stacked.

"What do we do, sarge?" Shawaski asked.

Robinson looked around. There seemed little alternative but to go inside. Inside! Barry Martinez! He had almost forgotten why he'd come here. "Inside," he yelled over the sound of burning metal and the screams of the dying.

As one, they turned and ran to the doors. On the way, Blamire took care to stamp on Ellen's brain. Robinson thought he heard it sigh, but there was so much going on it might just have been the wind.

Inside the terminal, people were crowded on the seats in the center of the departure lounge. Robinson, Blamire, and Shawaski stopped inside the doors and stared. The people stared back.

"Who we lookin' for?" Blamire hissed. His voice sounded unfamiliar. Robinson glanced sideways and, just for a moment, Blamire's hair seemed to be longer than it had been.

"A guy," Robinson answered, "just a guy."

"Well, take your pick."

Martinez was standing over by one of the desks, dialing a number into a telephone.

"Wait here." Robinson ran across the lobby.

As he pulled up alongside Barry Martinez, Martinez said "Fuckin' telephones," and slammed the receiver on its cradle.

"Hello Barry."

Martinez span around and linked eyes with Robinson.

"Phil!"

"Surprised to see me?"

Martinez shrugged.

"Going on a trip?"

Martinez nodded and looked over Robinson's shoulder. "What you doin' here, Phil?"

"Brought you a message. From Ellen."

Martinez had finally noticed the M-16. "Hey, now don't do nothin' stupid, Phil." He pronounced "stupid" with a double-o, backing away from Robinson and raising his hands in supplication.

"You been fucking my wife, Barry," Robinson said softly. "I don't allow that."

"It—it wasn't nothin', Phil. I mean it. We was . . . we was just foolin' around. She di'n't mean nothin', honest."

Robinson reached out and took hold of the other man's shoulder, nodding slowly. "I know, I know," he said.

"What-whatcha doin' Phil? Whatcha gonna do, huh?"

"Let's go outside."

Martinez shook his head and pulled back toward the desk. "I ain't goin' anywhere with you, Phil." A woman appeared behind the desk and gave them a big smile. Robinson smiled back.

"Come on, Barry. She's outside."

"Outside? Ellen?"

Robinson gave a little nod, conspiratorially, chuckling. "Yeah. She's waiting for you."

"Phil—"

"Come *on!*" He grabbed Martinez's jacket lapels in one hand and pulled him away from the counter. As he did, Martinez thrust his hand into his pocket, pulled it straight back out and hit Robinson in the stomach. Then he pulled his hand away.

Robinson laughed, looked down at his shirt-front, saw the blood, frowned. Martinez hit him again. This time, Robinson saw the blade, saw it go into his stomach, saw the other man lift his hand high, heard him grunt, saw him take it out again, saw the blood and bits of stuff dripping from the blade. Then he felt the pain.

Robinson staggered backward, bringing the M-16 up. He faltered, saw Martinez shoot a look to the left. He took hold of the barrel, steadied, and pulled the trigger. There was a burst of flame and sound and the woman behind the counter danced a jig, red blotches appearing across the front of her blouse. A little badge which said *Jackie* snapped in two and dropped to the floor. Martinez jumped sideways and started to run, crouched down, zigging and zagging.

Robinson steadied himself, looked back to the doors. Shawaski and Blamire had gone. But the old man was there. His hand was in the air, palm outstretched.

How!

You know how.

He turned around, saw Martinez running for the stairs. He fell back onto the floor, in a sitting position, and suddenly realized that something was dripping from his mouth. Martinez's figure was starting to blur now. He held the M-16 on his lap and, jamming two fingers between the trigger and its guard, he pulled, lifting the gun at the same time.

The first couple of shots took off the end of his left foot and he shouted. By then, though, the gun was up in the air. A whole crowd of people between him and the stairs started jumping around, blood lashing the desk fronts and the stair rails. Martinez took the last burst in his back and skidded the last few feet. He was still trying to regain his footing when his head hit the bannisters.

The magazine was empty.

Robinson looked down at his hands. There was a lot of blood.

Somewhere behind him, he heard the rhythmic beat of a drum.

When he looked around he saw the old man.

Walking toward him. Holding something.

That was one big knife! He fell back into the slime and waited. When he felt the hand grab hold of his hair and start to pull, he closed his eyes tight and bit hard into his lip. Back in 'Nam, they'd always said that when things looked bad you bit into your lip. Stopped the pain, they said.

They'd been wrong about a whole lot of other things, too.

The Visitor

Soldiers' Field wasn't really anything to do with soldiers, at least not these days. And Beatty seriously doubted that it ever was.

No, these days Soldiers' Field was to do with shit. Dog shit. And lots of it. Beatty wrinkled her nose at the thought of all those turds scattered about the grass and dotting the small concrete apron around the wooden benches to her right, in front of a red-brick wall which bore the sloppily scrawled legend SARAH CAPPELL SUCKS COCKS. The wall also boasted a hurriedly prepared spray-painted rendition of a large distorted penis and balls poised before a cartoony mouth, and marked the end of the field.

Beatty pulled her cardigan tightly around her, pocket-enclosed hands crossing her stomach. Was it "Soldiers' " or was it "Soldier's?" Beatty could never figure out where to put the apostrophe. But then, who really cared? OK, so dad had said that, now she was in the third year, she'd have to work harder if she was going to pass any of her GCSE exams. But then he had said the same thing when she'd moved up into the second year. And anyway, her brother Alan still couldn't tell the time without a lot of prompting, and he was ten—and he couldn't tell his left from his right. But mum always said it was just a mental block and that he'd suddenly figure it out for himself one day, and, anyway, "You shouldn't keep picking on him like that!"

The sky was noticeably darkening now, and a wind had come up, blowing across the grass and bending the almost leafless trees toward the ground. Over where Ned was sniffing, a large bundle toppled over from its upright position and rolled toward him. Ned barked and hopped back, obviously surprised. "Don't be stupid, Ned," Beatty called into the wind. The bag almost righted itself and, just for a second, it looked as though it was going to unfurl completely and envelop the hapless dog. But that couldn't be, because that would mean that the bag had to move against the wind. It looked awfully solid for an old sack, Beatty thought. Ned growled and the bag tumbled away with a fresh gust, though Beatty thought there was hardly enough force to send it scurrying toward the large hedgerow the way it did. Once at the hedge, the bag fell away, through the privet, and out of sight.

Beatty watched the hedge intently, waiting for some sign of movement. Maybe someone was in the bag. Maybe it was one of those pee-doe-file men that dad said hung around the toilets across from where she lived. Dad said they talk to you really nicely and then show you mucky pictures. She'd asked what the pictures were about but dad had just said to never mind, and "Just make sure you don't talk to anybody when you're out." She was always told to be in before it was dark and yet they never bothered if her being out in the dark suited them. Like "just nipping" to the corner shop for a tin of peas, or "just bobbing" down to the park with Ned. Anyway, she knew what the pictures were about. She'd seen Helen Carter's brother's books that he'd brought back from London. Big black men with cocks nearly down to their ankles, being ridden around somebody's front room by spotty girls with big tits, dressed like nurses or policewomen.

Beatty wondered if *her* tits would ever grow. She shrugged her shoulders inside her coat and felt the reassuring tingle through her jumper and vest. Thirteen years old and still nothing much there at all. Helen Carter's tits were really coming on now—in fact, even the brown bits around Helen's nipples were much bigger than her own, she thought, with dismay. Especially when Helen spat on her finger and rubbed the spittle around and around them. And she knew, too, that Helen rubbed them with her mum's Body Shop cream, some kind of thick paste made from cabbages or carrots or something. They smelled really funny, sort of like a cross between perfume and Lifeguard soap. Maybe Helen got her brother Richard to rub them for her. She wouldn't be surprised. Her dad always said that the Carters were a "funny bunch." She watched Ned crouch down in the darkness at the end of the field and heard him growling softly at the hedge.

Beatty couldn't see anything. Behind the hedge was a large wall, and behind the wall the Dunstarns began, "Street," "Close," "Drive," "Lane," "Avenue," and who knew what else. Cobbled streets of terraced boxes, stretching out the length of Allbeck and down the long hill into the industrial estate at Allbeck Park—a park which was as much about grass as Soldiers' Field was about soldiers— and into the outskirts of Leeds.

"Come *on*, Ned," she shouted impatiently. She could now only just make out the outline of the labrador, way across the grass. He had turned his attention back to where the bag had been, and was excitedly—or anxiously—nuzzling the grass, as though he was foraging for something. She could hear him sniffing: strange that she could make out the sounds so clearly. She turned around and looked back along the crescent path to either side. Beatty had only strayed a few feet off the path but, suddenly, she felt dangerously exposed. It was like she'd felt when she was out of her depth in the swimming baths when she was still learning to swim. She had an intense desire to walk backward to the path, all the time keeping her full attention on Ned and that hedge. And the disappeared bag—wherever it was. Ned was still growling, head thrust down as though he was worrying something. Shit most likely, Beatty thought. Probably an interesting collection of runny off-white lumps, the kind which always reminded her of the butterscotch topping stuff which mum put on plates of mashed-up banana, and gave to her and Alan for occasional special Sunday teas. Suddenly, she wished she could see what it was because it looked as though Ned was eating it, throwing his head back in the way he always did when he was grinding up biscuits and particularly difficult pieces of bone.

It was totally dark, now. Black. The blackest black of the night because the streetlights still hadn't been turned on. But, no, that wasn't right. The lights *were* on. She'd just seen that they were on when she'd turned around to look back at the path. She couldn't look back again, because then that would leave her front unprotected. At least her back was safe because nothing would come up behind her with all the lights on. But had she been mistaken? Was it just the lights in the windows of the houses on Allbeck Drive that she had seen? Maybe, even now, as she was thinking about the lights, something was gliding and rustling its way across the path beneath the cover of the darkness and the trees, rustling its way toward her back. Her totally unprotected back.

She removed her hands from her cardigan pockets and strained her eyes into the blackness. There was Ned. She could see his crouched form over in front of the hedge. His was the blacker shape against the other blackness behind it. She squinted. Her eyes were playing tricks now. She could have sworn that she'd seen Ned rise up, like he was standing on his back legs, but when she concentrated she saw that he was still sniffing. She could hear him. "Come on, Ned," she called. No way was she going to walk over there to get him. Her school shoes would get covered in shit—"Barkers' eggs" was what Alan called it and mum would throw a wobbly. And anyway, she didn't like the way the hedge was rustling even though the wind had momentarily dropped.

Ned gave out a loud cough which sounded like a cross between a bark and the anguished whooping noises which Alan had made last winter when he got that really bad flu. Then she felt him. In one agonizing instant, one pulse-stopping tiny fraction of a second, she felt the familiar nuzzling of Ned against her legs. She couldn't look down. For an instant, she couldn't move. She just kept watching the crouching shape that she had *thought* was her dog, watching as it reared itself up again and then shambled off, merging with the thicker shade behind it. At her feet, Ned whimpered. But it was without any trace of affection. It was a "Let's get away from here" sort of noise. And when she looked down, she saw that only a little bit of his snout—the bit on his left—was still in place. The rest of his mouth was completely exposed, teeth and gums bared to the night, with the top of his muzzle covered in runny sores which seemed to pulsate by themselves. Somewhere, she could hear a car horn "parrp," and there was a brief squeal of tires followed by an engine revving. Then the silence returned. That was the worst bit, because the silence meant that there was nothing to distract her . . . nothing to stop her returning her full attention to Ned's wrecked face, bathed, as it was, in the glow of the long flourescent red sausage—it had to be a sausage, hadn't it? Surely it couldn't be anything else—that he was holding clamped hard against his teeth. Was it really moving, or was it a trick of its own glimmering shine? Certainly the shine and the madness it illuminated in his eyes seemed to say it all: Why did I do this? they said.

Thinking back on it all later that night, tucked up securely in her bed, it was some time before Beatty could remember how she and Ned had got back home. So much had happened back at the house that the simple incidentals had temporarily faded from her memory.

She pulled the sheets tighter beneath her chin and looked around the room. It was still dark, despite the soft glow of the little night-light which dad had dug up from the loft following her terror at the thought of being in the bedroom, alone in the blackness. Strangely though, the light failed to dispel her fears. Even the bright shine around her room door, from the big bulb in the hallway, proved to be insubstantial. The worst of it was that she couldn't explain to her parents why she felt so scared. She could hardly bear even to think of it herself. Certainly she could not tell her father that Ned had eaten something which glowed red and smelled even worse than the dog's mouth usually smelled, even after he'd had a long bum-licking session (or was that just her mind playing tricks?), something that looked awfully like the spray-painted drawing of a cock which adorned the wall at the edge of Soldiers' Field. She also couldn't tell him that the thing was wriggling in Ned's mouth, like it had a mind of its own, or that there had been stuff coming out of the little hole in the end, and that wherever it had touched Ned's muzzle it hissed and steamed, making the dog's skin and fur drip onto the grass in thick runny globs. Helen Carter said that such stuff was called spunk, but she had also said that it was supposed to be a white color, like milk, whereas the stuff coming out of the thing in Ned's mouth glowed red, like steel being smelleded. She'd screamed at Ned to drop it. Drop it! Drop it! But the dog, whining all the time, had growled at her as she had made to step toward him: he'd never done it before. Beatty had not known whether to cry or laugh. Laugh at the sheer ridiculousness of the whole thing. Laugh at the fact that she was standing on the side of Soldiers' Field while her dog munched on a radioactive cock. Well, what else could it be?

And then, in one strange instant, the thing fell from Ned's mouth. Beatty had watched it, almost as though it was falling in slow motion, as it landed with a soft plop on the grass. She was sure that Ned was as surprised as she was. She couldn't understand it: one second Ned was gripping it with all of his might and the next he just let go. She was sure that, if Ned could actually have spoken—and could actually have made his mind work amidst the barrage of pain from his melted face—he would not have been able to explain why he did it. In much the same way, Beatty would have had trouble explaining why she stooped down and delicately lifted the thing up, between her thumb and index finger, and dropped it into the fluffy depths of her cardigan pocket. She could still hear Ned's insistent, almost pleading whine. Could still see, especially when she closed her eyes, the dog start to stagger, his back legs collapsing to one side, as he slipped away from this world. It was for that reason—

plus the fact that her heart pounded with the knowledge of what lay in the drawer of her bedside table—that sleep would be a long time coming.

Downstairs, over the steady drone of the television, Beatty could hear her parents talking. Her father's voice occasionally increased in volume sufficiently for her to be able to hear the actual words, and then drifted away again as he was soothed by Beatty's mother.

Outside, the trees waved in the wind, grown stronger since she had arrived back home, casting playful skeletal shadows on the other side of her curtains. Every few minutes a car or something would go by and cause a greater darkness to blot out the shape of the branches, passing first from the one side to the other, and then the other way. It was strange that the shadows seemed so slow and lazy, and that she never even heard an engine. Perhaps she was tired after all. How strange a room is in the dark. Maybe it needs the light to settle it, just like some humans do. Perhaps without that light, a room becomes restless, too. That would account for the little sounds. Nothing much, really, just little creaks and rattles, rustles and whispers. Beatty thought she heard the drawer open, almost believed she could feel rather than hear the skin-cracking grin of something savoring freedom, pulling back its mangled red foreskin and exposing a glinting orange eye as it waddled its way onto the top of her bedside table, to which her back was turned. But then the downstairs toilet flushed and she realized it must have been either mum or dad pulling the chain. Strange, though, that the cistern was taking so long to fill up.

Why had she snuggled down facing the window? The shadows were annoying her, making her drowsy. And the knowledge that the thing was in the drawer behind her, itself hastily snuggled among Care Bear paraphernalia and rainbow-colored Kleenex tissues, caused a warm tingling between her legs, almost like when she got cystitis and felt like she wanted to pee all the time. But she didn't feel like she wanted to pee now.

* * *

Beatty only realized that she had been asleep when she actually woke up. She opened her eyes wide and stared at the curtain. It was light outside, and she could hear the familiar comforting drone of the radio from downstairs which mixed perfectly with the faint earthy aroma of frying bacon. Funny how a sound and a smell could be so perfectly matched.

Morning had sneaked up on the world while she had been asleep—dreaming, she suddenly remembered. What had the dream been about? Her earlier thought about sounds and smells fitting together reminded her. A man had called to see her in her room though she didn't know how he could have got in. Somehow, it didn't really seem all that important. While she watched, the man had gently opened her bedside table drawer and removed the object. Peering wide-eyed over the tightly held bedclothes, Beatty had seen the thing—it definitely *was* a cock—wriggle in the man's proffered hand, wriggle like it was looking for something. It made strange little sucking noises and gave off a thick heavy odor which, despite what she had thought after returning from Soldiers' Field, was not at all unpleasant. Rather, it was oddly exciting, and very thick and pungent, like the smell of the massed purple flowers which towered above the boggy marshland down by the river. The way the thing moved was like it was blind, searching by means of other senses. Searching? What was it searching for? Beatty closed her eyes and tried to remember what the man had looked like. The sunlight through the curtains made it difficult to recreate the nighttime scene in her room, but, hazily, the dream came back to her.

He was tall, dressed curiously in a strange mishmash of styles and colors. She could make out the hues and textures of gently and hypnotically moving fabrics, undulating like fields of corn under a soft breeze. It seemed as though the man's head almost touched the ceiling. She remembered thinking that there was no way a man so big could crouch himself down to the size of an old bag, at least not unless all of his bones were broken. Somehow, this realization made her feel much worse; and already her pulse was pounding, heart thumping. Surely he could hear her. Maybe

94

the thing could hear her heart! Certainly, it seemed to be growing more agitated, and Beatty could see the faintest reflection on the end of it where no reflection existed only a moment ago. It looked wet.

The dream became clearer. With a slow, languid movement, the man stepped softly back from beside Beatty's bed and pushed the door closed. Replaying the dream like a video, Beatty watched the door drift slowly toward its frame, silently, without the usual creak which always accompanied it when *she* tried to do it stealthily. The light from the landing faded until, as the door closed with a soft click, it disappeared altogether. The room became suddenly black. Then she felt the man move nearer again. She couldn't actually see anything, but she knew he was moving nearer. Then a car did go past—she could hear the engine this time—and, just for a brief second, she saw his face.

It was finely boned, old and wizened, long and tired looking. He looked more like a skeleton of a man than a man himself. The skin was pulled tight across bulbous cheekbones and a long thin nose. His lips were also thin: in fact, they didn't really look like lips at all, but just a slit in the middle of his face. Behind the slit, she saw the promise—threat?—of teeth, glinting in the brief light as though they were actually moving around in the man's gums. But that couldn't be so. Just as it couldn't be so that she could feel a soft cooling intermittent spray from the thing in the man's hand. The sound it was making made her feel strange in her stomach. No, not her stomach: it was lower down. Whether she swallowed hard in her dream or here, now, recalling the dream, Beatty didn't know. Because the final part was unfolding in her memory. It was only now, as the light was beginning to fade again, and the man was pulling back the cover of her bed, exposing her body and the small frilly blue nightshirt that had ridden up around her waist, that she caught sight of the horns. And smelled the smell. She remembered closing her eyes and spreading herself wide and listening, as the little slurping noises became more muffled. The feeling below her stomach went away completely, and she just felt wet. Extremely, deliciously wet.

Beatty turned quickly, eyes open again, and stared at the

table. Nothing looked any different, but she knew that the thing had gone even without opening the drawer.

Kneeling up in bed, she leaned close to the bedside table and listened. There was no noise, but then why should there be? Even if the thing was still in there—and she was sure that it was not—there was no reason for it to be making any sounds. Holding her breath so that she could concentrate her full attention on the thing that either was or was not in the drawer, Beatty turned her head to one side. That was when she saw the mess on the sheet.

It was clearly blood. The reddest red she had ever seen. It fascinated and horrified her at the same time. Her periods! She had started her periods during the night! So that was what the dream was all about. Beatty jumped from the bed and looked between her legs. She had started all right. She held her legs apart with both hands and, bending over as far as she could, stared at the congealed blood around her vagina and the pink trails and smudges on her inner thighs.

"Beatty . . . Alan . . ." Her mother's voice boomed up the stairs. "Come on now, or you'll be late." The kitchen door clicked shut and the momentarily freed blandness of the songs which always featured on Radio Two was again contained within the hissing of frying bacon.

Breakfast proved to be the usual traumatic experience of spilt milk and forgotten schoolbooks. But in addition to all that there was Alan's crying—genuine for a change—and her father's presence at the table. Beatty's father had usually left for work by the time she arrived downstairs in the kitchen, but today was a special day. Today, there was no Ned wandering around sniffing at people's plates, and getting under everyone's feet. Alan just sat and sobbed. It hardly seemed the right time for Beatty to tell everyone that she had started her periods, but, of course, she had to say something. After all, her mother would see all the mess when she went in to make up Beatty's bed. Maybe she should just say nothing. Pretend that she hadn't noticed. But that just wasn't believable. The sheet looked like someone had been impaled. The thought made Beatty wince and she knocked the spoon out of her cereal bowl and it clattered to the floor loudly.

Beatty's mother spun around from the stove, clutching her hand to her chest. When she saw what had happened she merely shook her head. "Be careful, Beatty," she said in quiet tired exasperation.

"Sorry, Mum," Beatty said softly. "Mum?"

"What is it now, love?"

"I've started my periods. The sheets are in a terrible state." It seemed like a rather blunt way of informing her parents, but there seemed no other way than just coming right out with it. Beatty's father looked up from his bowl of Alpen, chewing, and grimaced.

"Beatty!" he said, his mouth full. "Not at the table, please. And not in front of your brother."

Alan did not even seem to hear.

Her mother turned down the gas under the frying pan and came over to Beatty's chair, smiling. "I don't know: it doesn't rain but it pours. How do you feel?" she asked, stroking her daughter's head.

Beatty considered for a moment before replying. "Fine," she said, at last. "I think."

"Any pains?"

Beatty shook her head.

"Well, you might get some tummy ache later," her mother said. "It might be a good idea to take some aspirins with a cup of tea." She moved over to the cupboard above the oven and removed a smoky colored glass bottle. Almost as if in response, Beatty's stomach gave a loud rumbling noise and she doubled over with a groan. It felt like her entire insides were being torn apart.

The telephone rang out in the hall, and Beatty's father jumped up from the table. "That'll be the vet," he said. Suddenly, Beatty's momentous news was forgotten, and Alan started crying again.

The walk to school was strange for Beatty, for a number of reasons. Firstly because Ned always used to walk slowly down the path and then stand wagging his tail, his head cocked on one side, as she turned into Allbeck Drive. It felt funny to think that Ned would never see her off to school again. But just "funny," not sad. In fact that in itself was funny, the way she had not really been upset at Ned's death. Maybe the tears would come later.

Secondly, she just felt altogether strange. Like she had just got out of bed after a long bout of flu or something. Everything looked unfamiliar and new, almost alien. But then, when she concentrated on something, it suddenly seemed natural again. She couldn't explain it, even to herself, so she didn't even bother trying tell her parents.

But the funniest thing of all was when she was walking past the park. It looked normal enough, but yet she sensed that it wasn't. She stopped at the corner of Weaton Crescent and just stared over at the wide expanse of grassland, while the lollipop lady stood waving her sign in the middle of the road. "Are you going to school today or what?" the lady shouted over to her. Beatty didn't answer, at least not straight away. Her attention was concentrated on a large bag-shaped object that seemed to blowing along the bottom of the hedgerows.

At school, the pain grew worse. Much worse. Beatty started to sweat uncontrollably. She had taken off her jumper and loosened the catch on her skirt, but nothing seemed to help. Even sitting on the toilet didn't ease the stabbing dull ache. Helen Carter told her that it would be crippling all day, and that Beatty should go home. But Beatty did not want to go home.

She didn't want to be in the house at all today. In the house on her own. It was mum's day out with Auntie Margaret—her auntie had told her mum that they could postpone wandering around the shops in Leeds until another day, what with Ned . . . with Ned dying and everything. But her mum would hear nothing of the sort. She knew, she said, how her sister looked forward to these trips to town, particularly since Uncle Eddie had died. And anyway, getting out would do her more good than moping around the house all day.

The scenes at home before Beatty had left for school had been terrible. Moving Ned's basket out by the dustbin, clearing out all the packets of biscuits and tins of dog food

. . . it had seemed to go on forever. And it was funny, but it seemed that, wherever she looked, Beatty could see the usual tell-tale wisps of matted dog hairs stuck to the sofa and the chairs, or wound together like spiraled clouds beneath the table in the kitchen.

A sudden sharp pain interrupted Beatty's train of thought, and she let out a high-pitched squeal. Mrs. Crawford turned around from the blackboard and stared myopically over her glasses. "Beatty? Would you like to be excused, dear?"

Beatty could not answer. Deep down inside her stomach she felt as though something was writhing around, twisting and turning frantically. Yes, that was it. It was a frantic movement. Almost impatient. The phrase "like a bull in a china shop" sprang into her mind, and she didn't like it. A low rumbling fart-like sound echoed from her lower abdomen, and some of the other children sniggered. Angela Fraser screwed up her face, as though smelling something extremely unpleasant. "Oh, gross," she whispered loudly. Beatty didn't hear her, nor did she hear Mrs. Crawford suggest more emphatically this time that she really should leave the class. All Beatty could hear, from far down in her body, was the sound of something moving around inside her. Something growing. Something with a mind all of its own. "Oh, God, help me," she moaned. Another violent movement and a faint far-off sound from inside her blouse, like someone biting into a slice of melon, brought Beatty to her feet screaming.

Sitting on the toilet seemed to do the trick this time and, after a couple of gurgling noises which failed to produce anything, there was a considerable amount of "action" as her father always put it. Within a few minutes, Beatty felt much better. It was only when she had pulled up her pants and was getting ready to flush the toilet that she grew worried. Looking down into the bowl, in that brief second before pulling the cistern lever, Beatty saw things which in no way resembled poopsies—it was the word she always used to describe her own excrement, being decidedly more ladylike than "shit" or "turds."

Rather, the blood-flashed coiled grayness heaped in the

toilet pan looked considerably more important. In the swirling anxious water which prepared to sweep them away forever, they looked like things that she really shouldn't be leaving behind. It just goes to show how much an upset can really affect you, she thought.

The ache and the cold sweats and dizziness grew stronger and more frequent as the day went on, with Beatty spending less and less time in any of her classes. After lunch—most of which she left, and the rest threw up almost immediately in one of the ground-floor toilet sinks—she went to the sick room and just stretched out on the narrow cot. Mrs. Carroll said that she should go home and even offered to take her in her car, but Beatty didn't want to go home. By this time she had been for four more of the unusual poopsies, each more novel and more colorful than the one before it. Now she could feel something definitely growing. Maybe it was a cancer. At least they could cure some cancers, she thought. But, deep down, she didn't really think that it was anything that anyone could cure. She could feel it uncoiling, filling up newly vacated space inside her, flexing and straining, moving around, still impatient.

By the time school finished, Beatty was almost gone. She could feel herself growing stronger but, almost as though she was nodding off to sleep, she kept losing her grasp on what was happening around her. It was as though she was getting smaller within her own body. And then, on the way home, hardly able to control her own feet, the complex machinery of memories, hopes and experiences that was once Beatrice Carrier, ceased to exist. Like the dot on television, after the last program of the day, she simply dwindled away, briefly into a white shadow of what she had been, softly questioning, reluctantly accepting . . . and then, nothing. But the figure marched on. Renewed, vigorous . . . reborn. Going home.

What was left of her daughter had been in the house almost two hours before Victoria Carrier returned from a fairly somber shopping spree with her sister.

Two hours was a long time. A long time for developing and growing. And too long to remain without sustenance.

Luckily, the girl's small sibling had come home only an hour after the shell of Beatty had entered the house. As a feast, the child left a lot to be desired, but as a snack he proved more than adequate.

The thing that was now Beatty was almost whole. Perceptions were growing and increasing by the second. The twin screens of reality—the child, screaming his reluctance to lose them, had called them eyes—were merging, coming into focus. She stared at the flapping tatters of skin on the small leg that she now lifted to her mouth. Tasty. She opened her mouth wider to allow the membrane to prepare the food. The thing now occupied her entire throat and peered through between her teeth to the world beyond. When it saw the leg, held delicately outside this small cave in which it now found itself, it sprayed its juice in a fine shower. The skin immediately began to sizzle and smoke, bubbling into small blobs which then burst with tiny pops.

She was tearing a piece off the leg with her teeth—which were fairly blunt and almost useless—when the woman entered the room and screamed. Victoria Carrier screamed at the blood and the mess and the entrails. She screamed at the sight of her daughter, her head bulging, hair almost completely gone, eyes hanging from their sockets like a gruesome Hallowe'en mask, bare belly bursting from her ripped blouse and school skirt, with a pool of gray and bloody lumpy wetness around the patch of floor on which she was sitting. Then, as she turned away from the sight of Beatty with a huge chunk of fresh meat in her mouth, she saw the small pile of bones on the floor beside the bed, some gnawed clean, some still fleshy, some still enclosed in pieces of fabric that Mrs. Carrier recognized as being Allbeck Juniors' school uniform.

She was still screaming, shaking her head, when, turning back to face Beatty, she saw—and heard!—her daughter's face split open across the middle. The split went through the mouth and around each cheek toward the ears: there was not much blood, a part of her noted almost absently. Then there was a frantic shuffling and heaving about Beatty's body and, suddenly, the top half of the head lifted, borne upward by some huge glistening thing, a dull but pulsating orangy-red in color, that seemed to be pulling itself out of the rest of the torso. It was about then that Victoria Carrier mentally checked out. When the thing, now freed from Beatty's head and for all the world resembling some ridiculous-looking three-foot-tall penis—wavered in front of her face, pulled back a long frilly foreskin and threw up what seemed like a bucket of hot red paint all over her.

It was the smell that made her smile. An earthy, primal smell . . . a mixture of age and newness. As she writhed and moaned on the floor, the smoke and spray from the exploding pustules on her face drifting in front of her eyes, she felt herself getting wet. In a last gesture of assistance, she lifted her bottom from the carpet.

In front of her, the thing had pulled itself completely out of the useless, empty carcass of her daughter, and now wobbled above her. Settling down between her spreadeagled shuddering legs, it noted, lifting the hem of the blue and gray checked skirt, that this time there would be much more room.

Head Acres

September 5

Took me bloody hours to load all my records into the flat from mother's car—she just sat there and listened to Dire Straits. "Dire" is right! I asked if she wanted to come in for a cup of tea but she had to get back—the Swintons are having a barbecue and that cow Sarah Billington (or whatever she's called now) will be there! Hoo-rah! She left just after three o'clock. I spent the rest of the day reading the *Sunday Times*—played a little Mozart and fell asleep in the chair. Must have been tired because it was turned 8:30 when I woke up. Had some bread and jam and listened to Shostakovich's *Piano Concerto Number Two*. Now I'm going to bed. It's almost 10:15. Shattered.

September 6
Vaughan Williams—*The Lark Ascending*.

It's good to be back. Today was just for settling in. My head of year is called Hollister. I spoke to him about doing extra work outside of lectures but he feels it's too early to say yet—and, anyway, he says I'll have enough to go at without taking on extra studies at this stage. It hasn't changed my mind. Everyone was full of the start of the new term and about what they did on their holidays. Nobody bothered asking me—thank God! The flat is okay but a bit dirty, and the hot water seems to please itself—I'm toying with the idea of looking for somewhere else. Wonder if father will provide the necessary? I'm writing down the best piece of music I hear each day—might prove interesting when I tie them up at the end of term. Today was a toss-up between Vaughan Williams's *Fantasia For Greensleeves* and his *The Lark Ascending*—I ended up going for the Lark. He's just *soooo* restful! Writing this in bed at 9:30.

September 7
Fairport Convention—*What We Did on Our Holidays* album.

The holidays thing from yesterday must have stayed in my mind because I pulled out Fairport without even thinking. Took me bloody ages to find it. Made for a rocking breakfast! Today was a good day all round. Discussed the relationship between instincts and archetypes—instincts being physiological urges perceived by the senses. At the same time, they manifest themselves in fantasies and only reveal their existence by symbolic images. Jung called them "collective archetypes," archaic remnants of a collective consciousness—sort of like a primordial sideshow. I call them "head acres." Hollister says music is probably the single greatest motivational tool known to man. When he was talking, it all made such obvious sense. I think I've always known that. Hollister called me back at the end of the lecture and said he'd spoken to Mr. Tuscatti who said I was his best student last year. I didn't know what to say. Anyway, Hollister loaned me a book—*Songlines* by Bruce Chatwin. Brilliant book! Stayed up until turned two o'clock reading it.

September 8
Beaver and Krause—*In a Wild Sanctuary* album.

No hot water and tired all day. James Booker asked if I wanted to go to a party on Saturday—I told him I was busy. He's so typical of them all. Just one thing on his mind—well, *two* things: beer and girls. It seems as though all they want to do here is get drunk and laid—and not necessarily in that order. Hollister gave us nearly two hours of filmed examples of music being used to manipulate. Lots of film scores and television advertisements. He told us about how Mozart always calmed him down if he was tense—I wanted to tell him that it worked for me, too. And I wanted to tell him about Vaughan Williams, and Terry Riley's *Rainbow in Curved Air* but didn't fancy everyone asking what the hell it was. I know from the bits of conversations I've caught that my musical tastes are a bit out on a limb! I overheard Lisa Morris in the cafeteria telling Angela Clayforth-Darby and the rest of that set that Happy Mondays was the only thing that relaxed her. Then she whispered something and they all fell about laughing. I think it was something to do with sex or drugs maybe. They're just like a bunch of old hippies! I'm going to play Andy Williams tomorrow. (What the hell made me think of Andy Williams?!) Read *Songlines* until 1:30.

September 9
Andy Williams—*Can't Take My Eyes Off You.*

Couldn't get the hot-water tap to work again this morning. Had to boil water just to shave in. I'm thinking of growing a beard—a big scruffy one like Robert Wyatt or Elvis or one of Z Z Top. Phoned father and he said it was okay for me to look for somewhere else—up to £30 a week. Can't be bad! I'm going to go hunting at the weekend. Mass Hysteria was top of the menu today. It's fascinating the way that the conscious mind and the ordinary sense perception can be so easily eclipsed. The funniest part though is that I seemed to know it all already but just needed to have it explained. I asked Hollister to give us more examples—he'd already told us about the Balinese sword dancers and how they go into trances and sometimes turn their swords on themselves—and he told me to stay behind. When I went to see him he told me about this religious cult in America— Tennessee—that plays music and sings songs and hand-claps while passing around live poisonous snakes. Some of them actually get bitten and die! Wonderful! He asked me how I was getting on with the book. I told him I thought it was great. He's going to dig me out some others. More from father's Andy Williams collection tomorrow, I think. Went to bed early but read until gone 11 while listening to his *Born Free* album. It's 11:55 now. Sleep calls.

September 10
Kevin Ayers—*Song From the Bottom of a Well.*

Woke up this morning (dah dah da dah!) feeling not like any Andy Williams at all. Last night I dreamed some pretty strange dreams but they all disappeared as soon as I got out of bed. Can't remember what they were about at all now, but I do remember there was a lot of desert in there somewhere. The hot water was on but I'm still going to look for somewhere else—gives the old man something to do with his money! Played Kevin Ayers's *Whatevershebringswesing* album and went into a kind of trance. Played it twice and felt like not bothering to go in to lectures at all. Glad I did though. More on head acres. The energy of collective archetypes can be focused through ritual to move people to collective action. The Nazis knew this, of course, and they used versions of the Teutonic myths to help rally the German people behind them—maybe the same could be achieved in single units . . . like working on one person at a time, maybe for a long time. Jung always said that man had yet to gain control of his own nature—maybe it's just that he needs help! I think music could be the way. Going to bed now to read more *Songlines.*

P.S. It's 2:40 and I've finished *Songlines.* The Aborigines chant their way through life, actually singing routes and paths into existence. Chatwin believes that it's a power inherent in humans . . . something that we've always had but forgotten. That must be why music can be so inspirational. But it's not just music, it's sound. After all, music is only a collection of sounds. It starts in the womb with the music of the mother's heart and then it goes on all through life. For the Aborigines, it clearly serves to open some kind of collective sentient consciousness and reveals knowledge that ancestors possessed. And that's what they mean by creating the paths—they're not *really* creating them but simply unlocking the race memory of them. But maybe after you've unlocked everything within yourself you can actually start influencing what's outside. It's an interesting concept: would the laws of science and nature respond to the Aboriginal chants? And if so, how could we know whether it was knowledge or power we already possessed? What actually would happen when you've exhausted the power inside? I think I'd like to experiment.

September 11
Philip Glass—*Serra Pelado*.

Saturday. Had a lie-in and felt pretty good. Got the bus out of Leeds to Bradford, an old mill town that seems to be filled with Pakistanis. Property seems much cheaper to rent than in Leeds (wonder why!). Saw an old place on the outskirts (Manningham Lane) which looks as if it might fit the bill. But the best part is that the owner (Mr. Jerrold) says I can have the cellar as well for just £2 a week extra—that's only £19.50 a week all in! He says it's "a bit rough at night" but that there's apparently "no shortage of skirt!" I told him that that was nice but I'd probably be too busy. I went into Bradford itself to look around in the afternoon and went back out to Manningham Lane just after seven o'clock. See what he means—prostitutes all over the place! Doesn't matter though cos I won't be going out at night. Came home and started *Songlines* again. Haven't been able to settle all night worrying about what I was going to use the cellar for. Philip Glass's *Powaqqatsi* has finally helped calm me down.

Peter Crowther

September 12
Philip Glass—*The Thin Blue Line*.

Sunday morning. Stayed in bed and read *Songlines* while listening to *The Thin Blue Line*. It made me cry. Then I put on *Powaqqatsi*—the word comes from the Hopi Indian words for sorcerer (powaq) and life (qatsi)—it's an entity that consumes the life force of other beings in order to further its own life. That's me! That's what I've decided to be. Except I'm furthering my own knowledge and what's knowledge if it's not life? Read *Songlines* all day and went to bed early. Listened to Terry Riley's *In C*, thinking about singing things into existence like the Aboriginals. If you can sing things *into* existence doesn't it follow that you could sing them *out* too? Sleep beckons. I know what I'm going to do! Can't wait for tomorrow!

September 13
Miles Davis—*Sketches of Spain* album.

Straight in today. Didn't wash. Couldn't wait to get started. We looked at the "compass of the psyche," Jung's way of looking at people. He was able to assess the mental makeup of people simply by applying this formula.

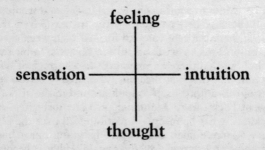

It's really just a cross. On the one line—the horizontal in my drawing—the end points are "sensation" and "intuition," while the line which crosses it (the vertical) spans from "feeling" to "thought." This will be important when I put together my playlist—but first I need a subject for the experiment. When I got home tonight I was too tired and too excited to read. Went through the records trying to find something which could relax and motivate me at the same time: it had to be Miles. I'm writing this while listening to *Sketches of Spain*, chanting to the beat with my legs crossed. It's not very comfortable but it's what the Haitians do to convince themselves they're possessed by Ghede. Rang Jerrold on the way back home and told him I'd take the flat. So tired. That's it for today.

September 14

Amazing. It might just have been the wind, of course, but today I chanted changes in the weather. They were only slight variations but I'm sure it was something to do with what I was doing. I sat on the outside wall humming a kind of mantra and concentrating. When I thought of heat and desert, the wind dropped; when I thought of cold and rain, the wind built up again. On tonight's weather report, the man said that parts of Northern England had their most unsettled day since records began. They even interviewed him and asked how the weather bureau had been unable to predict it. He said that it happens sometimes and that it's to do with pressure drops in the North Sea and the Atlantic occurring at the same time as huge buildups on the land masses. Sounds like the "experts" telling people who have seen flying saucers that all they've really seen is the reflection of Venus on the clouds. The most interesting thing was that I didn't eat all day! And I never had to go in to use the toilet. I feel tired now, though. Haven't played any music at all today. Just made my own. Bed.

September 16

Couldn't be bothered to fill you in yesterday, dear diary. I started looking for a subject but they're all so engrossed with themselves it was a complete waste of time. Today was the same. I missed this afternoon's lecture but read

Songlines sitting cross-legged on a bench—wait for it!—which I spent 20 minutes singing into existence in Beckett's Park. Just like that! One minute it's not there, and then it is. I couldn't believe it. Thankfully, nobody saw me. Yesterday's highlight was Dire Straits' *Love Over Gold* album which I played (I think) because I was thinking of mother. It's actually not bad but *Private Investigations* is brilliant. Today it was Cal Tjader's *Soul Surfing*—nothing to do with surfing. Feel a little strange tonight—maybe I'm coming down with cold. I'll probably sleep it off.

September 16

Spent a long careful time in the bathroom this morning, listening to Nigel Kennedy "fiddle" his way through Brahms's *Violin Concerto in D* while I, in turn, attempted to sing my stuffiness away. Nothing much happened except that when I went to brush my teeth later there was no water! A letter arrived from Jerrold. I can move in next Monday, the 20th. Missed morning lectures cos I felt so grotty. Looked for a subject but no go—felt a little better in the afternoon so I went in for Hollister's lecture. The ego's emergence can best be symbolized not by battle but by sacrifice . . . death leading to rebirth. Byron gave his life willingly during the revolution in Greece; St Lucia sacrificed her eyes and her life for her religion; an inscription on one British World War I memorial reads: "At the going down of the sun and in the morning we will remember them." Hollister read an extract from a book by Leopold Vaschimone called *Cyclical Cantata and Rhymic Stigmata* where he states that, according to reliable witnesses (!) Jesus hummed all the time he was on the cross. Everyone laughed except me and Hollister. He loaned me a book by Lawrence Block called *Random Walk*, about a man who suddenly just goes walking for no reason, pulling all these different people to him. One of them, a woman, is going blind but she realizes she can see much better the worse her eyes get. The pipes were making funny noises tonight. Must sleep.

P.S. My cold has disappeared.

The Longest Single Note

Big day tomorrow. Big day today, too. I've found him. He's perfect. I found him yesterday hanging around the market. At first I thought he was waiting to meet somebody but after a couple of hours I realized he was just passing time. I told him I was moving in to Bradford and asked where the best place to eat was. He took me down to a McDonald's and we chatted about nothing in particular. His name's Edward and he lives in Shipley. I told him we ought to get together for a drink. He said he'd meet me at the market again next Saturday afternoon. Didn't go into lectures at all on Thursday and Friday. Hollister came around on Friday night to see what was the matter. I said I still had a cold but I know he knew I was lying. He brought me the Vaschimone book and another one called *Stranger Than Science*, an old Pan paperback by Frank Edwards. Julia Ward Howe, who wrote *The Battle Hymn of the Republic*, says "I wonder if I really wrote it. I feel that I did not. I was just an instrument. It really wrote itself." That night I dreamed I was on the Potomac River, with mist swirling all around me. The next morning everything was damp in the flat—I'll be glad to get out of here.

Played Jefferson Airplane's *Spare Chaynge*, some Beatles and *Delibes Larkme*—the full 138 minutes, not father's highlights cassette!

September 21
Stravinsky—*The Rite of Spring*.

Shattered today. Took the day off yesterday to move and I'm not going in today. I've made great progress, wandering around the property chanting up routes and a few barriers—mainly to cope with any unexpected noises. There are still a few things I've got to sing in yet. I've made several paths around the flat which now seem comfortable, though I did trap myself for a while halfway down the cellar steps—I only managed to get going again by remembering that wood has a certain sound. It took a mixture of *Night on Bare Mountain* and *Hey, Hey We're the Monkees* before

I could actually move. The thing is that, once I was safe again and able to think through it all, I realized that I had not read anywhere about wood having its own sound. But it has. And so do all the metals as well as water and trees and plants. This is what I meant by race memory—I think I must be tapping into things that have lain dormant since the days of the cavemen. How exciting! Maybe that's how the ice age started: maybe it was nothing to do with meteors or exploding or imploding suns, maybe it was some kind of tribal chant put out by the savages of the time. Savages! That's a laugh . . . the real savages are those prats down at the University.

Sang the cellar in. All I need to do now is clean it all up. I'm starting to make up a lot of my own songs now— they're a mixture between chants and tunes . . . I'll call them "chantunes." I can sing away the need to pee now— haven't been since leaving Leeds, though there's a lot of staining down my legs and crotch. Ah, hubris! Man's greatest fallibility is that which he makes to the sin of pride!

September 23

Painted a quadrangular motif on the cellar ceiling to symbolize the all-important center of the psyche. Remembered to eat today. Everything's ready for Eddy. Spent the last two days writing a playlist, putting things on tape. I've got about 30 hours' worth already. I just hope it's enough. Favorite musical piece of the day has been the Andante from Shostakovich's *Piano Concerto No. 2*. Needless to say I've included it on Edward's tapes. Tomorrow I'm going to have a Love session, I think—haven't heard *Forever Changes* for ages. I think I'm putting off going to bed . . . there's so much movement around the place. I think people are walking my paths. Who are they? Why can't I see them? Can they see me?! Maybe I need a protective chantune.

September 24

Letter from father. Hollister has written to him expressing concern at my lack of attendance at lectures. Bastard!

I've a good mind to go around to his house with his books and do a little impromptu gig outside his window and heal his mouth and nostrils up. But I've too much to do preparing for Edward tomorrow. After the start to the day I decided against Love and went instead for Charlie Watts's Orchestra playing live at Fulham Town Hall, with *Stomping at the Savoy* and a purely masterful rendition of Lionel Hampton's *Flying Home*. That got rid of a little pent-up energy. Sitting up in bed now, writing this, listening to the faint rustlings and almost imperceptible movements along my pathways.

September 25
The Rolling Stones—*Beggar's Banquet*.

Hey, please allow me to introduce myself. Dear Diary. I am me. And what I have done—or started to do—today will make history. Met Edward as arranged. We went around Bradford and then went to see *Terminator 2*. When we came out it was dark and I suggested we go for a drink near where I lived. I realize now, too late of course, that Edward thought I was gay. I don't know why I didn't think of it before. Of course, I was merely immersed in my experiment but he was sexually motivated. Maybe that's not fair. We're both motivated by knowledge and the attainment of it. That must be true of everyone. All activity, all experience, all conversation . . . is knowledge. But each applies to—or titillates, or satisfies—different areas.

When we got back to the house he threw his arms around me once we were through the door. I realized straight away (thank God) and so I didn't do anything about it. But I managed to hold him off a while until I poured us a couple of glasses of wine—his was heavily laced with some of mother's "calmers." He's asleep now. Dead to the world. It took me some time to get him down into the cellar, but I managed it. It took longer because of the paths, of course. There's only one way in and out of the cellar and it's not simply straight ahead and then either down or up the stairs! I sang in a special route this morning—took me just over an hour—a long and circuitous route that involves going back on yourself and then forward and then left and then back and then right and so on. I've written it all down. And I've sung in a barrier of rocks and stone outside the cellar windows and at the head of the stairs. You can't see it, of course, but it is there—and you can't hear a thing out there. I checked by playing tapes loudly before I brought Edward.

Anyway, I'm going to go down now and watch—he'll be waking up soon. I've set up a chair in the side room, in front of the spyhole, and laid on some sandwiches and a flask of tea. I'm not hungry or thirsty at all these days but I just fancied the thought of making an event out of it— like the picnics that mother used to take me on when father was away. Oh, what a night it's going to be. I'm so excited!

September 26
The Beatles—*The Long and Winding Road*.

. . . That leads to your door! Edward woke up at 2:14 am. His face was a picture. I started the tapes straight away. He sat up on the cellar floor, shook his head and then looked all around. Then he called my name. Several times. Percy Faith and his orchestra was on at the time, playing *Shenandoah* from his *American Serenade* album. He stood up and tried to move to the door but couldn't because he doesn't know the path. I suppose he could find it in time, purely by accident—what is it they say about an infinite number of monkeys being able to type the entire works of Shakespeare? But, anyway, Edward doesn't know the path and so he has to stand or sit or lie right where he is. He might suddenly find—because he's got his legs or arms or knees in a particular position—that he's got more room or can suddenly move in a direction he couldn't move in be-fore. But it's short-lived. As I'm writing this he's sitting cross-legged on the floor staring at the door which is about eight feet away from him. He's already done the "mime" bit, moving his hands up and down against the invisible barrier in front of him, but he's given it up now. He gave it up when he had a pee and watched as the stream of urine started gushing out in front of him and ended up kind of bending around and hitting the floor about two feet to his left. That fazed him. He's been in there almost three hours now. I'm just about to start the third tape. A lot of my excitement has faded now, and I'm very tired. When I start this next tape I'm going to have a doze. He's just shouted for me again.

September 28

Missed a whole day. We've played 38 hours of music now. Edward has cried constantly for the past few hours. Occasionally though he seems to be paying more attention to different pieces of music. I've wired up my two-cassette player so that it will play for four hours at a stretch without me doing anything to it. That gave me time this morning to get out and have a breath of fresh air. It's starting to smell down there—Edward has relieved both bladder and bowels several times. But that should be it now. By the time we hit the end of the next tape all of his orifices will be sung closed. The playlist I put together has already sung away his desire to eat or drink. (I caught sight of myself in the mirror this morning—I don't look too good. Maybe I ought to have something to eat myself.) Going to grab some shuteye now.

September 30

It's eight o'clock pm. We're approaching the 100-hour mark now—less than seven hours to go! Apart from the odd twitch, Edward hasn't moved since early this morning. He's still breathing though. Just. But now he doesn't seem to be aware of anything but the music. He tilts his head constantly at the sounds, crying occasionally, staring wistfully into some strange distance and even letting out the odd smile and chuckle. He no longer seems to want to leave. My detailed notes showing half-hourly (except when I'm asleep) developments are coming to the end of the second exercise book.

October 1

Something is happening. Edward is shuddering as though he's cold. His skin is almost opaque, with a white glistening sheen. He's been humming in his sleep and is currently lying curled up in a fetal position about two feet above the floor! I don't know when this happened—he was like it when I woke from a doze at 5:37 this morning (it's all in the exercise book). He's starting to sing changes within himself, I'm sure of it. I think I'm going to have to go in.

I've been in. His breathing is very slow. Hardly any pulse. Skin clammy. He was completely unaware of me. Still humming, but not to the music that's playing at any time. They're odd little ditties and chants . . . quite folksy with unexpected basso profundo outbursts. There in the middle of his room the activity along the pathways is incredible. I crawled under and around him to see if I could sense or feel anything holding him up but there was nothing. I cut him. He didn't feel it. So then I cut off his right index finger. No reaction. No bleeding. I pierced the skin of his thigh with a needle and then slipped it through his testes. Still nothing. We're almost at the end of the tapes now. Must rest.

October 2—4:10 am

I thought it was an earthquake or something that had woken me up but it was Edward. He's standing up straight now, still suspended above the floor, and all his clothes have gone. They're not on the floor beneath him. His eyes are wide open but only the whites are showing, and his arms and legs are stretched out as though he is tethered to a wagon wheel. The final tape has about 30 minutes left to go. I'm going in.

—4:52 am. I'm now in the room with Edward. He died— or perhaps moved on might be a better expression—20 minutes ago, at 4:32 precisely. It was incredible. His face shone and he cried tears that were filled with bracken and bits of grass, that left orangey dust-colored streaks down both cheeks. Just before the end he stopped his humming (up to that point he had built it into a frenzied cadence that all but shook his body apart limb from limb) and opened his mouth. There was nothing inside—well, I say "nothing" when in fact there was everything. Space, is what there was. Billions of stars and all the milk-stain streaks of cosmic debris that litter the heavens. And it seemed to be lit, just the way that Edward's face was lit, burning with a fierce luminosity . . . like a bulb that's about to burst. Then he went. He just closed his mouth and rolled down his eyelids and . . . I think he just went off, down there inside himself, inside everyth—

October 3

I'm still here. It's a little after 1:15 am and I'm still in the room with Edward. I've been here nearly 20 hours now. Edward is still hanging up there, arms and legs stretched out to grasp and embrace everything. "Teach me everything," he seems to be saying. "I want to know everything."

I've forgotten the route.

And the detailed map is on the other side of the spyhole. The tape stopped as I was finishing my last entry. The silence is not particularly disturbing in itself, only in the way it accentuates the activity along the paths. I've been trying to find my way out but I keep getting stuck. Got as far as the outer wall a little while ago and then couldn't get any further. Then I couldn't get back to Edward. He's about three feet to my right now . . . I could actually reach out and touch him if it wasn't for the damned paths I sang in. I'm humming to ease the silence. I can't stand the silence. It lets me hear the things on the paths. They seem to be gathering—mainly near where Edward is hanging, but something brushed past me not too long ago. Maybe they're attracted by his body. Like dead meat attracts all kinds of predators. It's probably just my imagination but I'm beginning to feel a little vulnerable. I must stop the silence. I'm going to stop writing now so that I can concentrate.

Fell asleep. Had a really weird dream. There were all these Aborigines and I was with them. They were all frightened, pointing to the sky. And when I looked up it wasn't there. It sounds stupid now, writing it down on paper, but the sky had gone. It was like looking into a whirlpool, just a mass of swirling energy. And something was coming, swimming through the energy toward us. And in that stupid way of communication in dreams—talking to each other without really speaking—the Aborigines told me it was God. They didn't call it that, but I knew. I can't remember what they called it. They said they had sung it into existence long, long, ago, but it had been too powerful. Too destructive. So they had sung it out again, banished it. And I asked them why it was coming back. What did it want? And they all looked at me and said nothing. That's when I woke up.

I've no idea how long I've been here, nor what time or even what day it is now. Edward has mostly gone. It started with just bits of him being pulled away from the inside but then it got so that there were more and more bits disappearing into a kind of starry void with Edward's shape. I can't make out what it is that's taking him—it's invisible. Looking at Edward now is like looking out of the porthole of a rocketship traveling through outer space. But I can hear something . . . some kind of rhythm, distant but much nearer than it was when it started. It's a tune . . . or a mixture of tunes and chants—who's singing them I have no idea. As I watch there are tiny vine-like tendrils snaking around the edge of Edward's shape—it's strange . . . I recognize so many songs and sounds . . . they're drifting in like wafts of air through an open doorway. I'm constantly jostled by the things on the paths. They're gathering in front of Edward who is now completely "spaced out." The last piece—his left cheek and eye socket—has just been pulled away, toppling off into the distance like a jettisoned lump of garbage. The vines—for that's what they look like, like the constantly slowly snaking arms of a clinging ivy . . . except that these are not moving slowly! They're pulling at the edges of the hole that was Edward . . . pulling it wider. And the sounds are growing louder and lou—
    Wait.
    They've stopped.
    Everything is quiet now, even the activity on the pathways has settled down. I think we're all waiting for something to hap—
    Beautif—

Home Comforts

The sign comes up on our right. *Merrydale*, it says, *4 miles*.

I look across at Melanie, her face set to the windscreen and bathed a faint green in the dashboard light. Her mouth moves around, saying nothing in particular, just chewing syllables. Quiet.

The turning comes up quicker than I expected in the gloom and I almost miss it, spinning the wheel into the gravel and earth at the side of the road, watching the headlights wash across trees and earth and the last far-off gleams of the sun going down. Rain washes the windows and runs down in thick rivulets that the single wiper can't easily clear. For a second I think we're going to get stuck, but the wheels, skidding noisily just the one time, catch on something solid and the old Dodge jumps back onto the road. Now we can see a tree-lined lane in front of us, stretching down a hill. No streetlights. No noise. No signs of life.

Never any signs of life,

"Maybe here, honey," I whisper to Melanie, placing a hand that she once recognized gently on her knee. "Maybe this is the place." I put the hand back onto the steering wheel. There had been no response to it.

We start down the lane.

A few minutes later we roll onto a main street that must have once looked like something out of a *Saturday Evening Post* cover. Now it looks as lost and forlorn as we must look, drifting into town through the mud and the rain, our bellies empty of food, eyes empty of warmth, minds empty of compassion.

I check the gas gauge. It's low.

"Gonna have to get some gas, honey," I tell Melanie, though I know she isn't listening. I snatch a sideways glance and see her head making those staccato movements as she checks the storefronts and the barn doors, and we roll on down the road to what looks like it might be, or maybe once was, the Merrydale town center.

Up ahead there's the remnants of a picket fence surrounding a square of overgrown grass. Behind the square is a wooden walkway, its slats sticking up into the nighttime sky, and a General Store, a barber shop and a couple of others I can't make out. The windows are smashed in, a couple of them boarded over and the wood pulled open. The darkness behind the wood is absolute. A pure color. Complete black.

Round back of the square, to the left, I see a Texaco sign swinging in the wind. In my head I hear its rusty whine, like a baby left too long by itself, all hoarse and cried out, dried up of tears and passion. I pull off the main drag, into the shade of the buildings, and the rain seems to ease off. I drive around the square and now I see the garage. There's an old DeSoto, tires flat, windows smashed, parked half in and half out the station window where once a kid, or maybe some old guy who'd spent his whole life in Merrydale, would sit listening to the ball game or the Wednesday night fight or rap music, watching and waiting for cars and customers.

Suddenly the rain seems more insistent, wetter, relentless. The night looks darker and colder and even less hopeful. But we left hope, Melanie and me, a long way and a long time back.

I park the Dodge and get out. As I open the door, Melanie grabs my arm and shakes her head, groaning. She points into the back seat. "It's okay, honey, it's okay," I tell her. "I'm just gonna see if there's any gas in those pumps, is all." But no, she won't have it. She hangs on to my jacket, fingers white, eyes wide and staring. I tell her okay, and I reach in back for a couple of the stakes. Lift the old strapped hammer and shrug it over my head and my right shoulder so it sits around me like a gun. And I step out into Merrydale.

The wind is whistling and the rain coming down in intermittent sheets. A few steps away from the car and I'm soaked.

The pumps are smashed up, the nozzles removed and cast across the forecourt. I walk over to the DeSoto, look inside. There's a mummified body on the back seat. It's a woman. She doesn't have any eyes, just black, staring sockets. Her clothes are pulled up and her scrawny breasts exposed . . . her pants are down, legs pulled wide apart. For a second I think maybe I saw something move down there . . . something small with a long tail . . . but I convince myself it's just the clouds across the moon making shadows. Something I don't want to feel turns around inside me, calls to me to let me know it's still there. I take a look back at my car. Melanie is hunched forward in her seat, nose against the windscreen, watching me through the rain. I smile and shrug, walk away from the DeSoto to the pumps.

On closer inspection I see that I might be able to put one of them back together. I glance around to make sure I'm still okay and then crouch down, lay the wooden stakes on the pavement, pick up the nozzle, and heft it to the pump. It just needs screwing in again. I do that.

Melanie knocks on the windscreen. She's telling me to get the stakes. I wave and she stops knocking. Then I pick up the stakes and jam them inside my jacket pocket. The pump gun lever seems to be stuck, so I give it a tap with the hammer to free it up. I give it a gentle squeeze and nothing happens. Squeeze it some more. Still nothing. I curse my stupidity. No electricity. Just before I wrench the nozzle back out again, I see the crank-bolt on the side of the pump. Of course! There had to be a way to get the gas moving manually in such an out-of-the-way place. I look around on the floor for something to use, but there isn't anything. I lay the nozzle down and walk back to the Dodge.

Melanie leans over and lifts the catch. I pull the door open and crouch down beside the car. "Honey," I say, real soft and slow, so she won't start to panic on me, "I'm gonna go into the filling station, get a wrench or something to crank up some gas."

She shakes her head.

I reach over and take her small white hand in mine, stroke it once or twice. "Melanie, honey, we *need* gasoline. I have to try. Now you just sit tight right here and I'll be back before you know it." She blinks at me like she doesn't believe it. For a second I see how much she looks like her mother. How much she looks like my beloved Mary. But her memory seems tainted now.

I stand up and slam the door, turn my back on them, on Melanie and Mary. Walk over to the office.

Most of the glass is gone, littered across the inside of the room. In back there's a sign saying *Washroom*, but I ignore the privacy it promises. Near the counter is a comic book stand, no comic books in it, and a book rack with no books. Down on the floor I see a dog-eared paperback all puffed out with water damage. I pick it up and read the cover. It shows a baseball and a bat. *Gone to Glory.* Guy called Robert Irving or Irvine . . . I can't make it out. Something about it being "a moroni traveler mystery." I toss it back onto the floor and slide across the counter to where the pump controls lay covered in dust and dirt.

From the other side of the counter I can see the Dodge. I give a wave to Melanie, but she isn't looking my way. I see her profile. Watch her 11 years turn into 34 years, see her face turn from a girl into a woman. I jerk my hands up to my face and jam fingers into my eyes, stop the thoughts.

It would be so easy to just walk out of the office, walk out of the filling station, take it on the lam from beautiful, downtown Merrydale and hightail it up to the interstate, catch a ride on a truck heading for St. Louis or maybe Kansas City, chew the fat with one of the good-ol'-boy truck-drivin' boys while we listen to some sounds on his radio or shout back yells and thoughts at the voices that come over the CB . . . and, outside, the night speeds by us and he offers me some of his sandwiches and maybe a slug of Lone Star beer he's had cooling in the box beneath his seat. And he pulls his old steam whistle that honks into the darkness, lets everyone know we're alive . . . and we're comin'!

I take the hands away.

There are no trucks on the Interstate. There are no sounds on the radio, no voices on the CB, no ham on rye and no cold beers. There're just a few survivors and a few drinkers. Guy back in Racktown, little place due south of Columbus, had told me that there weren't too many drinkers left, he figured. He hadn't seen one in more than a year. That maybe it was all over now and it's time to rebuild.

I tell Melanie what the guy said. "Now ain't that just the best news you've heard all year?" I ask her. But she doesn't respond. Guy watches her and then asks me if she's okay. "Sure she's okay," I tell him. "Sure she's okay." And Melanie just stares ahead, past the old man, watching the road out of Racktown across the state of Ohio and into Indiana, next stop Indianapolis, and, after that, Springfield, Illinois and, after that . . .

Melanie can see me now. I wave at her and she waves back at me. The wave looks strange, woodenlike.

The old guy's voice comes back into my head.

"So what's wrong with her, then?" he says. "She your daughter?" I nod back to him and smile, proudlike. "Yep," I tell him. "So what's wrong with her?" he asks me again.

"She's been hurt." I tell him.

"Hurt?" he asks. "Yeah," I tell him. "Drinker got her." I say it real low so that Melanie can't hear me too well. "Back home, Macon, guy got her in the house and . . ." I let my voice trail and let him figure the rest. "That's what we're doin' now, her and me," I tell him. "Trackin' that bastard down."

He shakes his head in my memory.

"Look," I say to him. And I reach over to pull Melanie's scarf down from her neck. They're still there, on her neck, the bruises. Both sides. "Skin ain't broke," the old guy says.

123

"No," I agree, "and that right there is the one almighty blessing." And I pull up the scarf again. Melanie doesn't move, she just stares at the road. "But she got broke in other places," I tell him sadly. As if on cue, Melanie clasps her hands on her lap and draws her knees tight together.

"Trackin' him down, you say?"

"Right in one," I say. I take a sip of the lemonade he's given us. It tastes like I always figured champagne would taste, little bubbles tickling my face as I drink.

"Like a detective on an old TV show," he says.

I grunt, thinking back to television shows.

"You got any idea which way he's headin?" he says.

I shake my head.

The old guy nods. "Happened back in Georgia, you say?"

"I say."

"Long ways," he says.

I nod in agreement and look up at the sun, squinting.

"Long ways for such fresh-lookin' bruises," he mutters, and shakes his head, giving Melanie the once-over, looking down at her tiny, clasped hands. "Funny," he carries on, "I ain't never heard of a drinker doin' that."

Pretty soon after that we got back inside the Dodge, Melanie and me, and we rode on out of Racktown.

Melanie has settled some now, I see, my mind coming back to the filling station office. Now that she can see me.

I try to cast my mind back to before the sickness, before the "drinking" plague . . . the plague made that AIDS thing seem like a summer cold. It's like a dream to me now.

And I think back to Mary. In my mind I watch her getting sick. Lord knows where she got it from, or who gave it to her. She just got it. I think back to how we kept her locked up during the nighttime, when it was dark, and she was thirsty, thinking maybe it would just wear itself out, the sickness, like a fever. And how, during the daylight hours, we kept her safe and warm and dark. She had lost all recollection of who she was early on, become just like an animal. And Melanie and me we fed her the occasional animal I caught out in the woods. Let her drink to her heart's content.

But old man Snapes caught onto how he never saw Mary during the day. I told him she was sick with the flu—there was one going around at the time, which was a big help. But after a while most everyone else who'd caught it was getting better and Mary still didn't make an appearance.

I shake my head at the memory, but it's all churned up now and I have to run it through.

I think back to the night when they came for her. Old man Snapes and Corley Waters and a couple of boys I hadn't seen before. Knocked on the door, large as life, like they were making a social call, and then pushed past me and Melanie with their stakes and their hammers.

"Where is she, Jake?" Corley Waters shouts. I don't say anything, just grab hold of Melanie and glance at the bedroom door. They see the bolts, of course. And they go in, close the door behind them.

But we heard it, Melanie and me. We heard every thud and every scream.

A few minutes later, they drag her out in a sheet, blood all over it, and a few of the stakes are still in her. "You shoulda told us, Jake," old man Snapes says to me. His eyes look sad and tired as they look everywhere but right at me. "Woulda been easier."

And then they left, leaving the house quiet and still.

Melanie doesn't say a word. She just walks to the bedroom door and pulls it closed, pushes the bolts home.

Somewhere behind me I hear a noise.

I spin around and stare into the gloom.

Back away from the counter, the office lets onto a corridor with a door at the end. The noise came from in there. I glance back outside and wave at Melanie. She gives me that dull wave again, like a puppet, someone working her strings.

I creep slowly away from the window, into the corridor and toward the door. I hear it again, softer this time.

My hand is shaking as it reaches out for the handle, tests it, and finds it moves. I turn it all the way and push gently. As it opens, I can hear more noises now. Seems there was a whole lot of little sounds but, with the door closed, I could only hear the heavier ones. I get my head up against it and look inside.

It's light in there. The light is coming from a candle that flickers in the little breezes and drafts that find their way into the back room. It's a storage room . . . or was once. There's a whole line of shelving made out of metal scaffolding. On the shelves are a load of boxes and clothes, some hanging there on hangers. The room is done out like a home. On the floor, in front of the candle, a man is cleaning something. It's an animal. Looks like he's preparing something to eat. I can't make out what it is but I see a tail. Then I know why the woman's been left in the DeSoto. Bait.

Next to the man a woman is lying across some blankets and carpets. They're about 30 years old, maybe younger.

I watch the man.

I see him smile at the woman.

He smiles at her the way I used to smile at Mary.

He smiles at her the way I tried to smile at Melanie that first time, back in Macon. When I pushed her down and held her hands and made believe she was Mary. When I told her I needed some home comforts. Man can't get by without home comforts, I told her. That was when she stopped talking to me. When she stopped saying anything at all.

I pull the hammer off my shoulder and push the door open wide. It slams against some of the shelving right behind it and I march into the room. The man looks up at me, but I walk straight to the woman. She's making to get up, but the hammer catches her in the face and she falls right back down. I swing the hammer high and bring it down right into the face . . . that face that took the man's smiles. It bursts like a watermelon. The woman lies still.

"J-Jane?" the man says, making it a question. He knows there's no chance he'll get an answer from that pulp, but he just has to ask. For a second I feel a little sympathy. For a second. But I have other things to think about.

I reach down and grab the man's shirtfront, hoist him to his feet. As I drag him out of that back room, he's shouting back over his shoulder to the woman. Then he's shouting at me, asking me what I'm doing, telling me he isn't a drinker. He uses God's name a lot, and Jesus', too. But they don't have any place in this. They don't have any place in anything anymore. I don't say anything.

I drag him through the office and out into the night. My blood's pumping inside me and I feel something uncurling inside my pants.

Melanie gets out of the Dodge.

"I got him, honey," I shout to her. "Daddy's got the bastard what messed with you."

"What . . . what the hell are you—"

"Shut the fuck up," I tell him, smacking him across his face with my free arm, letting the hammer drop to the fore-court where its clattering echoes a while and then fades away.

Melanie is out of the Dodge now and leaning against the hood. Her eyes are wide and expectant, her hands are rub-bing themselves together.

I lift the man and toss him onto the hood, pull a stake out of my pocket. He holds his hands up in the air, covering his chest, pulling his knees up like a baby. He's shouting at me, but I don't hear. The thing in my pants is screaming now. I hold the stake over his chest and Melanie hands me the hammer. "Thanks, honey," I say to her and she smiles at me one of those special smiles.

"Jesus Christ," the man shouts, trying to grab my arm. But he just isn't strong enough.

"Is he the one, honey?" I ask her, ask her the way I've asked her all the other times.

She nods, quickly, emphatically . . . like she's nodded to me on all of those same times.

"I never seen her bef—"

The hammer comes down on the stake and drives it into the man's chest, stopping him in mid-sentence. The blood spurts like an oil-gusher. When I lift my hand from him he stays right where he is, jerking his belly up and down, not saying anything, and I figure the stake has gone right through into the Dodge's hood. I pull out another stake and hand it to Melanie. She holds it over his left hand side and I hit it squarely. The man is still now.

"He's dead," I tell Melanie, exhausted. "I killed him for you, honey. He can't hurt you no more."

Melanie takes my hand and squeezes it tight. The way she's done it after all of the others. The way she did after the boy in South Carolina and the old man in Racktown. Like after the youngster in Raleigh and the young feller in Charleston.

She squeezes and leads me around the Dodge to the back seat, pulls open the door. I get inside first, sweeping all of the wooden stakes onto the floor. Before she climbs in after me, Melanie helps me with my pants.

When we're through, I ask her, "Are you sure he was the one, Melanie honey? Do you think we could've made a mistake?"

Melanie frowns and looks down at her hands, pulls her dress over herself. Then she nods.

"Then he's still out there," I say to her, "the bastard."

Within an hour I've found a wrench and gotten some gasoline out of the old pump. Our luck is in.

With the sun starting to show across the hills, we leave Merrydale for points north.

As we pull onto the deserted freeway, I think back to what that old man said, back in Racktown. About how maybe I was like a detective in one of the old television shows.

Watching the road trailing into the distance I half imagine I hear end-credits music drifting across the blacktop and the roof of my old Dodge. At my side, Melanie stares out of the side window . . . like she's hoping to see something different to what we've just passed by.

I pat her on the knee, but she doesn't respond . . . just gives out a little shiver.

After a few hours, a sign comes up on our right. *Hannibal*, it says, *28 miles*.

I look across at Melanie, her face set to the windscreen. Her mouth moves around, saying nothing in particular, just chewing syllables.

Quiet.

Rustle

"Okay, where do we start?"

The man shrugged. "You tell me."

"Why don't you try to tell me what it's like."

"Tell you what it's *like?*"

"Yes."

"What *what's* like?"

"This other room."

"Well . . . it's a room. It's just . . . a room."

"You say it's just a room: what kind of room?"

"*Kind* of room?"

"Yes, is it a bedroom? Is it a—"

"No, it's not a bedroom. Not exactly."

"Not exactly? What do you mean by 'not exactly'?"

"There's no bed in it."

"Right. No bed. But you said 'not exactly.' Why?"

"There are things in there."

"Things?"

"Yeah, sleeping things."

"There are sleeping things in the other room?"

He nodded.

"What . . . like pajamas? Sheets? What?"

"No." A trace of exasperation. *"Things!"*

"Tell me what kind of things."

"I don't *know* what kind of things. I've not seen them. I've told you, I don't go in there."

"So how do you know there are things in there?"

"I've heard them."

"Doing what? Talking?"

The man giggled. "No, not talking."

"What then?"

"Sleeping."

"You've heard them sleeping?"

Another nod.

"What . . . like breathing? Snoring?"

"Yeah. Well . . . breathing, you know, breathing heavy . . . like you do when you're asleep."

The doctor looked over at the policeman. The policeman shrugged. The man between them rocked slowly, back and forth, his hands clasped between his knees.

"So when do you hear them, these things?"

He hesitated and then said, "When I take them a girl."

Doctor Malloy scribbled something on his pad.

"How many girls have you taken them, Edward?" The man sitting at the back of the room uncrossed and re-crossed his legs, the material of his uniform rustling in the stillness of the interview room.

The doctor looked up and leaned to the side, shaking his head. "I would rather you just let me talk to Edward, Inspector."

The policeman sighed and settled back on his chair.

"Can you answer that, Edward? Can you answer the Inspector's question? Can you tell me how many girls you've taken into the room?"

He sighed. "I've told you, I don't—"

"I know, I know . . . you don't go in the room."

"Right."

"So, how many girls have you taken into *your* room?"

"Eleven."

"Eleven girls?"

"Yeah. Eleven."

"You sound very sure."

"I am. I keep count."

The doctor made a note of Edward's use of the present tense and said, "When do you take them?"

"When? Like what time?"

"No, I mean how often."

"It varies."

"Why does it vary, Edward?"

"It varies because it depends on when they want another one."

" 'They' being the sleeping things, the things you haven't seen?"

"Yeah."

"They let you know when they want another one?"

The man nodded and looked around the room.

"How do they let you know that?"

"The room appears."

Doctor Malloy removed his glasses and pulled a handkerchief out of his trouser pocket, started to clean the lenses. "The whole room—just appears?"

"No, just the door."

"A door appears. All by itself?"

"Yeah."

"Where does it appear, this door? What is it like?"

"It's just a door. It's purple. A purple door. And it appears in different places. Sometimes it appears in the sitting room, sometimes in my bedroom. One time it appeared in the kitchen while I was cooking."

"The door just appears by itself? No walls attached to it?"

"Yeah, by itself." He chuckled. "You can walk right around it, right around the back." His face suddenly lit up and he chuckled again. "Like . . . like Doctor Who's telephone box."

"Is there anything around the other side?"

"No, there's just the door."

Doctor Malloy replaced his glasses and then tore a sheet of paper from his pad. He held out the sheet of paper to the man. The man accepted the sheet and frowned questioningly.

"I want you to draw me the door."

"Why?"

131

Peter Crowther

The question came back so fast that it surprised the doctor. "Just draw me the door, Edward."

"I don't have a pencil."

The policeman rose to his feet slowly and removed a button-topped Biro pen from his jacket pocket. "He can have this," he said. The doctor nodded and Edward turned around to accept the pen.

As the man began to sketch, Doctor Malloy said, "Over how long have you been taking the girls?"

"Mmmm . . . ? About two months. Maybe three."

"Where do you get them?"

"From outside. From the streets. Nobody misses them."

"You persuade them to go back to your apartment?"

The man nodded without looking up. "Yeah."

"Do you take them back to have sex?"

The man stopped drawing and stared at the paper.

"I said—"

"I heard you."

"Well?"

"I suppose that's what they think we're going to do."

"And do you?"

"No!"

"Where are the girls now, Edward?"

"I told you, they're in the room. Behind the door." He threw the paper across at Doctor Malloy and tossed the pen over his shoulder at the policeman. "There!"

Doctor Malloy picked up the paper and looked at the carefully drawn door. It was like any door, a round handle, beading surrounding four inlaid panels, and a number between the two upper panels. The number was *17*.

"This is very good, Edward."

The man did not respond.

"What's the number?"

"Seventeen."

"Yes, I can see that it's seventeen. What does it mean?"

"Mean?"

"Did you ever live in a house that had the number seventeen?"

The man thought for a minute and then shook his head.

"You're sure? When you were a child, maybe?"

"I'm sure."

Doctor Malloy slid the sheet into his pad. "So, you take the girls back to your room and then what?"

The man clenched his lips like a little boy trying to hold his breath.

"Do they see the door?"

"Of course they see the door!"

"And you open it and send them in?"

"Yeah."

"Do they go—do they struggle? Do you have to push them?"

"No. They just step inside."

"Don't they think that it's strange, you asking them to step through a door that's just standing in the middle of the apartment?"

He shrugged. "They haven't said so. I think maybe they've had stranger requests."

"What is it like inside the other room?"

"I—I haven't been all the way in."

"But you told us that you took girls *into* the room, Edward."

"I meant I took them up to the room. Not inside, just up to it."

"Have you never been inside at all?"

"Once."

"Is it different than the part of your own room that's around the other side of the door?"

The man nodded enthusiastically.

"So it's kind of like a magician's door?"

"Yeah, like a magician's door. That's just what it's like, yeah."

"How far did you go inside?"

The man's eyes opened wide and his bottom lip began to tremble slightly. "Nuhvurfah," he mumbled through clenched teeth.

"I'm sorry, I didn't catch that."

"I said, not very far."

"What's it like in there?"

"Dark. It's very dark. And big."

"Big? How big?"

"I don't know how big. But it is big. It stretches into the distance. And it smells."

"What of? What does it smell of, Edward?"

The man stared at the doctor. His eyes seemed faraway, lost in thought. "Dirt," he said at last. "It smells of dirt— you know. . . ." He waved his hands around and then clasped them tightly together. "And it smells of . . . of blood and warmth."

"Blood, you say. What does the blood smell like?"

"It smells like blood. How else—"

"No, I mean do you think it smells of blood because you know that there's blood in there?"

He shook his head emphatically. "No, I told you. I've only been in there once and I couldn't really see much."

"But you could see *some*thing?"

"Yeah."

"What could you see?"

"Shapes. Moving around."

"You saw these shapes when you went into the room by yourself?"

"Yeah."

"Do you see them when you put the girls into the room?"

He shook his head.

"Do the girls see the shapes?"

He shrugged. "They don't say anything if they do."

"You put them inside the door and then what happens?"

"The door closes."

"Do you close the door?"

"No."

"The girls?"

He narrowed his eyes and considered. "No, I don't think so."

"Do the shapes close the door?"

"They must."

"These shapes: what exactly are they like?"

The man shuddered involuntarily.

"Don't—Don't worry, now. Just take your time. Try to describe them to me."

"Heaps." It sounded like hiccups.

"Heaps?"

"Piles of clothes . . . washing."

"So, just blobs of . . . of material?"

He nodded. And then pointed quickly to a point on the floor behind where the doctor was sitting. "There," he said, "like that."

For a second, Doctor Malloy felt completely disorientated, so that, when he turned around, the gray and lifeless bundle on the floor some four or five feet to his side looked for all the world like one of the sentient and malevolent entities that the man had described. The thing seemed to hug the ground as if reluctant to leave . . . or, maybe, preparing to pounce. But it wasn't a blob or a creeping thing. It was the crumpled raincoat that he had dropped across the chair behind the door on his way in. He swiveled around and looked at the door. There was the chair. There was nothing on it.

He looked back to the coat. It was some eight or ten feet from the door. He was sure he hadn't just dropped it on the floor. It was most unlike him if he had.

"Did you move my coat?" he said, turning his attention to the policeman at the back of the room.

The policeman frowned and jabbed a finger at himself. "Me? No, Doctor. Not guilty I'm afraid."

He looked at Edward. "Did you move my coat, Edward?"

The man shook his head fiercely.

Doctor Malloy shrugged.

The air conditioning gave the slightest rustling sound, like a cloth being pulled across something, being pulled away to reveal. . . .

"And then what happens?"

"What happens when?" The man seemed puzzled by the sudden question.

"When the girl has gone through the door." His voice was slightly louder now, drowning out the air conditioning.

"The door goes."

"It goes?"

"Yeah, goes. Disappears. Vanishes."

"And then what."

"I tidy up the flat."

"In what way do you tidy up?"

"Their clothes. I put their clothes into a cardboard box."

The doctor watched the man carefully, weighing up his words before he spoke. "Edward, where do the clothes come from?"

Edward frowned and jerked his head as if trying to fathom out a difficult problem. "From the girls."

"From the girls?"

He nodded.

"Do you have them take off their clothes when they get into your apartment?"

Edward shook his head.

"So they go into—they go through the door with their clothes still on?"

"Yes. With their clothes on."

He leaned forward slightly and lowered his voice. "Then where do they come from, Edward?"

"Come from?"

"The clothes. If you send the girls into the room fully clothed and, as you've already told me, you don't go inside the room, then how do you get the clothes back on your side of the door?"

"They . . . they're left outside the door."

"So how does it work? The door opens and something drops the clothes out on your side?"

"N--no."

"Do you go through the door and get the clothes?"

"I told you, I don't—"

"Then how do the clothes appear?"

Edward crinkled up his mouth tightly and stared into some unfathomable distance just over the doctor's shoulder.

"Edward, I want to help you. Do you believe that? Do you believe I want to help you?"

He nodded. "Yes."

"Then we must be truthful with each other, yes?"

"Yes, truthful."

"Okay. Do you kill the girls, Edward?"

Edward shook his head.

"Do you have the girls take off their—"

"No."

"—take off their clothes and then—"

"No!"

"—and then you kill them and you cut them up—"

"No!" He turned around to the policeman who watched him impassively. "Tell him . . . tell him I don't kill them . . . I—"

"—and then cut them up and get rid of all the pieces. Except for the clothes."

Edward was sniveling. "I never killed anybody. Really. I take them in there because the things want me to."

The doctor sighed and leaned back on his chair. He waited for what must have been two full minutes and, when the man's sobbing had subsided, said, "And they just dump the clothes outside the door, right?"

Edward nodded and breathed in with a shudder.

"They leave the clothes and they go." He phrased it so that it wasn't a question. Edward did not respond. "Where? Where do they go? Where does the door go to when it leaves your apartment?"

"I—I don't know. I've never seen it."

"Why not? Doesn't that strike you as strange? This door keeps appearing and disappearing in your house and you never see it either arrive or leave? Can you understand how difficult it is for me to believe you, Edward?"

"Yes. I can see that. But it's all true."

The doctor scribbled something on his paper.

"I'm always asleep," Edward said.

The doctor stopped writing and looked up.

"I'm always so tired when . . . when the girls have gone through the door." He sighed heavily. "And I go lie down, sleep. When I wake up the door has gone and the clothes are left behind. I gather up the clothes and put them in a cardboard box."

"Is that the box we found, Edward?"

"Yes."

"Inspector, what clothes were in Edward's box?"

The man turned around and stared at the policeman. Unperturbed, the policeman read from a notebook lying open on his lap. "Nine pairs of women's underpants—G-strings, panties and the like—four brassieres, four suspender belts, six pairs of tights, six individual stockings, two headscarves, one beret, five sweaters, five blouses or shirts, two waistcoats, one dress, four skirts, five pairs of trousers—three are blue denim, one bright yellow, plus a pair of ski-pants—four coats, two zip-up jackets, six handbags, three pairs of baseball boots, one pair of sandals and seven pairs of shoes, two flat-heeled and five high-." He closed the notebook and nodded to the wall by his side. "There. All present and correct," he added.

Doctor Malloy looked to the wall. There was the box, brown cardboard, its leaves standing at angles to the sides. Draped over the front leaf was a pair of blue, lace-edged panties.

The policeman stood up, tutted and walked across to the box. As he nudged the panties back into the box, the air conditioning gave out a low thrum.

"And how many women did you estimate that to represent, Inspector?"

"We worked it out to at least eleven, working on the footwear," he said as he regained his seat.

The man had turned around again and was now watching the doctor. Doctor Malloy felt tense.

"Edward, when we came into your flat there was no door anywhere."

"No."

"But you had the girl with you."

"She was a policewoman."

"Yes, I know she was a policewoman, but you didn't, did you? You didn't know that."

"No."

"And we were listening to you talk to the policewoman. That's why we broke into the flat. Let's hear that tape now." He nodded to the policeman. "Inspector?"

The policeman got to his feet again, sighing, and walked across the holding room to turn on the cassette player.

"We've forwarded it to the part where you both reach the flat," Doctor Malloy said.

There was hissing and crackling, the sound of the material of the policewoman's sweater rubbing on the microphone, and the distinct rap of footsteps.

"*God . . . is it much further?*"

"*Nearly there.*"

"*I should bloody hope so.*"

"*Yeah, nearly there.*"

"*Twenty, you said, yeah? Twenty quid?*"

"*Yeah, I'll give you twenty pounds.*"

"*And no funny business, right?*"

"*No funny business.*"

The sound of a key being placed in a lock and turned. Elsewhere in the room, the pipes surged and a sharp but soft breath came from the cassette player.

"What was that?"

"What was what?" the policeman said.

Doctor Malloy pointed at the machine. "That! A . . . a sigh or something."

"I didn't hear anything," came the response.

Doctor Malloy reached over and pressed STOP.

The machine stopped.

They listened.

Nothing.

Just the air conditioning rubbing and pulling, twisting and turning itself, like stretched fabric.

"Wind it back."

The policeman walked across to the table and rewound the tape. To Doctor Malloy, the high-pitched gabble sounded like the noise that came from his spin-drier as it tumbled his shirts around and around and. . . .

The policeman pressed PLAY.

"*. . . there.*"

"*I should bloody hope so.*"

"*Yeah, nearly there.*"

"*Twenty, you said, yeah? Twenty quid?*"

"*Yeah, I'll give you twenty pounds.*"

"*And no funny business, right?*"

"*No funny business.*"

The sound of the key again, entering the lock, turning. But this time there was nothing else. Doctor Malloy settled back and listened. When he looked down at his hands, he saw they were white, grasping his pencil so hard that, as he released his grip, a sharp pain washed through his finger ends.

"*I don't do funny business,*" the woman's voice said.

"*I don't want you to.*"

"*What do you want then?*"

"*I'll tell you when we get inside.*"

"*No, I want to know now.*"

A handle being turned.

"*No, I'll tell you inside. Look, the door's open. It's safe for you to come in.*"

Footsteps.

When the man's voice starts again, it sounds further away. "*Look, nothing to be afraid of. Come in.*"

Slow footsteps. They stop and start, stop and start.

The woman breathes out and her sweater rubs the mike. "*Look, I'm not sure about this.*"

More footsteps. "*What aren't you sure about? Look, there's nothing here. Noth—it's gone!*"

"*What's go—*"

A door slams and cuts off the last word.

"*—king door. It's gone.*"

Hurried footsteps move away. The man's voice is distant again. "*It's not here!*"

The woman's voice is faint and urgent now, the feigned roughness completely replaced by a soft and insistent fear. "*I think you'd better come up,*" she says amidst rustling noise.

"She's talking straight into the mike there," the policeman pointed out.

"Where was it?" Doctor Malloy asked. "The microphone?"

The policeman tapped his armpit. "There, nestled into her bra just underneath her arm."

The doctor nodded.

"Now, *please!*" the policewoman's voice begs.

The man's voice comes back again, louder now. "*It's not anywhere.*"

"*What's not anywhere, love? Look, I told you no funny stuff, didn't I?*"

Somewhere in the distance more footsteps sound, several sets, running, growing louder.

"*Where is it?*"

"*Where's wh—*"

"*Where is it? Did you see it?*"

Footsteps getting louder.

"*Did I see wha—*"

"*Where is—*"

The sound of thumping and breaking, splintering.

Footsteps now very loud. Several new voices. The sound of scuffling. Was it scuffling . . . that noise, that sibilant crumpling sound?

"I think you know the rest," the policeman said as he turned off the cassette player. He walked back across the room and sat down.

The man stared at his hands, rocking gently. "They knew," he said softly.

"What's that, Edward?" Doctor Malloy said. "They knew?"

"The things. They knew she was a policewoman. That's why they moved the door. They knew even before I did."

"So where is it now?"

"Wherever it goes when it's not in my flat."

"And where's that?"

"I don't know."

The air conditioning wheezed and fell silent.

Frowning, Doctor Malloy watched two uniformed policeman accompany Edward Clegg down the corridor toward the cells.

Behind him, in the holding room, Inspector Andrews picked up a brassiere that had fallen out of the box. He must have knocked it out earlier. "Problem?" he asked.

"I don't know. Something . . . there's something about what he said."

"Like what?" The Inspector came out into the corridor pulling a packet of Gold Leaf cigarettes from his pocket and put one in his mouth.

"He *didn't* know his pick-up was a policewoman."

"So?"

"So why didn't he carry on the way he had done with all the others?"

Andrews blew out a plume of smoke and grunted.

"And where *are* the women?"

"He's got rid of them."

"Yes, but where? No signs of any struggles. No signs of any blood. And no sign of any bodies, despite the entire force combing the area for the past three weeks."

"So what are you saying?"

"Oh, I don't know."

"You're not telling me you believe him are you? That what he's telling us is true?"

"That's two questions. The answer to the first is yes, I do believe him. But, to the second, of course I don't believe his story is true. Only that *he* believes it is."

A shrill sound rang out and Inspector Andrews switched off the beeper on his lapel. "Trouble," he said as he started to run along the corridor in the direction that Clegg had just gone. Doctor Malloy followed.

Just around the corner they reached the steps leading down to the cells. Two flights down, Clegg was sprawled on the floor, crying and fighting with his escort.

"I'll go down," Doctor Malloy said.

When he reached the men he said, "What's the problem, Edward?"

"I . . . I didn't tell you everything."

"Do you want to tell me now?"

Clegg sniffed and nodded.

"What is it that you want to tell me?"

"The things . . . when I wouldn't tell you how I knew they wanted the girls?"

"Yes."

"They whispered it to me."

"Now?"

"No, back at the flat."

The two constables looked at each other and raised their eyes.

"They whispered through the door?"

"No. The first time. The first time I found the door, I went through it."

"So the time you told us about was the first time that the door appeared?"

"Yeah."

"And you haven't been in there since?"

"No way!"

"Why?"

"Because of what they whispered. And that's why you can't put me down there." He nodded his head in the direction of the dimly lit corridor of cells now just one flight below where they were standing. In one corner, the corner where the overhead light was at its dimmest, a pile of towels lay jumbled against the wall.

"What did they say to you, Edward?"

"They asked me to bring them women. Told me if I didn't they would come and get me. They said they'd seen me now and so they knew what I looked like. They said I had to give them women and that if I didn't then they'd come and get them themselves."

Doctor Malloy waited.

Clegg looked at the impassive faces of the constables.

Doctor Malloy said, "And what else did they say?"

"They . . . they told me that they'd take me as well."

"Take you where, Edward?"

"Wherever it is . . . behind the door. They said they'd get me."

"They can't get you here, Edward."

The man looked up at the doctor and shook his head. "Yes they can," he said.

The constables led him away.

"You think you should do this?"

"Yes. There must be something there that could tell us what he's doing with the women." Doctor Malloy pulled on his overcoat and wrapped it tightly around himself.

"But we've been through the place from top to bottom. There isn't anything."

The doctor shrugged. "I think I should take a look."

"You want me to have someone go with you?" Inspector Andrews handed a pair of keys on a ring to the doctor.

"No, I'll go by myself." He dropped the keys into his pocket and walked toward the exit.

Inspector Andrews was lighting another cigarette when the call came through. He listened to the voice on the other end of the line, frowning. He grunted an acknowledgment, replaced the receiver and stubbed out the cigarette.

When he got down to the cells the constables had cut the body down from the hot water pipes that threaded across the cell's ceiling.

"How?"

One of the constables held up a pink brassiere.

"Jesus Christ. You'd only just brought him down here," he said in exasperation.

The constable nodded and shuffled his weight from one foot to the other. "Nothing we could do, sir. You didn't ask us to stay with him. I asked him if he wanted a cup of tea or anything and he said yes. Few minutes later I brought the tea and there he was."

They all looked down at the body and then up at the pipes.

"Doesn't seem possible, does it?" the second constable said to nobody in particular.

The inspector shook his head.

The first constable was turning the brassiere over and over in his hands. "Funny," he said.

"*Funny?* I don't think it's fu—"

"No, not *him, this!*" and he held out the brassiere. "No make."

The inspector took it from him. "No make?"

"And no size details, either. There's nothing on it."

"Is it one of the items from the box?"

"I think so, yes. Where else would it have come from?"

"That's a very good question, Constable," he said. "More to the point, how the hell did it get down here?" He turned the brassiere in his hands and checked along the back straps. The constable was right. There were no manufacturer details on the garment at all. He looked up and said, "The other clothes still upstairs?"

The constables looked at each other. "We haven't moved

anything," said the one who had made the discovery of the tagless brassiere.

Inspector Andrews stuffed the garment into his pocket and turned sharply around.

Doctor Malloy turned up his coat collar against the cold wind and ran from his car to Edward's apartment building. He went through the main doors, up the stairs two at a time and then stood outside Edward's door. The key felt strange in his hand. He inserted it into the lock, turned and pushed the door.

Walking inside, he was aware of something different.

The place was completely black. No light anywhere.

He turned to the wall at his side and flicked the light switch. As the room burst into brightness, he half-expected to see the door waiting for him. But the room was empty.

Doctor Malloy kicked the door closed behind him and put the key back in his pocket. The answer was here, he was sure.

Something was here, whatever it was. He could feel it.

He walked across the room to the kitchen and pushed open the door. Empty.

He felt his heart beating.

Get out, a tiny voice said deep in his brain. He ignored it and walked back across the room, stamping his feet on the floor and listening for any change in the sound.

Suddenly a telephone started ringing.

He looked around for the telephone, trying to pinpoint the sound, but couldn't see one. Then he realized it was coming from the room opposite the kitchen. The bedroom. He walked across and pushed open the door.

Even in the small amount of light thrown in from the main room, he could see that the place was a mess. There were clothes everywhere.

The ringing was louder now and he saw the telephone. It was next to a lamp sitting on a small cabinet beside a bed which was strewn with shirts and trousers, socks and ties. He shook his head and flicked the light switch on the wall beside him. It didn't work.

He walked across the bedroom and lifted the receiver. He placed it by his ear but didn't speak.

The familiar voice of Inspector Andrews said, "Malloy?"

"Yes?" He stood with his back to the door and stared at the wall watching the line of light cast by the door shimmer on the wallpaper.

"Listen." The Inspector sighed. "Our man's topped himself."

"What? How?"

"Hanged himself with a bra."

"Oh, wonderful!" He pushed his hand into his trouser pocket and flicked his fingers against the key.

"But get this. None of the clothing has any manufacturer labels."

"Huh?"

"Not one. None of the underclothes, none of the blouses or the jeans, not even any of the shoes."

Doctor Malloy watched the line on the wallpaper, the thin boundary between light and darkness, slowly move to his right. The door was closing.

He reached out and flicked the switch on the bedside lamp. The close light made him feel better. Safer, somehow.

"Malloy?"

"I'm still here." He pushed a pile of clothes onto the floor and sat on the cleared edge of the bed. "I'll tell you this . . . your boys ought to clean up after they check a place."

"Clean up? How do you mean?"

"Clegg's bedroom. It's a mess. Clothes everywhere."

"Clothes everywhere? I'm not with you. The place was neat as a new pin when we left. And there *weren't* any clothes."

The door finally drifted shut with a soft click.

Doctor Malloy frowned. "No clothes? None at all?" He reached down and picked up a shirt. It felt faintly warm to the touch. He fumbled one-handed until he exposed the back of the collar. There was no label.

He turned his head to look at the door and felt something slip inside his chest. There were two doors.

One of them was the door that Doctor Malloy had come through when he entered the bedroom. The other was completely unattached to anything, standing a few inches away from the wall. It was purple and had the number 17 boldly emblazoned between two inlaid panels.

"It's here," he said into the receiver. But even as the words left his mouth he knew that the Inspector wouldn't respond. He leaned forward and looked under the table. The telephone wire had been torn apart. Several pieces of clothing were gathered around the two pieces of wire, and others—Malloy saw a striped regimental-style tie and a pair of green boxer shorts slide over the lamp socket—were slowly making their way toward his feet.

In front of the purple door, a pile of sheets was gathering—they were almost as high as the door handle.

He stood up and dropped the receiver.

There was a sharp tearing sound and the light went out.

Then, in the blackness, there was only the soft click of a door opening—though no new light was introduced into the room—and a flurry of insistent, excited rustling.

Cankerman

"Again?"

The boy nodded, his face tearstained and screwed up as though at the memory of something unpleasant.

"Nasty dream," Ellen Springer said, stifling a yawn. It wouldn't do to appear unconcerned. She knelt down beside her son's bed and eased him back under the covers. The boy shuddered as his tears subsided. A shadow thrown by the hall light fell across the bed, and Ellen turned around to face her husband, who was standing stark naked at the doorway, scratching his head.

"Was it the lumpy man again?" he said to nobody in particular. The lumpy man was a creation of David's, and a particularly bizarre one. He had first appeared in the sad time after Christmas, when the tree was shedding needles, the cold had lost its magic, and already a few of the gaudily colored gifts deposited by Santa Claus in David's little sack had been forgotten or discarded. Only the credit card statements provided a reminder of the fun they had had.

Ellen nodded and turned back to finish the securing exercise. "There, now. Snuggle down with Chicago." She tucked a small teddy bear, resplendent in a Chicago Bears football helmet and jersey, under the sheets. Her son shuffled around until his face was against the bear's muzzle. "All right now?" He nodded without opening his eyes.

Throughout January and into February David had woken in the night complaining about the lumpy man. He was in the room, David told his parents each time, watching him. He had with him a large black bag, and the sides of it seemed to breathe, in and out, in and out. The man posed no threat to David during his visits, preferring (or so it seemed) to be content simply sitting watching the boy, the bag on his knees all the while.

"Okay, big fella?" John Springer said, leaning over his wife to tousle the boy's hair. There was no answer save for a bit of lip smacking and a sigh. "We'll leave the hall light on for you. There's nothing to be frightened about, okay? It was just another dream."

Stepping back, Ellen smiled at her husband, who was standing looking as attentive as four A.M. would allow, his right hand cradling his genitals. "Careful, they'll drop off," she whispered behind him.

John pretended not to hear. "Okay, then. Night night, sleep tight, hope the—"

"He's still here, Daddy."

"No, he's *not* here, David." He recognized the first sign of irritation in his own voice and moved forward again to crouch by the bed. "He never *was* here. He was just a dream."

The boy had opened his eyes wide and was now staring at his father. "My . . . my majinashun?"

"Yes." He considered correcting and thought better of it. "It was your majinashun."

"He said he'd brung me a late present."

John Springer heard the faint pad, pad of Ellen moving along the hallway to the toilet. "He said he'd brought you a present?"

David nodded.

"What did he bring you?"

"He got it from his bag."

"Mmmm. What was it?"

"A lump."

"A lump?"

David nodded, apparently pleased with himself. "It *was* like a little kitten, all furry and black. At first I thought it was a kitten. He held it out to show me, and it had no eyes or face, and no hands and feet."

"Did he leave it for you?"

David frowned.

"Let me see. May I see it?"

The boy shook his head. "I don't have it anymore."

"Did the man take it back?"

Another shake of the head and a rub of small cheek against the stitched visage of the little bear.

"Then where is it now?"

For a second John thought his son was not going to answer, but then suddenly he pulled back the bedclothes and pointed a jabbing finger at his stomach, which was poking out pinkly between the elastic top of his pajama pants and a Bart Simpson T-shirt.

"You *ate* it?"

David laughed a high tinkling giggle. "No," he said between chuckles. "The man rubbed it into my tummy. It hurt me, and I started to shout."

"Yes, you did. And that's what woke your mommy and me up."

David nodded. "You called my name, Daddy."

John looked at him. "Yes . . . I called your name."

"It scared the man when you called my name."

"I scared the lumpy man?" He moved into a kneeling position on one knee only and affected a muscle-building pose. "See, big Daddy scared the lumpy man."

David chuckled again and writhed tiny legs beneath the sheets. John felt the sudden desire to be five years old again, tucked up tightly in a small bed with a favorite cuddly toy to protect him against the things that traveled the night winds of the imagination. Then he noticed his son's eyes concentrating on something on the floor behind him.

"What is it?"

David shook his head again and pulled the sheet up until it covered the end of his nose.

"Is it something on the floor?" He turned around, sticking his bottom up into the air, and padded across the room to the open door, sniffing like a dog. There was a smell. Over inside the doorway, coming from the mat that lay across the carpet seam. It smelled like the rotting leaves that he had to clear from the outside drains every few weeks during the early fall.

There was a shuffling from the bed. "He went under the mat, Daddy. Lumpy man hid under the mat when I cried."

David's father turned around and stared at his son, who was now sitting up in bed. Then he looked back at the mat. Ellen wandered by toward their own bedroom and glanced at him. "Isn't it time *you* went back to sleep, too, Mister Doggie?"

John smiled and gave a bark. He lifted the mat and looked underneath. Nothing. He felt suddenly silly. He had looked under the mat more for himself than for David, he realized. It would have been easy to tell the boy not to be frightened; that a big man could not hide beneath a small rug. But just for a few seconds he had been frightened to go back to bed without investigating the possibility that there was ... something ... under the rug. But the smell ...

"Has anything been spilled around here, Ellen?"

"Mmmm? Spilled? Not that I can think of, no. Why?"

"It just smells a bit weird." Actually, it smelled a *lot* weird. It stank to high heaven. He laid the rug carefully back in place and got up. "Nothing there." He turned around and snuggled David back into his sheets. "So off to sleep now. Hoh-kay?"

"Hoh-kay," said David.

John wandered out of the small bedroom and swung back along the hall to the toilet. Within a minute or two he was back in bed, his bladder comfortably empty, with Ellen complaining about the coldness of his feet. He lay so that he could see into David's room. The little mat lay between them, silent as the night itself, and despite John's tiredness sleep was long in coming.

That was March.

David left them in September.

The problem was a Wilms tumor, a particularly aggressive renal cancer that showed itself initially as an abdominal swelling on David's left side. Ellen discovered it during bathtime. The following day the tummy aches began. That weekend David started vomiting for no apparent reason. By the following Tuesday he had shown blood in his urine.

The Wilms was diagnosed following an intravenous pyelogram, in which a red dye was injected into a vein in David's arm. It was confirmed by a singularly unpleasant session on the CT scanner, which looked like a Boeing engine and hummed like the machine constructed by Jeff Morrow in *This Island Earth*.

The prognosis was not good.

David had a tumor in each kidney. He had secondaries in lung and liver. The kidneys were removed surgically, but on the side that was worse affected they had to leave some behind because of danger to arteries. He went through a short course of radiotherapy and then a course of chemo. He felt bad, but John and Ellen kept him going, making light of it all each day and dying silently each night, locked in tearful embraces in the hollow sanctity of their bed.

The cancer did not respond.

David's sixth birthday present was for the consultant to tell his parents that it had spread into his bones. It wouldn't be long now.

Morphine derivatives, Marvel comics, and Chicago the bear kept him chipper until the end, which came just before lunch on the third of September in the aching sickness-filled silence of St. Edna's Children's Hospital. Both Ellen and John were there, holding a thin frail arm each. Their son slipped away with a sad smile and a momentary look of wise regret that he had had to abandon them so soon.

Ellen started back at school late. When she did return she had been sleeping badly for almost two weeks.

The cumulative effect of the long months of suffering, during which a life was lived and lost, had taken its toll. And though the grass had already started to grow on top of the small plot in Woodlands Cemetery, no such healing process had begun over the scarred tissue of Ellen Springer's heart. On top of that, she had inherited a difficult class at school.

Their lives were undeniably empty now, though they both went to great efforts to appear brave and happy, affecting as close a copy of their early trouble-free existence as they could muster. David's room had been redecorated, the Simpsons wallpaper stripped off and the primary colors of the woodwork painted over in pastels and muted shades with names such as Wheat and Barley and Hedgerow Green. The bed had been replaced with a chair and a small glass-topped coffee table, and on many evenings Ellen would sit in there supposedly preparing for the next day's lessons, though in reality she would simply sit and daydream, staring out of the small window into the tail ends of the ever-shortening days. Another Christmas would soon be upon them, and neither of them was looking forward to it.

The lumpy man and his black bag had been forgotten, though John still had the occasional nightmare. Ellen never mentioned David's dreams—in fact, she tried never to mention David—and John had never told her about his and David's conversation that long-ago night when the lumpy man had brought their little boy a late Christmas present.

The first night after the funeral had been so bad that they could not believe they had actually survived it. Despite a sleeping pill—which she had assured John she would be stopping soon—Ellen had tossed and turned all night. She had told John that David had been in their room watching her. John had tried to reason with her. It was the healing process, he had told her, the grief and the sadness and the loss. David was at peace now.

She had cried then, cried like she had not cried since the early days following all their conversations with doctors and surgeons. How they had begged for their child's life during those lost and lonely weeks.

Ellen did not stop the sleeping pills, nor did John try to persuade her to do so. But her nights did not improve. Then, after five or six days, she had told him that it was not David who visited their room at night while she was asleep. It was somebody else. "Who?" he had asked. She had shrugged.

He had managed to get her to a doctor for a checkup.

She had not wanted to go back into a medical environment, but she had relented. Too tired to argue, he had supposed. Or just too disinterested. John had spoken to the doctor beforehand and had persuaded him to refer her to the clinic for a full scan. The local hospital agreed to let her through—despite the fact that there was no evidence to support any theory of something unpleasant—because of her traumatic recent history. She had taken the test on a Monday, and they had the results by mail the following Friday. It was clear.

They celebrated.

That night John had a dream. In his dream a tall man wearing dark clothes and an undertaker's smile drifted into their bedroom and sat beside Ellen. He stroked her head for what seemed to be a long time and then left. He carried with him a huge, old-fashioned black valise, the sides of which seemed to pulsate in the dim glow thrown into the house by the street lamp outside their bedroom window. *Soon*, he seemed to say softly to John on his way out though his misshapen lips did not move. John awoke with a start and sat bolt upright in bed, but the room was empty. Ellen moved restlessly by his side, her brow furrowed and her lips dry.

The following two nights John stayed awake, but nothing happened. During the days at the office he ducked off into empty rooms and grabbed a few hours of sleep. The work was piling up on his desk, but problems would not show up for a week or two. John was convinced it wouldn't take that long.

On the third night the lumpy man came back.

His smile was a mixture of formaldehyde and ether, which lit the room with mist, its gray tendrils swirling lazily around the floor and up the walls. His face was a marriage of pain and pleasure, an uneven countenance of hills and valleys, knolls and caves, a place of shadows and lights. And his clothes were black and white, a significance of goodness and non-goodness: a somber dark gray tailcoat and a white wing-collared shirt sporting a black bootlace tie, which hung in swirls and ribbons like a cruel mockery of festivity and inconsequence. His hair was white-gray, hanging in long, wispy strands about his neck and forehead.

Ah, it's time, his voice whispered as he entered, filling the room with the dual sounds of torment and delight. And as he listened John Springer could not for the life of him decide where the one ended and the other began.

Feigning sleep, curled around his wife's back, John watched the lumpy man move soundlessly around the bed to Ellen's side and sit on the duvet. There was no sense of weight on the bed.

The man placed his bag on the floor and unfastened the clasp. There was a soft skittering sound of fluffy movement as he reached down into the bag and lifted something out. John felt the strange dislocation of dream activity, a sense of not belonging, as he watched the man lift an elongated roll of writhing darkness up onto his lap. He laid it there, smoothing it, smiling at its feral movements, sensing its anticipation and its impatience.

Not long, little one, his voice cooed softly through closed, unmoving lips, and, leaving the shape where it lay, he reached across and pulled back the duvet from Ellen's body.

Ellen turned obligingly, exposing her right breast to the air and the world and the strange darkness of the visitor in their room. The man lifted the shape and, with an air of caring and gentility, lowered it toward the sleeping woman.

John sat up.

The man turned around.

And now John could see him for what he really was, a bizarre concord of beauty and ugliness, of creation and ruin, of discord and harmony. There were pits and whorls, folds and crevices, warts that defied gravity and imagination, and thick gashes that seeped sad runnels of loneliness. *Go back to sleep*. His voice echoed inside John Springer's head.

No, he answered without speaking. *You may not have her*.

John sensed an amusement. *I may not?*

No, John answered, pulling himself straighter in the bed. *You have taken my son. You may not have my wife*.

The man shook his head with a movement that was almost imperceptible. Then he returned his full attention to Ellen and continued to lower the shape.

No!

Again he stopped.

Take me instead.

The lumpy man's brow furrowed a moment.

Surely it cannot matter whom you take, John went on, sensing an opportunity, or at least a respite. *You have a quota, yes?*

The man nodded.

Then fill it with me.

For what seemed like an eternity the lumpy man considered the proposition, all the while holding the shifting furry bundle above Ellen's breast. Then, at last, he pulled back his hand and lowered the thing back into his bag.

John felt his heart pounding in his chest.

The man stood up from the bed, his bag again held tightly in his right hand, and moved around to John's side.

John shuffled himself up so that his back was against the headboard. *Who are you?* he said.

I am the Cankerman, came the reply. He sat on the bed beside him and rested the bag on his lap. *And you are my customer.* John licked his lips as the lumpy man pulled open the sides of the black valise and pushed the yawning hole toward him. *Choose,* he said. John looked inside.

The smell that assailed his nostrils was like the scent of meat left out in the sun. It was the air of corruption, the hum of badness, and the bittersweet aftertaste of impurity. Gagging at the stench that rose from the bag, John still managed to hold onto his gorge and stared. There seemed to be hundreds of them, rolling and tumbling, climbing and falling, clambering and toppling over, pulling out of and fading into the almost impenetrable blackness at the fathomless bottom of the Cankerman's valise.

All were uniformly black.

Black as the night.

Black as a murderer's heart.

Black as the ebony fullness that devours all light, all reason, all hope.

Cancer-black.

Choose, said the Cankerman again.

John reached in.

They scurried and they wobbled, squeezing themselves between his fingers, wrapping their furriness around his wrist, filling his palm with their dull warmth, their half-life. They pulsated and spread themselves out, rubbing themselves against him with a grim parody of affection.

Big ones, small ones, long thin ones, short stubby ones. All human life is there, John thought with detachment. And he made his choice.

There, deep within the black valise, his arm stretched out as though to the very bowels of the earth itself, his fingers found a tiny shape. A pea. A furry pea.

He pulled it out and held it before the grisly mask. *This is my choice*, he said.

So be it, said the Cankerman, and he closed the valise and placed it on the floor. Taking the small squirming object from John's outstretched hand, he allowed himself a small smile. *No regrets?*

Just do it.

The Cankerman nodded and, leaning toward him, placed the black fur against John Springer's right eye . . . and pushed it in.

Pain.

Can you hear a color?

Can you smell a sound?

Can you see a taste?

John Springer could.

He heard the blackness of a swirling ink blot, smelled the noise of severing cells, and saw, deep inside his own head, the flavor of exquisite destruction.

Good-bye.

When John opened his eyes the room was empty. He lay back against the headboard and felt exhaustion overtake him.

Ellen's hand brought him swimming frantically from the deep waters of sleep into the half-light of a smoky fall morning.

"I let you sleep," she said simply.

"Mmmm." He licked his lips and squinted into her face. "What time is it?"

"After eight."

He groaned.

"Hey, I had a good night."

John looked up at her and smiled. "Good," he said. "I told you: Nothing lasts forever."

"You were right. But it'll take me some time." She stood up and walked over to the wardrobe.

"I know." He watched her sifting through clothes. On impulse he closed his left eye, saw her outline blur, and felt a sharp pain deep inside his head. "Love you," he said . . . softly, so that she might not know how much.

Dumb Animals

Sonny Curtis didn't know anybody who had died in Vietnam. Didn't know anybody who had even been.

But he still found himself leaning against one of the big, black sections of the Vietnam Veterans Memorial, the one with all the names printed on it, looking around the edge for anybody who might have followed him. There was nobody.

And even though Sonny hadn't lost anybody in that war there were still tears in his eyes and, as he leaned back against the cool stone, the tears made the parkway and the trees shimmer. For a second, it reminded him of New York, like seeing the buildings through the steam drifting out of the manhole covers around Times Square. For that one second, it was like he was back in the Apple. But he wasn't.

This was Washington, D.C., and Sonny was a long way from home. It was cold and dark, the dead days of a new year. Not a good time to be away from the things that were familiar. He ran a hand down his shirtfront, his favorite shirt, a heady mixture of ocean blues and meadow greens, swirls of corn stalks and patches of soil, triangles and many-sided structures and shapes, all depicted in bright hues and thoughtful pastels . . . and his hand touched the wetness. Sonny had blood on him. Blood on his best shirt.

He pulled the shirt out from his body and looked down at it. The blood looked black in the glare of the solitary lamp, black and glistening, like oil or just plain dirt, swirling among the swirls already there, covering and dripping over and through the shapes, weaving its way into the cotton.

The only good thing about the blood was that it wasn't his.

Beside him, Frank's cat mewled in its basket, complaining at being jostled so much and at not being able to get out and roam around. Sonny moved his head back so the top of it rested on the stone and stared at the stars.

He had ducked out from the smoky bar on Henry Bacon Drive, left hand tightly holding a mess of bills and Frank's cat basket, right hand still gripping the long stiletto shiv . . . legs going full tilt, listening to the voices echoing after him

You come back here!

Hey, he knifed Troy . . .

Get him!

The accents of those voices, now replaying in Sonny's head, were deep and yawny. They lacked the characteristic drawl of the capital and its slow, long vowels and short, slurred consonants. They were Southern voices, he now realized. As foreign to the town itself as they were to him.

He had hit the street on a run, grateful of the darkness, and ditched the shiv behind some garbage cans outside back of an eatery on the corner of 21st Street, listening to the sound of its clatter fade only to be replaced by the lonesome pounding of his own shoes, running down the empty street. *Troy,* he had thought as he ran, pulling in air whenever he could, then holding it in so's he could hear if anyone was following. What kind of a name was that? Sounded like something off of one of the daytime soaps. And he had been unable to stifle a small, throaty chuckle . . . and equally unable to recognize it for the hysteria it was.

Sonny had arrived in Washington, D.C., in the late afternoon, when the light was dying, on a Greyhound which let him off with the other seven passengers at a depot on

New York Avenue. He hadn't intended to come to Washington. Hadn't intended to come anywhere. Sonny had just wanted to get out of New York. He hadn't intended to hurt anybody. He had just needed some money. The story of his life.

What was it Bill Clinton had said just a few days earlier? Sonny had watched the inauguration on the television at Frank's place, back in New York. He had watched the new president refer to 'this beautiful capital' and he had felt a sudden kinship when the man had gone onto criticize the people there for being obsessed by 'who is in and who is out, who is up and who is down.'

That was him, Gerald Jerome Curtis—'Sonny' to his friends and other people who knew him—out and down. Sonny had never felt much of a kinship with anybody before, let alone a president. But he had felt it then. Maybe that was why he had picked the Washington bus, picked it out without realizing why he was doing it.

Anywhere would have been fine. Anywhere but New York. There were people in New York who wanted him.

Sonny had heard Frank on the telephone. Frank had thought he was asleep, crashed out on the sofa in front of the television with the cat, but he wasn't. He was too worried about creasing his shirt. And while the forty-second president of the United States was telling everybody that people deserved better . . . and that 'in this city there are people who want to do better,' Frank was telling people where Sonny was. Telling them to come around and 'get the lousy queen' out of there. Telling them to come around quick.

And so he lifted the serrated knife that they had used to cut up the tuna and anchovy pizza Frank had ordered from the store around the corner and then sneaked up on Frank. And while in the room behind him Bill Clinton told America that the era of deadlock and drift was behind them, Sonny had pulled Frank's head back and sawed right through the neck in one sweep. Then he had let the body drop and said *Fuck you* into the mouthpiece—three times—smashed the bloody handset on the cradle until it shattered and then kicked the shit out of Frank Ryerman's still warm corpse while he figured out what to do next. On the sofa in Frank's room, the dead man's cat watched with a casual disinterest, torn between the picture on the television and the action in the room.

While Sonny thought, the president was still speaking. Sonny had listened a moment and then walked back into the room and switched off the set. He had since read that the inaugural speech had been fourteen minutes long. Will Rogers had said all the same stuff more than a generation earlier and used only fourteen words: 'There ain't but one word wrong with every one of us,' Rogers had said, 'and that's selfishness.'

He had to go. He had to get out of that room . . . out of that city . . . somewhere where they wouldn't find him. The cat licked its paws and watched him as he watched it.

Sonny grabbed his jacket from the floor and knelt beside Frank's body, checking his pockets for money. There were a few bills plus a handful of change—twenty-seven dollars and sixty-three cents. Sonny looked up at the cat, then caught sight of the basket on the window ledge behind it. *There ain't but one word wrong with every one of us* . . . Sonny stood up quickly and moved across to the window ledge. He grabbed the basket and then the cat, dropped it inside and fastened the latch. Then he ran out of the room, ran along the corridor, down the stairs and out into the early morning streets, feeling the wind in his face and listening to the sirens caterwauling, sometimes in the distance, sometimes like they were pulling right up alongside him.

And so it was that, on a particularly grimy sweat- and piss-smelling seat of the Port Authority Greyhound terminal, Sonny Curtis decided to go to Washington. To be near the president of the United States of America.

Two men on the bus had been talking loudly about the new president. "We gonna see a new beginning now," the first man had said, said it proudly as though he was going to do something himself. "We gonna see some fairness now."

The other man had shaken his head while Sonny watched. "No way," he'd said. "Way I see it, this ain't no new start. Ain't no new nothing. All we done is we've gotten ourselves into bed with the last guy in the bar. That's all."

Sonny had wanted to butt in right from the start, but he had waited, held his silence and stared out at the early morning countryside. He knew diddly about Bosnia and Serbs, knew even less about unemployment—it had never done him any harm had it?—or inflation or gross national product. But even his lack of knowledge couldn't keep him quiet forever, not when they were bad-mouthing the president for crissakes. It was a matter of pride, of keeping the flag flying.

Sonny had leaned forward, resting his right arm on the seat in front, and called to the men. "Hey," he had called, soft so's he didn't wake the old woman who slept across the aisle, muttering to unseen gods or demons as her head slipped on the seat-back with the movement of the bus, first one way and then the other. "Hey, you can't say that about the president," Sonny had said.

The men had looked around at him. "And who're you," one of them asked, "his fucking bodyguard?"

"Hey," the other had said, "maybe it's Kevin Costner."

"Jee-suss H. Christ," the first one said then, pointing at Sonny's chest. Sonny looked down at himself but couldn't make anything out. "Is that a shirt?"

"Holy shit," the other added. "That ain't no shirt, man, that's . . . that's—"

"That shirt's like to've made Picasso puke, man."

The second guy slapped his knee, shuffled himself around so his knees stuck right out in the aisle.

"Whassamatter, man . . . you lose a bet?"

"I know who he is, man! He's Captain Bad Taste."

And they had giggled like a couple of high school girls.

Sonny had wanted to pull the stiletto out of his Levis boot and thrust it forward so the point could draw just a single droplet of blood from one of the bulbous sacks of skin beneath the first man's eyes. *This is who I am*, the knife would have whispered around the redness, *who the fuck are you?* But, instead, he clenched his hand, made a fist. "I'm a citizen of the United States," Sonny had said over the drone of the bus's engine. "And I say that any man who cares about a cat can care about a country."

Sonny had read somewhere that Mr. Clinton had called in psychiatrists to took after his cat, Socks. Seems that all the pressure of being photographed and bustled around had upset the animal—The First Pussy, the magazine had called it. Ray Dringling had said, while nursing a beer in The Stopover bar down on 41st Street, that the magazine had got things confused. "The first pussy is curled up inside of Hillary Clinton's pants," he'd said and Sonny had wanted to slap him right in the mouth, had wanted to stop Ray's hysterical giggle and knock him clean off his stool. But he hadn't.

He gripped his shirtfront tightly.

Hillary Clinton had style. She would like his shirt, Sonny thought. She was a new woman . . . she was going to repeal the law that said to be good you had to be dull. Like Georgette Mosbacher said, "If you're blond, you're dumb. If you wear mascara, you can't read. If you use hairspray, your brain has atrophied." That was how Washington used to be. But not anymore. Not now the Clintons were in the White House. Now it would be style, not eccentricity. No more Barbara Bush in her puff-sleeved frocks and trainers; no more Margaret Tutwiler and her Popeye the Sailor dresses; no more Laura Ashley blouses or velvet hairbands; no more, even, Eleanor Roosevelt-style fox furs or Mamie Eisenhower big-skirted frocks and white glove ensembles; not even anymore of Jackie Kennedy's pillbox hats.

Sonny had seen Hillary Clinton and Tipper Gore out on the campaign trail, all Donna Karan bodysuits and tight-waisted jackets, and Ralph Lauren trouser suits in pin stripes. They would set the fashion standard for the working woman. They would set the fashion standard for the country.

Camelot II: this time it's funky! Sonny recalled the line from the *New York Times* and smiled. It would happen . . . no point in getting all hot about it. He relaxed his hand on his shirt.

And on the bus, when the first man had twirled a finger at the side of his head, making the other man laugh, Sonny had sat back and put a hand on the top of Frank's cat's basket. Watched some more scenery drift by outside while he listened to the woman across the aisle beg with somebody called Herman to let Miriam be. Slowly, moving gently to the movement of the bus, Sonny fell into a shallow sleep and a dream. In his dream Sonny caught the two men years later in a little town just north of Mexico City, and he pulled their pants down and cut off their balls and fed them to Frank's cat.

Remembering his thoughts on the Greyhound, while sitting crouched down in the chill air of the nighttime capital, and with Frank's cat mewling beside him and blood streaked down the front of his best shirt in all the world, Sonny realized what might be troubling the animal. He knelt down and unfastened the basket's catch, lifted the cat out. It struggled and tried to scratch his hand but Sonny held on tight. "There," he whispered, "there now. Whassamatter, huh?" He stroked the cat's back, felt it arch beneath his hand. "You hungry? Is that it?"

Sonny glanced up at the park. Sure, that was it. Why hadn't he thought about it before? The cat must be starving. He hadn't given it anything to eat since they'd left Frank's place and that was almost twenty-four hours ago. Come to think of it, Sonny hadn't had anything either.

"Hey," he said. "You like my shirt? Huh?" The cat shuffled and tried to break free. Sonny held it tight and lifted a paw to his shirtfront, wiped it in the bloodstain. The cat settled for a moment and licked its paw. Then it jerked backward and it was all that Sonny could do to stop it jumping from his lap and running off into the trees.

He dropped the cat back into the basket, trying not to listen to its frantic whining, and secured the catch. He had money now, money to buy something to eat. He shuffled over to the edge of the monument and peered around at the streets beyond. Nobody in sight. "Come on, cat," he said, getting to his feet, "let's go get us some food."

He had gone into the bar to get something to eat, too, he remembered. Maybe a sandwich, maybe a slice of pizza. Anything really. And three guys playing pool had seen him standing at the bar holding Frank's cat's basket. He had seen them notice him. It was like a second sense to him, honed over so many years of having to watch in every direction at once.

And the biggest of the three guys—the one whose name was Troy, he discovered later—had come up to him and pulled open his jacket, whistling. "Hoo-EE! I want it. I want that shirt."

Sonny had pulled his jacket closed and shrugged. "Ain't for sale."

"But I want the shirt." The man had looked around at his friends and pursed his lips. "Figure it make me look real fine," he added. "But I don't figure it make me wanna fuck cats." He looked down at the basket and scrunched up his nose like he was smelling something bad. "That yours?"

Sonny fastened his jacket and said nothing. The man was thickset and very handsome, a rugged tuft of blond hair curling over his ears and a cigarette which had been jammed behind the left one. For a second, Sonny felt attracted to him and strangely proud that the man should want his shirt.

"I said, is the cat yours?" he said again.

"Maybe they on a date," one of the other men shouted.

Sonny looked around the bar, taking in who was where.

"That right? One of your friends tell you you oughta get yourself some pussy so you went right out and picked up this . . . this fucking dumb animal?" the first one had asked.

"Cats ain't dumb animals," Sonny had said. "By the year 2000 there'll be sixty-nine million cats in the United States."

The man's eyes had opened wide and, just for a second, the fact had interested him, had kindled the almost dead, infinitesimally small light that still smoldered in the dark recesses of the man's brain. But only for a second. "Would you like to be there to see it?" he said softly.

Sonny frowned.

"Would you like to be there to see all of them fucking dumb animals?"

"Look, I ju—"

"Sell me the shirt."

"Hey, I don't wan—"

"Sell me the shirt and you can walk outta here."

Sonny had glanced around at the man behind the bar, down the far end of the room. The man turned around and made like he was tidying some bottles on the shelf behind him. Sonny looked back at the man. "How much?"

The man had smiled. "That's more like it." He turned around and laughed at the others. "That's more like it," he said again, louder.

Sonny had bent down, put the cat basket on the floor beside him and lifted his pant leg just high enough to pull the shiv out of his Levis boot. When he stood up the man was holding a handful of bills, pulling them back and starting to count. Sonny had grabbed the bills with his left hand and slid the shiv into the man's gut with his right, sweeping the blade up toward the ribs, grunting. Feeling it catch on bone, he pulled it out.

Time had stood still then . . .

the men at the pool table watched, open-mouthed
the man in front of Sonny looked down at his stomach
the barman leaned on the bar . . .

. . . and then it had started again.

The man grabbed his belly with both hands and howled, sinking to his knees, the cigarette dropping from his ear in exaggerated slow motion. He was no longer attractive.

Sonny bent down and hoisted up the cat basket with his left hand, still clutching the bills, dropping a few on the floor.

And he had turned around and run.

You come back here—
Hey, he knifed Troy—
Get him!

Sonny opened his eyes. "What?"

"I said, what can I get you?"

He shook his head and stared at the woman like he was coming out of a dream. On the wall behind her were lots of pictures of hamburgers and packets of fries, milkshakes and cartons of soda. He had walked down to a fast-food place without even thinking about what he was doing. He pulled his jacket tight around the bloodstained shirt and considered the menu. "Gimme a Big Mac, side order of fries, a Coke and . . . and a Captain Nemo." The woman nodded tiredly and turned around to the dispensers behind her.

Sonny knelt down in front of the serving area and whispered into the cat basket. "How's that sound, huh, cat?" he said, wishing he could remember the cat's name.

He paid the woman with a twenty and watched nervously as she held it up to the fluorescent light to check it wasn't a forgery. Then he walked across to a window seat and placed the basket next to the glass.

Feeding bits of the fish sandwich into the basket, Sonny watched the street outside. Just as he thought it might have been an idea to take a seat at the back, away from the window, a pickup—yellow or white, he couldn't make it out—drifted by and slowed right down. He leaned over against the glass and watched the pickup drift in front of the McDonald's and pull across to his side of the road, pull into a parking bay.

Sonny looked around at the people behind the serving area. They were talking about something, laughing, paying no notice to him. He looked along the back wall for another exit. There wasn't one. Over to his right there was a man wielding a wide cloth-covered broom along the floor. Two booths in front of him sat an old man staring into a mug of coffee.

Tap, tap.

The noise startled him at first, and then he realized what it was.

Sonny turned to the window, turned to the smiling face beyond the glass, saw the big hand tapping the window, watched the hand unfurl a single finger, saw it beckon to him to come outside. He turned back to the counter and saw one of the pool players from the bar, hands thrust deep into jacket pockets . . . but there was more than just hands in those pockets.

"You ready?" the man called over to him.

Tap, tap, insistent now. Sonny looked back at the window. The face nodded, still smiling, the head jerked backward, telling him to come on.

Sonny stood, put down his Big Mac, suddenly realizing

he had been holding it all of the time, and got to his feet. He reached over and picked up the basket.

Outside, the men greeted him like an old friend.

They took his arms and walked him along the road and across the street toward the Lincoln Memorial.

Then they crossed over into the park, toward the Vietnam Veterans Memorial. Nobody said anything.

When they got to the two black walls they stopped. "Put the cat down," the big man said.

Sonny did as he was told. "Are we going to talk?"

One of the other men laughed. " 'Are we going to talk, mithter?' " he said, singsong, mimicking Sonny's voice.

"Now take off the shirt," the big man said.

"It's cold," said Sonny. "I'll catch cold."

"It's the least of your worries," one of the others said.

He started to unbutton the shirt, slowly. "Look," he said, "I didn't mean anyth—"

The man slapped him across the face. "I didn't say talk to me, you little faggot, I said take off the fucking shirt."

Sonny tried to ignore the sting on his left cheek and continued with the buttons.

"Jacket."

"Huh?"

"Take off your jacket."

Sonny took off his jacket and laid it across the basket. Then he finished the shirt buttons and took it off, held it limply, looking across the men's faces, trying to make eye contact. All of them avoided his eyes except the big man. There were four of them. Too many.

"Give it to Earl."

A swarthy man chewing gum stepped into the light and smiled at him, held out his hand. "Thankth, mithter," he said, as Sonny dropped the shirt into the hand, watched it move away from him.

"Why . . . why d'you want my shirt?"

"Troy," Earl said.

"I—I thought Troy was dead."

Earl glared at him. "He is," said one of the others, stepping forward so Sonny could see him. "Gonna bury him in it."

Sonny looked around at Earl, holding the shirt out away from him like it was infected with something. The thought of that shirt—his best shirt in all the world—being put into the ground filled Sonny with horror. "Look . . . I said I was—"

"Gonna teach you a lesson," the big man said. He turned around and muttered to one of the men. The man pulled something out from under his jacket and handed it to him. When the big man turned back to face him, Sonny saw that it was a cushion. The man then pulled a gun out of his pocket. Sonny watched in fascination, trying to identify the model. Hands held each of his bare arms and someone jammed the cushion up against his stomach. "It's nothing personal, right?"

"No," Sonny said, looking from one to the other. "I didn't do nothing." Then he remembered. He had done plenty. "He made me do it," he corrected.

"Thay pleeth," Earl said, and, just for a second, Sonny saw the chewing gum, gray and teeth-marked, turn over on his tongue.

"Plea—"

The big man jammed the gun into the cushion and pulled the trigger. Twice.

Sonny was pushed backward, hard. He felt the wall of names cold against his back. Then it seemed to get warmer. Just for a second.

The big man held a finger to his mouth and looked around the side of the wall at the street. Freed from the arms that had held him, Sonny slid down the wall and sat roughly on the grass at its base. He tried to move his hands up to his stomach but they wouldn't respond. His stomach felt like it was wide open, the wind blowing into it, blowing all the insides down across his pants. He closed his eyes, tried to speak. "P-please . . ."

The shots had not been loud, more like a branch snapping. The big man nodded to the others and put the gun into his pocket, then the four of them stepped across Sonny, the gaudy shirt that one of them carried flapping in the late night breeze.

There was no pain. Sonny opened his eyes and watched them go, heard the cat mewl. "Please . . ."

The big man turned around and started back.

"Where you going?" one of the others asked.

The man didn't answer, just stepped over to Sonny and knelt down beside him. He pulled the gun out again and held it up to Sonny's temple. "Need another?"

Sonny moved his head slowly, side to side.

"What then?"

"Th-the cat. Let . . . go."

The man returned the gun to his pocket.

"What? What the fuck?" The man called Earl had come back and was standing behind the big man, watching Sonny's face over the man's shoulder. "What are you doing?"

"Letting the cat free."

"It's just a fucking cat, leave it," hissed Earl.

The big man had reached the basket and was unfastening the catch. He looked over at Sonny, made eye contact. "Have a heart," he said to them, keeping his eyes on Sonny as the cat pounced out of the basket and dashed toward the trees.

Sonny listened to the sound of their feet on the grass, growing distant. "Any man who . . ." he whispered to the darkness, ". . . can care for—"

Then both he and the night were silent again.

The Longest Single Note

"All music is life and all life is music," Uncle Nigel said to me almost matter-of-factly as the train chuckitty-chunked its way through the late-morning countryside.

I suppose I should have been surprised. Not at what he said but at the fact that he was even there at all. After all, the whole purpose of my journey was to attend his funeral . . . or, at least, that's how it had started out. But, somehow, I wasn't surprised. England seems to lend itself to strangeness.

I hadn't been back since my father's funeral, two years earlier, which was also the last time I'd seen Nigel, his grief sitting uncomfortably—even incongruously—on his round and usually jocular frame. Dad's death had hit him hard, though he had tried to cover up his grief for my sake. He needn't have bothered. Dad and I hadn't been much of an item since my university days, and my leaving for the States had been the last straw.

That was seven years ago.

In the intervening time, we had become estranged like lovers who tire of each other's company. I knew something about that, too.

Nigel and I had maintained an infrequent contact, exchanging occasional letters filled with pleasantries and politeness but which were as devoid of breath and life as my father had been, lying still and silent in the lounge of his old house.

The final letter didn't even come from Nigel but, instead, appeared one day, in the box outside our house in Wells, covered in the faint, birdy scrawl of Aunt Dorothy. Just looking at it, you could tell it was bad news.

Nigel was ill, the letter said, Very ill. Cancer. My uncle had lost a lot of weight and they were simply waiting for the end. It couldn't be long. By the time Susan telephoned Dorothy, the letter and its contents were five days old. Nigel had gone.

Long before the arrival of that letter, my house had become a pioneers' trail and, Susan and me, we had become two ragged, road-weary wagons passing each other on a long, tiresome search for something we'd misplaced. We didn't know what it was, nor did we even understand it: we just knew it was missing. Ringing Aunt Dorothy was one of the few things Susan had done for me in more months than I cared to think about. I didn't even want to think of what *I* had done for *her*. I knew it didn't amount to very much.

It was Susan's idea that I come over and attend the funeral. At first, I hadn't wanted to but then I got to see the trip as some sort of pilgrimage. Back to the old country, travel the old roads, see my past again . . . neatly folded and stacked away like old clothes in a hidden drawer. Maybe the thing I'd lost was in that drawer. Tucked between a pair of threadbare denims and a shirt I could no longer get into, smelling as fragrant and as natural as a lavender potpourri. Everybody needs a touchstone, something on which you can rest a hand and say . . . *yes, that's it . . . that's all that matters*.

I decided I had to find that touchstone . . . find myself.

With a minimum of preparation—and even less communication between Susan and me—I drove to Boston, caught the flight to Heathrow and arrived in England on

173

the kind of summery midmorning that I'd forgotten could even exist.

The journey from Heathrow to the King's Cross train station was filled with hustle and bustle, the tube train a kind of mobile Tower of Babel, packed with seemingly endless dialects and accents and languages. I felt immediately at ease—what are tourists except people searching for answers?

Me, I was also looking for the question.

The chaos of King's Cross gave way to the sober calmness of a train bound for Leeds. There I had to change for a local connection to get to Harrogate. My old hometown.

It was while we were passing through Peterborough that Uncle Nigel appeared, looking as large as ever I remembered him being when he was alive.

I turned away from the window, with its endlessly spinning stream of captured fields and trees, to look at him. He smiled and gave a small nod and then looked back out of the window. "It's all about us," he said with a soft satisfied sigh. "From the simplest birdsong to the most complex orchestral composition. It breathes. It lives." I closed my eyes tightly and then opened them again. Uncle Nigel closed and opened his own eyes a couple of times in an affected squint. "Yep, you're still there, too," he said with a chuckle.

"But *I'm* alive," I whispered, though there was nobody within earshot. By virtue of the fact that I was in a smoking compartment, the rest of the carriage was almost empty. Only one other passenger—an elderly man chain-smoking B&H and reading *The Times*—accompanied me through the countryside and he was down near the split into nonsmoking. The sunshine streamed through the windows, dappling the seat backs and bare tabletops, and shining off his bald head. All around him, swirling slate-blue smoke drifted lazily to the sound of the train's momentum.

"And I'm dead but I won't lie down."

"What's it like? Death, I mean."

The smile fell from Uncle Nigel's face and he seemed to stare at me more intently. "It's quiet," he said. "What is it that they say? 'Quiet as the grave.' Well, that's what it's like. No sounds. No music."

I shook my head and started to get up. "I'm imagining this," I muttered to myself. "Jet-lag . . . something I ate maybe."

"You're not imagining it, John. They're all gathering down at the house now. They're rehearsing their platitudes, their eulogies, straightening out their crumpled black ties, pressing dark trousers and somber dresses, practicing their expressions of grief and sympathy. None of it actually means anything." He made a facial expression as though he had just eaten something unpleasant and then, setting his jaw firmly, gave the merest hint of a smile. "More to the point, I'm not going."

"Not going!" I said, sitting down again. "Not going where?"

"I'm not going in the ground."

I remembered when he and my father would sit for hours listening to music. They would put one record after another onto the turntable and then sit silently, reverently, almost living a particular song and then discussing it while one or the other of them ferreted out another record. Music had been their passion, their raison d'être . . . a mythical chalice they would turn over and over in their hands, admiring it anew each time. Without it, they were nothing.

Sitting there in the train carriage on my way to my uncle's funeral, talking to his ghost—I presumed that was what he now was—I remembered a conversation with my father—back when we were still speaking—when I had asked him which of his senses he would be prepared to give up if he had to. It was one of those silly hypothetical questions concerning a situation that simply would not happen. But rather than dismiss it as so many would, my father had thought long and hard, stroking the memory of his beard as he decided upon the appropriate answer. The loss of his hearing—and, as a result, an inability to appreciate his beloved music—was what he had finally told me would cause him the most anguish. And then he had added, "But my memory comes a close second."

We sat for a while, my dead uncle and me, watching out of the carriage window until I resolved to find out what really troubled him. "Is it so difficult to cope with," I said at last, "being dead?"

My uncle stretched his legs under the table and shuffled himself back into his seat. "As I said, it's quiet and it's dark." He shrugged his shoulders and straightened his jacket lapels. "We come from darkness, you know."

He closed his eyes and in a lilting voice, sang the opening lines of Simon and Garfunkel's "Sounds of Silence." When he opened his eyes they seemed to focus from far away, as though they were returning to him—to the train carriage—from a long way away. And they were glassy and moist.

"Darkness is an old friend for us all," he said softly.

I nodded. It had been a perfect rendition of the song, even down to the fact that I had imagined the rhythmic picking of a solitary acoustic guitar.

"And how about this one." He cleared his throat and opened his mouth slowly. Suddenly there was a waft of music, of distant instruments—a guitar, two guitars maybe—playing what sounded almost like a Scottish refrain—and then Uncle Nigel started singing in a gentle, warbling falsetto.

It was another song that seemed to concentrate on darkness but it was one I did not recognize.

"A band called The Youngbloods," he said, recognizing my blank stare. "From an album called *Elephant Mountain*, 1969. And what about this one . . ."

The carriage turned suddenly cold and alien, and there was the strongest sensation of something awakening, turning over in the seats around us. My uncle closed his eyes and seemed to drift into a trancelike state. His expression was one of pain, but bearable almost beautiful pain. The sweet pain of loss, of grief. And the sounds that issued from his mouth reverberated inside my head. For just a few magical seconds, it was as though Uncle Nigel's bridgework had scooped up a radio transmission from the ether and sent the sounds floating from his open mouth. It was all there, voices and instruments. Jim Morrison couldn't have performed it better himself.

As though coming around from a séance, Uncle Nigel opened his eyes and gave me a half smile. It seemed almost like an apology. "Morrison had it right, you know?"

I frowned.

Uncle Nigel waved a hand languidly. "Paul Simon talked about darkness being an old friend—which is true—but Morrison had it bang on the button about music being our *only* friend. He meant it's our *truest* friend."

I shook my head. I still wasn't following.

"Because it's music that gives light to the darkness."

I looked nervously at the surrounding seats. Whatever had caused the restless movement around us had ceased now that he had stopped singing, and the carriage seemed to have regained much of its earlier warmth.

"They were one of Dad's favorites, The Doors." I slid in an attempt to fill the sudden void of silence.

He nodded, half closing his eyes.

I looked out as we sped past a small station lying weed-festooned and overgrown, forgotten from the great clamp-down of the 1950s. "Have you seen him? Since you . . . went over? My dad, I mean."

"I know where he is," he said.

"Is he all right?"

"As far as he can be, yes."

"What does that mean? Either he's all right or he's not."

"He's all right."

I cleared my throat. "Does he ever . . . does he ever mention me?"

Nigel smiled. "Now and again."

Neither of us spoke again for a few minutes. Then my Uncle said, "Know why we fear the dark? Because"—he went on without waiting for me to respond—"with the darkness comes the silence. It's why we're so scared of death.

"We come from darkness, and it's to the darkness we return. But in between we have discovered the music. And it's the loss of the music that scares us the most."

Uncle Nigel brushed at a tiny piece of lint on the front of his jacket and then folded his arms. "Darkness is nothing. It is the none-ness of being." He paused and then continued. "Light, on the other hand, is energy. In turn, energy is life. Life is movement, no matter how small. Movement is sound, no matter how faint or distant. And sound, dear John, is music, no matter how free-form or avant-garde it might be.

"It is the thing we search for all of our lives . . . search for it as though it were a mystic talisman, a keepsake." He looked out of the carriage window and threw his smile beyond the glass and his half-seen reflection . . . threw it to the countryside that lay humming in the sunshine. "It may be the rubbing of two twigs or the leaves of the trees on a windy day," he said. "It could be the noise of that wind through the feathers of a mountain bird; a rockslide or a rainstorm; waves breaking on the shore; a car engine, a baby's cry, the sound of footsteps on the pavement . . . the sound of this train." He turned back to face me. "Do you hear the music of the train, John?"

I did. It went *chuckitty-chunk, chuckitty-chunk.* "Yes," I said, "I hear it. But what has all this to do with you not wanting to be buried?" Just saying it made me feel incredibly stupid. The man at the end of the smoking compartment suddenly stood up and walked away, presumably toward the buffet car. It was as though he was leaving a theater in protest at the banality of the performance he had paid good money to watch.

Nigel waved the question away with his hand. "Whenever I walk along—sorry, *walked* along—Shaftesbury Avenue I always used to think of a piece by Les Dudek called 'Central Park.' It seemed to epitomize the throngs of people, the hustle and the bustle. And when the evening gloom came to the house I would often walk out into the garden and think of The Moody Blues' 'Twilight Times.' It was like all things in my life had musical references." He laughed and threw back his head. "Hell, my life itself was one long musical reference. I loved life, John. Loved it. I didn't *want* to die."

"Nobody want—"

"Yes, I know, nobody wants to die. But with me it was something more. Who else do you know that placed such store in music?"

"Well, my—"

"Apart from your father, I mean."

I shrugged and shook my head.

"You see, it's lost on most people. They don't grasp the significance. Life is the longest single note of all, John. We are a musical species. We come from darkness and silence into a world of noise and light. We translate all of our existence into musical as well as visual images. Soundtracks for films, music in church and at funerals—I wonder what they'll be playing at mine. It certainly won't be Jimi Hendrix, and more's the pity. It'll be something . . . something funereal. You see! We even have a word for *that* kind of music. Lost and cold music specially produced to reflect off the alabaster strangeness of someone we once knew but no longer even recognize." He stopped for a few seconds and looked back at the fields and hedgerows speeding by. "You wouldn't have recognized me at the end."

"I'm sure I would have," I said. It seemed that he needed the reassurance of his own identity.

"I was thin, God was I thin. Like a skeleton."

"What is it that you want of me?" I asked.

He seemed not to hear the question or, if he did, he chose to ignore it. "Have you noticed how, in a western movie, when somebody walks into a saloon, the fellow playing the piano stops? It's the threat, the imminence of death. That's why he stops playing the piano. He stops the music."

"Yes," I said. God help me, it was beginning to make a kind of sense suddenly, a fractured logic.

"And how *all* movies always have to have a music soundtrack. Even in the days of silent films, we had to have somebody sitting playing the piano to emphasize what was happening on the screen."

Chuckitty-chunk, chuckitty-chunk, went the train.

"What do I want of you?" he said after a while. "I want you to dig me up."

The man down the carriage returned with a lidded plastic cup and a shrink-wrapped sandwich. He sat down and I watched him remove the lid from the cup and then start to eat his sandwich. I turned to look at my uncle and shook my head. "Why?"

"Why? Because the ground is dark and silent, that's why."

179

"But you won't be in the ground. Well, your body will be but you—" I waved a hand in his general direction. "Whatever you are, you're here now, and your body is . . . I don't know, lying in state I suppose. So why should you be affected?"

"John," he said, "I came to you because of your father. Because, of everyone I know—even Dorothy—you might understand what I've tried to tell you. It's quiet over there, deathly quiet. And the reason is that you carry with you the sounds of where you rest. Why do you think they stole Gram Parsons' body? Why do you think they did it?"

"Who's Graham Parsons?"

"Not Graham, *Gram*. He was a singer . . . a musician."

"They stole his body after he was dead?"

Uncle Nigel nodded. "And he wasn't the only one. There've been others, but Gram is the only one that's actually documented."

"Who? Who's stealing all these bodies?"

He laughed. " 'Who' isn't important, it's 'why' that matters."

I was entranced. "Okay, why?"

"To leave them where it's light, where there's some sound." He said it like he was explaining one-plus-one to a five-year-old. "And that's what they take with them."

"To Heaven?"

"Heaven is just a state of mind, John. Like 'Great,' or 'Marvelous.' 'The flip side' is how *we* think of it . . . we whose lives have revolved around music."

"Okay . . . who's 'we'?"

He looked at me, kind of frowning and mashing his lips together. I was immediately aware of the train slowing down—not slowing as if it were coming to a station but rather just becoming less frenetic, less agitated. Everything suddenly became very calm. "This is 'we,' " he said and then he pointed out of the window.

I had heard about Woodstock and the other huge music festivals held in the 1960s and 1970s from my father. And I had seen the film. Well, looking out of the train window that day was like looking out on the audience at Woodstock. Only, the people standing out in the fields were not merely watchers, they were listeners, innovators of sound. People to whom music had been everything.

There was the Big 'O,' the Big Bopper, Benny Goodman, Elvis, Janis, Mario Lanza, Morrison, Jimi, Buddy Holly, Dennis Wilson—Uncle Nigel was pointing them all out because, don't ask me how, the train had slowed right down and we must have been doing only about five miles an hour. I looked around at the man down the carriage and he was sitting holding a cigarette half in, half out of his mouth, with his lips curled in a seemingly endless snarl, a thin freeze-framed trail of smoke curled around his face.

"There's Nat King Cole," my uncle said, "and Liberace, John Lennon"—I recognized him straightaway—"Karen Carpenter, who's no longer thin at all, Keith Moon, Glenn Miller, Rick Nelson, Bing Crosby . . ." The list was endless, names I knew and names I had never heard of before.

Suddenly I felt my uncle's hand on my arm. I turned around and looked at him, wearing a kind of dumb smile and suddenly fighting an overwhelming urge to cry. "Go out to the door and open the window," he said.

"Huh?"

"Go on, go out to the door and open the window."

I did as he said. The noise washed into the train like a scent of nightstocks, far-off and fragrant, impossibly beautiful and warm. Like a billion bees humming, or a zillion tree branches waving, or a thousand trillion waves strumming a distant beach.

And, as we passed the thousands of people, black people, white people, people all colors, I saw my father.

I went to Uncle Nigel's funeral that afternoon.

It was like he said it would be, somber, affected and depressing. For me, though, it was difficult to be sad. Even when Aunt Dorothy came up to me and wept against my shoulder.

They played a couple of hymns which I recognized but didn't know the names of. It was all I could do to stop myself from standing up and shouting "Hey, he doesn't want this. Put on some Hendrix!" But I managed it.

I didn't go back to the house. Instead I rented a car and

bought a large spade, some sacking and a cassette of Electric Ladyland. Then I rang Susan and told her that I loved her. She was shocked, asked me if I was okay. I said I was. We spoke for a while, nothing important in itself but, somehow, just speaking was the real important thing. "I think I've found it," I told her.

"Found what?" she said.

"Me . . . us . . . I don't know. Whatever it was that we'd lost."

Before I hung up she said, "John?"

"Yes?" I said.

"I . . . I love you, too."

That night I went down to the grave again.

It didn't take me too long. The earth was still soft and I managed to get it all put back the way I had found it. Uncle Nigel was right: he had lost a lot of weight at the end. His body couldn't have been more than about ninety pounds.

We drove until we hit open countryside, playing "Crosstown Traffic" and "Voodoo Chile" at full volume. Then I parked the car and hiked for another forty minutes or so into some real wild woodland. There were no paths, so no evidence that people ever came here. Just as he had said. I took him deep into a dense wood, getting ripped and lacerated by the clinging branches while, all the time, I was protecting his body slumped over my shoulder. When we got to where he'd described, I propped him against a huge birch tree.

I heard a voice say "Thanks, John," but he never showed himself. Maybe it was just in my head.

On the way back, still playing Hendrix, I thought back to the train journey and our conversation. And I thought of what Uncle Nigel had done with my father's body.

There's a small gully out among the rocks near Pateley Bridge with a special little collection of bones resting in the bottom where nobody can reach them. Being daily windblown, rain-washed and sun-dried. Listening to the sounds of existence.

And as the trees drifted by outside my window I thought of what Uncle Nigel had said about life being one long note.

Join the Leisure Horror Book Club and
GET 2 FREE BOOKS NOW—
An $11.98 value!

— Yes! I want to subscribe to — the Leisure Horror Book Club.

Please send me my **2 FREE BOOKS**. I have enclosed $2.00 for shipping/handling. Each month I'll receive the two newest Leisure Horror selections to preview for 10 days. If I decide to keep them, I will pay the Special Members Only discounted price of just $4.25 each, a total of $8.50, plus $2.00 shipping/handling. This is a **SAVINGS OF AT LEAST $3.48** off the bookstore price. There is no minimum number of books I must buy and I may cancel the program at any time. In any case, the **2 FREE BOOKS** are mine to keep.

Not available in Canada.

NAME: _____

ADDRESS: _____

CITY: _____ **STATE:** _____

COUNTRY: _____ **ZIP:** _____

TELEPHONE: _____

E-MAIL: _____

SIGNATURE: _____

The Longest Single Note

I thought of Susan, waiting for me, and I wondered what
my own note sounded like.

I think it sounds like this . . .

For Percival Crowther 1913–1972

Fallen Angel

At first Yellen thought the man was watching *him*.

He pulled back against the hedge, folding his body into the sharp branches, and waited. The man staggered a little and bent down. Yellen stared, trying to make out his movements through the gloom. The man had rested something on the ground and was now straightening up, muttering. The sounds of indistinct words floated across the street. Yellen glanced quickly to the left and right to see if there was anybody else around. The street was deserted.

Yellen had been casing a small one-up-one-down that stood out among the other houses by virtue of a gleaming silver satellite dish, standing proud on the patchy stucco like a ripe boil. He had heard the sound of footsteps and had dodged gracefully across the sidewalk into the hedge. He looked back at the man and wrinkled his nose. The hedge smelled of pee.

Across the street the man rose to his full height and took two faltering steps forward . . . then another one back and slightly to one side. He wore a long topcoat which, as he swayed side to side, feet held so firmly in place that they could have been nailed to the sidewalk, flapped open to reveal a dark jacket and light-colored pants. His shirt collar was unbuttoned low, necktie sprawled to one side in an explosion of crumpled material. The top half of his body continued to ripple as though an electric current were passing through it. Yellen recognized the current as being 80-proof. He slid his right hand into his jerkin and eased the .38 out of his waistband while the man shuffled around so that he faced the wall, his back to Yellen, and made a big deal out of unzipping his fly.

A faint hybrid sound of pooling water and bursts of mumbling echoed through the night, it sounded like someone trying to tune into a distant radio station.

After what must have been a full minute and a half, the man shook himself, bent forward, fumbled up his zipper, and then turned around. He looked straight across at Yellen, but his eyes clearly didn't see anything except the night and the loneliness and the New Jersey air. The man threw his arms into the air and shouted to the sky.

"Thus st-strangely" he stuttered hoarsely, "are our souls constructed . . ." He paused, shook involuntarily, and then continued, "And by such . . . by such slight ligaments are we bound to posterity or ruin!" He staggered back a step or two and, as if attached to a single string which had suddenly been severed, his arms and head fell forward to sides and chest. He kept this way for several seconds, swaying, and then lurched down sideways to retrieve whatever he had set on the sidewalk. Yellen retreated further into the hedge and concentrated on the object as it came into view. It was a bag.

It looked like a doctor's bag but bigger. One of those old black valises that carried prescription pads and Valium and painkillers. *And what else?* Yellen wondered. *Maybe a few uppers?* He held the gun down by his side so he could bring it up at full arm's length and fire if he were forced into it. He almost wished he would be. But, no, the man hoisted the bag up under his arm and leaned an unsteady head so that it met the object . . . and kissed it tenderly. Then he turned around to face the way ahead.

Yellen squinted. The bag looked heavy. Important. Precious.

The man started to shuffle his one-two-one way along the sidewalk and Yellen moved forward from the hedge, sliding the gun into his jacket pocket. He watched the man for a few seconds and then turned back to look at the house. It was still dark. He knew what was in there. VCR, television set, bunch of compact disks, receiver. The usual. It was the sign he had grown accustomed to looking for. It usually meant objects which he could easily turn into cash. He looked back at the man's weaving figure, heard a distant belch, and his eyes locked onto the black bag. But maybe there were better pickings to be had.

The man reached the end of the block and turned into the next street, shuffling back before proceeding, like a bad vaudeville act or Snagglepuss, the old cartoon lion. Then, with a throaty *burrrup* and a stream of Shakespearean-type mumbling, he was gone.

Yellen rechecked that he was still alone and unobserved and then took a final look at the house. His mind was already made up even before he acknowledged the decision. He folded himself into the air and the shadows and ran crouched and silent-footed across the street.

He got to the end of the block and peered around the corner. About fifty or sixty yards up the sidewalk the man was doing more of his soft shoe shuffle, trying to make a ninety-degree turn over the shards of a large fence. He negotiated the barrier with difficulty and staggered off the sidewalk. Yellen followed.

He followed the man across some stumpy grassland, festooned with ditches and rocks so concealed by the night that even he, stone cold sober, experienced some difficulty in maintaining his balance. The man, however, now seemed to have found his feet and glided effortlessly across every obstacle with seeming surety.

Eventually the steady hum of humanity, that almost indiscernible and often reassuring presence of civilization, faded behind them as they picked their way across the barren land. Here a tree sprouted from the earth, there an occasional bush; up a small slope, down a sharp ravine . . . until, at last, the sound of the man's shoes clattered again onto man-made material. Yellen stopped and watched, breathing heavier now.

The man was on a street. It ran straight to the right and into the far distance where it joined the main drag down into Westfield. To the left it ran a few yards before curving away and down what appeared to be a hill. Yellen couldn't be sure. The light was very bad, fed only by three street-lamps, unevenly spaced, and a gibbous moon that played hide and seek with the passing clouds.

The man stamped his feet, almost losing his balance in the process, and then crossed the road he was on and walked toward a large house that seemed to fill the whole horizon. A thick patch of cloud slipped across the moon and then slid off toward distant Miami, the sudden increased glare of light catching the full splendor of the property and etching it against the dark sky to the north. The house stood alone on the road. Yellen looked at it and marveled.

The tapering roof of an octagonal tower adjoining one side of the main roof—a smoke-topped chimney rose from the other—gave the house the appearance of a clenched fist, its index and little fingers stretching up in a combination of exclamation and caution. It was, Yellen recognized from his college days, a Queen Anne style mish-mash of tower, bay windows and porte cocheres. There were many examples of the period around Westfield, but this, surely, would qualify as being one of the finest. Possibly *the* finest.

Moonbeams glinted like fairy dust down a tapering roof which alternated between rows of fish-scale shingles and rectangular slates. More shingles adorned the gable, and the porch—within which the man now fumbled in coat pockets, the bag still held firmly beneath his arm—featured a frieze of spindles and inverted taper columns, up which a veiny confusion of ivy tendrils had crept. The windows were a patchwork of Elizabethan straplines, with small multicolored panes surrounding a larger clear-glass center.

And there, attached to the highest tip, a jumble of thick cables stretching and bowing down from it to the darkened depths of the grounds, was the biggest receiver dish that Yellen had ever seen.

As he crept stealthily across the road and into the drive of the house, Yellen kept his gaze fixed on the object, watching its perspective change and its size increase until, as he crouched behind a thick bush, the thing seemed to dominate the sky. It was at least three—maybe four—times larger than the usual dishes householders fixed to their properties. Black or dark gray in color, it boasted a stamen-like centerpiece of glass pipettes which themselves formed a fairy-ring periphery to a thick and bulbous apparently metallic protrusion that angled into space. As he watched, Yellen thought he saw the spike glowing. A sound from the porch made him crouch lower and fumble in his jacket pocket for the gun.

Through the bush, Yellen could see that the man had now turned from the door, which now stood partly open, to face the drive and the road beyond. He held the bag tightly to his chest with both hands, stepped out onto the path and looked up at the receiver dish. "As I stood at the door," he said, loudly and in now more succinct tones, "all of a sudden I beheld a stream of fire issue from an old and beautiful oak, which stood about twenty yards from our house."

As if on cue, the spike now proceeded to glow and throb and a distant symphony of metallic *tings* sounded through the gloom. "And as soon as the dazzling light had vanished, the oak had disappeared," he continued, "and nothing remained but a blasted stump." The man staggered a little and then, resting the bag on his outstretched left arm, he unfastened the clasp and pulled the sides apart. Looking inside, his voice lower now but still distinct, he said, "I never beheld anything so utterly destroyed."

And then he reached into the bag and pulled out, his hand clasped around one leg, what appeared to be a floppy doll. The object flailed at the movement, its free leg and both of its arms and its head swinging freely.

The man dropped the bag to the ground and held the doll aloft. Turning his head so that it faced the dish—or, perhaps, Yellen thought, some greater entity far beyond the confines of the house—he intoned, "Yet from whom has not that rude hand rent away some dear connection, and why should I describe a sorrow which all have felt, and must feel?"

He turned around and lowered the doll, taking it into both hands and pulling it to himself. "Nay, ne'er mind *describe* . . . why must I *countenance* it? Why *should* I countenance it?" And then he turned back to face the house and went inside, pushing the door closed with his body.

Yellen waited, heart beating fit to burst, and watched the porch. The door banged against its casing and then, slowly, drifted open once more. He removed the gun from his pocket, felt the reassurance of body-warmed metal, and then replaced it again. With a quick look around him he stood up and ran to the porch, up the few steps on tiptoe, and through the doorway into the darkness beyond.

Once inside, Yellen flattened himself against the wall behind the door and listened. He could hear echoing footsteps fading somewhere in front of him but, his eyes not yet conditioned to the impenetrable blackness, he couldn't make anything out. Why doesn't he turn on a fucking light? Yellen thought. Suddenly the sound of the footsteps changed. The man was on some stairs. But was he going up or down? Yellen put his head flat to the wall and closed his eyes, straining to hear. It was up.

He removed his shoes and placed them carefully by the door. Then, his vision improved, he moved forward deeper into the house.

The doorway opened onto a pentagonal hallway from which a series of doors, all but one closed, stood in the center of each wall with the main door behind him. The open door led onto what seemed to be a corridor. It was there that the footsteps could be heard. He checked his gun again, walked across the floor to the corridor, and slipped stealthily through.

At the end of the corridor was a cross passage. Once there, Yellen glanced carefully around the corners. To the left, the corridor led to what seemed to be a rear entrance to the house. The righthand wall of this smaller corridor featured a series of picture windows which showed a long, rambling garden, completely untended and overgrown. At the rear of the garden, adjoining a wide, rough pathway, was a car. Its wheels had been removed and the axle ends rested on small piles of stone. The car appeared to have no glass in its windows. The glass door at the end of the corridor opened onto a small room, also completely glassed, and Yellen could make out various handles and pieces of equipment.

In the other direction, to the right at the end of the main corridor, a shorter passage led to another open area, though this one was considerably smaller than the main hall. Yellen saw a banister end leading upward to the right and out of sight. Now, at least, he knew where the stairs were. He started to move toward them.

As he walked, straining to hear the footsteps and continued mumbles from somewhere overhead, Yellen was suddenly aware of the state of the house. It had been allowed to go completely to ruin.

From all of the walls large strips of wallpaper hung free, reaching to the floor and myriad piles of broken plaster and fast food wrappers and containers. From all around he seemed to hear soft scurryings, scratchings and rustles, and the almost soundless movement of gently billowing material. As he reached the foot of the stairs he checked the gun again and moved around the banister to face the risers leading upward.

The flight of stairs had approximately twenty-five risers and Yellen could clearly see the next floor. The stairs opened onto another cross corridor before continuing around to the right, up again. He started up, suddenly sharply aware of a pungent smell.

The smell was not exactly unpleasant, but it was strong. It hinted of body odor, a thickening draft of parmesan cheese sitting atop a bowl of steaming hot vegetable chowder. By the time he had reached the top of the stairs, it just smelled like shit.

The cross corridor led, to the left, to a long passage which featured three doors, two on the left, one on the right. The right one was glass paneled and led onto a small balcony overlooking the rear garden. At the far end of the passage was a wall and, on the left, a dark patch which suggested the corridor made a sharp turn to further rooms.

To the right, the corridor ended, by the foot of the next flight of stairs, at a door. The door was open and a light was shining from inside. Somewhere, something was humming. It was an equipment-type hum, the sound of confident strength, of well-tended machinery.

Something small ran over Yellen's feet and it was all he could do to keep from crying out. He kicked out and skipped toward the door. As he passed the next flight of stairs, the smell he had noticed earlier hit him like a hot sheet thrown over his face. He stopped and looked up the stairs.

The flight led to another level, another blank wall and, presumably, another cross corridor. Looking up, he could hear sounds ... groans and moans, shufflings and—he turned his head to one side to concentrate—an occasional clank, like bottles, or glasses being chinked together in a gesture of good health. But the smell coming down from up there spoke of anything but good health.

Yellen glanced over at the open door, listened, and then stepped onto the first stair.

His heart was now beating like an electronic drum, faster than should be humanly possible.

He took the second stair.

And then the third.

Each step led him deeper into that smell of depravity and filth. It was as though he were descending into a blocked sewerage system and not simply climbing a staircase.

When he had reached the top, he looked back. There was nothing much to see, just the faint glow coming from the small room to the right of the foot of the stairs. He turned around and swallowed hard to keep from throwing up.

This time, the corridor ending at the left and front, a passage led to the right and along to a large pair of doors across which a heavy plank had been fixed into two large, rusting metal hooks. The moans and groans were coming from behind the doors.

Yellen considered going back downstairs and out into the night. The temptation was strong. Hell, if he were so bothered about finding out what was behind the doors, he could even come back another day, tomorrow maybe. With help. In the light.

Because the night, and particularly this house, spoke of monsters. *Monsters!* Why should he think of monsters, for crissakes. He hadn't even used the word since he was a kid and couldn't get to sleep because of the big man who could fold his body into sections and sleep in the large bottom drawer of his chest. The drawer where his mom put Yellen's underwear and socks. The drawer which Yellen would never go into unless the penalty was sufficiently dire. After all, what were a few skidmarks in your smalls or the occasional lump of toe-cheese rattling around your socks when the alternative was to have a spindly arm and toothy grin telescope out of the colored interior of a chest drawer to grab you and kiss you, and pull you into the feigned softness of what was, in reality, a material hell.

Something shuffled up to the other side of the doors and bumped into them, letting out a tired groan. The doors had rattled briefly, softly, and were still again. Whatever it had been could now be heard shuffling away again.

Yellen took a deep sigh, strode to the doors, and lifted the plank free. He placed it against the wall and reached for the handle. As he did so, the left hand door opened slowly.

Yellen wasn't even aware of throwing up.

His gorge moved quickly and without deliberation, traveling from his stomach, up his throat, and into his mouth from where it splashed in one silent burst and then dribbled in two or three additional pulses.

Yellen shook his head at the thing that faced him in the gloom. It was—or once had been—a girl, maybe 14 or 15 years old. She stood before him as if in supplication or submission, completely naked, scrawny breasts covered in sores and scratches, a thick pubic thatch hanging from her crotch like a Scotsman's sporran.

The girl's skin was yellow, like matted breakfast cereal, boasting a series of sores, tears, lumps, and crisscrossed stitches that wept thin funnels of matter into crusted configurations on her cheeks and jowls. One of her eyes was closed in a puffy ball of rainbow hues. The other, a watery orb that stared, seemingly without recognition nor emotion, out of a thin and skeletal white socket, blinked once and fell still. The skin on her cheeks and down onto her neck was stretched so tight that Yellen could see the musculature flex and vibrate as she turned her head, first one way and then the other. It was with profound regret and shame that he saw he had been sick onto the top of her head, where his vomit ran and mixed with long tendrils of thinning hair.

The girl opened her mouth wide, separating lips so black they looked like heavy pencil slashes gouged beneath a turned-up nose, and let out a soft, querulous hum. Then she turned from him and shuffled back into the room. As she moved away from him, slopping her trailing feet through rivers of brown and yellow and green ooze, Yellen saw the caked mess of shit on her backside.

Now, in spite of the smell, Yellen moved into the room, There were maybe fifteen or twenty of the unfortunates in there, some standing, some sitting, and some lying down amidst the debris and the filth. Some were younger, some maybe older than the girl who had admitted him, but all were children. A handful in the far corner, beneath a series of barred and whitewashed windows, were only babies or toddlers. One of them watched Yellen, his black-rimmed mouth a shitty stain, as he paused in the act of eating a long runny stool that dripped onto his legs. It would, he thought, be crediting the child with too much to say that there was a spark of intelligence in those watery eyes. His actions were purely reactive.

A sound behind him made Yellen spin around.

The man stood in the doorway, swaying slightly, a beatific smile etched on his face. In the current circumstances, the smell of bourbon was tantamount to being the finest Chanel perfume.

The man held onto the door with his left hand and waved the other expansively to the scene inside the room. "With how many things are we upon the brink of becoming acquainted," he said in a slow, deliberate voice, "if cowardice and carelessness did not restrain our enquiries?" One of the children moaned and the man lifted a finger to his mouth and shook his head paternally.

Turning his attention back to Yellen, he said, "To Monsieur Frankenstein, this was a rhetorical question, my friend. I, however, put it to you fully." And with that he stepped back and ushered Yellen out of the room. Yellen walked as if in a dream, back onto the landing, and the man closed the doors and lifted the heavy plank back into its place.

"What are they?" Yellen asked as he followed the man down the stairs.

"They are the chosen ones," he replied, the words drifting over his shoulder like motes of dust. "I know what you are thinking, my friend."

"I'm not your friend," Yellen snapped.

The man reached the foot of the flight and nodded. "Quite so. But I do know what you are thinking. 'Its astounding horror would be looked upon as madness by the vulgar.'" He spoke the words reverently and Yellen saw that they were slightly out of the flow of the man's first sentence.

"Are those . . ." Yellen waved his hand. "The things you keep saying, are they quotations?"

The man nodded again, bending slightly from the waist as though before a dignitary. Standing straight again, albeit falteringly, he said, "Shelley."

"The poet?"

"Mary Shelley. The author *and* poet. *Frankenstein*. Are you acquainted with the work?"

"I've seen the movies," Yellen said.

The man sniggered. Then he gestured to the room at the foot of the stairs. "Come," he said. "All will become clear."

As he walked toward the room, the man removed a hip flask from his jacket pocket and, throwing his head back dramatically, took a deep swallow. Then he returned the flask to his pocket.

The room was huge and bare.

In its center was a padded black table, above which hung a chandelier-type object bedecked in wires and tubes. The wires ran from the head of the object and across the ceiling to a high point on the wall, below which a window looked out onto the path by which they had come to the house.

Yellen, patting his pocket for the reassurance of his gun, recognized the scene and surmised that the wires were attached to the receiver dish.

On the table itself lay the doll which the man had carried in his valise. Only it wasn't a doll.

The child was perhaps five years old, his skin pale and withered, a single heavily stitched scar traveling the full width of his stomach. Yellen stared at the child, not daring to believe what he was seeing. "You're mad," he said. The words sounded so ineffective, so clichéd and so entirely inadequate.

The man walked in front of Yellen to the shelving that covered the walls surrounding the room. Yellen now saw that the shelves bore what might well be hundreds of large bottles and jars and tanks, each with something floating in thick-looking solutions. " 'I hope the character I have always borne will incline my judges to a favorable interpretation, where any circumstance appears doubtful or suspicious.' " He reached down a bell jar, containing what Yellen thought could be livers or kidneys or something similar, and unscrewed the top. "That was what Justine Moritz, the closest of close friends to Elizabeth Lavenza, Frankenstein's virtual sister, said as she stood accused of the murder of Elizabeth's son, William." He took a rubber glove from the shelf and pulled it on with a loud squeaking sound. Smiling at Yellen, the man said, "Nobody ever understands." He lifted one of the things from the jar, replaced the lid—one-handed and with difficulty—and returned it to the shelving.

"What are those?"

"Things no longer required by their previous owners," the man replied. "You could say they're not wanted on the voyage." He chuckled and stepped across to the table where he dropped the piece of tissue or whatever it was into a around surgical tray which lay beside the child's body.

"Where do you get them?"

The man turned around and leaned against the table, removing the hip flask with his ungloved hand. " 'A churchyard was to me merely the receptacle of bodies deprived of life, which, from being the seat of beauty and strength, had become food for the worm.' "

"Oh, my Go—"

The man threw the flask across the floor, "Oh . . . spare me your platitudes and your pathetic pleas for help." He moved toward Yellen, waving a finger at the ceiling. "There's nobody there, can't you people understand that? The lights are on, but there's nobody home. God?" He laughed, making the word sound like an invective. "He doesn't exist—or, if he does, then he's singularly lacking in compassion.

"*I* am the light . . . *I* am the way. It's because of *me* that those children still survive."

Yellen shook his head.

The man turned back to the table and began rubbing a cloth across the corpse. "The girl that you saw is my daughter." He stopped and leaned on the table, head bowed. " 'I saw the yellow eye of the creature open; it breathed hard, and a convulsive motion agitated its limbs.' " He returned to the washing. "She was my first," he added. "Fourteen years old, raped and stabbed to death, her vagina clipped almost up to her abdomen with cutting shears. I try not to think of what order her injuries were sustained . . . try not to think that the killing insertion to her heart came last."

He dropped the cloth back into the bowl and pulled a cord overhead. The chandelier began to lower slowly. Turning to face Yellen, he said, "And yet you talk of God." The words came in a haze of spittle and disgust.

"You *are*—"

"Mad? So you said. 'All men hate the wretched; how, then, must I be hated, who am miserable beyond all living things.' " He suddenly concentrated his gaze on Yellen and frowned. "Incidentally, why are you here?"

Yellen shrugged. "To steal."

The man copied the shrug. "Makes no matter." The chandelier beeped and came to a shuddering halt. "Ah," the man said, "we're almost ready." He waved for Yellen to join him. "Here, you can help."

"You have *got* to be joking!"

"I never joke, Mister Thief. Hold not another in contempt lest you are yourself free from blemish. I, my dishonest guest, live to give. You, on the other hand, are a taker."

Yellen removed his gun. "Well, I'm going to do some giving right now."

The man watched the gun impassively. "And what do you propose to do with that?"

"I'm . . . I'm going to go back to that hellish room and put those things out of their misery. Will bullets—"

The man dropped to his knees on the floor and clasped his hands together. " 'She died calmly—' "

"Shut up."

" ' . . . and her countenance expressed—' "

"I said . . ."

" ' . . . affection even in death.' "

". . . SHUT UP!"

" 'His yellow skin scarcely covered the work of muscle—' "

Yellen ran across the room and swung the gun against the man's face, sending him sprawling against the table. The table skidded away and then held against two restraining straps fixed to the floor, jerking its passenger off to land with a dull thud.

"Jesus Chri—"

"There's no him, either," the man said, holding a shaking hand to the gash below his left eye. "There's just you and me, thief. Do what you must."

Yellen lifted the gun and fired. And he kept firing.

The first shot went through the man's hand and cheek, splaying brain onto the floor milliseconds before the back of his head touched it. The second and third went into his chest. The fourth, his stomach. The fifth strategically placed—Yellen had walked while firing and was now standing directly above the man—in the center of his forehead. There wasn't a sixth, only a click . . . followed by many more clicks until Yellen's finger eased from the trigger.

When he went back to the room at the top of the house for the final time, he carried the cold body of a small boy. He had already dragged the man's body up the stairs and propped it against the door beside two cans of petrol that he had found in a small hut in the garden.

On the top of the can sat two books: one containing matches and one containing words.

Entering the room again he smiled frequently. Nobody inside responded. Nobody tried to leave.

He placed the boy's body with the other toddlers and dragged the man into the center of the room.

Then he walked around spilling petrol everywhere, singing, "Hush little baby, don't say a word, daddy's going to buy you a mocking bird." It was a song his mother had sung to him many years ago.

As the flames took hold, he flicked through the pages of the other book, trying to find something appropriate.

He found it and paraphrased: "Farewell my beloved friends: may Heaven in its bounty bless and preserve you; may this be the last misfortune that you will ever suffer."

Then he left the conflagration and rejoined the night.

"When I placed my head upon my pillow, sleep crept over me; I felt it as it came, and blessed the giver of oblivion."

—Mary Wollstonecraft Shelley (1797–1851)

Incident on Bleecker Street

With a sharpened crackle and a soft but resonant ping like a throaty memory hitting a far-off spittoon, the thief barrels out of a hole on Bleecker Street, a hole temporarily darker than the blackness which surrounds it, his coat-tails trailing out behind like a thick woolly scarf, arms pin-wheeling and boot heels clacketing along the slippy and slidey gray-snowed sidewalk, the myriad reflected possibilities of his next action freeze-framed in the darkened glass of a pawn-broker's window which almost but not quite hides the murky recollections of once-new shoes and lonely trumpets as well as the comforting promise of a dull-metalled .38, propped forlornly against a sloppily dressed mannequin with half its face missing and wearing a green-and-ocher checkered wide-lapelled suit that once looked nearly new.

Winter in the city and the cold hangs over the blacktops like an Arctic curse freezing even the coughed-out steam from the manhole covers which appear just now and again beneath passing yellow cabs on their way uptown or maybe even further downtown, to maybe take someone home or maybe to a dinner party or maybe even way up to the Hundreds where the black folks walk their stiff-lipped and

Peter Crowther

loose-jointed struts to the million syncopated rhythms and fractured rhymes straining out of the screen doors and skylights and jammed-open windows to waft over the brownstones and the moaning traffic and the trees until they turn into half-formed wraiths pulled apart by the rising moisture of the East River.

January in the Village, cold to the touch and hot and sticky beneath your clothes so's your undershirt sticks under your arms like a tired child wet with spent energy and the crotch of your Fruit-Of-The-Looms hangs down low and damp and the smell of sleepily diminished movement echoes on your nose hairs with thoughts of what you did today, all long spurts and brief longings. The thief, he looks to his side and catches sight of himself first walking back that way then walking down this way then crossing the street and then staying just where he is right now watching himself watching himself. The images fade and die and are replaced by other images fainter now and slower somehow drifting into one another walking backward maybe until the choreography gets right and what's going to be is be and will been and maybe even was did going to have to have happened and then it is what it is but not what it was because that's why the thief is here and then he looks back at his own self from the pawnshop window and he smiles. Time to make it all different and what will be.

A soft and snowy Tuesday on Bleecker Street, more than a breath from the weekend and the long Sunday but still a long scratch to Friday night when the coffee houses smoke out in the open and the poets rage and curse and the guitars strum through the steamed-up windows and the uptown people, blacked out like curfews, all berets and beards and sandals and turtleneck sweaters, drift in on the subways and the buses because it ain't hip to ride the Yellows into the Village. Somewhere across the city a Greyhound rolls into Port Authority all dust-sided and grime-screened, lavatory smelling of mis-hits and travel sickness thrown out passing a thousand small towns of front-porch plans and dime-store maybes, thoughts and hopes and memories pulled up out of loose-fitting screen doors with Camel smoke and TV dinner smells as the bus rolls on by on its way to here from there. The joker rides the bus his head lolling on the glass away from the fat lady who sometimes snores and who sometimes eats Tootsie rolls and sometimes stares past him at the windows seeing maybe a stream of missed opportunities, maybe even a thin girl staring back and shaking her head tutting silently as only reflections can tut because only they can see the reality while the real can only see what they want to see.

Here is now but not the now that was because the now now, the new now, is a different now and the thief he's stolen the now that was and that always was ever since even the pure and virgin second that it became the now that was now just the promise or threat of a thought away. He fingers the knife, this thief, rubs a calloused finger along a blade sharpened with determination and good, honed with pure and simple righteousness that seems fit to shine out of his pocket into the late evening like a beacon to the joker so's he can risk a rhyme and strum a story preach a parable charm a couplet drop a letter right where he stands for others to pick up and turn over in their hands to maybe make something out of, something lasting, something that maybe means something or will do one day.

But the joker doesn't feel the light doesn't hear the shine doesn't smell the salvation like the pages of dusty bibles crackling through the Village air high above the city. He only sees the promise of the streets stretching out in front of him like girls to be charmed and vines to be emptied, a glass near brim-full swirling strange and sweet possibilities.

Elsewhere in the city and in the towns across this wide and long great country that is so familiar but so constantly alien the melting pot bubbles a moment or two and all of the people turn in their beds or think of going to them but fight off the moment because this day is now and the next need not happen so long as they can hold onto what they got here and what they got right here might just be a whole lot better than what might just be waiting crouched around the sunrise. The thief breathes in this stolen night air, fills his lungs brought with him from a city which looks a lot like this and even has its name but isn't the same not at all even though he's stood on Bleecker many times and heard or thought he's heard the same sounds he hears right now which are the sounds of the night and he shows the blackness his blade and just for a moment he thinks maybe he'll go back where he came from and let the now that was return. He cries, this thief who wants to give not steal, to give a grail of dignity, bestow a truth of identity, seek out with a shiny blade the goodness that once was. He cries just the way he's cried so many times over the years when he's thought of what it would have been like to stand right here and right now but then he called it "then" and he dreamed of meeting the joker before he met the city and let it turn him into a clown.

Way over on the wind-washed sidewalks of Port Authority the joker steps off the bus behind the fat lady who pauses wondering should she turn left or should she turn right but knowing deep down in the rolls of herself that it will be the wrong decision so why not just go with it because if either is wrong then both must be wrong and maybe one day she'll do the one right thing and stop herself from doing anything ever again. But that day is many days away and it's just the now that matters even though she doesn't know that the now she has now is not the now that could have been and has been these long years while the thief has been coveting this night in his memory-darkened bedroom of walled images and oft-played songs and words that he thought maybe once meant something but which had gotten bleached in the suns of many days which didn't mean an awful lot but just measured the passage of nows.

The joker drifts out of Port Authority all chords and breaks and changes, out onto the night-time street like an idiot wind wafting across the sidewalk and tinkering in the gutters among the cigarette stubs and bus tickets, lingering every now and again to form an image of words and rhythms which are still yet a little bit Minnesota, still a little bit dustbowl, but now a little bit of Wisconsin, too, and soon they'll be a little bit New York, because he learns fast, this jokerman and shrugs his guitar over his back like it's his whole life he's carrying and he thinks, yeah, maybe it is.

In the hour of days and weeks and months and years and

loves and hates and friends and enemies it takes the joker to get across town, the thief thinks back or is it forward? to what the joker has done/will do with that guitar and the tears they fall fast and silent in the cold night air and he thinks that maybe he should go home to where it's positively incidentally and absolutely safe though not dangerous anymore and anyway it's alright, maybe he's only dreaming. They share thoughts, these two, share nows and thens and dreams and realities and possibilities and the thief he envies the joker his innocence and he whispers a single word soft and low into the crystallized air, a single word a poem comprising four . . . but that's not him, that's someone else, a would-be, a charlatan, a copyist who doesn't feel what he feels now or then, or is it soon or now? he doesn't know anymore. The knife comes out like it's got a mind all of its own and swishes all around him making ready to drink its fill and then the joker's there in front of him, all bushy hair and fur-lined coat and denim jeans bound for glory and humming a song about how hard it is/will be in New York town and then the thief he spins around and buries the knife as deep as it will go, deep inside the fur-lined coat deep inside the soft flesh deep inside the poet's guts and stops the words the tunes right there on the sidewalk on Bleecker Street.

And the joker slips and falls, his guitar rattling against the wall as the thief withdraws the blade and strikes again feeling, this time, a little bit of righteous bone scrape his entry and already the thief feels the words and songs and tunes and rhythms start to fade like it was as if they had never existed and in that one instant he knows they never had, not now, this now, his now, their now. And it seems, suddenly, like such a waste and such a loss to the world but wasn't this what they wanted from him? Those folks who doubted, those who decried, those who begrudged those days, these days.

Drink deep the death you've earned the thief thinks to the jokerman as his life ebbs and seeps. *Hold aloft the artifact of your brief life . . . the holy gift I give you . . . the gift of unfulfillment . . . now they will think of what you*

*might have been and not dilute what you once were with
what you became.*

A hard rain has started to fall.

It patters noisily on the huddled shape which leaks
around the boots of the thief and the thief watches the
boots closely as the first signs show and the cracks on the
sidewalk shine right through and he feels released just as
he knows he's said/will say he would be so many times and
then the air is alive with a million trillion chords and se-
quences and words and lyrics, all playing together in the
thief's head, and he thinks what did I mean? what was I
thinking then/now? but then the tunes fade one by one until
all that's left is a few notes blowing in the wind.

As the thief becomes just a memory of something that
never happened, the notes and the bridges and the refrains
are all gone too, and the night drifts slowly along Bleecker
Street into the jingle jangle morning, while up along the
traveled years the memory of a maybe hero is born and the
promise of a greatness only hinted at is preserved.

Morning Terrors

He awoke like clockwork, jerking upright in bed, images racing through his mind in a steady stream, sweating feverishly and gripping his bottom lip with his teeth. He was already whining.

The luminous display of the clock on the mantelpiece, strangely twisted out of true and shimmering as though about to disappear, registered 3:08. To his left, the curtains were wafting gently, billowed inward by a gentle breeze which muttered around the outside of the house. He could see them out of the corner of his eye but refused to look at the window full on. Not yet. That would come soon.

He shook his head and whimpered, protesting like a cowed child. ". . . no," he whispered faintly, as though trying not to let anyone else hear him. ". . . no, please, no." The bed creaked and strained as the figure next to him moved slightly. He swallowed and tried to concentrate on the mantelpiece but already felt the first signs of detached curiosity that would cause him to turn around.

The wall in front of him looked wet and slimy and uneven: that had happened a week ago Tuesday. The wardrobe that should be next to the mantelpiece was not there:

that had gone for the first time on the Friday. Nor was the old wicker crib-and-stand in front of the radiator attached to the right-hand wall: the first time that went was the following Sunday.

Last week it had stopped here . . . changed back in the blink of an eye. The week before, it had stopped at the mantelpiece. The first week, as soon as he had woken up. But last weekend it had lasted until he had first looked at the curtains. Then, just a few days ago, the first pains in his chest had started.

Last night he had noticed the duvet.

He lifted his hands to his face and started to sob quietly, sniveling mucous out of his nose.

Between his fingers he could still make out the orange light that shone through the curtains. He breathed in deep and wiped his eyes with his fingers, roughly. And then he turned to face the window.

It was the same again. Orange. The sky outside the window shone orange through the paisley floor-length curtains into the room. No sign of the streetlight which lit the road between his house and number 20. No vague outline of the houses across the road. No faint sound of the late-night/early-morning trucks on the motorway. Just orange, pulsating.

And hissing distantly.

Staring at the window, willing it to change, he caught sight, in the lower periphery of his vision, of the shape which was no longer his wife curled up on the other side of the bed. In front of him, wrapped tightly in what had once been a duvet, the figure moved, growing increasingly restless.

"Shhhhhh," he said softly, ignoring the tingling feeling which jabbed through his chest.

Now, he thought. *Come back now.*

This was where it had ended last night. A sound started in his throat, long and guttural, building in pitch, as he started to lower his head to look down fully at the bed.

As he lowered his eyes he saw again that it was not a duvet which covered him and his wife but an old skin of some kind. Patches of the thick and course hair had worn through in some places and, in others, stains shone darkly, spotted occasionally with what looked like pieces of meat and dried grass. It smelled like the insides of the dustbins out in the yard.

The figure beneath the skin was huge. It was not—could not possibly be—Katherine. And it was misshapen, becoming larger at the feet end than at the middle, where the skin fell inward. At the top, it was enormous.

He had seen hints of all of this last night. Tonight he had seen it close up. And now he saw one more thing: the top of his wife's head protruding from the duvet.

And it was starting to move as though waking up.

"Nonononojesusjesusjesusjesusjee—"

Katherine's hands were on him suddenly, shaking roughly.

His eyes still closed, he heard her voice and almost cried. "There, there, sweetie," she said gently. "Another dream?"

He opened his eyes and looked around, realizing vaguely that he had turned on the lamp on her side table.

He was half kneeling in front of her, facing the window. The curtains were still blowing and he could make out the muted white glow of the light outside. Somewhere in the distance a horn sounded, followed by the haunting lonely call of a big truck, dopplering from and back to nothingness.

He looked at the clock. It registered 3:14.

Next to the mantelpiece stood the wardrobe.

In front of the radiator stood the wicker crib-and-stand, filled with all of Katherine's toy animals.

He looked down at the unmistakable swirls and splashes of the duvet. And then he looked up, through blurred eyes, at his wife. She stared at him wide-eyed and shook her head, settling back into bed and rubbing her hands through her long brown hair. He shuffled from his kneeling position, slipped out of the bed and padded across the carpet to the hall and the waiting toilet. His bladder felt like it was going to burst.

As he let loose a thick, strong-smelling stream into the water below, Katherine's voice called to him from the bed-

207

room. "I don't care what you say, Terry, but it's doctor's for you in the morning."

He groaned with relief as he finished and flushed the toilet.

"You hear me?"

"Yes, I hear you," he said. He rubbed his chest. It felt strange, almost tight. And it was sticky to the touch. Must be sweat. At least the pain had gone. He rubbed his hands down the sides of his legs and ran softly back to the bedroom.

Snuggling into Katherine's back in the now-restored darkness, he pulled one of his pillows so that it went down the outside of the bed behind him, protecting him from the room beyond.

He kissed the back of her head. "Love you."

"Love you too, sweetie," she said, her voice drifting back to him over her shoulder. "But you must go to the doctor's tomorrow."

"I will."

"Promise?"

"Promise."

And, his vision concentrated on the shine of the outside lamp, he slipped off into the dreamless sleep of exhaustion.

"Okay, you can put on your, er, shirt again."

Terry sat up, swung his legs over the side of the bed and reached for his shirt. "So what's the verdict, doctor?"

The other man sat down behind a wide desk and laid his stethoscope gently in an open felt-lined box. "Well, there's nothing wrong with your heart," he said, carefully avoiding looking Terry in the eye. It didn't bother Terry at all. The man was very shy and never locked eyes with anybody. There were seven doctors in the practice, not counting the endless run of trainees who spent a few months learning the ropes, and Terry got to see the doctor with whom he was officially registered. He had been seen by this fellow before.

He stood up and tucked his shirt into his trousers, giving an exaggerated breath of relief. "So I'll live?"

Doctor Platt allowed himself a nervous smile and pushed

his glasses farther back on the bridge of his nose. "I think it's, er, safe to say that."

Terry finished tying his necktie and folded down his shirt collar while the doctor keyed something into the computer. "So what about these dreams?"

"Well, those are probably caused by stress, tension, any number of, er, things." He scratched absentmindedly at his beard and made a further adjustment to his glasses. "How are things at work, er, what is it that you do again?"

"I'm in advertising," Terry said. He hated having to explain the complexities of his job with the bank, and advertising seemed to be the likeliest catchall.

"Busy?"

Does a wooden horse have a hickory dick? "Very," he replied.

"Well, it's probably just morning terrors. You probably need to, er, take a rest."

Terry nodded and sat down on the edge of the bed.

The doctor finished what he was doing at the computer screen and looked over it at the wall behind. "Everything okay at home?"

"Everything's fine at home." Terry was feeling better already. The pain in his chest—which had lingered with him for the past three days, steadily growing worse—had gone completely today.

The doctor stroked his beard and then turned to face Terry, his eyes locking onto the chair back just to Terry's right. "Well, I'll give you something to help you sleep," he said, "and some cream to clear up that, er, irritation on your chest."

"Irritation on my chest?"

"Yes, just around your, er, nipples." Doctor Platt cleared his throat and reached for a pen.

"My *nipples*?" Terry was beginning to feel like a parrot.

"Mmmm, it's just a bit of soreness. Nothing to worry about, probably been caused by rubbing, maybe a shirt or . . ." He let his voice trail off.

"Or?"

"Well, er, just by a shirt." He turned his attention to the little prescription pad and wrote quickly. "See if your, er,

209

wife has recently changed washing powders. That can often cause irritation." He finished writing and placed the top carefully back on his fountain pen. "Hadn't you noticed it?"

Terry shook his head. "No, not at all."

"Well," he held out the slip of paper to Terry while continuing to talk to the chairback. "That's, er, all right then."

"Your *nipples?*" Katherine laughed loudly as she removed her coat. "And what did he say about the dreams?"

"He said what I expected him to say, that I was just run down and that I need a rest." Terry watched her watching him. "He gave me something to put on it, anyway," he added. "A cream. And he gave me something to help me sleep better. He said it was just a case of morning terrors."

She walked over and turned on the gas beneath the kettle. "And are you satisfied with that?"

"Yes. Yes, I'm satisfied with that," he said, scratching at his left nipple without even realizing that he was doing it.

This time the clock had gone completely.

He felt groggy, half-doped. Must be the pills. Certainly he did not feel so concerned at waking up in what must still be the middle of the night.

The room was again bathed in an orange glow but tonight it was not silent. Tonight there was a muted sound of activity. Nothing that he could separate and identify: more a *sense* of things going on around him. And there was another sound, a low and pained moaning ... several moans all joining together, drifting and wafting. He stared at the wall in front of him and suddenly realized that it looked to be farther away. He allowed his eyes to travel upward.

The wall now bore no resemblance at all to the wall of his and Katherine's bedroom. As far as he could make out in the dim orange light, it was a rock wall that went all the way up and over. Like the wall of a cave. And he could sense movement on the floor in front of him and around him.

Terry yawned and rubbed his arms around on the duvet,

feeling the coarseness of the hair and picking at the occasional lumps matted within it. He turned to face the window and saw, instead of the paisley curtains, a thin veil, ripped and holey, hanging in front of a large opening. In his stomach he felt the first delicate flutterings of anxiety. There was something about the veil, something familiar . . .

A sound behind him, out on the stairs leading up from the ground floor, disturbed his thought. He did not turn around at first but listened intently. It was a dull and rhythmic sloshy clumping, like the sound he would expect a deep-sea diver to make with his weighted boots as he moved through some kind of overgrown swampland.

Time to wake up. He turned to look down at Katherine and saw that the bed was empty at her side.

The clumping grew louder.

He stared at the pulled-back hairy skin-duvet and then looked up again at the veil where the windows should be. The orange light showed it all exactly. It was like a patchwork quilt, only it wasn't made with material.

The clumping came nearer.

He recognized the small dark areas as hair. The lumps and holes were eye sockets and ears, boneless noses and empty fingers, limp toes and—He shook his head and felt the unmistakable warmth of urine between his legs.

His heart beating in his chest, he thrust his right hand beneath the covers.

The clumping was very near now.

His hand grabbed for his penis and . . . it wasn't there!

He leapt up from the bed into a standing position, ignoring the fact that the bed was surprisingly hard, like rock, and he screamed. Outside the bedroom, on the stairs, the clumping speeded up, louder and louder. He kept screaming, relishing the familiarity of his own voice, and turned to face the darkness where the bedroom door used to be. Something was moving toward him out of the gloom, getting nearer.

And now there was another sound, something calling to him, though not in any language that he knew. Nor was it a voice he recognized, if it was a voice at all.

He closed his eyes as if in prayer and pressed his hand

tightly between his legs, silently mourning the loss of a close friend. There was a blinding light and then darkness.

Katherine's face shimmered above him, the familiar patterns of the bedroom wallpaper providing a comforting backdrop behind her head. He grunted and lifted himself up quickly, thrusting his hand down to his crotch to grab hold of his flaccid penis. He sighed and fell back when he felt it, turning the limp appendage around and around in his hand.

"Terry? Terry, what is *wrong* with you?"

"It was the dream again," he said simply. "But worse this time. This time I had no penis."

She rose up in front of him. "That's it," she said sharply. "That does it, Terry. I've had enough. You need help." Terry shuffled back onto the bed and winced when he sat in a cold wet patch. He clasped his hand to his chest and lifted it away immediately. It was sticky. He sniffed at his hand and almost gagged. It smelled sweet. He returned the hand to his penis and groaned. "The bed's all wet," he said.

"Yes, it's wet. It's wet because when I came in from making myself a cup of tea you were standing on the damned thing peeing all over the place."

He rolled over onto his side and curled his legs into a fetal position. "I'm tired," he said. And he went to sleep.

The following day began uneventfully with a silent breakfast, during which the usually attentive Katherine allowed Terry to see to himself ensuring, with a minimum of fuss, that the two of them spent as little time as possible in the same room. As Katherine got into her car, Terry assured her that he would contact the doctor again. But this time he would insist on speaking to his own doctor. She waved a dismissive acknowledgment and drove off.

He never saw her again.

Terry rang the office and explained that he had had another bad night and that he would be in a little later than usual. It was his intention, he said, to try to catch up on a little sleep and come in around lunch time.

He cleared away the breakfast things and tidied the table.

Then he went upstairs and had a long shower. The water felt good, hot and good, swilling away the memories of the previous night. He tousled his penis lovingly, soaping it until it was erect. He considered masturbating there in the shower but the thought of it made his chest hurt. Well, not his chest actually, but rather his nipples. He looked down at them under the stream of water. Were they bigger? They felt bigger, both to the touch and also deep within him. When he had got out of his dressing gown to get into the shower, his chest hairs had all been matted and sticky, as if he had spilled something on them. But he had washed his chest well and now everything seemed as it should be.

Out of the shower, dried and shaved, Terry felt like a new man. Almost. He decided against going back to bed and instead put on the kettle for a cup of coffee while he dressed. But then it all caught up with him and he turned off the kettle and went up to bed without taking off his clothes. As he lay down, pulling the duvet around him, he failed to notice the two wet patches on his shirt front.

Sleep came immediately.

What awakened him he didn't know, but awake he was. Wide awake. And the orange light was there again.

Terry kept perfectly still and waited until his eyes adjusted to the gloom. As he lay there, now very aware of the rough and hard surface beneath him, he could hear the moans again. They were clearer now, more distinct. He was still curled up facing the bedroom door, only the bedroom door was no longer there. Now there was only blackness stretching away from him. Without moving, he lifted his eyes until he could make out the curve of the roof way overhead.

He moved his hand beneath the hairy skin which covered him and felt his trousers. His chest felt sore and heavy but more than that, it felt wet inside his shirt. He tried to keep his breathing slow and silent but adrenaline was pumping around inside him so fast he fancied he could hear it swirling through his body like a swollen river. Without shifting the skin-cover, he moved his hand to the front of his trousers and felt for his penis. It wasn't there. "Oh, God," he whispered. This time was different. He knew that. This time there was nobody else in the house to break the dream. He had to escape. From what, he had no idea. He only knew that he had to escape.

But if Katherine were not in the house, then the bed should be empty. He pushed back with his left leg, feeling with his foot for some sign of another body lying next to him. There was nothing. At last, he turned onto his back.

The room was misty.

No clock, no mantelpiece, no curtains, no wardrobe. Nothing that he could recognize as being his. Only strangeness. He looked to his side and saw that the bed was indeed empty. Over by the huge opening to the room the skin-veil shuddered and wafted softly. He sat up.

The moans seemed louder now, coming from all around him, and there was a smell of something dead or dying, like rancid meat or bad eggs. He looked around.

Shapes were moving on the floor, writhing and twisting. It was from them, he realized, that the moans emanated.

Terry pulled back the skin-cover and swung his legs out of the bed until he felt the floor. Then he stood up, maintaining a crouched position both to preserve his anonymity and also to be prepared for flight at the first sign of danger.

Each of the shapes was covered in its own hairy skin. He moved to the first one and lifted the cover gently. Beneath was what remained of a young man, a faint stubble on his chin and the light of madness shining from his eyes. The man let out a louder moan and, for a second, Terry was tempted to let the cover fall back but he just shook his head and hissed "Shhh!" The man's eyes focused on Terry and he stopped shaking his head. "Help me," the man said.

Terry pulled the cover fully back and immediately bit hard into his bottom lip. The man's body was falling in on itself. His skin was intact but inside it there seemed to be little left of any substance. His head lay on a makeshift pillow constructed of more hairy skins. Below the head the man's neck traveled to a mound of skin-folds. He was completely naked. His arms lay outstretched beside him like empty arm-length gloves, the fingers curled and twisted and entirely incapable of any movement whatsoever.

His body, too, was devoid of filling. No ribs, no bones, no meat, no organs. Empty. From his chest extended the remains of two large breasts, spread out across his flattened stomach like cartoon condoms, their teats bitten off and ragged. And below all that carnage the coup de grace was a woolly patch of pubic hair, matted and slimy and smelling like an old runny cheese. There was no sign of a penis.

"Help me," the man hissed and, for a second, Terry thought he detected a slight movement in one of those flattened glove fingers. He dropped the skin back over the man, thanking whatever god was watching down on this place that it fell mercifully across his anguished face.

"Who's there?" whispered another voice.

"Help us." Another.

Yet another started to weep.

All around the floor the hairy skins were moving, though each one moved only where it might be covering a head.

Terry straightened up and stared hard into the blackness where once his landing and the sanctity of his toilet had waited. From way, way off came the sound of a bell.

At once the shapes beneath the skins began to wail, screaming pleas and curses, begging, screaming. "Quiet!" Terry hissed, but it came out more as a shout.

Ahead, in the blackness, something was moving toward him.

Terry spun around and hopped over the figures on the floor, past the foot of the bed he had just left toward the skin-veil. When he got to it, and actually started to reach out a hand, he cringed. The veil was indeed constructed from a series of human skins stitched together. Faces stared sightlessly through empty eyeholes, stitched onto a stomach or buttock. But it wasn't just the sight of the grisly curtain that made Terry's eyes water and his throat fill with bile. It was the smell. And it wasn't coming only from the skin quilt. It was coming from a large vat standing just outside the opening. Terry could see it through a ripped nipple that boasted a ragged hole so large you could have thrown a football through it. He pulled back the curtain and faced the brave new world.

It stretched into infinity, a torn and twisted orange landscape of upside-down trees and smoking mountains. It was a land of nothingness.

Terry stepped fully outside and moved to the edge of the ledge he was standing upon. The ground was far, far below . . . too far and too steep to consider as a means of escape. He turned around and looked up. No exit there either. He took a step to the vat and peered over the rim.

Somehow he had known what would be in it. There were hundreds of them, all shapes and sizes and colors. And one of the ones on the top looked very familiar.

His scream was louder and more guttural than any sound issuing from a human being had any right to be. And it went on and on and on until he felt that he had completely drained himself of energy and sound and air.

Then he heard a movement from behind his back.

He spun around.

The thing stood its ground.

At first, Terry thought it was a huge balloon with two heads pasted onto the front. The faces watched him, the eyes burning into him. He broke his eyes from their stare and looked behind the thing, back into the cave. Trailing from where it now stood stretched a thick line of glistening drool. It had no feet and no other apparent means of propulsion. He looked back at it, shaking his head, and noticed that it had settled its bulk to the ground. Now it resembled a conical blimp of folds and creases, though the two heads still protruded.

And as its bulk had settled, the thing's insides had spread out so that different areas stuck out as whatever was behind pushed against the skin. Terry knew what those things were. They were bones. Nothing else mattered. Nothing else would exert any pressure.

Again Terry felt the warmth of wetness spreading down from his crotch. He lifted his hands to his shirtfront and began to undo the buttons.

Two huge breasts flopped out from within his shirt.

The thing lifted its mass to accept his offering.

He stepped slowly forward, lactating two fine-mist sprays of milk into the orange air.

Shatsi

When the wind is just right you can smell the dreams.

They're almost palpable, a thick mixture of smog, sweat and hope, drifting along Wilshire, Sunset and Hollywood Boulevards, pooling in the hollowed-stone footsteps and handprints of Marilyn Monroe and Hank Fonda, Jimmy Stewart and Jeannie Crain, and all the others that litter the sidewalk and courtyard of Grauman's Chinese Theater.

For Benjamin Wassermann, it would always be Grauman's. Fuck Teddy Mann.

Bennie Wassermann, whose resumé now has him as Sherman Tyler, sets the black valise down on the cracked paving stones beside the public phone kiosk and shuffles in his pocket for some change. He drops a quarter into the slot and dials. A woman's voice answers.

"Thank you for calling," the voice says. Then, "Herman Morris's office, how may I help you?"

Bennie has heard the line before, albeit with a different name maybe, but it always seems like the words or the phrases are in the wrong sequence.

"Hi there," he says, sounding real friendly. "Is Mr. Morris in right now?"

"Oh, I'm sorry, Mr. Morris is in a meeting this afternoon."

Bennie has to give it to her, her patter is well rehearsed. The woman sounds genuinely distraught that the guy can't take the call: the only problem is that Bennie knows he *can*.

"Can he be interrupted?" Bennie asks, oozing concern and sincerity, spreading on a little bit of Peter Falk in *Columbo*, the re-runs for which Bennie always watches on Channel 13. "It's important."

"I'm sorry," comes the response.

He waits.

"What is it regarding?" the voice asks, covering her ass. "Maybe somebody else—"

"It's a . . . it's a personal matter," Bennie says, sticking to his script, smiling as he delivers the hesitation. He pours sunshine into the mouthpiece, sunshine and professionalism. A Fuller Brush salesman with a hint of Jimmy Stewart, awkwardly playing with his hat brim, shifting it around in his hands. "But I think he'll want to take this call."

There's a two-second delay before the voice says, "I see. May I tell him who's calling?"

"He won't know me . . . *doesn't* know me."

"Well, as I said, Mr. Morris is busy right now. Is this something you could write him about?"

Bennie shakes his head and then remembers that the woman can't see him. "No, no this is something that really needs to be dealt with over the telephone."

"I see." But her tone says that she doesn't see. She doesn't see at all. "Well, may I tell him what it concerns?"

"It's personal," Bennie says. "I already told you that." A harder edge gleams in the words like a discarded razorblade catching the light, Martin Balsam in *Psycho*.

"Yes, well, as I told you, Mr. Morris is—"

"Tell him it's about his cat."

"Pardon me?"

Bennie shifts the handset to his other hand and frowns. In the mirror on the wall in front of him, Bennie thinks maybe he just caught a glimpse of DeNiro in that shitty remake of *Cape Fear*, even down to the Hawaiian shirt. He says, "Look lady, you heard me. Just tell him."

Another pause. "Hold the line please."

Bennie fishes a handful of coins from his pocket and drops them onto the open directory beside the phone.

A man's voice says, "What *is* this?"

Bennie is still Max Cady. "Mr. Morris?" he says.

"This is Morris. What is this? Something about my cat? Is she okay?"

Bennie says, "Mr. Morris the theatrical agent?"

"Who is this? Is this some kind of stunt?"

Bennie shakes his head and thinks Damon Runyon. "No, this is some kind of telephone call," he says.

There's a long silence on the line before Morris says, "So what about my cat?"

Bennie can't keep the grin out of his voice. "She's fine, Mr. Morris, just fine. She's missing you."

"Where's Rita?"

"Rita?"

"Yeah, Rita. She's looking after Shatsi. Is there something wrong with her?"

"Is that Rita or Shatsi?"

"Listen you dumb fuck, don't mess around with me. I'm asking you if my cat's okay."

"I already told you, Mr. Morris, the cat's fine." He moves the handset back to the other hand again, frowning at the moisture glistening on the plastic. "Your cat's name is *Shatsi*? What *is* that? Is that German? French? It sounds French . . ."

"Who are you?"

Bennie says, "Me? I'm a Samaritan, Mr. Morris. Call me . . . call me the patron saint of animals."

"You're a fucking animal you—What you doing to my cat?"

"Hey," Bennie giggles. "Hey, I'm not doing anything to your cat, Mr. Morris. I love cats. Really." He waits to see if Morris is going to say anything. When there's no response, he says, "Next to caviar, I love cats the best. Cat stew maybe, or cat carbonnade . . . or maybe ca—"

"What the fuck are—"

"Don't shout at me, Mr. Morris." He flexes his shoulders. That wasn't right, he thinks. A little too much Tony

Perkins, too vulnerable, too weak. He closes his eyes and, pushing a smile into his tone, he pictures Christopher Walken in *True Romance*, talking to Dennis Hopper. Reasonable but firm. "I don't like it when people shout at me," he says. "Like I say, I only like cats next to caviar or fillet steak. Thing is," he continues, the smile broadening into a real shit-eating grin, "I can't afford caviar. Can't even afford fillet steak."

"What have you done with Rita?"

"Ah, Rita." He pauses. "She the little Spanish bitch?"

"What have you done with her?"

"Rita's fine. Everybody's doing just fine, Mr. Morris. We're all fine here."

"Put her on. Put Rita on the line."

Bennie clucks, put on his regret voice, his *Oh gee whiz, I don't think we can do that* voice. "She's not here, Mr. Morris. Rita isn't here."

"Where is she?"

Bennie shrugs. "Back where I left her?"

"Oh, Jesus Chri—"

"Hey, now hold on. Don't go getting—"

"What have you done with Rita, you sick fuck?"

"Now you're shouting at me again, Mr. Morris, and I told you I don't like that. I'll call you again soon and we'll talk." He slams the handset down onto the cradle and glares at it, feels the muscles at the side of his jaw twitching. He turns and kicks the concertina door to the phone booth until it shakes, kicks it once more and watches the top pane of glass slide slowly out of place and down onto the floor. He lifts the handset again and listens, hears the dial tone and slams it down again, then kicks the pane to the back of the booth next to the valise, watches it shatter against the wall, his jaw still twitching.

Sick fuck? Was this any way for a theatrical agent to speak? He's heard that Morris was connected and that proved it. He picks up the valise and makes like he's going to throw it out into the street and suddenly feels a shift of movement inside. He leans against the glass and shakes his head, laughing a little, the twitching fading away now. He's getting too much into the part. Time to settle down.

"Looks like it's me and you for now," he says, his mouth against the shiny black leather. "Shatsi." He shifts the word around in his head until it feels right, like well-chewed gum. He puts the valise under his arm and steps out of the booth.

Somewhere over west, a siren wails like a banshee. Bennie figures it probably isn't for him.

Back in his apartment, Bennie tips some more bourbon into the funnel and watches it pool in the bum's mouth, thin rivulets pouring over the unshaven chin. The bum shakes his head from side to side and Bennie grabs hold of the guy's nuts, tight, like he's going to tear them right off through the stained crotch of his jogging pants. The bum makes to call out and that relaxes his throat. The level of bourbon falls rapidly and the bum swallows, reluctantly at first and then gratefully. He coughs and splutters while Bennie looks at the bottle. Looking down at the bum, Bennie dials the number on his mobile phone.

"Hello?"

"Mr. Morris?"

"Yeah, it's me. What do you want?"

Bennie smiles across at the cat and whispers, "Don't record me." Then he kills the call, waits a minute and dials again.

"Hello?"

"Hey long time no speakee Mr. Morris." He chuckles and then stops—it was sounding like Frank Gorshin's Riddler. "How you doin'?"

"Will you tell me what you want?"

"Hey, you're shouting again. No shouting, okay?"

There's no response, just the electronic hum of silent frustration, the all-pervading darkness of murderous anger seeping down the line.

Bennie says, "I said, okay?" He slaps the table with his free hand. Special effects.

"Okay, okay. Take it easy."

"That's better Mr. Morris. You recording me again?"

"No, I'm not recording you."

"You're lyin' to me, Mr. Morris. Are you lyin' to me?"

"No, no I'm not lying."

"Because if you are then it might be that little Shatsi here says nighty night to her master, you know what I'm sayin' here? Shatsi go beddy-by permanent, you understand?" He holds his breath, hoping he's not overdoing it.

"I understand. I hear you loud and clear."

"Good. Hey . . . loud and clear: I like that. It's like out of the movies, you know what I mean?" Bennie lets the silence hover and then says, "But you know all about the movies, am I right here Mr. Morris?"

"What do you want?" Morris's voice is calm and quiet. "Is it money?"

Bennie laughs and affects a nasal whine. " 'Izzit money?' " He laughs again. "You bet your life it's fucking money, Mr. Morris. Second thoughts, you bet your cat's life. Little Shatsi here. You catch my drift?"

"Yes, like I said, loud and clear."

"Yeah, right: loud and clear." Bennie throws in a giggle and is only a little surprised at how realistic it sounds. "I still like that," he says.

"Good. So everybody's fine?"

"Everybody's fine."

"Then," Morris says, hesitantly, "we have to make sure everybody stays that way, yes?"

"Right."

A pause. "So how do we do that?"

Bennie draws in his breath, making like he's thinking about it. "Well, it's gonna be expensive, you know what I mean?"

Morris says, "How much?"

Bennie says, "Pardon me?"

"How fucking much do you want?"

"Ah, well—"

Morris sighs and Bennie thinks he can hear other voices whispering somewhere near. He pictures them all crouched by the telephone or maybe a couple of handsets, everyone advising and suggesting. And Morris getting suddenly pissed at the whole thing.

Sure enough, Morris says, "Now listen to me, you shit-wipe, and listen good."

Bennie smiles and punches the air. He says, "Hey,

you're—" and sure enough Morris interrupts.

"*Hey* you're nothing, fuck-up. *Listen* to me. Rita is in the hospital and—"

"Rita?"

"My maid."

"Right. The Spanish bitch."

Morris lets it ride and says, "She saw you."

Bennie stays silent, breathes a little heavy . . . like he's trying to think back, trying to remember.

"She said you were like a superhero."

Bennie can't stop the snigger. "Like a *what?*"

"A superhero. Like in the comicbooks, she said. Big black cape."

Bennie looks across at the bed, across at the bundled-up black cape lying over the headboard. "That's some ID," he says.

"It is with the sneaker."

Bennie smiles. Bingo! "S-sn-sneaker?" he says, dragging the word out like he's suddenly gotten nervous.

"You left your sneaker on my front lawn."

"So what are you, huh? Prince Fuckin' Charmin'? You gonna go around town tryin' on an old Nike to everyone you see? Shee-it!"

"You drinking?"

The question catches Bennie on the hop. "Huh?"

"I said, are you drinking? Think about it, asswipe. It's an easy question. Look at your fucking hand and tell me if there's a glass in it."

"So what if I'm—"

Morris lowers his voice, like he's breaking a confidence, and says, "So this. You bring my cat back and we call it quits. Maybe I even let you have a bottle for your trouble. Like a reward for finding Shatsi? Plus I give you back your shoe and maybe a few dollars to fold up in your back pocket. What do you say to that?"

Bennie gulps in three or four mouthfuls of air, swallows hard and then lets out with a belch, right into the mouthpiece.

"What say we forget the reward and I eat your cat, Mr. fuckin' hotshot theatrical agent?" He thinks a second for a suitable exit line, smiles and adds, "My momma always tol' me never to drink on an empty stomach." He presses the "end" key and smiles across at the sleeping bum.

Outside the window behind the bed, the sky is black and moody.

"Okay," Bennie says, "time to go walkees." This time, he's using his normal voice.

It is almost midnight.

Bennie drags the unconscious bum out into the yard and lays him beside the car. Then he dresses him in the cape and bundles him into the back seat. He throws the valise in after him.

The drive takes a little under forty minutes. When he gets to the top of Beaconsfield Drive, Bennie turns off the ignition and lights and rolls down to the clump of trees and parkland adjacent to Morris's house. He sits there for almost 15 minutes to make sure he hasn't been seen, then he gets out of the car.

A minute later, he pulls the bum out of the back seat and drags him around the front of the car, lays him half on the road and half on the sidewalk.

Bennie gets back into the car and starts it up, drives forward over the bum. Slowly. He hears the bones crunch even over the sound of the engine.

"A Dodge is one heavy fuckin' car, man," Bennie says to the night, his voice a cross between the Fonz and Jim out of Taxi, in the days before Christopher Lloyd was a wacked-out scientist in the *Back To The Future* films or a Klingon spaceship captain in that *Star Trek* movie—the one where they rescued Spock from the planet that was blowing itself apart with the Genesis project doo-hicky.

Bennie gets out of the car and runs around to the crumpled body, kneels down beside it and feels for a pulse. The bum is as dead as dead can be.

Bennie takes the knife from his pocket, cleans it on his jacket, and slides it into the bum's outstretched hand, curling the dead-as-dead-can-be fingers around the handle. Then he runs back to the car and grabs the valise out of the back seat, pulls out the drugged cat and throws the valise back in. He slams the door. With the cat under his arm, he runs back to the body and goes into the performance.

"Oh my *God!* Oh my good *lord!*" Bennie shouts to the night. He stands up and yells, "Hey! Anybody! There's been an accident out here." He runs back to the car and leans on the horn, cringing at the sound as it rings through the early morning stillness.

He moves back to the body, stares down at it.

Somewhere behind him a light comes on.

He hears footsteps and muffled conversation.

Then the bum groans.

Bennie says, "Jesus Fucking Christ!" and kicks the bum in the side of the head.

Someone shouts, "Who's out there?"

He considers dropping the cat, getting in the car and driving the hell away from the whole mess. But he's come too far to stop now.

"There's been an accident out here!" he shouts, loud, so nobody can hear the dull thud of his shoe hitting the bum's head again. *What is he, this guy—a fucking Kryptonian?* "Over here!"

Bennie turns around and sees a dim movement over by the front door behind the gates. Still a ways off. He braces himself and jumps into the air, landing with both feet on the bum's head. It splits like a melon.

"What you say?" a voice asks.

Wiping his shoes on the grass as he walks toward the voice, trailing them behind him like he has two club feet—or maybe like Boris Karloff in the Frankenstein movies—Bennie says, "I knock this guy down and . . . and he pulls a knife on me. Guy's carrying a cat, for crissakes, and he pulls a knife on me."

"Who're you?" Gene Herman Morris says, his voice filled with sleep.

"Me? I'm—"

"What are you doing here?" Another voice, over to the left.

Bennie turns around and looks into the beam of a flashlight, shielding his eyes with his free hand. The beam moves off and illuminates the figure on the road.

Bennie waits, dreading some tell-tale movement, half expecting the bum to stand up and

Truth, Justice and the American Way!

just dust himself down. But the body doesn't move, not even when the guy holding the flashlight bends over him and lifts his one bare foot.

Bennie sighs with relief. That was just what he didn't need: a near-dead vagrant brought back to life by somebody tickling his feet.

The voice speaks again. "I said, what are you doing here?"

Bennie shrugs. "I was . . . you know, I was out driving." He points across at the house and waves his arm around the whole deserted street. "Hey, I often drive around the movie people's houses. You know?" He shrugs again. "I'm an actor myself but—" Another shrug. "I'm between roles right now." He laughs disarmingly. "Looking for the big break."

"Looking for the big break at one o'clock in the morning?" the voice asks. It comes from the figure alongside Morris.

Bennie turns around to make sure the bum's still on the ground.

"He dead?" he asks.

The man stands up, shines the flashlight at Bennie's car. "Yeah, he's dead. "Good car," the man says as he walks to the Dodge.

Bennie laughs. "*Old* car, more like. Still it gets me around."

The man is running his hand along the front of the hood, like he's caressing it. "No, I mean there's not even an impact mark."

"No?" Bennie shifts from one foot to the other. "Huh. Well, I hit him a good one." He shrugs. "Maybe I wasn't going fast enough to do any real damage."

"Did plenty of damage to him," the man says, swinging the flashlight's beam back to the crumpled body.

The Longest Single Note

Bennie decides that the statement doesn't need a response from him so he lets it go.

The two men in the shadows are muttering.

Morris steps forward. Bennie recognizes him from photographs in the movie magazines.

"So you're an actor?" he says.

Bennie gives another shrug, laughs a little and looks down at his feet. "Well, trying anyway."

"Maybe I can help you out," Morris says, holding his hands out.

Bennie does a surprised stutter, a kind of who and why, both abbreviated to wh—.

"That's *my* cat," Morris says. "Guy stole my fucking cat." He nods to the bum. "Can you believe that?"

Bennie hands Shatsi to Morris and shakes his head. "It's a weird world," he says, slapping his leg.

"Well, I figure I owe you," Morris says, tickling the cat under the chin, frowning at the lack of response he's getting.

"He looks traumatized," Bennie says, pleased with himself at changing the cat's gender without even thinking.

"It's a she," Morris says.

"Oh," says Bennie. "Sorry."

The man in the shadows steps forward. "So he pulled a knife on you *after* you'd hit him? Or before?"

More shrugs from Bennie. "I er . . . I hit him—well, first off, he just suddenly appears, you know? Across the street?"

The man with the flashlight is opening the Dodge's door. Bennie can hear the click.

"And?"

"Oh," says Bennie. "Let me think." He laughs and clasps his hands together. "It all happened so fast," he says. "Yeah, that's it," Bennie says, "I hit him and he goes down—" He claps his hands. "Boom. Like that, you know? And I get out of the car and go around to him and he pulls a knife!"

Now Morris says, "The guy pulls a knife on you when he's lying in the road?" He chuckles. "I guess you really pissed him off."

227

Bennie falls in with the chuckling. "I guess I did."

"Then what?" says the man.

"Well, I . . . I kicked him in the head," Bennie says, suddenly realizing that that all makes some kind of sense—it also explains the guy's head looking like a fruit crumble. "Yeah, I kicked him in the head—" He demonstrates. "—Twice, like this, and I take the cat from him." He flashes his open palms and smiles. "And then you guys appear."

A voice behind him—from the Dodge—says, "This is your car, right?"

"Sure it's my car," Bennie says, turning around. "You think I'm a thief? Hey, he's the thief," he says, pointing. "That guy over there."

The man is standing with the door open, leaning on the roof, looking across at Bennie. He lifts something into view. The valise. "This yours?"

Bennie feels whole sections of his guts tearing off and sliding down to the tops of his legs. He starts to laugh a little and gives a little shrug, looks around at Morris—who's even now taking a step toward them, frowning—and glances at the other man, who's watching him, a slight smile tugging at the corners of his mouth.

"Well?" the man says again.

Bennie nods. "Well, it's my sister's," he says.

The man nods. "Well, I guess that must make your sister pretty small."

"I didn't mean—" Bennie starts to say.

"There a problem, Joe?" Morris asks.

Joe slams the Dodge's door and walks around holding the valise like it's a trophy. "I think so, Mr. Morris," he says. "No sign of impact on the hood or the fender, car stinks of booze, bag stinks of pussy—and not the kind you'd want to spend a night with—and—" He points across at the still prone figure on the street "—guy there shleps across town with one bare foot and there's not a mark on it. That's what set me off wondering in the first place."

"Wondering? Hey, you know," Bennie says, indignantly, "I did you a favor, but this is all getting a little strange for me and I'd just as soon—"

Morris nods to the second man and the man takes hold of Bennie's arm. He has a firm grip.

"Like I said," Morris says, "looks like I owe you."

Joe has now reached him and taken his other arm, swinging the valise by his side. The first man has pulled something out of his pants pocket. Bennie can't see it fully but he doesn't think it's a contract. It looks too solid.

What's the phrase? *Cast iron.*

"Let's go inside . . . discuss your part," Morris says. "Frank, bring him inside. Get rid of the car, Joe. And clear the street."

As the other man—Frank—starts to walk him toward the gates and the waiting house beyond, Bennie tries to think of something to say.

"Say Goodnight, Gracie," Joe whispers as he lets go of his arm.

Too Short a Death

"Hey . . . hey!" The man on the stage was trying to make himself heard, laughing while he was doing it and waving his hands conspiratorially, as though he were Billy Crystal in the *Mr. Saturday Night* movie. But the sound that he was trying to drown out was not the sound of people enjoying *him* but rather of them enjoying each other or their food or their drinks.

"Yeah, Hillary Clinton." The man frowned and shook his hand as though he had picked up something that was too hot to hold. "You heard . . . you heard Bill wants six more secret service agents assigned to her, yeah? Well," he reasoned with a shrug, "after all, if anything happened to *her*, he'd have to become President."

In humor terms, it was one step—a small one—up from *Take my wife . . . please!* but somebody let out a loud guffaw and David MacDonald turned around on his seat to see who it had been. At one of the tables over by the coat-racks two men were laughing, but it was clearly not at Jack Rilla.

"Thanks, Don," Jack Rilla shouted into his microphone.

"My brother Don," he added for the audience's benefit. "Nice boy."

The man at the table—who was clearly no relation to the comedian—turned to face the stage and gave Jack Rilla the bird, receiving a warm burst of applause.

MacDonald had never enjoyed seeing somebody die on stage, so he turned back to his food.

He was enjoying the anonymity. All the effete photographers and the snot-nosed journos had gone, taken up their cameras and their tape recorders and walked. Gone back to the city.

He was no longer news. "The most innovative poet of his generation," *The New York Times* had trilled, mentioning—in the 18-paragraph, front page lead devoted to his quest—the names of early pioneers such as William Carlos Williams, Edwin Arlington Robinson, and Ezra Pound; Kenneth Fearing, to whom they attached the appellation "The Ring Lardner of American verse"; the so-called war poets, including Richard Eberhart, Randall Jarrell, and Karl Shapiro—the Pulitzer winner whose "Auto Wreck" had been widely (and wrongly!) cited as the inspiration behind MacDonald's own "The Downer", and even some of the Black Mountain College graduates, in particular Robert Creely and the college's head honcho, Charles Olson. This latter "revelation" enabled the hack responsible for the piece to tie it all back again to Williams and Pound, who, with their respective peons "Paterson" and "Cantos," were commonly regarded as being among the North Carolina college's—and particularly Olson's—chief inspirations.

A neat job, but, in the main, entirely wrong.

MacDonald loved e.e. cummings, born a generation after Williams but infinitely more eloquent in his embrace of nature and naturalness and, to the end, delightfully whimsical. Similarly, he preferred Carl Sandburg—whose "Limited" he had used in its entirety (all six lines!) as the frontispiece to *Walton Flats*, a surreal and fabulous (in the true sense of the word) novel-length tale of godhood and redemption which he had written in collaboration with Jimmy Lovegrove—to the Runyonesque Kenneth Fearing. And as for the "war poets," MacDonald rated Randall Jarrell above all others—Shapiro and his "V-Letter" included—even to the point of learning Jarrell's "The Death of the Ball Turret Gunner" when he was only twelve years old.

When it came to open verse, MacDonald settled for the Beats—Ginsberg and Ferlinghetti in particular—over the inferior Black Mountain scribes, a fact which seemingly never ceased to amaze the self-styled poetry pundits. But it was *their* amazement that so astonished MacDonald, just as it astonished him how nobody seemed to give credit to the "Harlem Renaissance" and the fine work produced in the field of poetry by the likes of Etheridge Knight (of course), plus forerunners of the stature of Langston Hughes and Countee Cullen, and contempories such as Nikki Giovanni and Sonia Sanchez. As much as anyone—if not more than, in many cases—these writers, in MacDonald's opinion, were fundamental in recording the consciousness of a country at odds with itself, as he had gone to great pains to explain to a surprised David Letterman on live television a little over three years ago. Quoting the final few lines from Giovanni's "Nikki-Rosa"—in which the poet comments on the patronizing attitude of the whites—MacDonald took great relish in Letterman's damp forehead.

Sitting at the bar, MacDonald recalled the piece.

> ". . . I really hope that no white person ever has cause to write about me because they never understand Black love is Black wealth and they'll probably talk about my hard childhood and never understand that all the while I was quite happy."

But the attention he had received in the press the following day was nothing to the coverage afforded his bold announcement that he was to forgo the novel on which he was working and, instead, go in search of Weldon Kees.

That was almost a year ago now.

The newspapers and the magazines had all followed: followed him to dry Californian towns, tracked him into the wastes of New Mexico, dogged his footsteps into the inhospitable Texas plains and now, back in the sleepy Nebraskan township of Beatrice, they had grown bored. After all, a fanatic is only of interest so long as he either looks like succeeding or looks like dying. Simple failure just isn't news.

Now no flashbulbs flashed as he walked still another dust-blown, night-time Main Street in some godforsaken town, in its own way just one more boil on the fat backside of indulgence, a lazy, going-nowhere/seen-nothing grouping of weatherworn buildings and choked-up autos clustered around an obligatory general store and wooden-floored bar . . . with maybe a railroad track where no trains stopped anymore thrown in for good measure.

Now no microphones were jammed between his mouth and some under- or overcooked indigenous delicacy as he continued his quest even through physical replenishment. Sometimes the questions had been more rewarding than the food. But the answers he gave were always the same, and the novelty had plain worn off.

Beatrice, Nebraska. A small, slow, company town lacerated by railroad tracks and gripped for eleven months of the year by permafrost or heat wave.

This was where he had started and, now, this was where it all ended. It was the latest—and, MacDonald now believed, the last—stop on this particular tour. Eleven months in the wilderness was enough for any man: Even Moses only spent forty days, for Crissakes.

Whitman's America had come to a dead end on the shores of the Pacific and, like the land itself, rolled lazily down to the waterline seeking only oblivion. MacDonald was tired. Tired of honky-tonk bars where he would search through a maze of good ol' boys and raunchy women, rubbing against tattoos and beer bellies, straining to see and hear through cigarette smoke and jukebox rhythms, carrying home with him the secondhand, hybrid musk of sweat and cheap perfume; tired of revivalist espresso houses in the Village, where he would search through intense poets and poetesses, all wearing only dark colors and frowns, the *de rigeur* uniform. They, like him, searching, always searching.

He pushed the plate forward on the table, the meal unfinished. It had been a bean-bedecked and fat-congealed mush that maybe could have passed for gumbo if he'd been about 1,500 miles to the southwest. He wiped his mouth across a napkin from a pile on the corner of the bar, their edges yellowed with age, and noted the faded photograph of a town square with picket fences that wouldn't have been out of place in an *Archie* comic book or a Rockwell painting. He'd walked through that town square—in reality, little more than a pause for breath between developments in what was merely a typical Nebraskan suburb—to get to the bar in which he was now sitting. There had been no sign of the picket fence.

Just like Rockwell himself, it was long gone. But he had seen from the swinging racks in the drugstore that Archie was still around, though his hair was longer now. Nothing stays the same forever. Maybe this town had been Rockwell once, but now it was Hopper, filled up with aimless people like Jack Rilla, the unfunny comedian, all living aimless lives, staring unsmiling out of seedy rooming house windows at the telegraph poles and their promise of distance.

Weldon Kees, where are you? he thought.

The bartender slouched over to him and lifted up the plate quizzically. "No good?" he said, his jowls shaking to the movement of his mouth.

MacDonald frowned and shook his head, rubbing his stomach with both hands. "*Au contraire,*" he said, effecting an English accent, "merely that you are too generous with your portions."

The bartender narrowed his eyes. "Aw *what?*"

"He said you gave him too much."

MacDonald turned in the direction of the voice to see a man in his early forties chasing an olive around a highball glass with a tiny yellow, plastic sword. The man looked like a movie star from the late fifties/early sixties, like maybe Tony Curtis or someone like that. He wore a plaid sportscoat, oxford button-down with a red-and-green striped necktie, and black pants rucked up at the knees to preserve two of the sharpest creases MacDonald had ever seen. Covering his feet, which rested lazily on the rail of his stool, were a pair of heavily polished Scotch grain shoes and, within them, a pair of gaudy argyle socks. MacDonald's eyes took it all in and then drifted back to the glass. There was no liquid it. He hadn't noticed the man before, but then he wouldn't have. The bar was crowded to capacity, a good turnout for the amateur talent night promised on a rash of handbills pasted around the town.

The bartender nodded and, with another puzzled glance at MacDonald, he turned around and slid the plate across the serving hatch. "Empties!" he shouted.

MacDonald swizzled the plastic palm tree in his club soda, twisted around on his seat and smiled. "Thanks. You want that freshened?"

The man turned to him and gave him a long, studied look, taking in MacDonald's plain gray jacket and pants, green, soft-collared sport shirt buttoned all the way to the neck, and nodded. "Yeah, why not, thanks. Vodka martini. On the rocks. Thanks again."

MacDonald raised his hand a few inches off the bar, and the bartender acknowledged with a short nod that looked more like a physical affliction.

"You here for the competition?"

MacDonald took a long drink and put his own glass back onto the bar. "That's right. You?"

"In a way," he said. "But really only to enjoy the efforts of others. I'm not actually a performer myself." The strange and self-knowing smile suggested hidden complexities in the statement.

MacDonald nodded and glanced at the stage, ignoring the opportunity to probe. At this stage of the journey he had had it with barroom confessions. Jack Rilla was telling a story about three men from different countries being sentenced to die . . . but being given a choice of the method of their execution. It was horrible.

"How about you?" the man said. "Are you a performer?"

"There's some that might say so," MacDonald replied, grateful to be able to turn away from what Jack Rilla was doing to stand-up comedy.

"What do you do?"

"I write poetry."

"That so?" The interest seemed genuine.

MacDonald nodded again and drained his glass as a crackly fanfare of trumpets sounded across the PA system to signal the end of the comedian. Nobody seemed to be clapping.

Turning around so they could watch the small stage at the end of the adjoining room, they saw a fat man with a Stetson starting to announce the next act. By his side were two younger men holding guitars and shuffling nervously from one foot to the other. The fat man led the halfhearted applause and backed away to the edge of the stage. The duo took a minute or so to tune their instruments and then lurched uneasily into a nasal rendition of "Blowin' In The Wind."

MacDonald shook his head and held up the empty glass to the bartender, who had apparently forgotten them and had now taken to slouching against the back counter. "Refills over here," he shouted. The bartender lumbered over and refilled the glasses, all the while mouthing the words to the song. MacDonald took a sip of the soda.

"Not too good, huh?" the stranger said.

"The service or the entertainment?"

The man jerked his head at the stage.

"I've heard better," MacDonald said. "It's probably safe to say that Dylan'll sleep easy."

The man smiled and nodded. "I knew a poet once," he said.

"Yeah?"

"Uh-huh." He lifted the glass and drained it in one perfectly fluid motion. MacDonald recognized the art of serious drinking . . . drinking purely to forget or to remember. He had watched somebody he used to know quite well doing just the same thing over a couple of years . . . watched him in a thousand bar mirrors. He called those his wilderness years. The man set the glass down again and cleared his throat. "What kind of poetry you write?"

"Kind? It's just poetry."

"The rhyming kind?"

MacDonald gave a half-nod. "Sometimes," he said. "Depends on how I feel."

The pair of troubadours finished up their first song, receiving a smattering of applause, and launched immediately into another. This one was their own. It showed.

MacDonald reached into his pocket and pulled out the plastic button. The number on it was 23. He looked at the board at the side of the stage: beneath the number 22 was a piece of wipe-off card bearing the legend *Willis and Dobbs*.

While Willis and Dobbs crooned about some truck driver whose wife had left him for another woman—modern times!—a small group of four men and two women chatted animatedly at the table right down in front of the stage. A tall spindle of metal stood proud in the table center and boasted the word JUDGES. They didn't seem to be talking about Willis and Dobbs. Maybe it was just that they didn't like country music.

Willis and Dobbs finished their song almost in unison and bowed while the audience applauded and whistled with relief. As the duo shuffled off the stage, the fat man with the Stetson shuffled on the other side, also applauding. As the fat man reached the microphone, MacDonald took another swig of the club soda and slid off his stool. "Wish me luck," he said to the stranger.

The man looked around. "You on now? Hey, break a leg," he said, slapping MacDonald on the arm as he walked past him.

The usual nervousness was there. It was always there. He made his way through the people standing up in the bar section and then walked down the two steps to the adjoining room where he threaded his way among the tables to the stage. All the time he walked he was memorizing the lines, though he knew them by heart. He reached the stage as the fat man told the audience to give a big hand to Davis MacDonald. The timing was impeccable.

He walked over to the microphone and nodded to the room, raising his hand in greeting. "Hi there," he said.

A smattering of nods and waves and mumbled returns acknowledged him. The man at the bar had turned full around on his stool to watch him. He raised his glass—which MacDonald saw had been replenished—and nodded.

MacDonald nodded back. Then he faced the audience and lifted one finger to his mouth.

As always, the silence was almost immediate. It flowed over and around the people sitting at the tables, flowed through and into them, touching their insides and calming their heads. The only way you could recite poetry and feel it—whether reading it yourself or listening to it being read by others—was to do it in silence. After all, who ever heard of a painter painting onto a canvas that already had something on it?

There were a few nervous shuffles as MacDonald paced from one side of the stage to the other, his hands thrust deep into his pants pockets. At last, satisfied that this was as good as it was going to get, he removed the microphone, pointed over the heads of the onlookers to some impossible distance, and began.

> "She's down!
> "Like a wounded mammoth, her body sags
> and, across the sidewalk,
> in a shower of fabled jewels,
> she spills the contents of her bags.
> "The empty street becomes alive
> with do-gooders, tourists and passersby,
> all holding breath.
> Transfixed, and with mouths agape,
> they see her features lighten under death
> while, alongside,
> the treasures once so richly cherished—
> a loaf, some toothpaste, matches, relish—
> lie discarded on the paving slabs.
>
> "And ooohs and aaahs, the silence stab.
> "It takes some time but, action done,
> the audience turns away its eye and,
> with a thought as though of one.
> thinks there one day goes I."

On the final line, MacDonald turned his back on the audience, walked slowly back to the microphone stand and replaced the microphone. A smattering of applause broke out around the tables. MacDonald nodded and raised his hand, mouthing the words *thank you, thank you.* He caught sight of the man at the bar. He looked as though he had seen a ghost.

After "The Downer," MacDonald recited his "Ode To the City."

"Beneath the legends of the stars
the drunks cry out in a thousand bars
while pushers prowl in speeding cars . . .
civilization is never far in the city.

"Bronchitic winos cough up more phlegm
to mouth the glassy teat again,
and venereal ladies stalk the concrete glens . . .
though love has long since left the city.

"The neons wink cold, thoughtless lies,
to flood the dark and strain the eyes,
while the flasher opens wide his flies . . .
because nothing hides inside the city."

MacDonald lifted the microphone from the stand again and walked across to the left of the stage.

"Smoke-bred cancers maim the flesh,
the addict chokes his vein to strike the next
while the abortionist clears away the mess . . .
as all life dies within the city.

"The dropouts pass around the joint
and the rapist hammers home his point,
but the suicide doth himself anoint
in the fetid, stagnant waters of the city.

"The kidnapper pastes together a note
and then binds his charge with silken rope
while frantic parents give up hope . . .
which so long ago left the city."

And now, as ever, the audience was his.

"In Mendaala When It Rains" came next, followed by "Dear Diary" and "Conversation." Then MacDonald paused and, unfastening the top button of his sport shirt, sat down on the front edge of the stage. "I want to finish up now with a couple of poems written by a man I never met," he said, the words coming softly, "but who I feel I've known all of my life.

"This man stole from us. He stole something which we possessed without even realizing . . . something which we could never replace. The thing he took from us . . . was himself." He shrugged out of his jacket and dropped it in a pile at his side. "On July twentieth, nineteen fifty-five, Harry Weldon Kees, one of *your* . . ." he pointed, sweeping his outstretched arm across the audience, ". . . your town's . . . most famous sons—disappeared from the north end of the Golden Gate Bridge.

"He left . . . he left many things behind him—not least a fifty-five Plymouth with the keys still in the ignition—but the worst things that he left were holes."

The faces in the audience looked puzzled.

"Those holes, ladies and gentlemen," MacDonald went on, "were the spaces that he would have filled with his poetry. Yes, he was a poet, Weldon Kees, and I'm here . . . here tonight, in Beatrice, Nebraska . . . his hometown . . . at the tail end of what has been almost a year-long search for him. Because, back in nineteen fifty-five, Weldon's body was never found. And because there have been some stories that he is still alive . . . somewhere out there. And if that's true, then I felt I had to find him." He stood up, shrugged, and said, "Well, I tried.

"Weldon . . . wherever you are . . . these are for you."

Reciting from heart, as he did with all of his "readings," Davis MacDonald recounted Kees' "Aspects Of Robinson" and, to finish, "Late Evening Song."

"For a while
Let it be enough:
The responsive smile,
Though effort goes into it.

Across the warm room
Shared in candlelight,
This look beyond shame,
Possible now, at night,
Goes out to yours.
Hidden by day
And shaped by fires
Grown dead, gone gray,
That burned in other rooms I knew
Too long ago to mark.
It forms again. I look at you
Across those fires and the dark."

"Thank you, ladies and gentlemen . . . thank you for listening to me." MacDonald replaced the microphone and ran from the stage, leaving tumultuous applause behind and around him.

When he got back to the bar and slumped onto his stool, he saw that the man next to him was nursing his drink in his hands and, his head tilted back, staring into the long but narrow angled mirror above the bar. MacDonald followed his stare and saw it all then: the bar, the back of the bartender's head as he moved by, the man's highball glass, and himself staring. But there was no reflection of the man sitting by his side.

He turned around quickly, mouth open, to stare right into the man's face and saw immediately that he had been crying.

"I'm Robinson," he said. "A friend of Weldon Kees."

MacDonald looked back at the mirror and shook his head. Then he looked back at the man and said, "How do you *do* that?"

"You tell a good story in your poems," he said. "I have a story, also, though I'm no weaver of words like you and Harry."

MacDonald slumped his elbows on the bar. "I think I need a drink."

The man stood up and straightened his jacket. "Come on, you can have one back at my place."

"Is . . . is Weldon Kees still alive?"

241

"No."

"Did he die that night? *Did* he jump off the bridge?"

The man shook his head. "Let's go. I'll explain on the way."

When they left the bar, the sidewalks were wet and shiny, reflecting shimmering neon signs and window displays. As he walked, MacDonald could also see his own malformed shape in the puddles but not that of the man who walked beside him. "I think I'm going mad," he said.

The man gave out a short, sharp laugh. "No, you're not."

MacDonald turned to him and grabbed hold of the arm in the plaid jacket—

Robinson in Glen plaid jacket, Scotch grain shoes,
Black four-in-hand and oxford button-down

The words of the poem he had just recited hit him suddenly and he pulled his hand back as though he had been burned. "How *can* you be Robinson? Robinson would have to be—" He thought for a moment. "He'd have to be around eighty or ninety years old."

"I'm actually much older even than that," the man said.

MacDonald looked down at the sidewalk, saw his reflection . . . alone. He pointed at the puddle. "And what about that?"

"The mirror from Mexico, stuck to the wall,

Reflects nothing at all. The glass is black."

He smiled and shrugged.

"Robinson alone provides the image Robinsonian."

"What are you?" MacDonald asked.

The man stared into MacDonald's eyes for what seemed to be an eternity, so long

His own head turned with mine
And fixed me with dilated, terrifying eyes
That stopped my blood. His voice
Came at me like an echo in the dark.

that MacDonald thought he was not ever going to answer his question. The worst part of that was that, while he stared, he simply did not care. "I think you can guess," he said, suddenly, releasing MacDonald from his gaze.

"Oh, come on!" MacDonald laughed. "A vampire? You're telling me you're a vampire?"

The man started to walk again. Over his shoulder, he said, "My kind go by many names. And, yes, vampire is one of them." MacDonald started after him, his mind ablaze with stanzas from Weldon Kees' poetry.

The dog stops barking after Robinson has gone.
His act is over.

And

These are the room of Robinson.
Bleached, wan, and colorless this light, as though
All the blurred daybreaks of the spring
Found an asylum here, perhaps for Robinson alone.

And even

This sleep is from exhaustion, but his old desire
To die like this has known a lessening.
Now there is only this coldness that he has to wear.
But not in sleep.—Observant scholar, traveler,
Or uncouth bearded figure squatting in a cave,
A keen-eyed sniper on the barricades,
A heretic in catacombs, a famed roue,
A beggar on the streets, the confidant of Popes—
All these are Robinsons in sleep, who mumbles as he
* turns,*
"There is something in this madhouse that I
* symbolize—*
This city-nightmare-black—"
He wakes in sweat
To the terrible moonlight and what might be
Silence. It drones like wires far beyond the roofs,
And the long curtains blow into the room.

MacDonald suddenly realized that he was running . . . running to catch up with the man. But, while the man was only walking, MacDonald was getting no nearer to him. *Good God*, he thought, *it's true. All of it.*

The man turned up some steps and stopped at the door of a house. As MacDonald reached him, the man stepped inside and waved for MacDonald to enter.

Inside, the house smelled of age and dirt. A narrow hall-way gave onto some stairs and continued past two doors to a third door which was partly open. "I'll get you that drink," the man said and he walked along the hall to the end door. MacDonald followed without saying a word.

The room was a kitchen. Dirty dishes that looked as though they had been that way for weeks were piled up in and beside the sink. In the center of the room, a wooden table with a worn Formica top was strewn with packets and opened cans. MacDonald saw several cockroaches scurrying in the spilled food.

The man opened a cupboard and pulled out a bottle of Jim Beam and two glasses. He poured bourbon into the glasses and handed one to MacDonald. "I first met Harry back in 1943. He was writing for *Time* magazine and *The Nation* where he did an arts column." He pointed to a chair littered with newspapers. "Sit down." MacDonald sat and sipped his drink. The man continued with the story.

"He was also doing some newsreel scripts for Para-mount—he'd just done the one about the first atomic bomb tests—and he had recently taken up painting. He was as good at that as he was at anything, exhibiting with Willem de Kooning, Rothko—" He paused and shook his head. "I'm sorry . . . are you acquainted with these names at all?"

MacDonald nodded.

"Ah, good. Yes, with Rothko and Pollock—and he was holding a few one-man shows. So, I guess it's fair to say that life for him was good.

"I met him one night in Washington Square. I say one night when, actually, it was well into the early hours of the morning." He paused and took a drink. "I was hunting."

"Hunting?"

"Yes. I was out looking for food."

"Are we back to the vampire shtick now?"

The man ignored the tone and continued. "I usually arise in the early evening. If it's too light outside, I stay indoors until the sun is about to set. Contrary to fable, we can exist in the sunlight although it hurts our eyes and causes headaches like your migraines. So we don't do it. Not usually.

"This particular evening, I had already fed upon a young woman down near Port Authority. She had just arrived in town from Cedar Rapids, Iowa, and she offered me herself for twenty dollars. That was a steep price for a prostitute back in 1943, I can tell you. But she was an attractive girl and she knew it. How could I refuse.

"I killed her in an alley, and drank my fill." He drained his glass and waved it at MacDonald. "More?"

"Huh? Oh, no. No more, thanks. I'm fine with this."

The man turned around and poured himself another three fingers. "Always the truth is simpler than the fiction, don't you find?" he said as he turned back to face MacDonald. "The truth is that we do not have to hunt every night. A complete feed will sustain us for many days—sometimes a couple of weeks—before we start to grow hungry again. Vampires, as you call us, are not naturally aggressive . . . any more than humans, we hunt and kill merely to feed.

"Anyway . . . where was I? Ah, yes. When I met Harry—he was calling himself Harry back then, and I guess I just never lost the habit—when I met Harry, he was working on notes for his second book. He was walking through the Square where I was sitting. I was completely sated at this time, having—" He waved his hand. "The girl and so on."

MacDonald nodded and took a drink, eyeing the open door at his side.

"Anyway, he sat down beside me and we started to talk. We talked about the city and the night—both of which I know well—and then he mentioned that he was a writer. I think that's what Harry regarded himself as more than anything else: a writer.

"And he asked me if I enjoyed reading. I told him not very much at all. Then he mentioned his poetry: Did I like poetry? I told him I really wasn't qualified to comment on

245

it. I did have some books, I told him, but, I said, frankly they might as well be filled with blank pages for all the good they are to me.

"Some time later, of course," he said, leaning forward from his place against the kitchen counter, "he wrote—in the first of what I came to regard as my poems—

The pages in the books are blank.
The books that Robinson has read."

MacDonald took another drink and hiccuped. "Did he know . . . did he know that you were a, you know . . . ?"

"Not immediately. But, eventually, of course, yes." He took a drink and rubbed his hand against the glass. "We were . . . we were alike, you know. Alike in so many ways."

"Alike? How?"

"Well, alienated. I suppose you could say that we were both outcasts from society. In those days I lived in New York.

"I have, of course, lived in many places—I won't bore you with the details: Harry covered some of them in his 'Robinson At Home' . . . uncouth bearded figure; keen-eyed sniper; a beggar on the streets; confidant of popes—but when I lived in New York, it grew too hot for me in the summertime. I used to go up to Maine, to a little coastal village called Wells. Do you know it?"

MacDonald shook his head. Holding out his empty glass, he said, "I think I *will* have that refill now."

The man took the glass. "Of course." He filled it to the brim and handed it back. "Harry didn't like me going off in the summer. He said it made him feel lonely."

"Lonely? Were you both . . . were you living together at that time?"

"Oh, gracious no. Harry was married—Ann was her name: nice girl, but entirely unable to cope with living with someone like Harry. And, of course, as he became more and more taken with my . . . shall we say, *company*, he became even less livable with." He sniggered. "Is there such a phrase as 'livable with'?"

MacDonald shrugged *why not?* and took another drink.

The man smiled in agreement. "So, Ann took more and more to drinking. In 1954 she went into the hospital and—oh, of course, by this time we were in San Francisco. Did I mention that? We moved across to the West Coast in 1950. Harry took up with some new friends—Phyllis Diller, the comedienne? And Kenneth Rexroth?"

MacDonald nodded to both names.

"Wonderful poet. Ken Rexroth. Wonderful." He took a drink.

"We moved out West because, as I say, Harry hated the summers in New York when I was away. You remember 'Relating To Robinson?'

(But Robinson,
I knew, was out of town: he summers at a place in
  Maine,
Sometimes on Fire Island, sometimes on the Cape,
Leaves town in June and comes back after Labor
  Day.)"

He laughed suddenly. "I tell you, I never—*never*—went to Fire Island. Or the Cape. That was Harry. He was just so pissed off with me for leaving him." He shook his head and stared down into the swirling brown liquid in his glass. "So pissed off," he said again, but quieter.

"So—San Francisco. It was fine for a while, but Ann grew more and more restless. Harry had taken up playing jazz. He was good, too. Incredible man. So versatile. But our relationship—and the constraints placed upon it by his being married—was starting to take its toll. You see, Harry was growing older . . . and I was not.

"In 1953, he wrote 'The lacerating effects of middle age are dreadful. God knows . . . what the routes along this particular terrain are, I wish I knew. The trick of repeating *It can't get any worse* is certainly no good, when all the evidence points to quite the opposite.' " He shuffled around and lifted the bottle of Jim Beam. "You see," he said, flicking off the screw cap with his thumb, "I wanted Harry to let me taint him."

"Taint him? How do you mean?" MacDonald watched

the cap roll to a stop on the dirty floor. Its sides were flattened.

"I mean . . . to make him like me."

"A vampire?"

"A vampire. He would have had eternal life, you see. It doesn't happen every time. Not every time we feed. That's another thing the legends have got wrong. We only taint our victims if we allow our own saliva to enter the wound. Most times, we do not.

"But, no, Harry wouldn't hear of it. He said that life was too precious—which was a paradox of a thing for him to say—and he couldn't face the prospect of hunting for his food. I told him that I would do all of that for him . . . but it was no use."

MacDonald took a deep breath and asked the question he had wanted to ask for several minutes. "Were you lovers?"

The man's eyes narrowed as he considered the question, and then he said, "Of a sort, yes. But not in the physical sense. We were soul mates, he and I. I had the information and the experiences of the millennia and Harry . . . Harry had the means to put them into words. Such beautiful words." He fell silent and, lifting the bottle to his mouth, took a long drink.

"By the time 1955 was upon us, we both knew that we couldn't carry on this way. In his poem 'January,' Harry wrote:

This wakening, this breath
No longer real, this deep
Darkness where we toss,
Cover a life at the last."

And MacDonald added: *"Sleep is too short a death."*

"You know it?" the man said, clearly amazed and apparently quite delighted.

"I know them all."

"Of course, you would.

"Well, that year, we decided that Harry would have to disappear. I suppose we had known it for some time. Harry had often toyed with the idea of his suicide—even before he met me. He kept a scrapbook of cuttings and notes, and a chronological list of writers who had killed themselves or simply disappeared. One of his favorites, you know, was Hart Crane. He threw himself off a ship."

"Yes, I know. His poem 'Voyages' is one of my own favorites."

"Harry's, too," said the man. He sighed and continued. "And so we decided that he would jump—or appear to have jumped—from the Golden Gate Bridge. The day he did it was one year to the day since his official separation from Ann."

"Where did you go?"

"Mexico. Mexico City. He lived in Mexico—*we* lived in Mexico, I should say—very happily. We led as close to a normal life as we could . . . which was very close indeed.

"Harry wrote poetry and short stories—many of them published under *noms de plume*—and we spent the nights together, talking. I would tell him of all the things that I had seen and experienced and Harry would put them into poems and stories.

"Then, in 1987, a journalist for the *San Francisco Examiner* wrote that he had met Harry in a bar in Mexico City back in 1957."

"That was true, then, that story?"

The man nodded enthusiastically. "Every word. Absolutely true. The journalist was Peter Hamill.

"Harry was pretty zilched-out that night, I remember," the man said wistfully. "He'd been drinking Jack Daniel's and then, because it was my night to hunt, he went off by himself—something he did very rarely—and polished off several bowls of marinated shrimp and most of a bottle of mescal. We thought nothing more about it until, like three decades later, for crissakes, the story appeared in the *Examiner*. Needless to say, we left Mexico City within a few days."

"Where did you go then?"

"Oh, different places. Central America at first, but then Harry got to hankering for the States so we moved up to Texas." He took another drink from the bottle. "Then, when Harry's health got really bad, we moved back to Beatrice."

"What was it? What was wrong with him?"

"Cancer. He was riddled in the end. He died three weeks ago. I don't think I'm ever going to be able to cope."

MacDonald didn't know what to say.

"Even in the final days, I begged him to reconsider. If he'd let me taint him, he could have conquered the cancer. Then we could have lived forever. But he wouldn't." The man dropped the bottle and slid down the side of the counter to the floor. MacDonald jumped unsteadily from his chair and went to help him. He found a cloth by the side of the sink and ran cold water over it, flicking pieces of food and a couple of dead bugs into the sink. Then he rubbed the cloth over the man's face.

"I want . . . I want you to see him," he said. His voice was shaky and slurred.

"See him? I thought you said he was dead?"

The man nodded. "He is."

"He's dead and he's still here? Here in the house?"

Another nod.

"Where?"

"Upstairs. In his room."

MacDonald turned around and glanced back down the corridor toward the front door. Suddenly the smell of decay which permeated the house made sense. Kees had died three weeks ago. The weather was warm.

The man shuffled himself back up to a crouched position. "I . . . I want you to see him *now*."

MacDonald took his arm and helped him up. "Okay, okay."

"C'mon, then, let's go." The liquor was clearly having an effect. On MacDonald, it seemed to be having no effect at all. He felt as though he had never had a drink of alcohol in his entire life.

They staggered down the dark corridor to the foot of the stairs. "You sure you want to do this?" MacDonald asked.

"Sh—" he belched loudly and hiccuped. "Sure. Harry'd want to meet you."

They started up the stairs, swaying from side to side,

MacDonald against the handrail and the man called Robinson buffeting against the wall.

At the top of the stairs, the smell was deeper and thicker. It was now pure decay.

"Thish way," Robinson said, and he took off by himself along the narrow corridor toward the end room. He reached it with a thud and took two steps backward, stretching his right hand out toward the handle.

MacDonald ran forward. "Here, let me," he said, against his better judgment. Robinson stepped aside.

MacDonald took hold of the handle and turned it. His first impression was that the air that escaped from the ancient pyramids must have smelled like this, only milder. It stank. He lifted his hand to his mouth and swallowed the bile that was even then shooting up his throat. He pushed the door open and stepped into the room.

It was almost pitch-black. The curtains were drawn across the narrow window, but a small night-light glowed beside a wide bed that ran from the side wall into the room. In front of the bed and along to the side beneath the window, stretched a long desk strewn with huge piles of manuscripts and sheets of paper. On the table was a typewriter, a confusion of pens and pencils and erasers, a half-full—or half-empty—bottle of Jack Daniel's, and an army of empty glasses, some upright and some on their sides.

On the bed itself was a body, though its resemblance to anything that might once have lived was tenuous. It was dark and wizened, and seemed to move and writhe where it lay. MacDonald realized that Harry Weldon Kees now provided a home for a multitude of insects and larvae.

The door clicked shut behind him.

MacDonald spun around and faced Robinson. "You . . . you're not drunk," he said.

The man smiled. "Sorry. I've had what you might say was a lot of practice in holding my liquor." Then he opened a cupboard by his side. "I have a job for you."

"A . . . a job? What kind of job?"

"I want you to kill me."

MacDonald laughed and made a move toward the door. "What the hell is this . . . ? I'm getting out—"

Robinson pushed him back and MacDonald stumbled against the bed, throwing his arm out to steady himself. MacDonald's hand sank into something which seemed damp and clammy. He felt things pop under its weight. "Oh, Jesus!" He jumped away from the bed and looked at his hand. It was covered in what looked like leafmold. He shook it frantically. "Oh, God," he said. "Oh, Jesus . . ."

"Here." Robinson reached into the open cupboard. He pulled out a flat-headed wooden hammer and handed it to MacDonald.

MacDonald took it and said, "Oh, Jesus!"

Then Robinson reached in again and pulled out a wooden pole, its end sharpened to a fine point.

MacDonald started to whimper.

"Here. You'll need this, too."

"No, I won't."

"You—"

"I'm not doing it. I'm not doing anything else, I'm getting out of this—"

Robinson took hold of MacDonald's jacket, crumpled it in his fist, and pulled the man toward him. "You'll do what I say you'll do . . . if you *do* want to get out of here."

MacDonald started shaking and stepped right back, away from Robinson. The man had spoken right into his face, breathed right over him . . . but the smell had not been of Jim Beam, it had been of blood. Heavy and metallic. "Why? Why do you want me to do this? Why *me?*"

"Because I want to sleep the long sleep. Because . . . because I'm lonely. And because you are here."

"Is . . . is there no other way?" '

Robinson shook his head. "At least one of the legends is true. A stake through the heart. It's the only way."

MacDonald looked at Robinson and fought off looking around at the thing on the bed. "What if I don't?"

"I'll kill you."

It didn't take long for them to get things organized. Robinson stretched out on the bed next to Weldon Kees and held the stake's point above his chest with his left hand. With his right hand, he held the hand of the body by his side.

While he thought about trying to make a break for it, MacDonald heard Robinson sigh a long, deep sigh. "It feels funny," he said. "Funny to be lying here at last, lying here waiting to die.

"I've come close a couple of times—well, more than a couple, I'd guess—but I've always managed to turn things to my advantage." He turned his head to Weldon Kees and smiled. "Old friend," he said softly. "You and me, forever now." He looked up at MacDonald, smiled at the man's shaking hands around the shaft of the hammer. "You've no idea, have you?" he said.

"About what?" MacDonald lowered the hammer, grateful for the pause.

"Loneliness. The ache of ages spent completely alone. I thought that loneliness was all behind me. I thought that Harry would eventually relent and let me taint him. But it was not to be. He even begged me not to bite him if he should slip into some kind of coma before the end. He said if I did, then he would never speak to me again." He shook his head. "I couldn't live without Harry's words. I cannot live without his words. Death can only be a release." He closed his eyes and shook the stake gently. "Do it. Do it now."

MacDonald lifted the hammer high. As he started to bring it down, Robinson's eyes opened and fixed upon him. "Burn us when you're through."

The hammer hit the stake squarely, as though MacDonald's hand had been guided right to the very end. The pole went into the body hard and lodged in the mattress beneath it. Robinson's body arched once, high in the air, and then slipped back.

MacDonald watched in fascination as the skin shriveled and pulled back, exposing teeth that looked nothing like what he expected a vampire's teeth to look like. The eyeballs jellied in their sockets and sank back out of sight. The flesh and muscle atrophied, the bones powdered, and within seconds Robinson's clothes sank back onto the dust. There was no blood.

As if in a daze, MacDonald put down the hammer and walked across to the desk. He lifted a pile of papers and scattered them about the desktop. He could not help himself. As he threw the sheets around, he tried to read some of the lines . . . some of the title pages. He started to cry.

He threw sheets onto the floor . . . high into the air, and watched them flutter onto the lone body on the bed. "Please . . . please, God, let me take just one sheet. . . ."

In his head, amidst the confusion, he heard a voice he did not recognize. It was an old voice, but it sounded gentle and wise. It said, *Take one sheet, then . . . but only one.*

MacDonald grabbed a sheet and jammed it into his sportscoat pocket. Then he picked up a book of matches, struck one, and ignited the whole book. He tossed it onto the scattered sheets, turned calmly around, and left the room.

The fire took longer to get going than he expected.

In the movies, the conflagration is always immediate. But here in reality, it took almost an hour. MacDonald watched it from across the street, watched the first flames reach up to the waiting curtains, watched the first glow in one of the downstairs rooms, smelled the first smoke-filled breeze blowing across the sidewalk.

Then it was done. And only then did MacDonald feel released from the power of Robinson's eyes.

As he started back to the heart of Beatrice, a gentle rain began to fall. MacDonald pulled the crumpled sheet from his pocket and, in the occasional glow of the streetlights, started to read. It was a poem. A complete work captured on a single sheet of paper. It was called "Robinson At Rest." It began:

Robinson watching a movie, safe
In the darkness. The world outside spills by
Along sidewalks freshened by rain.
He says to the man by his side, "Is that clock
    correct?"

*"No," the answer comes. "It's stopped
At last."*

And seventeen lines later it ended:

—Weldon Kees (1914–1993)

Bindlestiff

a man could get religion in a
God forsaken
place like this

— Wilma Elizabeth McDaniel

1

As the freight train rattled across U.S. 54, its lonesome howl splitting the night like a butcher's cleaver, Walker Lange leaned against the open doors of the boxcar and stared into the failing light at the hobos, spread out along the dust-covered blacktop in both directions like a badly-strung row of human heads.

The earth was sore with them, and with the endless storms of flying soil through which they marked their passage.

Sometimes they would hit like side-on tornadoes, these storms, boiling walls of dirt that towered thousands of feet above the earth and skirted the ground from horizon to horizon, thick curtains which covered men, animals, automobiles, and buildings alike.

Lange recalled being parked up on Route 270, three miles outside of Woodward, locked inside a cube of metal, glass, and sweat-stained upholstery with a wall-eyed thin man who spoke with a stutter and hailed from Dalhart, Texas. For forty minutes they had sat there, he and the thin man, in the silent and cold darkness of the man's '29 Chevy, while the winds howled against the glass and static electricity played all over the panels of the Tin Lizzie. Until, at last—somehow—the storm brought Lange on early, though there had been no moon to see, full or otherwise.

That had been near on a year ago now, he realized, and the time between changes was shortening.

The man's name was Nathan Calhoon and, as Lange had spread him out over the quilt-covered, broken seat-springs, the final stages of the change tearing across his face like runnels of sweat, Calhoon had tried to beg . . . *puh-puh-puh* . . . until Lange had bitten out his throat and spit it in one huge, stringy lump against the confusion of baling wire that was holding the door closed. He remembered sitting hunkered up on the broken-down front seat of the Chevy waiting for the man to die, smelling the sweet metallic scent of fresh blood, while he tore at what clothes remained around his changing body, half-howling at the thundering winds and half-listening to the air whistling through Calhoon's torn throat and bubbling around his neck in a fine but intermittent spray. Waiting to eat.

Lange shook the memories clear and leaned forward some more, staring through the late prairie-afternoon, over the heads of the lost people on the highway. Somewhere over there, way in the distance, there was a dried-out river that now ran only eddies of dust and despair. Way over beyond it, the good folks of Amarillo were turning on their lights to meet the gloom. But it would take more than an all-too-brief candle-lantern to cast off the dark shadows of depression that now roamed the land.

He looked through the other door, out toward the west, toward Albuquerque and the Rio Grande, and saw only the top edge of the setting sun.

Soon the moon would rise.

Shuffling back away from the open doors, Lange rested against the boxcar side and tried to control his steadily increasing breathing. He reached into his pants pocket and pulled out a much-folded sheaf of papers, worn by repeated reference and the constant friction of his trousers. He unfolded the papers and stared tiredly at the top sheet: *September 1935*.

His eyes ran along the sloppily crossed-through boxes until they found one that was uncrossed. *28*. He pulled the blunted pencil from his workshirt and drew two lines, intersecting them in the middle. Another day ended. The thirteenth day of the new moon, six days after the first quarter. Still more than one full day to the full moon.

And it felt worse than ever before.

Lange pulled his roll from the center of the car and dropped it behind him. He leaned back and fought off the urge to scratch his leg, opening himself to sleep but knowing that it would not come. Not properly. Not yet. Not for another two days.

Not until the hunger subsided.

When he closed his eyes, his head rolling in time to the steady movement of the train, Lange saw his beloved Manhattan, caught on the insides of his eyelids, freeze-framed in sepia, and crisscrossed with a multitude of tiny veins that pulsed and shimmered, and looked for all the world like a route-map of hell.

Overprinted upon this vascular cartography were the once-familiar lines of the Ninth Avenue El station. Lange could make out its spreading eaves and low-pitched roof, could see its nighttime shadows. Like a movie-house fanatic watching endless reruns of his favorite film, he replayed the scene from his memory.

It was a dark scene, dark but light. Full-moon light, the streets bathed in an almost blue-tinged whiteness that washed the two automobiles parked against the sidewalk curb. Behind one of them, he saw again the candy-stripes of the barbershop, and the signs in the windows of A. Zito's bakery advertising nickel loaves, and the clutter of pans and tools in Balkman's hardware store. He wanted to tell himself not to stand there looking, wanted to yell to his distant, time-lost self, *Get away!* But it was already too late for that.

He watched one of the shadows detach itself and lope along the sidewalk toward him, watched in dumb fascination as he had during every dream-torn night these past three years, watched as the moving blackness became whole, a manic mixture of flesh and hair . . .

And teeth, don't forget the teeth.

. . . and teeth.

He gave in and scratched his thigh, banishing the images to his subconscious as he had done so many times before.

2

He had been asleep.

In his dream he had been rolling around in what seemed to be a huge pile of hairy dough. His legs were trapped in a fleshy substance and, when he tried to lean his weight on his arms, they, too, sank in. The surface of the dough, though matted with thick tufts of wiry hair, was spotted with eyes, unblinking. Beneath the eyes, what at first appeared to be folded-over sections exposed themselves as slits with actual edges. As he watched the edges rippling beneath him, one of them opened wide. From the wet blackness inside the hole, Lange saw sharp teeth and a thick tongue, curling over itself repeatedly like a snake. Then it smiled at him . . . and sank itself deep into the softness of his right thigh.

He opened his eyes and looked around slowly, trying to place where he was and what had woken him.

Outside it was dark though the moon—so big!—cast a light across sidings that reflected silver as they drifted slowly by.

Slowly? Sidings?

The train gave out a triumphant howl and Lange felt it slowing down.

A station.

He pulled his bundle toward him and shuffled up onto his knees. He couldn't bend. His neck had already lengthened and bowed forward so that his chin nearly touched his belly. He pulled up the collar on his shirt to cover the swollen curvature of the top of his spine while, at the same time, attempting to shorten his back, arching it around the lumbar region so he could lean backward and see in front of him. It hurt like hell.

From experience, Lange knew that soon the only way he would be able to enjoy normal sight would be to crouch on all fours. But, for almost another day at least, he would be able to stand erect—though badly bent—affording himself forward vision only by pressing his head against one of his collarbones. By the time the moon was full, he would have no choice in the matter. By then he would be down on the ground.

Grimacing at the shards of stabbing pain which erupted in a dozen different places around his body and legs, Lange pulled himself to a standing position and lifted his bundle. He tucked it beneath his arm and limped to the door.

Outside, a sign passed slowly by. *Goodwill*, it said in a scrawling script.

Seconds later he was rolling down a ditch by the side of the tracks, breathing dust and cursing the night.

3

Behind them lay failed banks and closed factories, dead wheat and dying cattle, lost homes and forgotten friends. The past was a slowly dissipating memory clouded by a seemingly never-ending run of weary and tattered lineups waiting for free bread and soup.

Ask them where they hailed from and many would be hard-pressed to remember. *Now* was what was important, not then. And next was most important of all. *Tomorrow!*

Goodwill wasn't much of a name for a town that consisted only of tents and hastily-constructed board shacks. But the people who lived there had learned to carry home with them. Sometimes it took the shape of a Kewpie doll or a teddy bear, maybe missing an arm or an eye; sometimes it was an old cigar box filled with photographs of smiling faces—if you looked real hard you might even recognize some of those same faces sitting around a tinder fire. They were older now, and lined with hardship, but they were determined. Always determined.

As Walker Lange shuffled along a walkway, alongside which someone had erected a wooden sign that said Main Street, he watched the faces and the language of the bodies. Over against a slatted-wood barrier behind the tents, a young boy—couldn't have been more than seven or eight— was playing a fiddle, the tune shrieking out amidst the dull thrum of hopeless conversation and mindless movement, while, in front of him, an old man was shucking and clapping to the rhythms, his worn work boots carving small gulleys in the dust. Nobody else paid the man any attention.

Goodwill was in No Man's Land.

A little way up Route 54, in Guymon, someone had hung a sign that read "Home of the most lied-about weather in the U.S." In two years Guymon had recorded almost two hundred dust storms—one every three-and-a-half days. And it was going to get worse before it got any better.

Goodwill was No Man's Land because no man claimed it and no government recognized it. With the winds having taken down the house sidings and the stores, it wasn't even recognized as a town anymore. And that made ignoring it so much easier.

When the storms came racing across the prairie, they overran any buildings still standing, the birds flying in front of the swirling spires, looking desperate, the few surviving chickens going to roost and the occasional drunkard praying for redemption. A tidal wave of brown, a wall of soil and dirt and stone that lifted up at the horizon like a bedsheet and blotted out the sun, before storming forward to cover everything in its path.

Here and there small flowers of conversation lazily bloomed, hanging on the morning breeze like dandelion seeds.

"Folks over there say the drought's gonna last clear through to the '40s," a man was telling a ragtag group of men and women who seemed only half-interested. Behind him, a woman was stretching over the front seats of a

Model A shaking a measure of Lacto Dextrin into a tin spoon. All around the car a confusion of packets and cans were spread out in the dust like a crazy quilt.

A towheaded boy of some six years, clearly the soon-to-be recipient of the elixir—"a remedy for changing the intestinal flora," as some would have it—was sitting on the running board pulling at the clasps of his work-bib. As Lange drew up alongside him, the boy looked up and, for a second, their eyes met. The boy let go of the clasps and leaned back against the Ford, his eyes staring, lips pulling back in a rictus snarl of fear. "Ma!" he cried out.

Lange moved on quickly, trying hard to straighten his stoop while keeping his thickening mane of wiry hair tucked under his workshirt collar. Behind him he heard the gentle placatory noises of the mother quieting the boy, whose disturbance she understandably blamed on the proximity of the dreaded Lacto Dextrin.

A little farther on, a group of men were cooking a jackrabbit on a makeshift spit. "Hoover Hogs" the hobos called them, welcome dinner "guests" since the collapse of livestock prices. One of the men was talking, his eyes lost in the flickering embers of the fire. "Farmed shares in El Reno," he was saying as Lange shuffled by. "Dusted, busted, but never rusted," he finished off, the statement bearing all the hallmarks of careful rehearsal. The man chuckled to himself as he said it, looking up at the others for nods of approval. There were none. There was only the gentle heat of early morning. The man looked back at the fire and continued. "Drove west in '34. Picked peppers and butter beans at Oxnard, California." He shook his head. "Came home in '35. I'd rather be where people is friendly."

Lange imagined the man turning on the spit, his wrinkled skin frazzling gently in the even heat of the fire. He closed his eyes slowly, hoping none of the men would notice, and moved away.

He passed by a corral of automobiles, mostly Chevys and Model A's, more evidence of the "tin-can tourists." Lange smiled and recalled Will Rogers' words, which he had read in *The New York Times:* "We are the first nation in the history of the world to go to the poorhouse in an automobile."

The sharp crack of one of his shoulder joints realigning itself disturbed his thoughts and echoed in the air like a pistol shot.

Lange stood stock-still, his shoulders hunched over. Two men talking over by the raised hood of a Chevy turned around and looked questioningly at him. Over to the right, back the way he had come, one of the men beside the cooking jackrabbit was also staring. Lange forced a tired smile and hitched his bedroll bundle tighter on his shoulder. One of the men by the Chevy took a cautious step toward him.

Crack!

The men by the Chevy started at the sound. They stared at Lange, realized it had not come from him, and then turned around. The man by the fire also turned in the direction of the noise. Lange followed their gazes.

Over by the sidings, a group of boys were throwing rocks at a billboard advertising Burma Shave. Hanging over the board was a metal sign shaped like a hand, its outstretched finger pointing over to the entrance to the yards. The sign read *Gasoline 15 cents*. As Lange and the other men watched, one of the boys managed to hit the metal sign again—which went *Crack!* as opposed to the dull *Clunk!* when a rock hit the board. The boy did a strut in front of his friends before diving into the dirt to find more rocks.

Everyone returned to what they were doing. Lange breathed a sigh of relief which stopped short when he discovered that his tongue was getting too big for his mouth. He turned away in case he accidentally let it flop out down his chin, already feeling the tingling around his jaw which signaled the extension of his muzzle. He looked up at the sun; it was only around six o'clock. He had another fifteen, sixteen hours to wait until the change was complete and he could eat. Meanwhile, he had to find somewhere he could change without anyone noticing him.

He tried to move off, but his feet were already changing in his boots, insteps lengthening, balls padding out, heels lifting. The resulting movement was a drunken shamble, a sideways gait which almost had Lange sprawling across the ground. At the last moment, when a fall seemed inevitable, Lange caught hold of a woman's arm and steadied himself. As he relaxed his hold, turning to smile at her and nod his gratitude, the woman took hold of his forearm and helped him stand straight.

"Th-thank you, ma'am," he managed to sputter around his tongue, nodding and holding his head down low so she wouldn't see his misshapening face.

"My *Lord*," the woman said in a raucous but friendly voice. "What ails you, mister? Face looks like a mule kicked it."

Lange shook his head. " 'S nothing, really," he stammered and, pulling his bedroll around his front so that its end came up in front of his mouth, he nodded again and shuffled off.

"You find yourself somethin' ta eat," she called after him. "Build your strength up."

Lange waved his thanks without turning and hoped the woman would stay where it was safe tonight.

4

The rest of the day was filled with the fever of the change.

Lange had found an unoccupied lean-to over by the edge of the Hooverville, perched awkwardly on and around a pile of cross ties and buckets containing assorted spikes, joints, nuts, and bolts. Over in the back, where the shadows were darkest and longest, a tin-plate sign showed a smiling, crewcut-topped boy in a striped T-shirt. The boy was proclaiming *Today's the day!* in a large speech bubble that extended from his mouth to the edges of the sign. Behind the boy, on the picture, was a waiting locomotive, steaming like an impatient dragon, and in front of that, in a small group at the head of the tracks on which the loco waited, a man in a top hat was caught in the act of swinging a hammer at a spike protruding from the end cross tie.

The small print at the right-hand corner of the sign said:

The Longest Single Note

Yes, on Saturday 11 August 1931, Mayor Jonathan Johnson will officially lay the final spike that will link Goodwill to the thousands of miles of train tracks that cross the length and breadth of these United States of America! Come one and all and celebrate with us! Bring the family! The Boise City High School Marching Band will lead the festivities and there will be hamburgers and sodas for all!

The ceremony will begin at 2 o'clock—don't be late!

Leaning against the side of the lean-to, sufficiently back from view, Walker Lange did a rough impersonation of a smile. It was difficult. Hell, it was painful.

His mouth was now several inches away from the rest of his face, its sides elongating on either side toward his ears. His nose, now flattened onto his upper jawbone, had shrunk and turned leathery. And, as always happened during the early stages, it kept running down his muzzle, causing him to wipe it repeatedly with a piece of rag. As usual, this was becoming increasingly difficult as his hands turned pawlike. Already his fingers had disappeared, leaving in their stead small, bloated, nailless blobs of hairy flesh that were becoming hard to control as hands.

By his side was a pile of clothing, all useless now.

Lange's neck had lengthened to the crown of his head, linking spine with jaws. His ears had grown into small spires topped with fur. His legs and arms had shrunk into spindly sticks covered with stubble. And, beneath his body, coating his backside and the long, protruding muscle that was fast furring over, was a widening pool of urine and excrement. The smell, which had started out as astonishingly foul, was now beginning to seem perfectly normal . . . if not downright attractive.

Blinking his eyes quickly, Lange rolled over to allow the rest of the change. Outside the lean-to the moon had risen, bathing the pathetic collection of tents, shacks, and bag-laden automobiles in a faint light that faded and intensified as the clouds rolled across the sky. Lange watched a steadily dwindling succession of men and women walk to and fro amidst the tents. They wandered without purpose or intent; they moved without interest or hope.

He fought off the urge to cry out, knowing that the sound would be a mournful howl that would bring people to his hiding place before the change was complete.

He felt rather than heard the soft plop as his balls retracted into their new, thicker scrotum. He groaned and started to pant as his rib cage contracted, belly lifted, throat constricted. He laid his head down on the ground, resting it between his front paws, and stared at the moon.

He listened to the faraway footsteps of passing food mingled with the closer sounds of his body preparing itself.

Soon it would be time.

5

At last, the night was his.

The night and the moon and the moment.

His eyes picking up every detail, every scurrying movement, every color, he left the tumbled lean-to under cover of cloud, loping across the dusty soil to the billboard advertising Burma Shave, and dropped onto a dusty track.

To the right, the track ran away from the hustle of the Hooverville toward the never-ending flatness of the prairies and the undelivered promise of rain. Lange hunched up by the back of the billboard and sniffed the air; he smelled the desert and the sky, the steam and grease of the railroads, and the thick sweetness of human meat surrounded by warm blood.

Lange held his head low, folding his ears back, and turned to the left.

That way, the track ran beneath skeletal telegraph poles and their wires into a ramshackle grouping of buildings about five hundred yards in the distance. He set off, keeping to the shadows, constantly turning each way to check for movement or the scent of food.

Goodwill itself was a ghost town.

The main street ran for only a couple hundred yards or

so and then gave out to the desert again, the train tracks winding and glinting their way to a pocket of hills where the darknesses of nighttime sky and earth met.

On his left was a brick building: First National Bank. Its windows were boarded up, doors closed against the night. Maybe somebody was holed up inside there, safe against the others. Lange paused and sniffed. Nothing. He moved on.

The other buildings were wood-built. The sides of many of them had long since fallen down and were nowhere to be seen. Maybe they had been removed, maybe they had been buried by the storms. Lange neither knew nor cared.

The buildings' interiors were open for all to see, like dolls' houses, their rooms and landings and staircases standing empty and strangely lost-looking, covered in layers of dust that ran in the corners and against the room edges like yellow snowdrifts.

The Rainbow Hotel and The Home Café—its windows boasting *Room* and *Eat* and *Shop*—still contained some furniture, all covered in the constant spread of dust and dirt. He sniffed again and then ran across the street.

There was something here.

Lange clambered onto the boardwalk that ran by The Home Café and pressed himself against a tin sign that announced *Eddy's Bread* alongside a picture of a loaf in checkered wrapping. There he waited, and listened.

Someone or something was moving around inside. It wasn't noisy movement, but it was movement. Without even thinking, Lange raised his ears and sniffed. *Human!*

He checked the street around him until he was sure he was alone and then padded carefully through the ripped mesh of the screen door.

The blackness inside was absolute and Lange had to wait until his eyes adjusted. Eventually, he could make out a long counter which ran along in front of him and curved around at the left into another room. It was from there that the sounds were coming. He moved up to the counter and followed it around.

The back room was completely empty of furniture. But it had other things that were much more important. Over by the back wall, a girl knelt on the floor beside a long bundle. By her side a candle flickered, its halo-light lifting the darkness.

Lange could only see the girl's back, but she smelled no more than seven or eight years old.

The stretched-out bundle seemed to be shaking, and every now and then she reached over and stroked the head that stuck out of its top.

"There, now, there," she whispered.

The bundle coughed and shook some more.

"Shhh," the girl implored.

"E-Ellie? You there, Ellie?"

"Momma's not here right now, Daddy," she said, and Lange could hear the sadness welling up her young throat.

"W-We gotta take the kids, Ellie . . . head west." He coughed and Lange saw something fly from the man's mouth in a fine spray. "West is . . . west is best," he said.

The girl lifted something by her side and squeezed, the sound of water filling the room. She leaned over and wiped the cloth around the man's head and made a thing about tucking the clothes tighter around his neck.

Lange stretched out inside the door and watched.

"Ellie!" The man shouted and arched his back, then slumped back against the floor, coughing. "Ellie . . . oh, God, I's hurtin' real bad."

The girl hung her head into her free hand while smoothing the man's face with the other. Lange could hear her sniffling. "You'll be jes' fine, Daddy. Just hang on. Don't you go leave me, now, you hear?"

"Myrna? That you, Myrna?"

"Yeah, it's me."

"Where's your ma?"

The girl shook her head and straightened the bundle again. "She ain't here, Daddy."

Cough cough. "Well, where is she?"

She didn't answer.

"Is your brother there? Is Mikey there?"

Still no answer.

"Mikey! Sarah!"—*cough cough*—"You come over here when your daddy calls, you hear?"

"Daddy . . . they ain't here. Ain't nobody here 'cept you 'n' me. They're gone, Daddy. You must 'member that."

The man struggled to lift his head and was almost successful. He lowered it with a dull *thud* and burst into a long fit of coughing. In that split second, Lange had seen the man's face. Caught in the flow of the candle, the man's soul hovered like a trapped moth, dancing around the worn lines and cracks, and darting across the dirty stubble like moon shadows in a twilight meadow. As the coughing eased off, he spoke: a single word. "Dead?"

The girl nodded.

"I 'member now," the man's voice droned. "I 'member it all."

She leaned forward and gently put her arms around the bundle on the floor. "Oh, Daddy, don't you go thinking 'bout it now. Save your strength for gettin' better."

They lay there like that for several minutes. Then: "Daddy?"

The girl sat up. "Daddy? Kin you hear me?"

The silence rushed into the room like one of the dust storms, carrying all before it, leaving only desolation in its wake. She lifted the bedroll up over her father's face and then sat back, sobbing quietly.

Lange watched the girl, watched her back shake and her shoulders shudder. He felt the yearning deeper and stronger than he had ever felt it before. Meat! Fresh and young, tender and succulent. He wanted her like he had never wanted anyone—any*thing*—before. But yet he didn't want to take her.

His body was a battlefield of emotions, pulling one way and then straining the other. Hunger!

His tongue flopped onto the floor in a thick ooze of saliva as the girl rose to her feet. She turned around and started rummaging in the bundle at her father's feet, the wolfen shape of Walker Lange watching from the shadows as the girl's tears fell in tiny, juddering *plips* onto the material and the wooden floor.

In the two or three minutes that seemed to pass as the girl searched the bundle, Lange decided for and against leaping the few yards that lay between them at least a dozen times. In the end, as the girl found what she had been searching for, he had decided against it. The girl clasped the object in both hands, held it to her face. and then got to her feet and ran out of The Home Café on malnourished, spindly legs, passing within inches of Lange and not noticing him, disappearing into the night and leaving behind her only the soft, sweaty smell of her young flesh and the dull clatter of the screen door.

Lange waited.

The silence was deafening, broken only by the dead man's gases rearranging themselves in wheezy twangs. At last, he could wait no longer. He had done something tonight that he had never been able to do before: he had shown compassion. He had held back from cold-blooded murder and, in so doing, beaten the craving. He rose to his paws and padded carefully across the floor to where the man lay.

He sniffed.

The man was still warm, his blood still runny.

He pulled back the bedroll and stared at the face. The shimmering shade he had seen across the man's face had gone. Now it was empty. He hunkered down beside his head and licked his face, twice, tasting the dirt and the sweat. He pushed his muzzle forward and bit off the man's left ear, relishing the *crunch* his teeth made when they severed the muscle.

His heart was racing now, pumping his blood around his body faster and faster.

He rose to his paws again and settled back so that one paw was behind the head and one across the man's chest. Then he took hold of the throat and pulled back, tendons twanging, blood splattering as a long section of windpipe pulled free and lashed his muzzle.

He began to chew.

The scream cut through the night like a razor or the whistle of all the nighttime boxcars he had ridden across the land.

Behind the scream came words—*"Bad dog!"*—and footsteps . . . running footsteps.

Lange turned around and saw the girl.

She was running toward him.

She was waving something at him.

He rose up and snarled, pieces of her father's throat hanging from his jaws, and, for just a second, he felt a profound sadness that he would have to kill the girl after all. But the sadness was soon replaced by the excitement of the impending kill. *No more Mister Nice Guy*, he thought. Then he saw the candle by his side reflected in the object in the girl's hand. Rushing toward him.

A brooch, heart-shaped and bearing the single word *Ellie*, metallic . . .

Silver!

He pulled back without even thinking but it was too late. Much too late. The long, slender point of the pin entered his left eye and he felt his head explode in a turmoil of pain the likes of which he had never imagined possible.

Out around the tents and the boarded-up lean-tos of the Hooverville on the outskirts of the little, dead town that was once Goodwill, the hobos and the derelicts and the bums and the lost and lonely people of the dust bowl night turned in mid-sentence, mid-dream, mid-mouthful and stared in the direction of the howl that cracked the heavens and shook the ground like dimly-remembered thunder.

One by one, they got to their feet and silently, apprehensively, walked across the tracks and over to the dirt road that led to The Home Café. And as they walked, the howl rose and fell. Now it was a scream, ululating like a songbird singing through swallowed water; now it was a roar, deep and raucous, cursing its own existence as much as the world that allowed it to hurt; and now it was a mournful cry, craving help, begging sympathy, yearning for release from pain.

Inside The Home Café, the girl who was Myrna watched the creature that had been feeding on her dead father as it spun around the room, her mother's brooch hanging from its weeping eye like a medal. She stepped back against the wall and stared as the dog—*was* it only a dog? It sure seemed mighty big to be only a dog—caromed against walls and bar front, yelping, roaring, whining, screaming . . . *screaming?*

She frowned and leaned closer into the turbulence that flew all around her.

Words.

She heard words.

There, amidst the ferocity and the animal anger, she could make out human sounds.

She could not understand all of them but she clearly heard the word God, strung onto itself many, many times—*godgodgodgodgodgodgod*—like a frantic warble. But maybe it was just the thing barking.

Then she saw.

"Oh, my *Lord*," she whispered.

The dog, if dog it was, had developed human feet, small and still a little hairy, but they were human. Now it was standing on those feet, rearing itself up to its full height, pawing at the air in front of its face, spinning around, screeching.

Then she saw the paws become a baby's hands, pudgy and half-formed, covered in long, matted hair that seemed to disappear as she watched.

Then she saw the tail grow shorter.

The muzzle retract into the ruined face.

The long, deep, hairy belly pull back and flatten out into a man's torso.

And, beneath the belly, she saw . . .

Myrna closed her eyes and felt herself falling, heard the sounds of the dog receding, and she hit the floor. In the dream, which she entered immediately, she heard a deep voice whisper in her ear. Two words: *You bastard!* Then she felt a sharp pain in her arm as the roof fell onto her back.

6

When Myrna came around, the room had changed into a tent.

She could feel the outside, hear the sounds of the night turning into day, smell the morning coming on.

She turned her head and saw the telltale signs of the sun

272

rising, sending the darkness to hide beneath the rocks and in the gulleys for another day.

She sat up and called out, to anyone who could hear, "Hello?"

The tent flap opened and an old man's head appeared. "You awake, now, huh?"

She nodded.

The man crouched down and shuffled into the tent. "How you feelin'?"

"Okay, I guess."

"Head okay?" He pointed to her forehead.

Myrna lifted a hand and rubbed a spot above her right eye. It hurt when she touched it, but otherwise it felt fine. She told him that.

"How about yore arm?"

"My arm?"

The man nodded, his battered derby hat jiggling backward and forward on his head. "Yore arm was in a mess when we found you." He paused and added, "You and th'other fella."

Myrna heard the tone of his voice alter, noted the disapproval. "My daddy . . . you find my daddy?"

The man crouched down beside her, groaning at the effort. "Now, which one's yore daddy? He the fella without no clothes on, lyin' right there top of you? Or's he the one with his throat bit out, over to the wall?"

Myrna felt her stomach threaten to throw up, but all that happened was a deep retch and the sour taste of bile. "He . . . he was the one over the by the wall. The one with his . . . his—"

"Okay, yep, we found yore daddy. Now, what about th'other one, the one without no clothes on?"

She shrugged. "I—I don't know."

"You don't know who he was?"

She shook her head and started to speak again but remembered her arm. *You bastard!* She heard the words clearly: they weren't words in her dream, they were words spoken by the naked man . . . the dog-man. She remembered him changing right in front of her eyes. Then she remembered seeing his genitals, big swinging things that she remembered Mikey talking about with the other boys back home in Wichita, Kansas. Then she remembered him falling on top of her . . . and the pain in her arm. She turned and stared at the piece of dirty gingham wrapped around and around her forearm.

Werewolf!

She didn't know where the word came from, it just came. And she knew what the bite of a werewolf meant. She reached over and started to undo the rough knot in the cloth, grimacing at the stabbing pain as she touched the arm.

"Don't know what happened in there an' I don't know as I want to know," the man said.

She pulled at the cloth as he carried on speaking.

"Fella without no clothes on—"

She unwound the cloth slowly.

"—lying there large as life—"

As the pressure eased, Myrna felt her arm begin to throb.

"—his mouth stuffed fulla—"

The cloth fell away and exposed . . .

"—chunks of his own arm—his own arm, I ask you—and—"

. . . a tiny pinprick.

"—his other hand wrapped around some kinda jewelry he done stuck right in *yourn!*" He shook his head as Myrna began to sob. "Don't make no sense 'tall."

She looked up at the old man and forced a smile through the tears. "He wasn't talkin' to me."

The man frowned. "What's that yore sayin'? Who weren't talkin' to you?"

Myrna shrugged and allowed the smile to fade. Wrapping the cloth back around the wound, she said, "It don't matter, mister. Whut's done is done. Ain't no going back."

The man got to his feet and nodded at her. "You said a mouthful there, missy. Only place to go from here is for'ard."

As the man left the tent, Myrna saw the sun, briefly, hanging high in the sky like a Chinese lantern.

A Breeze from
a Distant Shore

*If life can be said to be any one thing, then surely it could
be thus defined: a long, sometimes interminable series of
arrivals and departures.*

Comings and goings.

*On this brief trip to the limits of human experience, we
are concerned with only one of these.*

The leaving.

*If, as all the best ghost stories from our childhood would
have us believe, there are occurrences that take place at the
very edges of our perceptions—and even more events just
waiting to occur—then consider this:*

*Always settle your bill while you have the time to do so.
Because, afterward, it may be too late.*

Unless you happen to be in The Twilight Zone.

Thomas Danby sat in his attic room overlooking the
street, feeling older than he had ever felt before . . . and
older than he might ever feel again.

He had turned into a teenager around the same time that

spring had turned into summer, when the skeletal branches of the trees had sprouted green and the sun had shimmered bright across the land.

Any birthday is a special time. But the first day of teenage is another thing altogether, a way-marker on the route from adolescence to adulthood, when the world finally and reluctantly unfolds its pastel petals and exposes the gaudy promise of the future.

But this year the birthday messages had included one he had not bargained for. A card. A card for *his father*.

This card was ominously lacking in good wishes, totally devoid of Gary Larson's wacked-out cartoons. It came in a small brown envelope from FOREST PLAINS GENERAL HOSPITAL, and the message it carried was brief: The tumor was inoperable. It was, the card concluded, only a matter of time.

Hey, but tell your son . . . Happy Birthday!

The summer had dragged on and on, baking the ground by the river and alongside the tracks with a special ferocity, turning the pavement around the mall into a hot tar covering that steamed like the fudge sauce on Pop Kleat's sundaes.

Jack Danby had stayed around the house. Doctor's orders.

At first, the big man's resolve had been bigger than the fist-sized growth that pulsed in his stomach. But soon the roles reversed.

Soon Jack's resolve was exposed for what it was: a collection of words and bluster, smart-aleck remarks and hollow bravado, nothing more. No match for a living thing that grew and strengthened during every minute of every day.

And as the optimism faded from Jack's eyes and the doctor's visits grew more regular, Thomas had become increasingly aware that the swelling in his father's stomach had begun to leak a special poison. One they had not bargained for.

And now the dog days of summer had fallen silent and the trees had turned their leafy covers into burnished golds, reds, and browns, and the sun had started wearing a shimmering rim of orange around its core.

Everything was tired now.

Everything wanted to rest.

And in the Danby household, the rest arrived at last, falling like a dust sheet over everything they knew and held dear.

Jack Danby had breathed his last breath in the world just three days ago . . . just sucked in, his face lined with pain, the skin stretched over his head like Egyptian papyrus and the remaining tufts of thin, wispy hair clustered about its top like tumbleweeds . . . and stopped. Dead.

Thomas' mother told him that the pain had fallen away like rain off the roof.

Replaying it all in his head, staring out of his window at the steadily darkening landscape of Forest Plains, Thomas Danby let his eyes roam across the symmetrical sprawl of green lawns and garage forecourts, watching the day take its course and the afternoon light lose its glare.

Across the house tops opposite, the fields rolled down to the railroad tracks and then across the valley bottom to the hills that surrounded the town. Everything looked quiet.

Peaceful.

A voice called out. "Tom?" it shouted, and he heard it as though through water or locked inside a dream. Thomas got to his feet wearily and leaned up against the glass so he could see down onto the street beneath. There was a man standing beside a red Camaro, mopping his forehead with a hank of white material. "Tommy? You up there?"

Thomas opened the window and called down, "Hey, Mr. Macready, how's things?"

"Things are just fine with me, boy," came the answer. The man rubbed the handkerchief around his face and squinted up at the attic window. "More's the point, though, how're things with you?"

"I'm okay, Mr. Macready," Thomas said. "We're both okay."

"Your mom?"

"She's fine. You paying a visit?"

Mr. Macready nodded, folding the handkerchief carefully with both hands. "Thought I'd just call around and pay some respects to your pa, Tom. Your mom in?" He thrust the handkerchief into his pants pocket and lifted his belt over his ample stomach.

Thomas shrugged. "I guess."

"I banged on the door a couple times but . . ." His voice trailed off like the hum of a summer fly.

"Hold on and I'll come down and let you in."

Mr. Macready nodded as Thomas turned around from the window. "I 'preciate that," he heard the man say, "I 'preciate that."

Stepping out of his attic room—his study, was what he liked to call it—Thomas was suddenly aware of the time of day. The staircase was cloaked in darkness, twisting away to his right and dropping steeply to the next landing.

Thomas took a couple of steps and stopped. The house was completely silent. *Awful* silent.

"Mom?"

No answer.

"Mom . . . you down there?"

His parents' bedroom door opened suddenly, and a thin, watery light spilled out onto the landing. "What is it?" Clara Danby asked in a weak voice.

Thomas realized that he had been holding his breath and, when he spoke, the words tumbled out like loose change dropping from a hole in his pants pocket. "Mr. Macready. He's at the door. Downstairs. Says he's come to pay his respects."

The figure of Thomas' mother came into view, pushing a strand of corn-colored hair off her forehead. "Oh, Lord. Whatever next!" she said to her feet. She looked up at Thomas. "You tell him I was in?"

Thomas frowned. "I didn't know. He said he wants to come in anyhow."

"I'll go down," she said.

"You want me to—"

"No, just leave us be." She walked along the landing and started down the stairs to the ground floor.

Thomas sat down on the attic stairs and rubbed at a scuff mark on his sneakers. He heard his mother opening the door, heard the *squeeeak* of the screen door and then heard her speak. "Hello, Pat," she said. "You come to see Jack?"

"Clara," said Mr. Macready. "Clara, how *are* you?"

"I'm fine, Pat, just fine. Come on in."

"If I'm imposing, Clara, then—"

"No, you're not imposing at all, Pat. I was just resting is all. Come on in. Jack's in the front room."

The door slammed, and Thomas heard footsteps walking along the hall. The footsteps stopped at the front room door, and Mr. Macready cleared his throat. Thomas imagined that the fat man would be adjusting his suit and necktie as though he were going to see the President on the White House lawn.

Then his mother opened the door.

"There he is," said Mr. Macready, his voice hushed to a whisper. "There he *is*." The footsteps started up again, into the room, and the door closed.

Thomas felt, for one brief moment, the coldness of the grave come seeping out of that room and along the hall up the stairs to the first floor landing and then up the attic stairs, where it spooled and wafted around his legs and feet like strands of sea anemone waving in the water. He lifted his feet and shuffled on his backside, back to his study.

He had come up here in the first place to get as far away from that room as was possible. It spooked him. Having his dead father lying there in his coffin, stretched out in their front room as though he were just having a doze . . . passing the time until dinner was ready and they'd all just sit down and eat. Just the way they had always done before . . .

He shook his head and listened. He could hear muted conversation drifting up through the house, could hear it, the sound of it, but couldn't make out the actual words. Thomas stood up and crept down the stairs quietly, avoiding those that he knew creaked when you stood on them.

He got to the first floor landing and tiptoed along to the stairs. He went down three or four and then sat down again. Now he could hear.

"—look no different, Clara."

"I know."

Peter Crowther

"I mean *no* different. It's downright amazing what those folks can do. Oh . . . I mean—"

"I know what you mean, Pat, and I thank you. I really do."

"No call for thanks, Clara. I'm just saying the truth is all."

"I know that."

"So, how *are* things?"

"Things?"

"You know, money things? You okay for money, Clara? You don't have no debts or anything I can help out with?"

"It's real nice of you to ask, Pat, but we're okay. Really."

"Really?"

"Really."

"So . . . so Jack left you okay?"

"Jack saw to everything, yes."

"Glad to hear it, glad to hear it."

There was a pause before Mr. Macready spoke again.

"Mind you, it's only what you'd expect from Jack Danby. Yessir, that is some man lying there, Clara."

"I know that."

"Yessir."

Thomas leaned his head on his knees and stared into some dark unfathomable distance.

"How *is* Tom?" The question sounded as though it had followed on naturally from what they were talking about . . . as though they could both see him sitting there on the stairs.

"Tom's fine, he's doing just fine."

"Glad to hear it," said Mr. Macready. "He's a good boy."

"Why, thank you."

"No, I mean it, Clara. A good boy."

Another silence.

When his mother spoke again, Thomas realized she had moved her position in the room. Moving around his father. Maybe they were circling him like a pair of satellites.

"It was bad for Tom, Pat," she said. "Real bad."

"Bad? In what way was it bad, Clara?"

"Oh, I don't know. It's bad losing your father, of course,

but this was different. Tommy lost Jack a long time ago. A long time before . . . you know."

There was no response to this.

"He just withdrew . . . pulled himself into himself. You know what I'm saying?"

"I can imagine," Mr. Macready said. "It can't be easy."

"It wasn't. They were hardly talking to each other way before the end. It was like . . . like Jack resented Tommy somehow. Resented his health . . . resented the fact that Tommy was going to be around after he had gone." There was a thud, someone hitting something. Then, "Am I making any sense, Pat?"

Thomas twisted his feet so they were pointing at each other and tried to stand one foot on the other so that it made one foot without any overlaps, staring at them.

Mr. Macready must have nodded to that because Thomas' mother spoke again without trying to explain what she had meant. "He hasn't cried."

"Tommy? He hasn't—"

"Not a tear. Not a single tear. He just sits up there in his study—he calls it a study, you know, the attic—and stares out of the window. Lord alone knows what he sees out there."

"Has he been down to see . . ." Mr. Macready's voice trailed off.

"No. Not once. I asked him if he wanted to come and see his father—I was standing here, right beside Jack, and Tom was at the door over there—but he wouldn't. He wouldn't come in. Wouldn't set a foot in here. It was like . . . like Jack had the plague or—"

"Now, Clara . . ."

"Oh, Pat, I don't know. I really don't."

"You want I should have a word with him, you know, talk to—"

"Oh, no. No, Pat. If he does it, it'll have to be in his own good time." Thomas stood up and crept back up the stairs, back to the safety of his own domain, a place secure against parents and well-meaning friends . . . a place untroubled by death and decay and formaldehyde.

His own good time.

Peter Crowther

In front of his window eyrie, high, high above the town, his elbows on the ledge, Thomas watched the night come. He saw it start on the hills, at first a shadow of the sun itself, setting for the day, but then the tendrils of twilight snaked out and down the slopes and across the fields to the railroad tracks. Then the station and the grain silos up in old Mr. Jorgensson's field, then the far end of Main Street, now bejeweled with tiny steetlamps.

Deep in the bowels of the house something moved and shuddered through the interjoining floors and woodwork. Thomas turned around and suddenly noticed how dark his room had become. He walked across to his table and turned on the lamp, feeling a sharp reassurance as his eyes saw the familiar objects scattered around him. Comic books, an empty glass holding the trapped white ghost of old milk, a plate with a sprinkling of cookie crumbs, pencils, eraser . . .

"Tom?"

His mother's voice.

"Tom, can you come down here?"

He walked to the door and shouted back down the stairs. "What is it, Mom?"

"Mr. Macready's going now, Tom."

Thomas didn't say anything. His heart beat faster as he tried to face going downstairs and facing old, fat Mr. Macready. To face having his hair tousled roughly or his back slapped firmly or being told to *take good care of your mom, now*.

There was a flutter of conversation that Thomas could not make out, but he recognized the tones. His mother's firmness and Mr. Macready's reasoning. Then, "Bye, Tommy," in Mr. Macready's familiar nasal twang. "You take good care of your mom, now, you hear?"

"I will, Mr. Macready," he shouted back. "Bye!"

The front door slammed, and Thomas went back into his room and over to the window. While he had been away, the night had arrived in earnest, stealing what little remained of the light and storing it away for another day.

Down on the street, Mr. Macready opened the door of his Camaro and waved up at the window. Thomas waved back and kept waving until the car had moved off and its

282

taillights twinkled in the distance where Sycamore Drive joined Beech Street. At night, with his head flat against the window, Thomas could see the far-off lights of the cars on the Interstate, traveling to places and from places.

He heard his mother on the stairs to the attic and turned around to see her coming through his door. "Tom, I declare I don't know what's gotten into you, I truly don't."

"What did I do?"

She moved into the room and sat down on the chair beside his table. "You know what, young man. You should have said good-bye to our guest."

"I did," Thomas argued, hearing the petulance in his own voice. "I shouted to him—"

"Yes, you shouted to him. Wouldn't it have been a sight more polite to come down and pass the time of day?"

Thomas shrugged. "I was busy."

"Busy doing what?"

"Things. Just things, Mom."

An uneasy silence fell between them, and Thomas dropped his head forward and looked at his sneakers. Even *they* seemed embarrassed. He felt his mother watching him, then he felt her shake her head and sigh and, lifting his eyes without moving his head, he saw her feet move across the room and back to the stairs. "I'm making us some sandwiches," she called back to him. "I didn't want to cook anything. Big day tomorrow."

Thomas couldn't quite see the connection between the two points, but he let it go. "Great," he said, though the tone of his voice did not match the words themselves.

Big day tomorrow.

That was true. Tomorrow they were burying his father. Planting him, Johnny Margulies had said. *Hey, Danby . . . when they planting your old man?* Thomas had shrugged at that one, delivered loudly in the school cafeteria, and wandered the full length of the hall to a table at the far end, where he sat alone and played with his food. He had felt the sniggers traveling behind him and stopping just short of his back, where they whispered and chuckled cruelly.

"You sleeping up there again tonight?" Clara Danby shouted.

"Yeah. I guess."

"Your bag still up there?"

Thomas looked around and saw the crumpled sleeping bag sitting over by a pile of comic books. "Yeah."

"You want to come down and get your food?"

He stood up. "On my way."

That night, Thomas left the window open.

He curled up in his sleeping bag and read a Marvel Masterworks hardback collection of old Fantastic Four stories, readily identifying with Johnny Storm. His Uncle Matthew had bought it for him for his eleventh birthday, and Thomas had already read the stories several times. He particularly liked the mole men.

When he had turned out his light, he lay staring at the night outside the window, wondering if there really were such creatures. And, if there were, did they ever burrow up into a cemetery?

Out on the highway a horn sounded sharply and then dopplered away into some distance or other. Was it coming or going? Where was it coming from? Where was it going to?

Questions.

He shuffled around and eventually fell into a troubled sleep in which mole men burrowed into his father's coffin, and when they splintered it open, there was only a big pulsating lump, like a misshapen potato, with his father's eyes staring out of it. *Tommy*, the eyes said, *I'm sorry*.

When he woke up, Thomas wondered why.

He had heard something.

What was it?

He turned over and pulled his right arm from inside the bag. The luminous display on his watch said 2:17. He listened. The house was quiet. So why was he awake?

Then there it was again.

Movement.

Was it his mother? Going to the bathroom, perhaps? He

waited to hear the cistern empty and refill, but there was nothing. All was quiet beneath him.

Then, again. Another movement.

Slithering.

The sound of material being trailed.

It lasted for only a few seconds, but he heard it.

Thomas pulled both arms back inside the bag and slid the zipper up until it touched his chin. He shivered and waited.

Nothing.

Outside, a soft wind had risen. He watched it tug at the open window, watched the glass shimmer silently to the window's gentle but insistent movements. Then the wind made a noise, only it didn't come from the open window. It came from the open door that led onto the attic stairs.

The noise was unmistakable.

It was a sigh.

And it was followed by another slither of material.

Thomas knew what it was. It was his father. He had pulled himself out of his wooden box with the mock-gold handles and had dragged his stiff legs out of the room and up the stairs.

Maybe he had already called on his mother. Thomas' heart was beating like a bongo drum, now.

Maybe he had crawled into her room and up onto her bed while she slept and he—*it!*—had opened his mouth beside her and let the cancer out. Maybe a piece of it was on his mother's pillow right now, skittering toward her, stealthily . . . heading for her open mou—

Thomas pulled down the zipper and threw back the open bag. He stood up and pulled on his jeans. As he fastened the buttons, he felt less vulnerable. He shrugged his way into his sweater and felt another degree better.

The noise had stopped now.

He went to switch on the table lamp and then thought better of it. The light would only expose him to anything that was coming up the stairs. Right now, he had night-sight. That made him and whatever it was even. And if it *was* his father then Thomas had the distinct advantage. *He* had speed.

He was alive.

He walked slowly to the door and edged his head around so that he could see the stairs. They were empty.

Everything below was in darkness.

Thomas had asked his mom repeatedly to leave the light on, but she had said that it was a waste of electricity. And they couldn't afford to waste money anymore. *Not now your father is*—She always stopped herself before she said it. The word.

Dead.

Keeping his feet to the edges of the stairs, Thomas crept down. As soon as the first floor landing came into view, he stopped and waited for any sign of movement.

There wasn't any.

He moved forward and down.

The landing was quiet and empty.

Thomas moved along to his parents' bedroom, now his mother's room. The door was partly open. Thomas pushed it and strained his eyes.

It was darker in there than it was on the landing. She always slept with her curtains drawn against the night, and the blackness that sat around her bed seemed impenetrable. He looked quickly behind to make sure nothing was edging its way toward him and then took one step into the room. Then another. Then one more.

He saw the shape of his mother curled on the bed. She was on top of the sheets, still wearing her clothes. Her face was half into the pillow, and her breathing was halfway to a snore.

Maybe that was what he had heard.

Certainly there was no evidence of any intruder. Could his father be an intruder in his own house?

Thomas frowned.

Could Jack Danby, dead or alive, be an intruder in his own wife's bedroom?

A sudden vision flashed in his head. In it, his father was rough-housing his mother, and she was laughing fit to burst. Thomas' father was staring at Thomas over her shoulder, and he was laughing, too.

Thomas shook his head.

The vision cleared, and the sound came again.

This time it was clear. It came from downstairs.

He backed out of his mother's bedroom and pulled the door closed behind him.

Somehow, Thomas was feeling not so scared anymore. A deep but significant part of himself was telling him the sound was nothing. But that same part was telling him to check it out. *Check it out, Tommy . . . check it out all the way.*

He reached the ground floor and stood for a minute or so, his head cocked on one side, staring at the closed door of the front room.

Suddenly he was at the door and turning the handle.

The door slid open silently, and, there in the center of the room, the furniture all pulled back away from it, stood the casket. The men from the undertaker's had left it on Thomas' mother's best table, its leaves pulled out full length to accommodate the entire thing.

And in the casket, Thomas knew, lay his father.

He tried standing on tiptoe so he could make sure his father was where he should be without Thomas actually having to go any further into the room. But he couldn't see that far, and the light was poor anyway.

There was nothing else for it. He moved forward, one foot at a time, into the room.

Then, there he was beside the casket. But he was still facing the far wall, just aware that the casket was actually in front of him and beneath him by virtue of peripheral vision.

He breathed in deep and held the breath.

Then he looked down.

He was asleep. That's all it was. His father wasn't dead at all, only sleeping. The pain had gone from the lines on his cheeks, their hollows filled by magic, their dark swathes cleared up and skin-colored again.

Thomas leaned forward.

No, he was dead. The skin looked unreal, like a waxwork dummy. It looked as though it were wet, or damp. Thomas lifted a hand and reached into the casket, trailing a finger over that face that he had seen so often and that was now, suddenly, so alien to him.

It felt cold under his touch.

He pulled back his hand and looked back at the door. The last thing he wanted now was for his mother to walk in and see him poking fingers into his—

As he faced the door, the sound came again.

It sounded like waves.

He turned back and stared into the coffin, half expecting to see his father's eyes jerk open.

But everything was as it had been. No difference.

But, still, he had heard it.

He leaned forward so that his face was inches above his father's and listened.

Then he pulled himself to his full height and leaned fully into the casket. As he did so, he rested his right elbow on his father's chest and his own face came down to his father.

That's when it happened.

As he rested on the body it moved upward slightly, like a jackknife, and his father's face came up to Thomas' so that the mouth touched Thomas' cheek.

And at that very instant, the lips trembled and a soft sound escaped from them. It sounded like a balloon letting out air.

The lips against his cheek were dry and yet . . . and yet they were soft. It seemed as though they had been waiting for this instant so that they could open and . . . and kiss him.

For it *was* a kiss.

A kiss.

A single word and yet so much more. A symphony . . . comprising four short letters.

Thomas jerked back and watched as his father's body settled back gently into the casket, the white satin crumpling beneath his head.

And coming up out of there, drifting lazily out of the casket, was a smell.

It was a scent, nothing more. A scent of stopped clocks and piano dust, of grass stains and sunshine . . . and just the vaguest hint of peppermint.

Thomas felt a huge stone being moved from his heart, and a wave washed up into his chest and up his throat.

His eyes started to sting, and the image of his father shimmered as though he were looking at him through a rain-streaked window.

He left the room without caring about noise.

And he left the door open so that his father might feel a part of the house once more.

A breath, a kiss, an emotion?
Call it what you will.
The scientific answer is both simple and rational.
A pocket of air, a collection of gases released by the application of pressure.
This and nothing more.
Words we make to control and sanitize the magic of life.
Words like "cause" and "effect."
"Action" and "reaction."
But maybe, just maybe, it was something even more elemental.
A freshening foretaste of adventures to come, perhaps, carried to this world of the mundane by the breeze from a far-off distant shore. A beachhead on that vast and wondrous continent that we call . . . The Twilight Zone.

For Rod Serling

For Those Who Wait

"Hey now. You just leave me be," the voice scrawked above the whine of Jed Washburn's harmonium. "I ain't done nothin' to you fellers, so just leave me be."

I turned around from the bar, my glass of Ed Mulaney's watered-down beer still in hand, and stared over toward the double doors. It was just some nigra-boy caught by the strap of his suspenders by Jerzik Kubat. Jerzik was holding a mess of cards with the other hand and a few coins scattered on the table in front of him told me right off that he weren't having too good a night of it. And that was always the trouble with Jerzik right there. He would get hisself as ornery as a treed cat when Lady Luck didn't seem to be stroking the cards for him as they came off the deck.

"Whass a matter, boy?" Jerzik snapped, making a real point out of the last word, and his smile showing no warmth or humor, only a need to take his bad fortune out on somebody. "You here to see if'n we wants our shoes shined?" This got a laugh from around the table and Jerzik lapped up the attention like a cat draining a bowl of cream.

I looked around the room and read the looks on the faces. It was always something that came natural to me, even back when I was a young'un, seeing what folks was thinking from the way they held their mouths or squinted their eyes or puffed out their cheeks. It was a talent that I'd turned to good use, changing over the expressions of the face for the expressions of the river. Weren't no difference when it all came right down to it: a river, just like a human being, has itself a whole mess of moods. One day it can be as pleasant as a young beau who's taken to courting, another it can be mischievous and playful, like a child barely in its britches or like one of the barrel-stackers at the Shavers and Dows cracker factory or the pork packing plant, while he's still a few drinks short of bein' full. And on yet another day it can be downright mean, ornery as a wounded bear and with no single soft spot of feeling or compassion.

For nigh on forty years I'd traveled the river—it was the night of my fifty-eighth birthday, though I hadn't celebrated the event since I don't know when—and I'd seen it as frolicsome as a newborn lamb, thoughtful as a wistful spinster and vicious as a bobcat with a cactus up its ass. I'd seen people all of those ways, too, particularly in taverns. And right then, they was all watching Jerzik Kubat's performance.

There were the Watrous boys, owned the feed and grain store out on First Avenue, the corner of Third Street. Jed and Ed was their names, I remember, hands like shovels in both size and color, the one of them writing down a heap of figures and the other telling him what to write. And there was Osgood Lamprey, old time fur trader and, so some would have it, a good source of other things as well.

And there were a passel of other folks, too, some watching and drinking, some watching and talking, giving odds on how long it'd be before Jerzik kicked that boy's black ass out into the street, and some just watching. Around left of the swing doors, tucked back out of the way, was an old feller, looked to be eighty-something if'n he was a day, pulling deep on a briar pipe that swung out of his mouth and up into the air, glowing red and puffing smoke, while in front of him on the table was a book, folded open. He looked tired and worn out, and his eyes were heavy-lidded, accepting of anything and surprised at nothing, leastways nothing like Jerzik Kubat.

He weren't a bad man, Jerzik, but whiskey and cards sat awkward with him, and he weren't in no mood for being awkward. As I recall, he'd been havin' a specially bad time of it, seeing as how he'd lost his youngest girl, Janey, of the croup during the long snows and one of his boys had taken to his bed. Times were sure enough hard in Cedar Rapids in the winter—as they were anywheres in Iowa in them days—without losing your loved ones in the process. Particularly when they was helpful around the place.

"Hey, Jezz, loosen up now," I said, smiling across at him as friendly-looking as I could muster. "Let the boy in if'n he's a mind."

Jerzik looked across at me, scowled. "Ain't nobody asking for your opinion, riverman, so stay quiet til somebody's a mind to ask you to speak." He sat back on his chair then and gave me a full stare. "What you doing in here anyways, riverman?" he said. "Not seen you take a drink with honest working folks before. You best mind your business and keep your own council."

He was right that I didn't do much in the way of sociable drinkin' in them days. Never have done. Oh, I saw most of the folks around the town and on the boat from time to time, but I'd never held much with drinkin' seeing as how it could change a man's personality so much. But I was in there that night because I had a special reason though I weren't about to explain that to Jerzik Kubat in the middle of Mulaney's Bar.

Luckily I didn't need to.

"Are we gonna play this hand or are we gonna jaw all night?" Marty Benholm placed his cards face down on the table and raised his hands. "It's your bet, Andrew," he snapped at the man on Jerzik's right hand side.

Jerzik put down his own cards, reached out and took hold of the feller's arm. He looked back at the nigra feller and said, "Well . . . don't they teach you no manners where you come from, boy? I asked you a question."

The nigra looked over at me. Right then I saw that he weren't like most of the other black fellas you come across.

Most of them, well, they're no more than boys in a man's body. Don't matter what age they are, they look beaten and fearful and obedient. But this one . . . this one looked different. He was about 50 maybe, maybe a little more, maybe a little less. But his eyes! His eyes were wide and knowing. And when they looked at me across the room, they were asking me a question, a question out of simple politeness. The question those eyes were asking was *do you want to finish this or me?*

"Ain't no point in looking for help from the sailor boy over there," Jerzik said, shaking the boy like he was a rag doll left out in the dust. "He ain't about to save your black ass from gettin' a kicking, comin' in here large as life when we workin' folks is havin' ourselves a little rest and relaxation. Where you think you are, boy? Down in the bayous?"

The fourth man started to chuckle at that. I watched him in the mirror set on the wall behind the bar. The black boy looked over at him, tired like. "You hear something I didn't there, sir?" he said. "Something funny?"

Jerzik was on his feet in a flash, his chair tumbling over backward and just missing Jud Washburn's shins in the process. In the mirror, I saw a hand swing out—a black hand, mind you—and then swing in, watched it connect and then Jerzik Kubat disappeared. When I turned around, he was already laying across another table beside the old piano. A second or two after, the table legs gave way and tipped old Jerzik onto the floor where his head met up with a silvered spittoon and made a ringing clank.

Marty Benholm got to his feet and slid the money off of the table and dropped it into his vest pocket. As he was doing that he said to the nigra, "You shouldn't oughta done that, boy. Now you done made him madder'n ever."

Andrew Walsh, a one-eyed farmer from Marion, picked up his few coins, slipped them into his pants pocket and lifted his beer glass from the table. The last man tidied up his own stash into a pile and pulled the table away from the action, making it judder across the floor with a noise fit to wake up the dead. From his position on the floor, Jerzik stared up in disbelief.

"I was you, I'd stay there and sleep it off," I shouted, resting my elbows on the bar. "Seems like it's not this black boy's backside gonna get kicked tonight, seems like it might just be yours."

"I told you—" Jerzik shouted without turning his attention from the nigra.

"I heard you and I'm tellin' you, Jezz, to stay down there or I've a mind to finish off what the boy done started here. And I mean that, I really do." I stood away from the bar and walked over, picked up the boy's strap—it held a couple of shirts and a pair of pants as I recall—and I guided him over to the bar. "Seems to me like you need a drink," I said. "Ed!"

Ed Mulaney slid his night stick under the bar, picked up a couple of shot glasses and a towel and swaggered over like he was just doin' a bit of cleaning. "What'll it be?" he said.

The problem with most men when they've had more alcohol than their bellies can handle is they make a lot of noise and they can't desist from tellin' folks what they've a mind to do. Jerzik Kubat fitted this description on both counts. I heard the clatter of his getting up and I heard him break up the chair he picked up, then I heard him moving across the floor and, just as I was turning around again, I heard him telling me what I'd a right to do and what I didn't have a right to do. Gets to a point when a feller's had just about all the orders he can take.

The first punch hit him square in the nose, the second, a left uppercut, landed in his gut and kept on going until I swear I could feel his spine a gratin' on my knuckles. The third, a haymaker, took out a tooth and sent Jerzik stumbling back against the card table which gave up the ghost and went over. Maybe it figured the floor was the safest place to be right then. The little feller with all the money went down with it, coins scattering all over the dusty floor like grain thrown out for the birds.

I turned around and licked the knuckles of my right hand. There would be a bruise there in the morning, like as not, and it'd play hell with holding the wheel. I cursed my getting involved in the ruckus and made a mental note to soak my hands in vinegar first thing in the morning. "What'll it be, the man said?" I said to the nigra.

He smiled one of them blackman smiles, all white teeth and pink tongue, his nostrils spreading out above his top lip and his eyes wide and laughing at me. No, not at me, with me. "That's mighty neighborly of you, sir," he said. "I think I'd like me a beer."

I nodded to Ed Mulaney. "Make that a couple," I told him. "And keep your hand away from that water ladle."

Over by the wall, Jud Washburn started up his harmonium again. I figure that's what Purgatory sounds like, some feller sitting around all day just a playing an old harmonium while, maybe, Maude Jessop stands right next to you telling you what might've been if'n you'd taken one of them other roads you consider walking along but never get around to doing. Me, my road was always clear cut: it was a watery road, clear and simple, stretching out from each dawn to each sunset.

Ed Mulaney slapped a couple of beers on the bar-top and the black boy grabbed one of them and took a deep swallow. "Thirsty work gettin pushed around," he said, his eyes a-twinkling with mischief and fun.

Jerzik Kubat had pulled himself off of the floor and was rubbing his head with hands that could swallow a coconut from one of the traveling carnies we'd started getting more'n our share of. Jerzik got to his feet and shot me a stare, turned around and stalked out to the street.

"He's gonna be plenty mad at you, mister," the boy said to me out of the corner of his mouth. "What you done'n'all."

"He'll be okay when the liquor wears off," I said.

"Liquor never wears off folks like that," a deep voice said from behind me. "It just rolls around and around, like the river, every now and again washing up bits of twig and the occasional dead vermin."

I turned around and looked into the watery eyes of the old feller with the pipe.

"Sometimes it flows peaceful and sometimes it flows rough, but it always flows."

"Mister Sam?" The black boy's eyes had opened wide

enough that they looked set to tumble out onto Ed Mulaney's polished bar. "Mister Sam! It's you!"

"There's nothing warms an old heart more than a black boy with good vision," the old-timer drawled holding out a wrinkled hand. "How you been keeping yourself? Seems to me it's like you always told me: human beings can be awful cruel to one another."

"Yessir, and that's a fact," the boy said, his face beaming with a toothsome smile, and he took hold of the old feller's hand. It was then I saw that the black boy was no more a boy than I was a farmer. His hands were rough-hewn and veiny, a couple of fingers missing nails and one of them missing its own end. My eyes traveled up the black arm and saw sagging skin around the elbow under the torn-off shirt sleeves, and then saw the rounded back and filled out belly, the scrawny neck and hanging chins, and the tell-tale hint of grayness on the stubble on his cheeks and the nigra curls around his forehead. "Never mind me, Mister Sam, it's how're you doin'?"

I stepped back to let the feller to the bar between us and he nodded at the courtesy. "It's like I always say, Jim, a man wastes more time complaining than suffering. Best to think there's always something worse could happen so just drink it all up and pay your bill."

"Sounds like good advice to me, mister," I said.

"There's no such thing as good advice, just interfering," he said turning his attention to me and, for a moment, there was a hint of a smile. "But I don't need to tell you anything about that now do I?" he finished, casting a sideways glance at the broken furniture.

"Sam Clemens," he said, holding out his hand.

I took the hand and shook it hard. "Bill Bowling," I said.

"Bill, good to make your acquaintance."

"I read the book, Mister Sam," the black boy said excitedly. Then the smile faded a mite and he hung his head. "But I had to have some help with some of it. After you left, I never did get no more schooling."

Sam Clemens blew out a mouthful of smoke that smelled like he'd got rabbit carcasses burning in the bowl of his pipe. "Heck, Jim, didn't I always tell you that learning was wasted on them as don't need it? Man like you—man who can read the land and the skies; man who can tell which way the hen'll run in the morning; man who knows when it's time to leave a place and when it's time to settle down—well, a man like you's got more to teach than to study."

"Study, Mister Sam?"

"Means learning, Jim. Just another damn fool word that means another word, dreamed up to confuse honest folks and lengthen sentences so that fools like me can stay up on their feet longer." He turned to me. "A riverman, eh. Well, Bill Bowling, I'd like to buy us all another round of this ale—a brew that, in truth, is as much river as it is hops—pass some time talking."

Now I wasn't ever a drinking man and I told the old feller so. He tugged at his mustache some and winked an eye. "Then how is it you find yourself here tonight?" he said softly.

"Oh, it's a long story," I answered and I lifted my glass and stared in it, watching the beer swirl and eddy.

"Splendid!" he said and slapped the bar with his free hand. "Three more of your fine ales, barkeeper," he said to a bemused Ed Mulaney. Then, to me, "Long stories is how I've made my living, such as it is. I always say that so long as you're telling a story, you're alive. Isn't that right, Jim?"

The black boy drained his glass and banged it on the bar. "That's right, Mister Sam," he agreed loudly. "You all as did say that, right enough."

The beers came and we moved back to the table by the swing doors. The old feller's book was still open where he'd left it to come and talk to us.

I took a deep swig as we sat down and saw right away that the ale was starting to have some effect on me. I was more aware of noise around the place, aware of it but noticing that it was somehow softer now, urging me to top it up with some sounds of my own. "I ain't ready to talk much yet, Mr. Clemens, but I will ask a few questions."

The old feller raised his hands and nodded. "Man that asks the questions owns the answers, Mr. Bowling," he said. Then he leaned nearer to me and took hold of my sleeve. "And I'll call you Bill if you'll call me Sam."

I nodded.

He took a drink and set down his glass. "Ask away, Bill
He slipped his pipe into his vest pocket and took out a b
cigar.

"How come you two know each other?" I said.

Sam Clemens shook his head and spat out a piece
cigar, made a big business out of lighting it, savoring th
taste and the smell before answering. "Now there's
story," he said at last.

"That's right, that's right," the black boy confirme
grinning like a cat with cream.

"That's right, Jim," Clemens said with a smile. There wa
a lot of sadness in that smile and I saw by the way th
Jim's own smile fell from his face that he had noticed
too. "And that story has been going on and on these mar
years since it started. I won't go into it all here now but
will say that the fates have a sense of irony—of humor, let
say—that quite takes away my breath. I've lost a brothe
a wife and two of my children, Bill. It seems, at times, a
though the world has no more that it can show me . . . b
I still have to look for more." He took a pull on his cig.
and washed it down with beer. When he set down his gla
again and breathed out, there was no smoke.

"There was a great poet," he said, hookin' his finge
into his vest pockets, "name of Coleridge, that said 'Th
man hath penance done, and penance more shall do.' Seen
to me that penance is what life's all about."

I saw the black boy take a drink. I wasn't sure he kne
what the old man was talking about. After what seeme
like a long silence, I said, "Penance for what?"

"Penance for living, I suppose. Seems to me that the gi
of life is like the treaties we been giving out to the indian
The pain is in the small print."

When I set my glass on the table I saw that I had draine
it, and right then it seemed more important to me than th
plain fact that the old man hadn't answered my questio
Hadn't even come anywheres near. I waved at Ed Mulan
and he started to pour three more.

I remember wanting to talk rather than to listen. To sa
what was on my mind and the simple reason I was in M

laney's Bar at all. "Tomorrow, I'll have lived longer than my father," I said, and immediately regretted saying it. I looked over at Sam Clemens and he was nodding, watching the table as though he were reading every single word that had ever been spoken around it, as if it were all etched into the grain of the wood. Then he looked right at me and I could see it in his face: a refusal to speak, a determination not to interrupt my flow until it was done. And I saw, too, that he was doing it for me, like he knew that I had to say my piece . . . get it out of my system like a snake bite or a bad steak.

"My folks came to Cedar Rapids when I was knee-high," I went on, holdin' my hand out over the floor, "not quite able to wipe my own backside. Ever since I can remember, I wanted to get out onto the water. Does the water hold any interest for you, Sam?"

"It does," he said. "For me, the water is everything I know, and everything I can remember. It's no accident that the world is made up of seven parts water just like we are ourselves." He held up his glass and added, "And that's even more true as we sup this beer!" I laughed and looked around to see if Ed Mulaney could hear what we was saying but he was busy tendin' to somebody else.

"Without even knowing why they do it—nor even that they do it at all—human beings are attracted to water," he went on. "Why, I remember—and I wrote this down somewhere, though I can't recall where—I remember my first visit to St. Louis. It was nothing more than a few shacks back then, and I remember I could have bought that town for six million dollars, lock, stock and barrel. And—though I might have been a dollar or two short of the asking price, you understand—there've been many times since that I wish I entered into that particular transaction." He smiled and winked at me. "Might've been a rich man now."

He rarely smiled, leastways not in the brief time that I knew him, lost in a Cedar Rapids tavern at the turn of the century, when the world seemed at once younger but somehow more wise, but his eyes . . . well they were a different story. His eyes looked like they was laughing all the time, laughing fit to burst at the plain foolishness of it all.

Ed's daughter, Rosa, brought over some fresh glasses an laid them on the table. I gave her a quarter and waved awa the change, diving into the drink as though it were som kind of lifegiving elixir. Maybe it was. It sure seemed lik it.

"So, go on, Bill. You were saying about your folks."

"My father was called Addison, Addison Bowling, an my mother, Mary. They moved on out to Iowa in 1848 came out from Akron, Ohio, drawn by the promise o cheap land." I took a swig and wiped my mouth. "And th water.

"The water was something that had always been specia to my father, and maybe that's why it's so special to me."

Clemens nodded sagely and blew a column of smok which Jim—never learned his last name—followed with hi eyes, watching it spiral up toward the ceiling of the tavern I continued after a minute or so.

"I was born in 1851, second of five children. There three of us left now; me, my brother Aaron and my siste Ellen.

"Soon as we got here, my father saw the power in th river and he visualized how it could be used. Before long he met up with another feller, name of Nicholas Brown and he helped him build a dam which was able to contro that power and turn it into energy. In less than a year the had a sawmill and a gristmill and a few years later, woolen mill. But it was the water that attracted my fathe not simply the way we could use its power."

"I can understand that, Bill," Clemens said matter-o factly. "The river and what its power can achieve is like th difference between a beast in the wild and in captivity There's a mighty fierce beauty in freedom."

Jim burped loudly and covered his mouth quickly. "I'r truly sorry for that, Mister Sam," he said, head shaking an eyes wide as uncurtained windows in the night. "I think . . I got excited . . . I guess it was when . . ."

Clemens laid a hand gently on his arm. "It was when started talking about freedom, wasn't it, Jim?"

Jim nodded.

"You see," he said, turning to me, "Jim here didn't know

nothing about freedom. When we met up he was a slave boy, him loading bags and other personal belongings onto the steamboats down in a little place called Cairo at the confluence of the Mississippi and Ohio rivers. He was owned—as were all black boys in those days—by a white man. In Jim's case, the feller was not as bad as many but a good deal worse than some. And we got to talking about the river and how, one day, Jim hoped the water would carry him off to freedom."

"And you tells me that freedom ain't something to go off into, it's something right there in your head," Jim added.

"That's right, Jim. A state of mind. Some folks go traipsing here and they go traipsing there looking for their freedom while all the time it's right there in their own heads."

"So he told me I oughta learn to read books," Jim told me, leaning right across the table. I started to think that maybe we'd been doing Ed Mulaney a great mischief complaining about the strength of his beer. He looked sideways at Clemens and, for a second or so, the whiteness of his eyes turned all pink and misty. "He said if'n I learned to read, he'd write a story about me. Ain't that right, Mister Sam? Di'n't you say that?"

"I did, I did, Jim."

"And did you?" I asked.

"Did he! Why, ain't you never heard of *Huckleberry Finn*?"

"*Huckleberry Finn*! Why, that's by Mark Twain," I said. Now I had never been a reading man up to that night and I haven't been much of one since, but I did know about Mark Twain. Anyone who knew the river knew about Mark Twain. The leader on the riverboats would take soundings of the river's depth, particularly on the more dangerous sections, and they would shout out the measures in fathoms. "Mark Twain!" was the call for the critical level, two fathoms, below which the riverboat would be in danger of running aground. I had been shouting the man's name up and down 1,200 miles of river for some forty years or more.

I looked at him, watched him revel in my sudden realization who he was. He nodded and said, "And you said you were here tonight because you'll have soon lived longer than your father, is that right?"

"That's right."

Jim frowned.

"Seems like as good a reason to sink a glass of ale as any I've heard," Mark Twain told me.

I shook my head and fidgeted with the glass on the table. "It feels . . . it feels funny," I said.

"Funny? How?"

"Well, like I don't have no right. It's like I'm getting something that he never had."

Clemens tossed the butt of his cigar over into the spittoon with expert aim and blew out a last cloud of smoke. "Let me tell you this: the worst thing in the world—and I mean the worst thing—is for a man to bury his children. You know that? You know that feeling?"

"No, I don't," I said.

"Well, then you're a lucky man, Bill Bowling. What you're going through tonight is a special time. It's a time of changeover."

"Changeover?"

"You ever hear the expression 'The child is father to the man'?"

I remember I thought for a minute or so and then shook my head.

"No, can't rightly say that I have."

Clemens smiled. "Well, it means that the parent can always learn something from his children. Most often it's the little things, usually things that the parent once knew but then forgot."

"Things like runnin' barefoot in the grass, Mister Sam?"

"Hell yes," Clemens laughed. "And what the summer smells like, and the sound of rain over in the next county, and the taste of the sea on the early morning breeze. Comes a time in every man's life when he needs to remember those things. There comes a time when the world hangs so heavy on a man's shoulders he feels like he's Atlas, doomed to spend the rest of his days just standing there with nary a soul to help with his burden."

We were silent then, for a time, all three of us. Mark

Twain a-puffin' on a fresh cigar, the black boy called Jim a-messin' with the stump of his half-finger and me a-twizzlin' my glass of beer around on the table. After a time, I said, "I thought it was about a white boy. The book— what was it called?"

"*Huckleberry Finn*, Bill, and, yes, it was about a white boy. But Jim was in there, large as life and half as handsome." He leaned over smilin', and laid a weather-beaten hand on Jim's arm. "I'm just foolin' with you, Jim."

Jim smiled back. "Oh, I know that Mister Sam."

Clemens looked at the two of us and said, "So, we're all at a crossroads tonight. You because you'll soon have lived longer than your father," he said to me, "and Jim here because he's between here and there, then and now." He stopped for a minute and then added, "And me . . ."

I think he was going to add something to that but he seemed to think better of it. Neither Jim or me said anything. Then he held up his cigar and banged his chest mightily. "Tobacco heart," he said. "Going to be the end of me and there's nothing anyone can do about it."

He looked across the room and then at each of us sittin' there, dumb as a pair of mules, and took a hefty pull on his cigar. It was as though he was a-darin' Old Death himself to leap up from under the table and cover him up in a black cloak. "But I don't mind," he said. "Gets to a point where a man comes to have had enough." He pulled a watch from his vest pocket and flipped open the cover. "My," he said, "it's time I was somewhere else."

I don't remember what else we said to each other—I don't recall it as bein' anything memorable anyways—but I always finish the tale with that last remark. It seemed to sum up the man's whole attitude. And I like to tell the tale too, but then you've prob'ly already gathered that.

It's not much of a tale, I don't suppose, but it's all true. And like I say, I like tellin' it because, just like Mark Twain told me in that smoky barroom all them years ago, tellin' stories keeps a man alive.

It's clear that I did go on to live longer'n my father—a good time longer as that night was nigh on twenty years ago, now. And Mark Twain died not long after we spoke. In the April.

I stopped piloting the riverboats more'n ten years back, hands racked with arthritis and back stooped from standin' over the wheel. But I still go down to the river most days and I watch her wander by.

Cedar Rapids is big, now, and the whole world is passin' by so powerful fast it's almost like the river itself. And I know now what Mark Twain was talkin' about on that night way back in nineteen and ten. It does get to a time when you feel like you should be someplace else. I feel like it now.

I saw Jim the nigra on a few occasions after that meetin' but we never spoke again. I haven't seen him for years now.

Sometimes I think back on that night, just like I'm thinkin' back on it now. And I think on all the things that Mark Twain told me. He was right on all of them except the one.

There was one thing that Mark Twain did get wrong. I know that now. When he said there was nothing worse than havin' to bury your kin, he was wrong. The worst thing in the world is not havin' any kin at all. And it strikes me that that's the way I've always felt, out there on the water.

It's a lost kind of feelin'.

Gettin' to the end of the river—so close you can see the trees and the bushes on the far bank—and knowin' there's nobody behind you waitin' on you to come back.

And nobody up ahead waitin' for you to join them.

Eater

"He's a *what*?" Doc Bannerman slammed his locker door closed and turned to face Jimmy Mitulak.

"An eater." The word hung in the air with the dying echo of the metal door as though it were a part of the sound. "He eats his victims," Mitulak went on, hanging his black shirt on the back of his door. He shook his head and clunked his teeth together, growling.

Bannerman rolled his eyes in despair. "This fucking city, it gets to me sometimes. Gets so I think maybe I can't take any more of it."

"But still you turn in with each new shift."

"Yeah." He drew the word out lazily. "But maybe one day . . ."

"Yeah, maybe one day you'll win the lottery," Mitulak smiled. "I'll know it before you do, though, cos that'll be the day I drive down Sixth and all the lights'll be in my favor." He pulled a crumpled, brown, short-sleeved shirt from his locker and struggled into it. As Mitulak slid his holster over his head, Bannerman saw a cartoon drawing of a bowling ball with a lit fuse coming out of one of the finger-holes and the words BOWL PATROL—and, in

305

smaller letters beneath, MITULAK—emblazoned on the back.

"Nice shirt."

Mitulak turned around and squinted at him. "You serious?"

Bannerman shook his head. "No."

"My sister, Rosie. She designed it."

"I didn't know she was a designer."

Mitulak lifted his jacket off the peg and closed his locker. "She isn't," he said as he slapped Bannerman's back and made a gun sign with his hand. "Keep an eye on him, okay?"

Bannerman nodded. "I'll keep *both* of 'em on him."

"You'd better," Mitulak shouted over his shoulder as he opened the locker room door. "He 'specially likes eyes."

Bannerman sneered a smile. "Who've I got?"

Mitulak was already halfway out and he didn't stop. His answer floated back through the gap between the door and the jamb, merging with the sound of footsteps already fading down the corridor to the parking lot. "Gershwin and Marty. See ya."

Bannerman changed into his shirt and pants and strapped his holster onto his belt. Then he made a last call into the bathroom and walked out into the corridor, made a right away from the back door and started up the stairs.

The holding cell where they had the beast was on the first floor, tucked against the wall in an open plan office where the uniforms could write up their collars. Just like in the movies. Above that was a flat roof, looking out onto the oily waters of the Hudson. Below, was a walk-through main desk and seven small offices. Below *that* was the locker room and the showers.

The 17th Precinct building was in a derelict area two blocks west of the Port Authority terminal and one block south of the Lincoln Tunnel. It was surrounded by warehouses filled with containers of frozen fish and electrical goods. No people. Particularly at night.

It was 3:03 a.m. when Denny 'Doc' Bannerman signed in at the front desk and walked slowly up the corridor to the rec room.

The Longest Single Note

His nickname came courtesy of a one-year spell doing medicine at N.Y.U. Medical Center. It was to there, the 18-story hospital building, that Denny's policeman father had taken a young punk spaced out of his head on PCP. The punk had laughed and cried, both at the same time, and, in an all-too brief second when nobody was paying him too much attention, he had pulled a two-handled telescopic wire out of his shoe, wrapped it around Jim Bannerman's neck and, with a swing of his hands, severed the big man's head and sent it scudding across the floor. Then the kid had leapt through a plate glass window, dropped two floors, smashing both legs, three ribs, both collarbones and the hood of a 1983 Studebaker before trying to scurry away across 20th Street like the stocking-clad torso in Todd Browning's *Freaks*. When the delivery van had hit the punk, witnesses said he was still laughing. Denny never went back to the hospital.

Bannerman pushed open the rec room door and cleared his throat. "Officer Bannerman reporting for duty," he said, clicking his heels to complement the officialese.

"Hey, how you doing Bannerman?" It made a change from Marty Steinwitz's usual greeting of *What's up, Doc?* which he usually supplemented with a munching chuckle à la Bugs Bunny.

"Just fine." Doc lifted the night's call-sheet from the desk. Steinwitz returned his attention to a thick slab of coagulated pizza which he lifted from a *Sbarro* bag perched precariously in front of him on a maze of papers and forms, alongside a polystyrene cup of milky coffee, its top edges pinched tight with teeth marks.

"What's the pizza?" Bannerman asked without turning his attention from the papers in his hand.

Steinwitz held up the steaming mess and belched. "Pancreas and large intestine."

Bannerman glanced up and grimaced. "Ho fucking ho."

Steinwitz shrugged and continued to eat, getting the mess all over the lower part of his face.

Bannerman read on. Pinned to the back of the call-sheet was the eater's record details. The guy was a bonafide headcase. No doubt about it. The record itemized the contents of his freezer—various entrails and intestines contained in see-through bags—a wardrobe of custom-made "clothes" and several items of undeniably avant-garde "furniture" which included an occasional lamp fashioned out of a moldering leg stump, two torsos bound together with garden twine and used, or so it would appear, as a footstool, and three arms, suitably bent at the elbow and attached to the living room walls in a grim parody of exotic boomerangs or headless geese flying to sunnier climes.

He wanted to feel revulsion but couldn't. That was the worst part of the job right there: the way it shaved off a person's ability to shake his head at the weird and the absurd. Here, nothing was weird anymore. Nothing was absurd. Things just *were*, that was all. He settled back into his chair, removed the gun from his holster for comfort and propped his feet on his desk. "There any coffee?" He opened a drawer and dropped the gun inside.

"I was just gonna make a fresh pot."

"Sure could use it."

Steinwitz nodded and bit into his pizza. "Just let me finish up my supper, and I'll get right onto it," he said through a full mouth.

Bannerman returned his attention to the call-sheet as he shook a cigarette out of a crumpled crumple-proof pack. "You seen him yet?"

"The eater?" The word came with a thick half-chewed wedge of what looked like cheese and anchovies that fell out of his mouth and landed with a thud on the open file in front of him on the desk top.

Bannerman lit the cigarette and threw the burning match into a full ashtray next to his arm. "Yeah." He blew out smoke. "His name's Mellor."

"I know," Steinwitz said as he gathered the expelled food between two pudgy fingers and slid it into his mouth. Just for a second it looked to Bannerman as though it were alive, like a long, stringy worm, folded in on itself time after time and hanging with thin bubbly veils of cheese, twisting in his grip. "What's he like?"

"What's he *like*? You mean, does he like have horns and a tail or something?"

"No, I mean what's he like? How does he talk? How—"

"Kind of deep." Steinwitz spoke in a throaty baritone, his ample chin resting on his shirt collar. "How the fuck do I know what he talks like. Go talk to him yourself, you're so interested." He lifted the glop to his mouth again and then stopped. "Hey, that's an idea. You like cooking . . . go compare some recipes." He sniggered and pulled off a piece of anchovy that looked like a wriggling worm and slurped it up into his mouth. The call sheet said they had found the remains of thirty-two bodies. It had to be some kind of record. The sheet also said that some of the bodies seemed to date back a long ways but that the condition might have something to do with the lime content of the ground in which they had been buried, or something like that. Basically, not a lot could either be done or determined until they had the forensic results back. Then they might be able to pin a few names to the remains.

Bannerman shook his head and blew out smoke. "Thirty-two bodies. Jesus Christ."

Steinwitz burped and wiped his mouth on the back of his hand. "*He* almost certainly wasn't one of them."

"*Who* wasn't—Oh, hey, that's funny, you know that? You ever think of going into Vaudeville?"

Steinwitz stopped eating for a second and looked straight at Bannerman. "That's what this is, isn't it?" He waved a greasy hand in a wide arc, taking in the room, the station and maybe even more beyond that. "A routine? A stand-up routine?" He seemed to produce another piece of food from the side of his mouth and started to chew again.

Bannerman shook his head and stared at Steinwitz. "I swear I don't know what's gotten into—"

"And, anyways, there's more than thirty-two."

For a second, it seemed mightily oppressive in the small room. Bannerman watched Steinwitz eat his pizza. It sure had a lot of tomato on there—the stuff was all over Steinwitz's hands.

"How d'you mean, more than thirty-two?"

"*Bodies.* More than thirty-two *bodies.* I mean what are we talking about here?"

"I know *bodies*, okay? I mean what makes you say there are more than thirty-two?'

"Because—" He paused for maximum effect. "—that's the way it is. There are more."

"Says who?"

Steinwitz smiled, his mouth a thick smear of pizza topping, and jabbed a runny finger against his chest. "Me says, that's who."

"And who are you?"

Steinwitz chewed, swallowed and stared. He smiled and said, "What about all the stuff in the freezer? Where'd that come from?"

Bannerman's shoulders relaxed. "Oh," he said, "yeah. Forgot about that."

Steinwitz wiped his mouth on a napkin and waved a finger. "Shouldn't forget about stuff like that," he said. "Gotta think about the promotions. Gotta think like Sherlock Holmes."

Bannerman threw the call sheet onto the desk. "Yeah, right. Sherlock Steinwitz."

Steinwitz laughed and stood up.

Bannerman laughed along with him, suddenly realizing that it sounded forced, unnatural.

Steinwitz said, "Coffee?"

"Yeah." Bannerman stood up and followed Steinwitz out of the room, watched him walk to the front desk. "Hey, where's Gershwin?'

Steinwitz reached across for the coffee pot and switched it on. He shrugged without turning around. "Gershwin? Oh, he went to check on the prisoner."

Bannerman shook his head. "Five'll get you ten he's on the goddamn telephone again. Who's he call at this time of night, anyway?"

"Beats me."

"I'll go and get him down here."

" 'Kay."

"You got the phones geared to come in down here?"

"The phones are fine."

Bannerman turned and walked along the corridor, away from the front desk. He pushed open the swing doors and started up the stairs. A half a minute later he walked into the squad room and paused, looking around the main office.

The desks were strewn with piles of papers, cardboard cups partly filled with cold coffee and greaseproof paper packages of unfinished deli feasts. He figured that the Marie Celeste probably looked a lot like this. Round-backed chairs sat at angles to desks, a television set picture glowed in the corner—Lee Marvin smashing a new car into thick concrete pillars, each impact making no sound at all—while a radio across the office advertised secondhand cars at knock-down prices. Bannerman smiled at the timing and looked across at the far wall. At the cage. It was empty.

He stepped into the squad room—suddenly wishing he hadn't removed his gun—and walked slowly between the desks, keeping his eyes wide. Then he saw the figure, lying on the bunk at the back of the cage, wrapped in a thick blanket, his face turned to the wall. He hated the relief he felt. He just hadn't been able to see Mellor because of the surrounding desks. That was all. What the hell was wrong with him?

"Hey, Gershwin? You on the goddam telephone again?"

There was no answer.

What seemed somehow even worse was the fact that Mellor hadn't moved.

Bannerman turned his full attention to the figure and called again, louder. "Gershwin?"

Still nothing.

He walked over to the cage and stared at the prisoner. Was he moving? Could he see the faint traces of the man's back rising and falling? Maybe he was in a deep sleep. After all, it must have been one hell of a day.

On the radio, a woman with a come-to-bed voice started talking about McCain's pizzas like they were sex aids.

Pizzas. *Sbarro* closed at midnight. And yet the pizza that Marty had been eating had looked hot, or warm at least. He remembered seeing it steaming. Bannerman frowned. The microwave. That was how he had done it. The frown disappeared. What was *wrong* with him?

He turned off the radio and the television set and lifted

a plastic mug from a nearby desk, rattling it across the bars of the cage, like he had seen Jimmy Cagney do a thousand times. "Hey, Mellor—you want anything?"

"How about a plate of liver 'n' eyeball risotto?" said a voice behind him.

Bannerman spun around to see Marty Steinwitz holding out a steaming mug of coffee.

"I brought it up to you in case you'd gotten involved with the prisoner. Here."

Bannerman took the coffee and nodded thanks. He took a sip. It tasted good and strong, though there was a faint metallic undertaste.

Steinwitz sat down heavily and rested his feet against an open desk-drawer. "That good?" he asked.

"Mm, hits the spot."

"New blend," Steinwitz said. "Chicory and soya."

"Ah." Bannerman nodded, feeling inexplicably easier.

"You seen Gershwin?"

Bannerman shook his head.

Steinwitz made a clicking noise with his mouth and then thrust a finger between his teeth and his cheek. "Maybe he's out in the storeroom," he said around the finger.

"Yeah." Bannerman took another sip of coffee, swallowed and noticed a piece of grit on his lip. He picked it off and studied it, then threw it into a nearby basket. "Guy's out like a light," he said looking across at Mellor. The figure had not moved during their entire conversation, he was sure of it.

"You ever wonder what makes them do it?"

"Kill people?"

Steinwitz nodded and clasped his hands on his stomach. "And eat them. That's the thing. Eating *people*."

Bannerman shrugged. "Maybe he gets a charge."

"A charge?"

"Yeah, you know—a thrill, kind of. Some kind of sexual turn-on." Bannerman drained the coffee and put the mug on the desk. "I can't figure it."

Steinwitz sighed and moved his hands behind his head, cradling it. "You ever wonder what it tasted like? Human meat?"

"Same as any other meat, I guess." Bannerman walked across to the cage and held onto the bars, rattling them, making sure they were securely locked.

"I think it's power."

"Huh?"

"The reason he does it. Maybe it gives him some kind of power, an edge. Maybe—" He stopped talking and turned his head sharply.

Bannerman followed the other man's gaze and looked at the door. "What? What is it?"

Steinwitz sat up on his chair. "Thought I heard something."

"Like what?"

"Dunno. Wait here a minute." Steinwitz stood up and walked across the room. When he reached the door, be opened it slowly and looked out. He turned back, shrugged, and mouthed *Wait*. Then he stepped out and closed the door behind him.

Bannerman waited.

Suddenly, the precinct house seemed impossibly big and him inside it impossibly small. Impossibly small and *very* vulnerable. He waited a little longer and then shouted, "Everything okay?", but there was no answer. What had Steinwitz heard? Bannerman wished his partner had at least given him some idea before he had just gone off like that. It wasn't like him. It wasn't like him at all. Damn me for leaving the fucking gun downstairs, he thought.

He strained to listen. He strained so hard he imagined he could hear the clock near the front desk ticking. But that was two sets of doors, a flight of stairs and two corridors away. Maybe it was his watch. Bannerman lifted his arm and looked at the watchface. It was a little before four a.m. He lifted it all the way to his ear and listened for a gentle ticking. There was no sound.

He turned around to the cage and watched Mellor's body for signs of movement. Had he moved? Had Mellor turned around and watched him while he had been watching the door? He didn't like to think that. He didn't like to think of Mellor quietly turning around, quietly standing up and oh-so-quietly shuffling across the cage toward his back. His unprotected, unsuspecting back. Sure there were bars between the two of them but were bars enough? Maybe the prisoner could have reached through those bars and grabbed him . . . maybe he could have ripped his—

He shook his head and scattered the black thoughts away like crumbs from the table. "Hey, Mellor!" He banged on the bars again. "Hey, sleeping beauty . . . rise and shine. Come on!"

The body just lay there, didn't move a muscle.

He was dead. That was it. The guy had up and died on them. Here they were, jumping at the slightest sound, and all because of some guy lying dead in the cage, stiffening up right now, probably. Maybe he should check on him.

Bannerman looked around for the keys and saw them hanging from the hook on the wall beneath a large, hand-drawn sign that said POKEY in big letters. He walked across and lifted the keys, feeling something slide in his stomach as he held their coolness in his hand. He jingled them and watched for some sign from Mellor. Nothing. He walked back to the bars and rattled the keys across them. Nothing.

He shuffled through the keys until he hit on the right one and then inserted it into the lock, started to turn it slowly.

"Hey, I ain't sure you wanna be doing that, man," said Gershwin from the door. "I ain't sure you wanna be doing that *a-tall*." He slammed the door behind him and strolled across the squad room. Bannerman watched him, suddenly aware of the dumb look he must have on his face.

"Where you been? Didn't you hear me calling you?"

Gershwin frowned, raised his shoulders and splayed out his hands. "Hey, I'd heard you, man, I'd've answered. What's up?"

Bannerman pulled the key from the lock and checked the cage-door again. Just to be safe. "I'll tell you what's up," he said. "Marty heard something downstairs and—"

"Wasn't anything."

"Wasn't—"

"I just saw Marty, downstairs. He said to tell you it wasn't anything."

"What *was* it?"

314

Gershwin answered with a shrug. "He didn't say. The wind? Who knows, man? Nothing."

"Where is he now?"

"Downstairs. He's still downstairs."

"What's he doing?"

"He didn't say."

Bannerman rubbed his face with his hands. "God, I don't know . . . This whole thing is spooking me."

Gershwin sat down at the desk that Steinwitz had been sitting at and pulled open the desk drawer, propped his feet on it. Just like Steinwitz. He clasped his hands behind his head and smiled. "What whole thing is that, man?"

Bannerman watched him for several seconds and then smiled.

"What's funny?"

Bannerman laughed.

Gershwin's face broke into a wide smile. "What is it, man?"

"It's you . . . you guys . . ." Bannerman shook his head.

Gershwin joined in the nervous laughter, only his contribution didn't seem to sound quite so nervous. "*What?*"

Bannerman felt the smile slip from his face and, as it slipped, he watched the smile on Gershwin's face slip, too. Yeah, *what?* he thought. What the hell was so funny? "Nothing," he said. "Forget it." He turned to the cage and felt Gershwin's eyes watching him. He rattled the bars, though he knew there would be no response. Then he looked across at the squad room door.

"You want another coffee?" Gershwin said.

It was like somebody had encased Bannerman's back in ice. He wanted to ask how Gershwin had known he had already had a coffee; he wanted to ask why Gershwin sat right down at the same desk as Steinwitz; how he'd known which drawer to pull out; how he'd propped his feet up in just the same way as Steinwitz; how he'd clasped his hands behind his head, just like Steinwitz again. But then he didn't want to ask those things. There was a large part of his head that said, No, *let's not play their game; let's not show them we're falling for it.* And there was a small part of his head, a tiny, darkened part, where the sun never shone and where things—even the most ridiculous things—were simply accepted . . . where questions were never asked. That part said, *Don't let him know you know.*

Know what? said the big, rational part.

Just don't let him know, came the answer.

Bannerman heard Gershwin stand up from his chair. "I said, you want another—"

"No!" Bannerman turned around quickly and, just for a second, the other man seemed to falter. "No," Bannerman said, calmer now. "Thanks."

"Is anything . . . wrong?"

Bannerman winced inwardly at the suspicion in the question. It oozed suspicion. He'd blown it. He glanced back at the door, irrationally considering his chances of making it. Then he looked back and started to laugh. At first, it was forced but then it just seemed to flow naturally. The ease with which it flowed amazed him. Hysteria, he guessed. He laughed so loud and so hard that it hurt. He leaned back against a desk and folded his arms across his stomach. "Is *anything* wrong! Hell, is anything *right's* more the question," he said between laughs that came dangerously close to out-and-out sobs. "We're holed up here," he said, "the three of us, with some whacko who eats people for a hobby—" He pointed to the body in the cage (*Who is it?* that dark part of his head wondered) "—and the dude up and dies on us while he's in custody." He took a deep breath. "Now, how's that gonna look in the morning? Huh?"

Gershwin watched him, his head tilted slightly to one side. "I'll tell you how it's gonna look," Bannerman said, standing up and walking toward the other man, hoping he wouldn't be able to hear his heart thudding, "it's going to look . . . *bad.*" He laid emphasis on the last word like it was cement.

Gershwin continued to watch.

Bannerman turned around and started toward the door, mentally counting the steps, mentally humming, mentally praying, mentally waiting.

"Where are you going?"

"To tell Steinwitz we have a problem," he said without

stopping. "A fucking big problem." He pulled open the door, holding his neck so tight that the muscles would ache for days. If he was lucky. He walked along the corridor to the stairs, forcing himself not to run, forcing himself not to turn around.

The door clicked shut behind him. There was no other sound. Walking down the stairs, he muttered to himself. He wasn't sure what he was muttering but he made sure the word 'problem' cropped up in it several times, and the phrase 'up and died on us', too. He imagined that Gershwin was right behind him, could almost sense his breath on his exposed neck . . . breath from his open mouth . . . his *wide* open mouth.

He walked along the downstairs corridor as loudly as he could. Bannerman, man with a mission, man without fear. Yeah! "Hey, Marty?" he yelled. "Marty, we got a problem. It's a fucking big problem, *mi amigo*." He kept walking. Through the downstairs doors. Towards the main desk. Still walking. "Marty," he yelled again, "you listening to me? You hear we got a problem?"

There was no answer. Of course.

The precinct house doors loomed ahead of him.

He kept on walking.

"Yeah, the problem we got is—" He reached the doors, reached out . . . "It's big, Marty. It's—" His hand touched the handle, grasped it firmly, and turned.

The doors were locked.

"It's one big fucking problem," he said in a soft voice that somehow seemed very alone.

Bannerman looked down at the lock and saw there were no keys. He hadn't expected any.

He turned around, half-expecting Gershwin to be standing watching him, a knife and fork in his hands, chanting *Chow time!* over and over. The place was empty.

He started to walk back the way he had come, mentally cursing the security of the station: barred windows, steel doors . . . you name it. "Hey, Marty? You gone back upstairs?" he shouted. Then, his voice lower, "What the fuck is the lieutenant gonna say when we hand over a dead body, for crissakes?"

Halfway along the corridor he turned into the side office he and Steinwitz—or whoever Steinwitz was *now*—were in earlier. He was still muttering when he picked up the receiver. Still muttering when he jabbed the numbers. But he stopped muttering—

—*the phones are fine*—

when he heard the silence from the earpiece. He had always thought that statements like *The silence was deafening* were ridiculous. But here it was, real, honest-to-God deafening silence. That explained what had been bothering him earlier: no incoming calls. No complaints about domestic fights; no robberies; no shootings or knifings. *Just . . . eatings*, the dark part of his head observed.

He replaced the receiver as gently as he could and leaned on the desktop with both hands. Then he saw the file on the desk, the file that Marty had been looking at while he ate his pizza. There were stains all over it. He leaned over and read upside down:

HOBBIES—Music, golf and cooking

That was

—*hey, that's an idea. You like cooking . . . go compare some recipes*—

his own personal file. Steinwitz had been reading his own personal fucking file! Bannerman reached out to pick up the file and throw it across the office but managed to stop himself. Instead, he pulled open the drawer of the desk he was sitting at. His gun wasn't there. He checked to make sure it hadn't slid to the back, but the drawer was completely empty.

He straightened up and considered his position. It didn't take long. Locked doors, barred windows, dead telephones, no gun—all the other firearms were locked up in a metal cabinet that only the lieutenant had a key for.

Steinwitz was walking along the corridor when Bannerman stepped out of the office. "What you—" Steinwitz started in Gershwin's Brooklyn drawl; then he cleared his throat and said, "What're you doing down here?" The replacement nasal tone was Marty Steinwitz's.

"Looking for you," Bannerman said, all but placing his left hand on his hip and wiggling his right index finger like a fourth-grade schoolteacher. He hoped Steinwitz's dialect-slip hadn't been intentional—which would mean Steinwitz wanted him to comment on it—and he hoped that, if it were unintentional, Steinwitz wouldn't think he had noticed it.

"Problem?"

Problem? Bannerman wanted to ask where Steinwitz had been, wanted to rub his nose in it. But

—don't let him know you know—

he didn't dare.

He forced himself to walk up to Steinwitz, stand right in front of him, like he was going past, then he stopped. "I was looking for you."

Steinwitz glanced at the office Bannerman had just left and returned his attention to his face. "I was taking a dump."

Bannerman nodded. "Thank you for sharing that with me. Was it a good one?"

Steinwitz pulled a face and rubbed his stomach. "Think I might've eaten something disagreed with me." (Was that the hint of a smile tugging at the edges of his mouth?) "What's up?"

Bannerman slumped back against the wall and thrust his hands—his increasingly sweaty and shaky hands—deep into his trouser pockets. "Oh, nothing much. Nothing except we've got a dead prisoner in the cage."

Steinwitz narrowed his eyes and watched him. "Dead?"

He's playing for time, Bannerman thought. He's weighing up what kind of a threat I am to him. He's wondering if he should stop the game right now. Does he know I know the phones are dead? Does he know I've tried the doors? Does he know I've seen that he was reading my personal file? Does he know I've been looking for my gun? He looked deep into Steinwitz's eyes, searching for a sign, a sign that he was wrong, that he was being stupid and everything was A-okay. But though the eyes were Marty's eyes—a conviction that came to him not without an element of surprise; after all, why would he study another man's eyes, even over the many years he had known him?—then again they weren't. They were the right color, sure, but they were darker and without depth. Fish eyes, lacking in . . . soul. He nodded. *He knows*, said the voice in his head. "Yeah, dead. Why don't you go see."

Steinwitz watched him, shuffled from one foot to the other. "Gershwin's up there," Bannerman added.

Steinwitz smiled. "Better take a look then, I guess."

"Why don't you do that." He stood up from the wall and started back to the main desk.

"You not coming up?"

Bannerman replied without turning around. "Yeah. First I'm gonna brew up some fresh coffee. Looks like it's going to be a quiet night."

"That's the way I like it," Steinwitz said softly behind him.

Bannerman nodded slowly as he walked toward the coffee maker and, just for a second, he felt like giving up. He felt like turning around and telling Steinwitz, *Okay, you win. But kill me first, okay?* But he didn't think that whatever it was that occupied his friend's body now would observe such a display of generosity. Such weakness. He kept walking and felt a wave of relief when he heard the door at the end of the corridor behind him swing closed.

As he reached the desk he turned to look behind him. Steinwitz had gone. He leaned against the counter containing the coffee maker, coffee and various mugs, and forced himself to think. What now? He looked up at the front doors, checking for signs of a key hanging somewhere next to them. Nothing. He looked across at the barred windows and, though he couldn't see them, thought about all the empty warehouses in the streets beyond. No life anywhere.

He had to get out.

Suddenly, he jolted upright. Downstairs! He could get out from the basement. What had taken him so long? He switched on the hot water and then walked calmly but quickly across to the stairs to the basement. Checking the corridor to the stairs leading up to the squad room, he placed his hand on the door leading to the basement, grimacing as he expected it to be locked.

The handle turned.

The door came open.

Another quick check to see that the corridor was clear and he slid inside and started down the stairs.

As he traveled down the air got fresher, cooler. He ran, now, taking steps two and three at a time. When he reached the bottom he stopped and looked back up the staircase. Saw the spare key hanging beside the door. Bannerman bit into his bottom lip as he considered running back up the stairs to lock the door. Would he get halfway up and the door suddenly open, though? *Chow time!* He decided against it and turned to the corridor leading past the changing rooms to the back door. Halfway along he stopped and listened for sounds of footsteps coming down the stairs, accompanied by Bernard Herrman's shrieking violins. But all was quiet.

He reached the back door, took the handle in his hand, turned the dead-lock and pulled. It opened.

"Where the hell *you* going?" Jimmy Mitulak said.

Bannerman stopped dead and stared.

"What the hell's the *matter* with you?" Mitulak said.

"What are *you* doing here? You should be home."

Mitulak frowned. "I forgot something. What are you, my mother?"

"What did you forget?" Bannerman said backing down the corridor.

"My bowling shoes. We got a match tomorrow—*today* now. Look, what the hell's the matter?"

"You could've picked them up in the morning."

"Doc, what *is* this? I gotta be in Buffalo by—Hey, since when do I gotta tell you everythin—"

Bannerman grabbed hold of Mitulak's jacket and pulled it open. "You still got your gun on."

"Yeah, I still got my gun on. Come on, now, what's—"

"Get inside."

Mitulak stepped warily into the corridor, still frowning.

"Let me see it."

Mitulak frowned some more.

"The gun, let me see your fucking gun."

Mitulak smiled and started to shake his head.

"Jimmy, I'm not playing around here. Let me see the gun."

Mitulak flipped the harness catch and removed the gun, held it out to Bannerman. "I hope I'm not going to regret this."

Bannerman took it gingerly, checked the cartridge. It was full. He secured the cartridge and handed it back to Mitulak with a visible sigh of relief.

"You wanna tell me what's going on?"

"He's out."

"Who's out?"

"The eater, Mellor. He's loose in the station."

"What?!"

Bannerman nodded. "But . . . it gets worse."

"How worse?"

"He's disguised."

"How can he be disguised? There's only you and—"

"He's disguised as Marty."

"Marty?"

"And Gershwin."

Mitulak started to laugh. "Hey, I don't know what you're smoking, Doc, but how about passing it around."

"Listen to me, goddamit!"

Mitulak's smile faded.

"He's taken their appearance. I know, I know," he said as Mitulak looked at him like he was going mad. "It sounds crazy, but he has."

"How?"

"How the fuck do I know how. Maybe he's a fucking Ymir or a face-hugger . . . maybe he can assume the identity of whoever he eats . . . you know? Like the Indians? They ate the hearts of their enemies because they thought it gave them their enemies' strength. Maybe this guy gets the full thing . . . hair, face, looks . . . everything."

"He's *eaten* Gershwin and Marty?"

Bannerman shrugged. "Maybe. All I know is that they're never together."

"Never together?"

"Never together in the room at the same time. And when Gershwin came into the squad room he sat down in the chair as Marty . . . propped his feet on the desk just the same way as he had been doing a few minutes earlier. And . . . yeah, and Mellor's dead. In the cell. He doesn't move or speak or anything."

"You just said that Mellor was loose."

"Jesus Christ! He *is* loose. But he's left his body in the cell, curled up so it's facing the wall."

"You sure it's him? In the cell?"

"Sure as I can be without going in there and checking him out."

"You haven't checked the body?"

"Hey, I've seen *Silence of the Lambs*, okay? I wasn't going to go in there and have him wearing my head like a Halloween mask."

Mitulak thought for a moment. "But, if Mellor's out and about, what's the problem with going in the cell?"

Bannerman was breathing heavily, almost panting.

"Well?"

"I wasn't sure then. I'm sure now. Okay? I didn't want to go into the cell when I thought that, maybe, Mellor was playing possum. But then all these other things happened—"

"Like Gershwin and Marty sharing a chair?"

"Yes! It sounds crazy . . . I know it sounds crazy, okay? But my gun."

"Your gun?"

"It disappeared. And Marty was reading my personal file . . . and the phones are dead . . . and the front doors are locked . . . Look, we have to do something, Jimmy."

Mitulak made noises with his mouth as he considered. Bannerman shook his head and ran both hands through his hair, turning around and walking to and fro in the corridor.

"Okay."

"You believe me?"

"Let's say I believe *you* believe, and leave it at that for now. Maybe it's worth checking it out."

Bannerman suddenly felt as though all of his problems were over. Then, just as he felt like hugging Jimmy Mitulak, he remembered that they still had to confront Steinwitz. Or Gershwin. Could he move both of them at the same time, this eater? He didn't think so. It would be one or the other.

Peter Crowther

"So what do we do?" said Mitulak, interrupting Bannerman's thoughts.

Bannerman glanced longingly at the back door and then turned to face him. "We go up."

Mitulak nodded. "Right." He slipped off the safety catch on his gun and hefted it slowly in his hand, like he was weighing it. "Right," he said again. "You lead the way."

Bannerman turned around and walked back along the corridor to the stairs.

Taking the stairs slowly, stopping after every couple of risers to listen for any sound of movement, took time. In fact, it took too much time. Halfway up, Bannerman started to wonder what Steinwitz was doing up there. Had he discovered that Bannerman—wasn't there? If so, where did he think he'd gone? Surely by now he would have checked all the possible hiding places—there weren't many, for crissakes—and would probably have concluded that he was downstairs. If so, then why hadn't the eater come down after him?

He stopped and listened: all quiet. He pressed on.

Maybe Steinwitz had suddenly remembered the downstairs door, and had gone out from upstairs and snuck around the back of the parking lot to wait for him outside. Shit! Maybe the eater had tried the door and discovered it was open . . . then sneaked in, sneaked along the downstairs corridor, taken a look around the corner of the staircase, real quiet, and seen Mitulak and him creeping up the stairs.

Bannerman stopped again and turned his head slowly. There was only Mitulak behind him. The rest of the staircase was empty. He shook his head and carried on. Two steps further and he was at the top, his hand on the door handle.

"Hey . . ."

Mitulak's sharp whisper near-on made Bannerman jump out of his skin. He held onto the handle tightly and hissed, "What?"

"You want maybe I should go first?"

"Why?"

"Because I got a gun. If this guy is around the corner

when you open the door—and if he knows you're onto him—he's gonna start shooting as soon as we show ourselves."

It made sense. "That makes sense," Bannerman whispered, and he changed places with Mitulak, staring intently at the door handle while neither of them was holding it.

When they were in place, Mitulak gently turned the handle and pushed. The door crept open silently.

"See anything?" Bannerman whispered.

"Nothing." Mitulak pushed the door a little wider and stepped onto the top step, folding his body into the door, his gun flat against the handle.

"Anything now?"

"Just wait, for—" He stopped.

Bannerman drew in his breath. "What? What is it?"

Mitulak jammed his head between the door and the jamb and tried to look up the corridor to the right.

"What is it?" Bannerman asked again.

"It's Marty."

"Jesus Chri—Where? Where is he? Can he see you?"

Mitulak pushed the door wider and looked around it to the left. Then he stepped back and turned to Bannerman.

"Now I believe you."

"Huh?"

"It's Marty. He's dead."

"Dead?"

Mitulak nodded. "Far as I can make out."

"Where is he?"

"Lying on the floor right in front of us."

"Any sign of Gershwin?"

Mitulak shook his head. "God. Marty. Dead." The three words came out slow and punctuated into tiny sentences, each with a poetic, grim resonance.

"What do we do now?"

"We go out. What else can we do?"

Bannerman grunted. There was nothing else.

"Ready?" said Mitulak.

"Ready."

"Right!" He pushed open the door and ran, crouched over, to the main desk on the left.

Bannerman stepped up onto the top step and looked around the door-edge. Marty stared up at him. He was naked, lying facedown on the floor about fifteen feet from the door, his head tilted to one side like he was watching the basement door. His legs were splayed out behind him, his arms stretched in front of him. One half of his face had gone, exposing teeth and gums and part of his cheek bone. His left arm ended just above the wrist in a fray of skin and cartilage. There was no blood.

Bannerman closed his eyes and blinked away the tears, then opened them again. The horror was still there. He pushed open the door and stepped out into the corridor without thinking.

"Hey," Mitulak whispered loudly. "What the hell you doing?"

Bannerman didn't answer. He walked across to Marty Steinwitz's body and looked down at it. There was a folded piece of paper lying on his back. He bent down.

"What is it?" Mitulak whispered.

Bannerman read the words on the note, four gramatically incorrect lines, carefully typed on one of the machines up in the squad room:

game over
you have gun now

now weer even
lets finnish it.

He waved the sheet to Mitulak. "Come read it yourself. He knows you're here."

Mitulak stood up from behind the desk, warily watching for any signs of movement from anywhere. "Huh? How's he know I'm here?"

"He knows I've got a gun." Bannerman shrugged. "How the hell do I know how he knows anything?"

Mitulak reached him and took the note. He read.

Bannerman turned Steinwitz's body over and jumped back. "Jesus H. Christ!"

Mitulak looked up from the note and then down at the

body. The whole of Steinwitz's chest had been ripped open, pieces of snapped bone jutting out.

Bannerman said, "He's eaten his heart."

Mitulak said nothing.

"Let's go. He's waiting for us."

Bannerman led the way along the corridor to the doors. They pushed open the doors together and looked up the staircase. Gershwin was hanging from one of the lights. He, too, was naked, his chest similarly destroying and both legs gone from the knees. As they got closer, they saw that his eyes were missing. A note taped across his stomach read:

getting warmer
the end is neye

Neither of them said anything.

At the top of the stairs, his heart pounding fit to burst out of his own chest, Bannerman turned the handle on the door.

"Wait . . ."

Bannerman turned.

"Let me go first. I'll go left, over toward the cage, you go right."

Bannerman nodded.

"Right!" said Mitulak.

Bannerman threw open the door and both men fell into the room, crashing in two directions behind the desks nearest the door. The hail of bullets Bannerman had expected didn't come.

Bannerman lifted his head above the desk and looked around. He couldn't see anything.

Mitulak did the same.

"Hey . . ." Mitulak said.

"What?"

"I thought you said the guy was dead in the cage."

Shit, Bannerman thought. He knew what was coming next but he had to respond. "He was."

"He ain't now, man," said Mitulak. "Cage is empty."

Bannerman stood up slowly, staring around the squad room. "He's gone back to his own—" He stopped. Over

327

by the far wall, Mellor was sitting against a radiator. He still had the blanket wrapped around him, like an Eskimo or an Indian Chief. Pulled down over his head was a large, brown evidence bag, one side of which was blown apart and stained a red so dark it looked almost black. The wall behind the bag looked like somebody had thrown a pizza at it.

"What is it?" Mitulak said.

"Just wait where you are," Bannerman said. "And cover me." He moved to the side and walked slowly around the desk. As he moved, more of the body came into view. Mellor was holding a gun in one hand. In the other hand was another note. He looked around at Mitulak. Mitulak frowned and mouthed *What?* Bannerman shook his head. *Cover me*, he mouthed. Mitulak nodded and waved the gun.

Bannerman edged his way along the side wall, keeping Mellor in sight all the way. At last he had reached a point where there were no more desks to provide cover. But he had watched the body very carefully and there was no sign of any movement. Either the guy *was* dead or he could hold his breath a very long time.

He crouched down onto all-fours and crept the final few feet toward the body. When he reached it, he leaned over and took hold of the barrel of the gun and gently pulled.

"You okay?" Mitulak whispered.

The gun came away, and Mellor's fingers plopped against his stomach.

"Yeah, I'm okay," Bannerman said. He put the gun in his pocket and reached for the note. Behind him, he heard Mitulak moving between the desks.

Bannerman unfolded the note, a roster sheet, and looked at the other side. It was blank.

"You still okay?"

Bannerman nodded, frowning. "He left a note."

"What's it say?"

"It doesn't. It's blank." He turned it over. It was this week's roster. He looked at the grid and the penciled names in the boxes. One of them was ringed, the one for tomorrow—*today*, now. The box was for 10 a.m.; the name in the box was J. Mitulak.

Bannerman looked at the evidence bag, reached up and lifted it off. The eater had left just enough of the face for Bannerman to recognize who it was, even without the eyes. "Jimmy . . ." he whispered, sadly. Behind him, he heard desks moving as though something large was making its way across the floor.

He saw it all, now, in his mind's eye.

He reached into his pocket and lifted out the gun.

Then he discovered that the cartridge was missing.

"Let's eat," said a voice behind him. It didn't sound like any accent or dialect he had ever heard before.

Mister Mellor Comes to Wayside

(From *April Fool*, a work in progress)

The old song as crooned by the late-great crooner-supremo Frank Sinatra has it that while it might be nice—oh *so* nice!—to go traveling, it's so much nicer to come home.

But that's just one man's view. It isn't everybody's.

And while Martin and Rosemary Fenwick were almost relieved to get home after their brief sojourn in Derbyshire—a break that had, if anything, highlighted their difficulties rather then relieved them—their young son much preferred to travel, full stop. Home to Freddie Fenwick was a long series of television programs, an uncomfortable bottom and a parade of stony faces from his mother, who, it had to be said, had resumed her strangeness and her distance to her son virtually as soon as she had stepped back into the house.

So, for Freddie, coming home was grossly over-rated.

It was much the same thumbs-down from Martin Fenwick who had now hit the magical age of 40 when, statistically, there was a hell of a lot more behind him than there was still to come. He was enjoying the thrill of a new relationship and even when he *was* home, he constantly dreamed of being away from it again.

Even Rosemary herself dreamed of being set free from the drudgery that life looking after Freddie had become. The novelty had very much worn off and she yearned for freedom. Homes were for the sick and the weak and the old.

Rosemary felt that she was none of these.

Mister Mellor—who had also, in his time, been misses, misseses and muzzes (though he had little time for political correctness) . . . as well as young children, animals (both wild and domesticated) and even the occasional insect—did not have a home. All places were the same to him.

Wherever he found someone to 'play' with was as close to home as Mister Mellor ever came. That was where and when he was most comfortable . . . most fulfilled. Because when he was 'playing'—at least each time he *started* 'playing'—he could not help but hope that this might be the one. This might be the one companion who could relieve the monotony.

He had never been there but, to Mister Mellor, home was the blackness and rest of death. In his own way, he had sent many people home in his time. It was what he did. And he did it well.

During the years since Freddie Fenwick's birth, Mister Mellor had not been idle. He had been visiting people in different areas and even in different countries. And he had been playing hard. But all the time he watched the skies and listened to the voices in his head.

The voices were a confused and confusing jumble of sounds . . . little more than static, really, that he interpreted to suit his own situation. The past three years had seen a marked increase in this static and he had been told, somewhat paradoxically, that he must build his strength and his fortitude so that he was better prepared to meet his ultimate foe . . . his savior.

This foe would be a child. Of that he was convinced. But where he would *find* the child, he had no idea.

Peter Crowther

After a lengthy sojourn around the United Kingdom—with an extremely pleasant stay in Northern Ireland, where real innovations were eminently possible—he had traveled to the United States. The means by which he effected these changes in direction were of as little consequence as they were of memory. He had met an old woman in Heathrow airport, that much he could recall. But then the specifics of how he became her—disposing of her body along the way—and took her place on a scheduled flight to LaGuardia airport in New York were lost in the mists of time.

He was not interested and so he did not remember. Memory was a waste of time and energy. On those rare occasions when he thought back, Mister Mellor grew despondent. It had been too long and the longer it took the less he believed there would ever be an end to it.

And now it was that he was still in the United States, although he had moved around quite considerably.

The first day of May had come and the promise of a summer to follow filled the countryside. Mister Mellor had been here for a couple of weeks, during which time he had not been idle. He had discovered a solitary homestead and he had spent time there, talking to the man and the woman and the three children and even the dog. They had been unable to help him. Now they were resting. The police would call it different when they finally found them but for Mister Mellor, 'resting' was a reasonable catch-all.

He drifted into the nearby town—with the rather quaint name of Wayside—with the first hot day, not fully-formed and completely undecided of what he wanted to be . . . crouched down on all fours and slinking in, feral and deceitful, alongside the wire-mesh fencing by the town dump.

For the past day he had been holed up in the fields and the valleys down along the Interstate between Carver and Durphin, playing with shapes and preening himself like a wily old cat just waiting for the right time to come along. That time was now, first day of the month, and he felt energized by his rest, felt frisky and ready for action.

He stopped at the sign and looked at it . . . looked at it for several minutes. This must be the place, he reasoned as he had reasoned many thousands of times before, reading significance into weather variations, town names, people names until he could no longer separate reality from the countless variations that may or may not lie ahead.

Wayside. It sounded right. Hell, it felt right. Wasn't there an expression about falling by the Wayside? There was, he was sure of that. Maybe that expression had been forged from the same piltdown goo that had birthed him, the perpetrator and the prophecy; Yin and Yang . . . the two elements that would provide the whole. He would fall in Wayside. It made sense.

It was just after six am.

The coming summer's light sang to the weeds in the cracks in the sidewalks of Wayside, casting shadows of the sycamores and the oaks that lined the Bluffs Road—strange name, he thought . . . another omen? Was he not the greatest bluffer in the world?—in the sharpest relief they would have all year.

Mister Mellor moved forward, changing as he did so, to start work.

Johnjo MacDaniels' wide-eyed pitbull, Driver, cocked a leg and peed against Maggie Henderson's old Dodge—the one her boy Drury had piled into the wall of Cy Simmons's General Store over on McLintock Avenue—and the steaming yellow liquid ran down the door and across the now crusted bloody handprints that littered the window like a frantic mosaic.

If he could have talked, Driver would have told a couple of stories to anyone who had the time or the inclination to listen. He would have told about how he'd like to stick his pecker way up inside Fred Krueller's Pekinese—so deep he'd split the little bitch into two ragged pieces—and about how some nights, when the wind was just right and whirling the dust and soft soil up into the air and a gibbous moon held court, a dark-stained spectral teenager reappears behind the wheel of that car and claws at the door with broken hands while, all around him, silent white flames lick across his broken face and tease the blackened upholstery.

But not now.

Now, smelling of sweat, axle grease and rotting vegetables, Driver sniffed the air and let out a throaty rattle the way all dogs do when they see or sense something that humans can't. The hair along his back and above his sawed-off tail stump rose up, bristling, and gave a low moan, occasionally snapping at the flies to show how tough he really was. Soon, Johnjo would step out of his trailer and tell Driver to shut the fuck up before he unscrewed the top off of his Old Granddad and mouthed the glassy teat for the first shot of the day.

It could even be that Johnjo would be feeling so plain mean and hung over, the way he did most every day when he woke up, that he wouldn't notice some things had gone from against the trailer. Things like a saw, a tire-iron, a couple of wrenches and an old pitchfork with a splintered handle. But they were so rusted up from years of ignorance that he probably wouldn't even notice. And Driver would be mighty pleased about that, seeing as how he got blamed for everything that went wrong around the place . . . from a blown tire on Johnjo's Cherokee to a busted faucet on the water supply. But Driver figured there comes a time when discretion makes for the better part of valor. He further figured that the well-dressed young man who tipped his hat to him and gave him a wink as he pulled together all of these things was not about to take kindly to a whole mess of barking and snapping. So he stayed real quiet.

And so neither the new season nor the well-dressed young man paid Driver any attention as the two of them, man and season, drifted off—slithered and slid, Driver might have said if he'd been able to speak—along Fairfax, toward the Good Neighbor grocery store where Wilhemina Sherbourg, the biggest and fattest woman outside of a carnival sideshow, lay spread-eagled on her queen-size bed, her flabby elbows reaching over each side toward the dusty floor.

The first ray of sunshine span and pirouetted through the torn curtains and drifted across Wilhemina's slumbering naked bulk, lighting the pock-marked flesh and the feeding bed bugs, each one bloated with chocolate- and pizza-flavored blood, and lingered on the wide spillage of breasts so big you could tear them off, hollow them out and then carry 30 or 40 pounds of apples home in them.

The Longest Single Note

But while the new season drifted past, heading on for the hills and the valleys, the plains and the fields, the tiny Main Streets and the mighty Interstates, something it had brought with it, like a seed on the breeze, slowed down and finally stopped at the paint-peeled door, sniffing, relishing the aromas that wafted through the gaps in the door, the grain in the woodwork and even the walls themselves.

Why this door and not another was not certain. More than that: it was not *known*. The truth of the matter was that there was no plan to such an event, no schedule to follow, no criteria to achieve, no standards to maintain, and no accounts to be settled. An entirely random visit.

Inside, a knock sounded at Wilhemina's door . . . gently insistent but somehow lazy, too. Kind of relaxed but inevitable, like the person knocking was in no hurry but, equally, was not going to go away. No way.

Wilhemina shouted, "Who is it?", half not caring and half not expecting any answer.

"It's your destiny!" a voice announced, a voice that sounded for all the world like one of those guys on the TV quiz shows, all toothpaste and toupee, set to offer her her wildest dreams and make everything she had ever dreamed about come suddenly wonderfully true.

Wilhemina could hear, from somewhere off in the distance, that damned dog creating a stink about something. Mutt sounded like it had its dick caught in a gate, making all that noise.

"I don't have no destiny," Wilhemina called, petulantly and sad, half lifting her head from her pillow, a once-white cotton affair marked with a hundred nights of dribbled saliva and lost hope.

"Oh but you *do*," the voice said, gently correcting her. "*Everyone* has a destiny," it said.

Wilhemina said, "Shit!", and rolled over across the bed to allow her gargantuan legs to spill off the mattress in wobbling folds of jello flesh, slightly grainy with yesterday's and the day before's dirt and smelling like old meat, sweet and dangerous.

She pulled on an old robe, tied the cord tight around her belly, and shuffled to the door. She leaned against the wood

335

paneling to hear if the guy was still out there but she didn't hear anything. "You still there?"

"Still here," the voice confirmed. "Destiny never goes away," it added.

"Whatcha want anyways? This some kinda sellin' stunt? Cos I can tell you—"

"No kind of selling stunt at all," the voice said. Then, after a pause, it said, "This is the real thing."

"Oh, hell," Wilhemina muttered as she shifted the deadbolt and turned the latch. She took hold of the door handle and gave it a good tug, seeing as how last fall's rains and the lengthy winter had warped the wood right in the frame. And as it opened wide, she gave a small gasp.

There on the stoop was a fine-looking young man, a big smile beaming on his face and his hat held in one hand. "And it's a fine good morning to you," he said. "Might I come in for a while?"

Wilhemina tried to speak but suddenly found that her voice had snuck off and hidden somewhere deep in the myriad folds of her ample bosom. She wanted to ask him who he was and what he wanted. She wanted to ask if she knew him—though she knew that she didn't—or who had sent him. More than anything, though, she wanted to know why a fella dressed so mighty fine was carrying a whole load of old tools, all rusted and broken, so's they made a mess of his good suit. But somehow, she didn't really want to know the answer to that one until it became absolutely necessary.

Wilhemina Sherbourg took a faltering step back into the hovel of her life while the young man answered that move with a couple of steps forward.

He kicked the door closed and breathed in deeply the collective aroma of sweat and dirt and old food. "My," he said, "now that smells good!"

He lay the tools down on the floor and turned, dropping the latchlock and shifting the deadbolt back into place. "Tell me," he said as he turned back to face her, "do you have any young ones—you know, children?—around the place?"

Wilhemina shook her head and suddenly felt like she needed to pee.

The man looked disappointed at first but then he shrugged and smiled, tossing his hat onto the chair alongside the door. "Ah well, not to worry," he said. "We can proceed without them."

Wilhemina took another step back and tried to speak. It was still no use.

"I see you're interested in why I'm here," the man said as he bent down to rummage through the things he had brought. He picked the saw and the tire-iron and stood up again.

"They say that inside every fat person there's a thin person trying to get out," he said. "Let's see if that's true."

And the two of them set to playing.

Forest Plains

All of the Indians are dead
(a good Indian is a dead Indian)
Or riding in motor cars
—Ernest Hemingway
(from *Oklahoma*)

"What then is the American,
this new man?"
—Crevecoeur

ONE

The dead man drove his car through the ghosts of his people.

He saw their spirits hovering over the blacktop like heat shimmer or the tail-ends of the morning haze that runs across the meadow in early summer, when the sun is still drying out the winter earth. When he got out of his car at a Mobil gas station twenty-three miles north of Kansas City, he could even smell them.

338

He rubbed his hands along his back, stretched and faced into the gentle breeze, sniffing. Alongside his head, flies and an occasional wasp buzzed by. Behind him, a screen door whined and then clanked twice. The sound of slurring feet approaching his back made him turn.

"Premium?" The old man reached for the nozzle without waiting for an answer and thrust it into the side of the Dodge. He had already started to squeeze the trigger.

"Premium'll do just fine." He turned back to face the wind and breathed in again, recalling the words of Chief Luther Standing Bear, passed down through the generations. *The world was a library and its books were the stones, leaves, grass, brooks, and the birds and animals that shared, alike with us, the storms and blessings of the earth.*

"Smell anything?" The old man stooped over the Dodge, dutifully wiping spilled gasoline from a rusting fender as the traces of his words hung in the air like the wind on a wire fence. He was watching the dead man, watery eyes squinting into the sun.

The dead man breathed deep, pulling the air into his lungs.

Smell anything . . .

He smelled cheap supermarket fats, and frying eggs, steaks and sausages.

He smelled pancakes, syrups and coffee, some of it freshly made, some of it old now—old in coffee terms—and losing its life warmth.

He smelled cigarettes—he identified eleven brands before giving up the game—and cologne, a handful of cheap perfumes and the faintest hint of prophylactic lubrication.

He smelled the fresh water of the Missouri River.

He smelled dirt and chemicals.

And, most of all, he smelled the past.

The old man's question swooped and dived amidst the gentle, regular *ting* of the gas pump as it fed the old Dodge. It ached to be answered and released. The dead man breathed deep again, filtering odors through the cloying smell of gasoline, and pulled in the prairie.

He smelled the Assiniboin and the Cree, the Massika and

the Maudan, the Arikara and the Blackfoot. And many more besides.

He smelled buffalo hides, skins of beaver, muskrat and lynx, some fox, a little weasel and mink.

He smelled teepee smoke and rat shit.

And then he smelled something else. It hung on the wind like a trapped ribbon, swirling and dropping, but always returning to the same point. He closed his eyes and sniffed some more, short sniffs, concentrating on the unfamiliar scent. Then he recognized it. It was death. Old death. *Wrong* death. It was death with pain, sudden and brutal. The smell made the dead man gag and he put his hand to his face.

Behind him, the old man replaced the gas nozzle and set to cleaning the windshield with a piece of gingham cloth, which he pulled out of his pants pocket. The cloth was filthy with grime and dust. The Cree Chief Piapot once said: *The white man who is our agent is so stingy that he carries a linen rag in his pocket into which to blow his nose, for fear he might blow away something of value.* The dead man smiled and stared at the rag. Maybe there had even been a time when that piece of cloth had been just a part of a larger garment.

He concentrated, just for his own amusement.

It had been a long time for that piece of cloth, and a lot of windshields and spilled gasoline, but it was there, buried beneath the grease and snot: the faint waft of young legs, feminine legs, the gentle, teasing odor of dawn-hair and pheromones.

He smiled to himself, pushing the smells back, away from him. "Breakfast," he said at last, the word springing out into the heat as though it had a life of its own.

"Huh?"

The dead man rubbed his stomach. "I smell breakfast. Know where I can chow down around here?"

The old man stepped back from the car, rubbed a grizzled beard that was more bush grass than meadow, and jammed the cloth into his pocket. The dead man saw a flash of colored stripes through the old man's fly as it gaped open and then closed back up. And he caught the stench of urine and stale jism, crabs and shit. He turned away quickly and drank in the scents of the land again. It was worse than ever, his 'gift'. It was getting so that he couldn't stop from pulling them all in.

"Well," the old man said, telling it like a campfire story on the back of a long day and a shared bottle, "you go on along here a ways—mebbe eight, nine miles—you come to a fork: left, lemme see now . . . left is marked Railroad Crossing." The old man smiled. "That's all it is. That's all that's down there."

"Right is where you need to go, town name of Forest Plains. Ain't much more'n a general store, an auto fix-it and a bar, but the store does an all-day breakfast that should set you up some." The old man chuckled and the dead man turned back to face him, his eyes asking the question. "Fact is," the old man said, still laughing, "they cook but the one meal but they do it all day. It can be any meal you want it to be. It'll be as good as any breakfast you ever had." He looked up at the sky measuring the time, and the dead man noticed that the old man did not wear a watch. "Be as good as any lunch you ever had, too." The old man thought for a minute and then added, "Nice girl there. Indian." He smiled a superior smile, exposing blackened gaps in old bridgework, and nodded to the dead man. "Should make you feel right at home."

"Sounds fine to me," the dead man said and he turned his head to look up the road. The wrong-death smell was still there. "Forest Plains." He turned the words over in his mouth until they started to feel right. That was the place. He could feel it as well as smell it.

"That'll be sixteen eighty-five for the gas."

The dead man pulled two crumpled bills from his jacket pocket, straightened them with his hand and then held them out. "There you go," he said. "Twenty dollars. Keep it."

"Hey," the old man beamed, taking the bills and folding them into his pants pocket on top of the gingham cloth, with all of its ingrained history. "That's mighty kind of you. Mighty kind." His eyes twinkled his gratitude. Maybe now the old man was regretting the Indian crack.

"My pleasure." The dead man walked around to the driver's door.

"Nice auto," the man said, earning his tip.

"Was once," the dead man said. "Now it's like me, dead but it won't lie down."

The old man nodded and watched him slide into the car. "What is it?"

"Dodge Royal, 1954." He rested his arm on the door and pointed his hand to the hood. "Got a 361-see-eye version of the Chrysler hemi vee eight under there."

The old man whistled dutifully.

Trying hard not to smile, the dead man turned the key. Its thirst sated, if only temporarily, the car rattled into a semblance of life and then the engine caught and held, blowing one thick plume of smoke straight back out of the tailpipe while another burst out by the side of the offside rear wheel.

"Looks like your muffler's shot," the old man yelled above the noise of the engine.

"Yup," the dead man agreed. "Car's dying, and there ain't nothing going to save her. But then,"—he smiled and shrugged his shoulders theatrically—"I guess we've all seen better days."

"Ain't *that* a fact," the old man said. "Don't forget, now: Forest Plains."

The dead man pulled out of the station and onto the blacktop, waving. "I won't forget," he said to the man's reflection in the rear view mirror. "Forest Plains."

TWO

When does a small town stop being small?

Maybe it's this way: towns are like people. They start off small, they grow big and then they die. One way or another.

Some die because somebody moves the highway—which is like removing the artery that feeds a human heart. The result is the heart stops.

Some die because they outgrow their strength. That's the

way it happened with New York and Los Angeles, with Philadelphia and St. Louis. There are plenty more.

With Forest Plains it was the first way.

One time, the blacktop took a dog's leg turn and rode straight on through Forest Plains. Only in those days it wasn't a blacktop, just a pair of wagon-wheel ruts running either side of thick grass, providing link routes for the trappers and hunters trading fish and furs at the rude log stores and warehouses along the river front some eighteen miles east. Back in those days, whiskey, groceries and other staples were exchanged for wool, buffalo robes, Mexican coins and ore. But then, in 1850, Kansas City was incorporated as a town and the end of the Civil War brought the railroad along with peace.

"K.C." thrived.

The Indians—who had given the town its name; "kansas" meaning "smoky"—were replaced by the cattle ranchers, driving huge herds across the endless ranges of the West to be shipped to market. And Forest Plains was forgotten.

Forest Plains.

Even the name itself is a contradiction, a dichotomy of the bare and the clothed, the arid and the wooded.

In the country surrounding Forest Plains, the land stretched effortlessly from horizon to horizon. Around Forest Plains a man could see the future and the past . . . where he was going and where he had been.

And, all the while, the town lay on a deathbed of its own making, pulling in sharp breath-rattles where once it had pulled in fresh, clean air.

Crossing over Main Street between Barry Lozier's General Store and Barry's storage shack on the one side, and Griffin Stolkin's auto repair shop and the boarded-up funeral parlor on the other, West Street became East Street before getting tangled up in both directions in sugar maple and red oak, sassafras and hickory. On Main Street itself, a dusty road bordered by buildings for only three hundred seventeen yards, and which later became limestone, unstriped asphalt, striped asphalt, two-lane concrete and, finally, the divided four-lane ribbon of I-70 and its predecessor, U.S. 40—along which a dead man steered his dying auto-

mobile, looking for a turnoff that said FOREST PLAINS—
the townsfolk talked about the coming season the way they
talked about the coming of every season, their voices hushed
but polite, their faces bathed in gentle but tired smiles.

Sitting on an upturned half-barrel on the boardwalk outside of the General Store, a girl stared up the road. Her
name was Sara—"Like the desert," she used to tell strangers until there were no more strangers who didn't already
know. Truth was Sara was like the desert in more ways
than a simple and contrived similarity in pronunciation. She
was aloof and self-sufficient, and yet secretly lonely and
dependent on the brief conversations of others.

Sara nodded to Bill McCandless and his wife, Irene, as
they stepped off the dusty street onto the boardwalk, intent
on passing her by in silence on their way into a store. The
woman ignored her but the burley man tipped his wide-
brimmed hat in response.

"Hot enough for you, Mr. McCandless?" Sara trilled in
a come-on voice. She had watched Bill McCandless's piggy
eyes trying to see down her blouse when she served him
coffee and a Danish every morning, delighting in every bead
of sweat that ran down that lined forehead. She turned and
looked up at him, shielding her eyes from the sun's glare
with one hand. With the other hand, she wafted the neck
of her blouse so that it popped a couple of buttons and
revealed a swell of rusty-brown breast.

Oblivious, Irene McCandless pulled open the screen door
and stepped into the cool darkness of Barry Lozier's store.
Her husband held the door for a few seconds, smiled and
nodded, and then followed obediently, the door clanking
behind him pushing a pleasantly cooling draft onto the
boardwalk where the sun absorbed it, quickly and without
mercy.

Fastening the buttons on her blouse, Sara turned back to
the road and chuckled to herself. She tried to imagine Bill
McCandless in the nude, his checkered shirt, with the ever-
present leather glasses-pouch and ball-point pens still
clipped to the pocket, hanging on the back of the wicker
chair in her bedroom; baggy blue work-pants draped across

344

the foot of the bed; voluminous Fruit-of-the-Looms and two holey socks lying in a crumpled pile on her rug.

In her mind's eye, she imagined his big, white belly, filled with Coors and Miller Light, and criss-crossed with blue lines like the map of the state. And then she imagined his tiny pecker flushed out with blood, its end bruised and purple, quivering with anticipation, nosing its way out of a straggly thatch of graying pubic hair like a prairie dog checking the day from its tumbleweed home. She slapped her knee and shook her head, laughing, her black hair flouncing across her knees like storm clouds. When she looked up again, she saw the column of dust approaching the town.

THREE

The dead man found the turning and took a right.

He drove alongside grassed-over railroad tracks for a couple of miles before the tracks, as though bored with his company, suddenly swept away to the left and disappeared behind the trees.

He passed a wide pond that was still and mysterious, its water green and furry near the banks. A wooden sign beside it said *Darien Lake*. The sign had been uprooted and now lay at the side of the road, partially covered by the long grass. The dead man smelled a young death there, but it wasn't the one he sought.

Another mile along the road, he passed an arrowed sign showing a smiling trout waving one of its fins, and faded red lettering that said: *Fish Camp—Tackle and Bait*. Hidden by the trees around the bend indicated by the arrow was an old shack, its boards mildewed and rotten. The split sign above the gaping and disused doorway said, in bold letters, *Bait and*. The rest was missing.

Eventually the trees gave out to rolling meadowland that stretched up on either side of the road, beside which wire-free telegraph poles stood in various stages of decay, leaning this way and that like good old boys with maybe one too many beers under their belts. Every now and again he

saw small homesteads nestled in among the greenery, each
sporting its own winding, dusty, single-lane track from the
road. Some of these homes were accompanied by a barn or
other outbuilding, while others featured old, choked-up autos rusting in the sunshine. By the time the rickety buildings
of Main Street came into view down the road ahead, he
had counted twenty-three of them. But not a single person.

He drove into the smells of Forest Plains a little before
midday, with the sun glaring down and the faint breeze
blowing heat and dust and the scent of old wrongs, much
stronger now, drifting through the open window of his car.

FOUR

He pulled his car up to the boardwalk in front of the
general store and slid out into the light. A young Indian
girl sitting on an upturned barrel watched him intently. He
nodded and smiled at her. She returned the nod but not the
smile.

The girl was in her early twenties, hair as black as a
raven's coat and eyes of almost as deep a blue. Her face,
too, was dark and brooding and the dead man noticed the
early signs of a downy brown mustache on her upper lip.
The additional hair suggested an impure lineage. She was
maybe three or four times removed from her tribe. Sioux,
he guessed; probably Lakota.

"Hey there," he said.

"Hey yourself."

He nodded to the screen door behind the girl. "This
where I can get the best breakfast or lunch I ever had?"

The girl's eyes remained on the man's face. "Call it whatever you want," she said, her words soft and couldn't-care-
less. "The food's the same, anyways."

"So I been told."

The girl frowned.

The man thumbed at the road he had just driven. "Fella
about ten miles back, in the filling station."

Her eyes registered her understanding, though she made
no other movement.

The man stood his ground. "You work here?"

"Yes, I do."

"You the cook?"

She screwed up her eyes and shook her black tresses emphatically. "Do I *look* like a cook?"

The dead man chuckled the start of an apology but she cut him off.

"Nossir, I am *not* the cook: that's Mrs. Lozier. Mrs. Fay Lozier. I just do the waitressing."

"But you know what I can have, yeah?"

"Same as you can have every day of the week, every week of the year."

He smiled, hitched up his pants and took a sideways glance along the street. Down the boardwalk a couple of old men sat on uncomfortable-looking wooden chairs, watching him. He nodded to them but they didn't respond; just sat there watching him like a couple of old dogs setting in the shade, watching humanity but not understanding it too well. The dead man turned back to face the girl. "And that is?"

She looked puzzled.

"The food."

"Steak and eggs, as many fries and pancakes as you can eat, and enough coffee to float the fleet." The words were well rehearsed.

"Sounds good."

"We ain't had no complaints." The girl leaned back against the wall, pulling the shade of the shingled roof down around her face so she could get a better look at the stranger.

He was tall, around six-two, and wore a tight-fitting, short-sleeved shirt decorated in a criss-cross pattern of interconnecting parallel lines, and a leather vest, complete with collar and tasseled silver buttons. Down below the shirt was a thick leather belt, worn and faded in parts, sporting an elliptical shield buckle with what looked like a bullet dent in the top right corner. The belt held up a pair of blue jeans with the usual white-faded, soft-looking area just to the left of his zipper. She could clearly see the gentle lump beneath it. On his feet he wore a pair of brown boots, down at the heel and coming away from the sole at the left toe-cap.

"You miss anything?"

She suddenly looked up from the man's feet and met his eyes with her own. He was smiling. No, she realized, his whole *face* was smiling, creasing itself up like a catcher's mitt beneath a thick shock of graying black hair. As she watched, he ran a thick, muscular hand through it to lift it from his forehead. It was brown, that face, and lined: deep brown—like the stones by the side of the railroad tracks—and deep lines, cut and worked into his skin over some . . . what? thirty years? She looked deeper. No, some thirty *thousand* years.

Because that's what it was: not just one man's face but the face of the entire Indian nation. It was a proud face, defiant, brave and trusting. But there was even more to it than that. Sara stared at it, like it was freeze-framed on the television, drinking in every whorl of skin, traveling along every meandering track, pausing at every feature.

Sure, those traits were there, but the negative sides of them were not. Or, at least, she couldn't see them. There was no obduracy, no intransigence, no cruelty, no naiveté. It was strong without being oppressive, fair without being weak. It was . . .

He laughed and shook his head, rubbing his chin. There was only the faintest sign of stubble, running down from each side of his full-lipped mouth like dust.

"Huh?" she said.

"Hey, I know I must look a little road-weary but you're acting like I growed myself a third eye."

The girl rose to her feet and flounced out her skirt, petulance and embarrassment coloring her cheeks like the finest rouge. "You got a name?" she asked, throwing the words over her shoulder as she pulled open the screen door.

The man nodded and smiled. "Yeah, I got a name."

She slouched back and placed her free hand on her hip, still holding the screen door wide. He could see the dim interior of the general store, could see the tables running down alongside the old counter, could hear the rusty whine of electric fans holding the heat at bay. "You wanna tell me what it is?"

The smells sailed out on the fanned breeze. Steak, eggs, potatoes, coffee . . . guilt. And death. Old death. *Wrong* death.

When you tell a man your true name you give him a power over you, the dead man's grandfather had told him. *It was the first thing we did that was wrong.*

He looked away and stared back up the road out of town. The road he had traveled in on.

The road that had brought him back to life.

He looked back at the girl, saw her questioning eyes. "Lazarus," he said at last.

She frowned. "That your first name or your last?"

"That's all of it." He shrugged. "Just Lazarus."

The girl kept on looking at him.

"How about you?"

"Sara," she said, "like the desert." And she walked inside the store.

FIVE

You cannot see a smell. Not really.

But think of how they do those heat detector glasses, the ones that show you where the thermal currents are. Well, if you've got the *nose*—and there are not too many around, not anymore—then you can see the smells, traveling up and down and around . . . coming from everywhere, going to everywhere.

For Lazarus, walking into Barry Lozier's General Store was like stepping into the tomb of some old, Egyptian king. The store itself stretched back and to either side from the door toward a bar that ran the full length across to the right and curved around to the left right in front of him.

In the recessed areas at either side of the door stood a couple of old single-bar display racks from which hung a collection of checkered shirts in a variety of sizes. The colors were different but the design was the same on all of them. Jammed between the castored feet of the racks were some old cardboard boxes, their flaps standing proud. In the boxes, Lazarus could see shorts and vests, ladies' underwear and soft-looking blouses, all enclosed in plastic.

The bar drifted around and ran down the left of the store to a pool table. The felt was ripped and stuck over with Scotch-tape. Four balls were waiting. A cue lay across the table widthways, another stood against it. Leaning against the counter in front of the table was a large man, muscle gone to fat, slow-footed and slow-witted. He carried the look of men who have lost their way and mean to make someone else pay for it. The man, who was in the process of lighting a cigarette—Marlboro (of course!); Lazarus could smell the tobacco—stood with his Zippo lighter lit, poised in the action of leaning into the flame. He was watching Lazarus.

A little way in front of him, sitting at the counter, an old man sat nursing a cup of coffee. He was not watching Lazarus but staring at a calendar thumb-tacked on the wall directly in front of him at the other side of the walkway behind the counter. The old man's mouth moved, fast and silent, twittering like a squirrel's, and he kept on adjusting his shoulder like his coat was slipping off.

Behind the counter right in front was Barry Lozier. Lazarus·knew this because the man wore an apron with the words I'M BARRY LOZIER . . . WHO'RE YOU? boldly imprinted across the large pocket that bulged around his stomach. Barry Lozier was also watching Lazarus.

The girl called Sara walked briskly around the raised flap in the counter and picked up a pad of paper and a pencil. She walked back through the gap and stood beside a recessed table over to the right against the windows. For a second, the dead man couldn't understand why he hadn't been able to see into the store from out on the boardwalk but then he realized that the scene on the windows was some kind of painted mural: a town scene not unlike the real Main Street of Forest Plains, but dated around fifty years earlier. "You gonna sit down or are you gonna stand there all afternoon?"

Lazarus smiled and walked toward her.

He stepped through the smells like an explorer working

his way through the fronds of a million spiders.

Here was a cheap perfume, there some aftershave and over here a waft of muscle-relaxant cream. Everywhere, the tendrils of sweat and dirt hung like rotting curtains. As he shuffled into the booth he caught the fishy smell of the girl's private parts and the unmistakable steely odor of blood. She had her period, he realized suddenly, the thought making his cheeks redden. In the booth in front of him sat a fat man in a checkered shirt—he had his back to Lazarus— and a woman wearing RayBan sunglasses and a couple of inches of face powder.

"What'll it be?"

"I'll have the meal," he said.

"Coffee?"

He frowned and chewed his lip. "Bring me a Coke, Diet."

The girl nodded, turned around without writing anything and walked back behind the counter where she disappeared through a swing door in the wall.

At the far end of the store, further along from where Lazarus was sitting, another man appeared. Right away, Lazarus saw that this man and the one over the pool table were some kind of double act: Fred and Barney . . . Scooby and Shaggy. He smiled. The man caught the smile and slowed up as he approached Lazarus. Lazarus nodded. The man nodded back, frowning, then walked on past toward the pool table.

A minute later, he came back and sat on one of the revolving stools along the front of the counter. His buddy, cigarette finally lit, sat beside him and swung around so he could stare at Lazarus.

"Where you headed?" The voice was higher than it should have been coming out of that body, another reason for the man's disillusionment with life.

Lazarus turned to face the man. "Oh, just traveling," he said. He smiled.

The man's face remained deadly serious. Beside him, his friend slouched on the bar, his back to Lazarus.

"You?" said Lazarus.

The man's friend's back seemed to tense though he appeared not to move.

Peter Crowther

The man lifted his cigarette and took a draw, letting the smoke curl up out of his mouth. "I live here," he said. He said it strangely, Lazarus thought, without any inflection on the word 'live'.

Lazarus nodded. "Looks like a nice town," he said, still nodding.

Behind the counter, Sara appeared out of the swing door. She carried a plate of steaming food and a smaller plate piled high with pancakes. These she set on the counter and then disappeared again.

Lazarus watched as the man with the cigarette lifted a fry from the plate and dropped it into his mouth. "Tastes good," the man said, chewing.

"Wayne!"

The man turned around and lifted his shoulders in a 'who, me?' gesture. "What'd I do?"

"You stole the man's food is what you did," Barry Lozier said in what sounded like an upstate New York accent. "You do it again and I'm gonna have to . . . to ask you to leave."

The man turned back and pulled on his cigarette. "It was just a crummy potato fry," he said to Lazarus.

"Yeah, but it was my crummy potato fry."

The man with his back to Lazarus seemed to twitch.

Wayne glared at him through his cigarette smoke.

Sara appeared again, this time with a tray. On the tray was a can of Diet Coke, a glass, mustard, relishes, catsup, pickles, syrup and a fresh pot of coffee. She walked through the gap in the counter and, setting the tray on Lazarus's table, unloaded everything.

Wayne tapped his friend on the shoulder. "Hey, John,"—he pronounced it *Jarn*—"know the difference between a squaw and a icebox?"

Jarn did not respond.

Wayne smiled, glancing across at Sara's back and registering Lazarus's eyes. "A icebox don't fart when you take your meat out of it." Wayne's wheezy laugh sounded like a busted fan, high-pitched and grating.

Lazarus glanced at Sara. She was ignoring the men. Lazarus decided he would, too. For now.

"Don't talk dirty, Wayne," his friend said. "There's no need to talk dirty." The man had not turned his head, he just kept on looking across the bar.

Wayne pulled a face and shrugged. "Only havin' a little fun is all."

"Yeah, well," John said and let it rest.

Sara turned around and picked up the plates and carried them to the table, set them down in front of Lazarus, and then stepped back, waiting for his reaction.

Lazarus leaned into the rising steam from the food. "Mmm-mmm, but that smells *good*."

"Like I say, ain't had no complaints," she said, lifting a strand of black hair off her forehead.

He held his head over the food, closed his eyes and breathed it all in. *All* of it. "Know what it smells like to me?" he said.

"Like steak?"

Lazarus nodded. "What else?"

The girl giggled, looked around at Wayne and John—the icebox crack forgotten—and frowned. "Eggs?" she said at last.

"Yes, eggs," Lazarus said. "Other things, too."

"What other things?" Wayne said.

Lazarus breathed in the food.

SIX

He breathed in Barry Lozier's General Store.

Sucked in Main Street, sucked it dry.

Drank in Forest Plains.

At first, it made him dizzy. It was like swimming in the torrent of a raging river, the water taking his head and ducking it down into the depths every few seconds. He couldn't breathe. It washed over him, buffeted him, shook him until he thought he couldn't take any more.

The girl whose name was like the desert watched the man. He was having some kind of a fit. She'd heard about this kind of thing before, read about it in *The Enquirer*. He looked like he was going to upchuck right over his dinner.

She stepped back against Wayne's legs and watched.

And Wayne watched,

And, next to Wayne, John watched.

And, from the other side of the counter, Barry Lozier watched.

In the adjoining booth, Bill McCandless grabbed hold of his wife Irene's arm and started to shuffle along the seat toward the aisle, pulling her with him.

Along the counter, the old man kept on staring at the calendar. A Vargas drawing of a girl in greeny-yellow dress stared back at him, pouting.

Lazarus felt sick. And hot. And cold.

The words of Chief Seattle of the Suqwamish and Duwamish rolled around his head, like a roulette ball traveling in a steadily decreasing circle as it lost its momentum. *All things are connected. Whatever befalls the earth befalls the children of the earth.*

"What the hell is *wrong* with him?" Wayne whispered.

Nobody answered.

Lazarus no longer heard the words around him.

As he opened himself fully to his gift, all extraneous noise stopped to be replaced by the sounds of the smells.

He heard the rush of the water in the river, and the keening cry of the eagles as they circled the peaks like feathered necklaces.

He heard the groan of the wagon wheels crushing the earth, and the sibilant sigh of the locomotive as it thundered along the singing rails.

He heard . . . many things. And each of the smell-sounds brought with it its own pain, a pain of change and of loss.

Gift! The word held a hollow ring for Lazarus. It was the only thing that he had ever possessed that he would trade without the slightest second thought.

But now, as always, he shed the last vestiges of reluctance, the final veil of refusal. As ever, exhilaration, a blur of spinning colors and sounds like old photographs on which the images started to talk and move as you held them in your hand.

He embraced them then, these pasts locked in the tiny

myriad spicules of scent and taste and aroma. And they ran to him like children to their father.

Pawnee. He smelled Pawnee, saw in his mind's eye the gently-graded terraces overlooking the river, smelled the sod and timber lodges. Their smell was strong, though there were also traces of Cheyenne and Arapaho, Comanche, Kiowa and Lakota. The Lakota smell was also strong.

He smelled the campfires and the stories told around them. He smelled the expressions on the children's faces as they sat, cross-legged, their faces aglow as much with wonder as with the reflected heat of the fire.

He smelled the old tales, breathed in the brittle but strong construction of their words, scented the syntax: tales of *Maka*, the earth, and of *Maka-akan*, his spirit; tales of *Hanwi*, friend of the Lakota, whose smiling face lights the *hanhepi* ... keeps *Gnaski* at bay; tales of *Ibom*, whose swirling winds destroyed many villages; and of *nagila*, the inner flame which, together with *nagi, niya* and *sicun*, binds the soul to the body.

Suddenly he was falling.

He could feel the heat from the fire, hear its crackle.

He could hear the rustle of the teepees and the swish of the horses ...

He pulled back sharply and raised his hands high.

"Taku Skanskan!" he shouted. "Lift me!"

Inside the store, the air was thick and cold. Nobody spoke, only watched.

Lazarus thumped his hands onto the table, rattling the plate of food. Then he was still again.

He was spinning upward, leaving the fires and the buffalo and the endless plains far behind him. But he was not traveling geographically, he was traveling temporally, the years spinning alongside him like windblown dust, traveling toward Forest Plains and Barry Lozier's General Store, all of which were as yet simply great trees still to be felled.

He smelled the tanners and the buffalo hides.

He smelled the wooden sleepers of the railroad.

Then he smelled Texas Longhorns and splenic fever.

He smelled floods and cholera.

Then he smelled the sweat, a lot of sweat . . . the birth of Forest Plains.

The smell of the automobile.

Civilization.

He smelled a hundred thousand people, their individual essences drifting on the time-winds like seeds. Men and women, boys and girls. He smelled their laughter and their tears, picked out their efforts with his nose, revelling in their triumphs and wallowing with them in their despairs.

He was getting closer. He could sense it.

They watched him, this strange Indian man. They saw the sweat on his brow, saw the black hair paste down against his skull, watched his eyes dart around their sockets beneath his closed lids.

Then he smelled the scent of death. There was a lot of death, but one death came through strongest.

It was a woman! Lazarus laughed a mighty laugh and thumped the table again. "The dead woman's here!"

Dreams.

Can you smell a dream? Lazarus could. It smelled like sarsaparilla, fizzy bubbles drifting up the passages of his nose.

It was a dream of escape, this dream among the many. Of getting out. This dream had a secondary smell, a scent of aspiration. It was a dream of the Big City, its towering spires and endless avenues stretching upward and outward. The images came first from picture books and then from books without any pictures. Some of the words he smelled in the woman's mind he recognized. They were names.

Whitman. Melville. Sandburg. Dickinson. Frost.

He smelled/heard her say the words, intoning them like secret karmic pledges, aural runes.

Then: more sweat.

Lazarus gagged, brought bile up into his mouth and swallowed. It tasted like battery acid.

He smelled the woman giving herself.

He smelled money.

He smelled—

"No!" He leapt to his feet, turning the table over and spilling his plate across the floor.

For what seemed like a long time, Wayne, John, Sara, Bill McCandless and his wife, Irene, plus Barry Lozier—even the old timer who had been talking to the breeze and watching a girlie calendar for a sign of movement—watched the food splatter across the floor. Nobody said a word, and it fell to the proprietor to break the spell.

"Jesus Christ almighty!" Barry Lozier shouted as he ran out from behind the counter.

Wayne backed away between the stools. "What's the matter with him? He havin' a fit?"

"You okay, mister?" Sara asked softly, resting her hand on Lazarus's outstretched arm.

He opened his eyes and nodded. "I've found her," he said.

SEVEN

His name was not Lazarus.

Nor was he a dead man.

But, in many respects, both were appropriate, though each was a paradox of the other.

For him, the country itself was a lifeless version of all earlier condition. It was not a condition which he had personally experienced but rather one which he had come across during many trips along the olfactory highways, which, to him, were as natural as the road he had ridden just hours before in his dying Dodge.

But these were highways without hard shoulders or white lines, bizarre blacktops in the ether which stretched far forward and long back, lacking directional signs or mile counters, bereft of warnings and advice. On these roads, one element was the same as any other—rain, snow, wind, sun—and nothing froze his bones, blew his hair, dampened his clothes or roasted his skin. All there was was the smell.

And the memories.

They had trooped out of Barry Lozier's General Store like an old-fashioned wagon train. The man the others knew only as Lazarus led the way, his hands stretched out to either side like aircraft wings which held some secret power of divination.

Nobody spoke.

Behind Lazarus, the girl with the heart of the desert stepped lightly but with a surety that she had never felt before.

Behind her came the two men, Wayne and John, the one bearing an expression of reluctant obeisance mixed with fierce skepticism; the other carrying on his face a flaunted and troubled frown.

Then came the McCandlesses, a double act, pomp and circumstance, two figures lovingly fashioned from Play-Doh, pudgy arms linked in something resembling an embrace, each of their small, fat faces lost in secret concerns.

Barry Lozier held open the screen door of his general store to allow the old man room to move through onto the street, while throwing his apron back into the store and shouting to his wife—the hidden cook of the greatest dinner or breakfast in the world—that he would be back later; that he didn't know how long he was going to be; and that she should close up for the afternoon. Once on the street, Barry slapped the old guy gently on the shoulder and jogged past to fall in beside Wayne and John.

The old man, now the octogenarian backmarker and resembling for all the world a bandage-less Kharis from the old *Mummy* movies, set each shaky foot onto the ground with an almost profound deliberation while balancing his tortuous gait with his spindly arms.

All around them, the wind blew along the street.

The smells came with it.

EIGHT

He had his eyes closed for he did not need the power of sight.

He knew the street was now deserted. The wind drove dust into his face, stinging his cheeks, but still he walked on.

The woman's thread was held tight but still he had to

concentrate. All around drifted the old aromas: sweet grasses smoked in pipes; coils of basswood bark steeping in drums of water; willow, oak and slippery elm; chokecherry stones and thornapples; dried squash and pumpkin seasoned with maple sugar. All the traces of an old Lakota village, long gone and buried beneath the dust of Main Street, Forest Plains. And something else. A woman.

He reached the end of the street and stopped, opening his eyes. Behind him, above the soughing howl of the early afternoon wind, the footsteps stopped.

Lazarus looked around where he was standing.

To the right stood a row of buildings—the doctor's office, Bill and Irene McCandless's house, and a window displaying bridles and saddles. Standing in the doorway beside the window, a tall man stood watching, rubbing his eyes.

To the left of Lazarus, a row of wooden fencing ran to the end of the street. It was to the fencing that Lazarus turned. "A shovel," he said. "I need a shovel."

Barry Lozier looked questioningly at Wayne and John, then ran across to the man standing in the doorway. As he reached the man, Barry was surprised to see he was crying.

"My mom . . ." the man said, the tears rolling down his cheeks.

"Max, what's wrong?"

"I can smell my mom, Barry. Breck shampoo. She always used Breck shampoo . . ." His eyes had a glassy sheen, staring over Barry Lozier's shoulders to the street beyond. But they were looking—or seeing—further than a few yards.

"Max—"

"She used to wash her hair four, maybe five times a week. Like Mary Martin in the ads in *The Post* . . . You know, Mary Martin from *South Pacific*?"

"I know, Max," Barry started to say, but the other man was not listening.

"She's out there."

Barry took hold of the man's arm as he started to move past him. "Max, your mom's dead." Max Saalfield turned to look at him. "She's been dead a long time, Max," Barry went on.

"But . . . I can *smell* her, Barry."

Barry Lozier turned to the street and, against his better judgment, breathed in.

At first it was just a smell of metal, like old tin cans or auto parts. And then, like a mist, it cleared.

"Jesus Christ," Barry whispered.

He smelled his old lead soldiers and the two-piece Ralston Purina truck his mother bought him from Dalton's Toystore in KC, way back in 1950. Then he smelled the sugar scent of Hunt's Catsup. "Tommy?" Barry Lozier said to the wind.

Tommy Lozier, who had delighted in covering every meal placed before him with thick oodles of catsup, had drowned in Darien Lake in 1974. Ten years old.

"Tommy?" he asked again, though his head asked a different question: his head asked what the hell he was doing, standing beside Max Saalfield in the afternoon street, the wind blowing all around him, the pair of them calling up the dead. But then, it wasn't him or Max who was doing the calling up. It was the Indian.

Barry looked across the street and watched Lazarus. He was kneeling down beside the fence, pulling boards apart and lifting the stones from the exposed vacant lot that used to house Dan Morton's Auto Emporium. He recognized, now, the smell of Dan's onetime "Special Buy," a deep red 1957 Chrysler Imperial hardtop that he would have given his right arm to buy. He could almost taste the wine-and-white vinyl interior and the wine-red carpeting in the trunk.

He watched Lazarus start to scrape the dirt away with his hands.

"We need a shovel, Max," Barry said.

NINE

It took just a little over an hour to expose the body.

TEN

"Her name was Julia."

Lazarus stood back from the hole he had dug by the side

of the fence and listened to the man called John.

"She and I were going together," John went on, speaking dreamily. "We made all kinds of plans for leaving, leaving Forest Plains and heading off to the city." He stopped and stared down into the hole. "Then, one day, she just upped and left. Didn't leave no note, no forwarding address, no nothing."

Except for the checkered blue dress and the thick thatch of black hair around her wizened, grinning skull, there was little to suggest the sex of the body. It lay just a few feet below the surface, curled up like it was asleep.

"Took all her clothes, too," John went on, pointing to the crumpled mess of clothing that the Indian had pulled out on the way down to the body.

Sara moved forward and looked down. She grimaced and pulled back quickly. "When was this?"

"Fourteen years ago," John said, maintaining his matter-of-fact tone. "Used to be there was a lot of trucks went by on the spur to the Interstate. I figured she'd just gone and left me for the city."

Lazarus knelt by the hole and reached down, taking hold of the frail hand crusted with dirt. He breathed in.

Hopes.

Hopes and dreams.

He smelled a determination to get out of the town . . . to take her man and ride the dusty blacktop to somewhere where there was no flatness. Because, the smell told him, there is no mystery to flatness. Only certainty. A certainty that nothing's coming. Nothing's going to change.

He pulled in a little deeper.

Sperm.

He smelled semen, more than one blood type.

As if one cue, John started to speak again. "She said she was only doing it for me."

"Doing what?" Sara asked the question softly.

"She . . ."

"She was a hooker," Wayne said. "I'm sorry, John."

John appeared to take no offense. "She said she was doing it so's we could get ourselves a little extra money. Looks like she pulled one trick too many . . ."

As John continued to speak, Lazarus brushed the dirt away from the woman's stomach and exposed the slit in her dress. It was a long gash that stretched all the way across from her stomach to her right side, the side she was lying on.

"It's strange, you know?" John went on. "I want to feel sad . . . to cry or somethin'. But, in a way, I feel kind of relieved. I mean—"

Lazarus lifted her right hand up and pulled it free of her body. It was clenched tight.

"—she didn't leave me—"

It was holding something.

"—after all."

He pulled the fingers apart, cringing at the dusty *crack* as they snapped and separated open.

"What is it?" Sara said.

"You find something?" said Barry Lozier.

"Bill—" Irene McCandless hissed.

Bill McCandless breathed in loudly. "Oh my—"

Lazarus turned the object over in the palm of his hand. It was metal. A string tie clasp. He dusted it and turned it around so that he could read what was written on it.

"Bill. *Bill!*" Wayne gasped.

Bill McCandless started forward. "That's my—" He stopped.

The clasp featured a name scrolled in lariat. *Bill.*

"You killed her?" The words were colder than an arctic wind, and the face that said them—John's face—looked whiter than snow.

Everything else happened fast.

Bill McCandless stood transfixed, shaking his head. "I nev—"

John leapt across and grabbed the older man by his neck, pushing him to the ground.

Irene McCandless threw her RayBan glasses to the ground and tried to pull her husband's assailant back but it was no use.

"John, I nev—" The punch landed in his mouth and split his upper denture. Almost immediately, a second punch broke his nose.

Barry Lozier threw himself across the two men and wrapped his arms around John.

Irene McCandless shuffled across on her knees to hold her husband's head. He wasn't moving. "Bill! Bill?" She shook his shoulders.

Behind her, John worked his way free of Barry Lozier and reached across for the shovel.

"*Bill!*" Irene shouted.

John lifted the shovel.

Lazarus watched.

"John, for crissakes . . ." Wayne snapped.

"*He* didn't kill her!" Irene McCandless screamed. "*I* did."

Lazarus caught the shovel.

The wind whispered, pulled back and regrouped.

ELEVEN

The woman sat on the ground, cradling her husband's head on her lap, rocking gently to and fro.

"I knew he'd been seeing her," she started. "Any woman knows when her man's cheating on her. But I didn't have no evidence." She straightened his hair. "Somehow, that made it okay, you know?" She looked around at the faces for confirmation and for sympathy. She didn't find any.

"Then, this one night, he came home and went to bed," she went on. "Bill sleeps like a bear in hibernation. When he closes his eyes, there's nothing gonna wake him up.

"Anyways, I went over to his clothes and checked them over—you know, for lipstick, rouge . . . that kind of thing?"

She had addressed this last question to Sara. Sara nodded and looked away.

"Well, I couldn't find anything.

"So, I was going back over to the bed and I caught sight of his tie-clasp—it'd fallen on the floor over by the dresser. I bent over to pick it up . . . and I smelled it." She nodded to the body. "*Her.* I could smell that scent she used to wear, could smell it all over my husband's tie-clasp."

"Jesus," Wayne said.

"*Jesus* is right," Irene agreed. She shrugged and shook her head. "What can I tell you? I went mad, I guess. I went right over and confronted her with the clasp. She took it from me, held it in front of me. Then she told me it didn't mean nothing." She looked at the other faces again. "I couldn't take that. Not from her. '*It doesn't mean nothing,*' she says to me."

"It was then I realized I'd taken the knife."

Bill McCandless started to move. He groaned but didn't open his eyes.

"Shhh," his wife whispered, stroking his forehead. She sighed and continued her story.

"Anyways, when it was done, I carried her down to this lot, dug the hole and rolled her in. Then I went back and took all her clothes, threw them in after her." She shook her head again and turned around, a half-smile tugging at her mouth. "It's surprising what you can do when you have a min—"

If anything, the hole appeared above Irene McCandless's left eye a split second before the sound of the gun. She was dead before she fell back against the ground, her husband's head still resting on her lap.

TWELVE

His name was Joe, Joe Yenne.

His wife had died giving birth to their daughter, an only child who lived four hours before deciding she'd rather stay with her mother.

The years following Maggie Yenne's death had been empty years, lacking both motivation and companionship.

Then the girl had come to Forest Plains.

Her name was Julia, and she used to treat Joe Yenne like he was somebody. She would talk to him when she served him coffee, telling him about what it was like in the Big City . . . even though, as she freely admitted, she had never been. And she would quote things to him, lines of poetry, words that spoke about Big Cities everywhere.

She quoted from Robert Frost and Ezra Pound.
She quoted from Emily Dickinson and T.S. Eliot.
From Carl Sandburg and Hart Crane.

Then they would laugh together, sharing secrets that only those people completely comfortable with each other could truly share. And the only thing that came between them was forty years, give or take a few months.

He told her he liked words, never having been much of a reader himself. And he made her a proposition.

He knew all about her dream to fly away to the Big City.

He knew all about John, too. He'd seen the way they looked at each other in Barry Lozier's General Store.

So he told her he would pay to have her read to him, read him poetry.

At first she had laughed. But he was serious, he told her.

Then she had laughed again, she read him *Oklahoma* by Ernest Hemingway. She chose that poem, she told him, because it summed up everything she wanted to escape from:

The prairies are long,
The moon rises
Ponies
Drag at their pickets.
The grass has gone brown in the summer—
(or is it the hay crop failing)

He had read and reread the poem from the book she had loaned him, committing that stanza to memory.

And sometime later, months later, she had revisited the poem with him following an unpleasant incident with a truck driver. Barry Lozier had thrown him out—even before the fella had had a chance to pay for his meal—but not before he'd made a few cracks, mean cracks.

Oh, the fella hadn't meant anything by them, but they'd hurt Julia just the same.

"Know what the difference is between a squaw and a proctologist?" the man had asked her. *"A proctologist only has to look at one asshole at a time!"*

And:

"What does a waitress say after sex? 'Gee, are all you fellas on the same team?'!"

She had told him the Indian's day in this country was

365

finished and that Hemingway had prophesied it in *Oklahoma*.

All of the Indians are dead
(a good Indian is a dead Indian)

"That's us, Joe," she had said to him, her eyes glistening. "Dead people . . . dead men, dead women."

When he told this part of the story to others, standing around her grave, a single tear popped from each of his eyes and ran down to the sides of his chin. He made no effort to stop them.

And then, one day, she didn't show up for work.

The next day was the same.

And the next.

And Joe Yenne was alone once more. With nothing to hold his interest during the long wait except Vargas girls on Barry Lozier's calendar.

THIRTEEN

Lazarus was the first to speak.

"Put the gun away," he said. "Take it home, and put it away."

"Hey, now wait a min—"

Lazarus turned to Barry Lozier and shook his head.

"Shhh," he said. He turned back to the old man. "Joe Yenne, I have something for you."

The old man nodded.

"It is a gift. The gift of knowledge."

He nodded again.

"But like all knowledge," Lazarus said, "its strength lies in its secrecy. Knowledge shared is power weakened. It is a mistake my people began to make and then saw their mistake. Better to die strong than to live weak. Do you understand?"

Another nod.

"Listen then." Lazarus leaned forward and whispered into the old man's ear.

This close to him, Lazarus could smell the old man's pancreatic cancer stronger than ever.

It shifted and growled like the mountain cat.

Turned and hissed like the cyclone.

He finished speaking and stepped back. He said, "Do you understand?"

Joe Yenne smiled. "Yes, I understand."

"Then you must go."

The old man turned around, the gun still hanging limply from his hand, and walked back the way they had come.

"We'll have to tell the sheriff," Barry Lozier said.

"Of course," said Lazarus.

Barry turned to look at the other man, surprised. "They'll go out to get him."

"Mm hmmm," he said. "But he won't be there."

"Where'll he go? He's just an old man."

"Oh, he's not too old for the kind of traveling *he* must do . . . and he's going too far for you to follow," came the answer. "For some time, at least."

FOURTEEN

"What did you say to him?" Sara asked as they watched John and Wayne carry Irene McCandless's body along the street.

Lazarus cocked his head on one side and frowned.

"Okay, okay, I know—mind my own business." She smiled and shrugged. "Will *he*—" she nodded to Bill McCandless, who was sitting against the fence staring along Main Street to the flatlands beyond, the opposite direction to that now being traveled by his late wife "—be okay?"

"He'll be as okay as he will ever be," Lazarus answered, "or as he has ever been."

It wasn't the kind of answer she wanted, but she knew it was the only one she was going to get.

Lazarus walked across to the hole, knelt beside it and reached down.

"What are you doing now?" Barry Lozier asked, the sound of his exasperation sounding clearly in his voice.

"I'm turning her around," Lazarus said.

"Turning her *around*?"

367

*"In spite of all the learned have said,
I still my opinion keep;
The posture, that we give the dead,
Points out the soul's eternal sleep."*

He turned around and looked up at the girl and the man standing watching him.

"A poem: it figures," Barry Lozier said, and walked off to get the shovel.

As Lazarus got to his feet and dusted off his hands Sara said, "I ain't never read much poetry. Is it . . . is it all like that? Pretty, I mean."

"Some of it is, some isn't. It's like everything else, means different things to different people. Like the desert," he added, smiling at her.

Sara returned the smile and glanced away. When she looked back, Lazarus had turned around and was starting to walk back along the street to where a dusty Dodge sat beside an empty general store. "Was it yours?" she called after him. "The poem?"

He turned back and shook his head. "No. It is called *The Indian Burying Ground*, by Philip Freneau."

Sara nodded. "*The Indian Burying Ground*. I guess she'd like that."

He twirled his car keys around on his finger, threw his head back and breathed in through his nose. Behind him, Barry Lozier was shovelling dirt back into the hole. When Lazarus lowered his head again, he was smiling. "She does," he said.

Sara watched him all the way back to his car, then watched the car as it, too, disappeared. Then all that was left was the magic light of late afternoon, the faint, tinkling echo of the dead man's car keys and the sweet smell of resolution.

Dedications

To Ray Bradbury who, with *Something Wicked This Way Comes*, spoke volumes about the importance and the wonder of father-and-son relationships; to Percival Crowther (1913–1972) who, in our relatively short time together, proved it was all true; and to Oliver and Timothy, with whom I have taken the circle around one more time.

And to all the people—be they editors, publishers or readers—who continue to show an interest in my work. Long may it continue.

BEDBUGS
RICK HAUTALA

From the subway tunnels of Boston to the rain-swept streets of Quebec City to the deepest snow-filled forests of Hilton, Maine, no one in these chilling stories by horror master Rick Hautala is safe from the darkness or the dangers that lurk in the shadows. Waiting for us. Reaching for us . . .

Over the years, Rick Hautala has terrified and captivated millions of readers around the world. *Bedbugs* is a career-spanning collection of stories that whisks you away on a guided tour of the darkest reaches of the human mind and soul.

T. M. WRIGHT
LAUGHING MAN

In their own way, the dead tell Jack Erthmun so much. Jack is a New York City police detective with his own very peculiar ways of solving homicides, and those ways are beginning to frighten his colleagues. He gets results, but at what cost? This may be Jack's last case. He's assigned to a series of unspeakable killings, gruesome murders with details that make even seasoned detectives queasy. But as he goes deeper into the facts of the case, facts that make it seem no human killer can be involved, Jack begins to get more and more erratic. Is it the case that's affecting Jack? Or is it something else, something no one even dares to consider?

----

the Maudan, the Arikara and the Blackfoot. And many more besides.

He smelled buffalo hides, skins of beaver, muskrat and lynx, some fox, a little weasel and mink.

He smelled teepee smoke and rat shit.

And then he smelled something else. It hung on the wind like a trapped ribbon, swirling and dropping, but always returning to the same point. He closed his eyes and sniffed some more, short sniffs, concentrating on the unfamiliar scent. Then he recognized it. It was death. Old death. *Wrong* death. It was death with pain, sudden and brutal. The smell made the dead man gag and he put his hand to his face.

Behind him, the old man replaced the gas nozzle and set to cleaning the windshield with a piece of gingham cloth, which he pulled out of his pants pocket. The cloth was filthy with grime and dust. The Cree Chief Piapot once said: *The white man who is our agent is so stingy that he carries a linen rag in his pocket into which to blow his nose, for fear he might blow away something of value.* The dead man smiled and stared at the rag. Maybe there had even been a time when that piece of cloth had been just a part of a larger garment.

He concentrated, just for his own amusement.

It had been a long time for that piece of cloth, and a lot of windshields and spilled gasoline, but it was there, buried beneath the grease and snot: the faint waft of young legs, feminine legs, the gentle, teasing odor of dawn-hair and pheromones.

He smiled to himself, pushing the smells back, away from him. "Breakfast," he said at last, the word springing out into the heat as though it had a life of its own.

"Huh?"

The dead man rubbed his stomach. "I smell breakfast. Know where I can chow down around here?"

The old man stepped back from the car, rubbed a grizzled beard that was more bush grass than meadow, and jammed the cloth into his pocket. The dead man saw a flash of colored stripes through the old man's fly as it gaped open and then closed back up. And he caught the stench of urine

He rubbed his hands along his back, stretched and faced into the gentle breeze, sniffing. Alongside his head, flies and an occasional wasp buzzed by. Behind him, a screen door whined and then clanked twice. The sound of slurring feet approaching his back made him turn.

"Premium?" The old man reached for the nozzle without waiting for an answer and thrust it into the side of the Dodge. He had already started to squeeze the trigger.

"Premium'll do just fine." He turned back to face the wind and breathed in again, recalling the words of Chief Luther Standing Bear, passed down through the generations. *The world was a library and its books were the stones, leaves, grass, brooks, and the birds and animals that shared, alike with us, the storms and blessings of the earth.*

"Smell anything?" The old man stooped over the Dodge, dutifully wiping spilled gasoline from a rusting fender as the traces of his words hung in the air like the wind on a wire fence. He was watching the dead man, watery eyes squinting into the sun.

The dead man breathed deep, pulling the air into his lungs.

Smell anything . . .

He smelled cheap supermarket fats, and frying eggs, steaks and sausages.

He smelled pancakes, syrups and coffee, some of it freshly made, some of it old now—old in coffee terms—and losing its life warmth.

He smelled cigarettes—he identified eleven brands before giving up the game—and cologne, a handful of cheap perfumes and the faintest hint of prophylactic lubrication.

He smelled the fresh water of the Missouri River.

He smelled dirt and chemicals.

And, most of all, he smelled the past.

The old man's question swooped and dived amidst the gentle, regular *ting* of the gas pump as it fed the old Dodge. It ached to be answered and released. The dead man breathed deep again, filtering odors through the cloying smell of gasoline, and pulled in the prairie.

He smelled the Assiniboin and the Cree, the Massika and

339

Forest Plains

All of the Indians are dead
(a good Indian is a dead Indian)
Or riding in motor cars
—Ernest Hemingway
(from *Oklahoma*)

"What then is the American,
this new man?"
—Crevecoeur

ONE

The dead man drove his car through the ghosts of his people.

He saw their spirits hovering over the blacktop like heat shimmer or the tail-ends of the morning haze that runs across the meadow in early summer, when the sun is still drying out the winter earth. When he got out of his car at a Mobil gas station twenty-three miles north of Kansas City, he could even smell them.

The man looked disappointed at first but then he shrugged and smiled, tossing his hat onto the chair alongside the door. "Ah well, not to worry," he said. "We can proceed without them."

Wilhemina took another step back and tried to speak. It was still no use.

"I see you're interested in why I'm here," the man said as he bent down to rummage through the things he had brought. He picked the saw and the tire-iron and stood up again.

"They say that inside every fat person there's a thin person trying to get out," he said. "Let's see if that's true."

And the two of them set to playing.

paneling to hear if the guy was still out there but she didn't hear anything. "You still there?"

"Still here," the voice confirmed. "Destiny never goes away," it added.

"Whatcha want anyways? This some kinda sellin' stunt? Cos I can tell you—"

"No kind of selling stunt at all," the voice said. Then, after a pause, it said, "This is the real thing."

"Oh, hell," Wilhemina muttered as she shifted the deadbolt and turned the latch. She took hold of the door handle and gave it a good tug, seeing as how last fall's rains and the lengthy winter had warped the wood right in the frame. And as it opened wide, she gave a small gasp.

There on the stoop was a fine-looking young man, a big smile beaming on his face and his hat held in one hand. "And it's a fine good morning to you," he said. "Might I come in for a while?"

Wilhemina tried to speak but suddenly found that her voice had snuck off and hidden somewhere deep in the myriad folds of her ample bosom. She wanted to ask him who he was and what he wanted. She wanted to ask if she knew him—though she knew that she didn't—or who had sent him. More than anything, though, she wanted to know why a fella dressed so mighty fine was carrying a whole load of old tools, all rusted and broken, so's they made a mess of his good suit. But somehow, she didn't really want to know the answer to that one until it became absolutely necessary.

Wilhemina Sherbourg took a faltering step back into the hovel of her life while the young man answered that move with a couple of steps forward.

He kicked the door closed and breathed in deeply the collective aroma of sweat and dirt and old food. "My," he said, "now that smells good!"

He lay the tools down on the floor and turned, dropping the latchlock and shifting the deadbolt back into place. "Tell me," he said as he turned back to face her, "do you have any young ones—you know, children?—around the place?"

Wilhemina shook her head and suddenly felt like she needed to pee.

But while the new season drifted past, heading on for the hills and the valleys, the plains and the fields, the tiny Main Streets and the mighty Interstates, something it had brought with it, like a seed on the breeze, slowed down and finally stopped at the paint-peeled door, sniffing, relishing the aromas that wafted through the gaps in the door, the grain in the woodwork and even the walls themselves.

Why this door and not another was not certain. More than that: it was not *known*. The truth of the matter was that there was no plan to such an event, no schedule to follow, no criteria to achieve, no standards to maintain, and no accounts to be settled. An entirely random visit.

Inside, a knock sounded at Wilhemina's door . . . gently insistent but somehow lazy, too. Kind of relaxed but inevitable, like the person knocking was in no hurry but, equally, was not going to go away. No way.

Wilhemina shouted, "Who is it?", half not caring and half not expecting any answer.

"It's your destiny!" a voice announced, a voice that sounded for all the world like one of those guys on the TV quiz shows, all toothpaste and toupee, set to offer her her wildest dreams and make everything she had ever dreamed about come suddenly wonderfully true.

Wilhemina could hear, from somewhere off in the distance, that damned dog creating a stink about something. Mutt sounded like it had its dick caught in a gate, making all that noise.

"I don't have no destiny," Wilhemina called, petulantly and sad, half lifting her head from her pillow, a once-white cotton affair marked with a hundred nights of dribbled saliva and lost hope.

"Oh but you *do*," the voice said, gently correcting her. "*Everyone* has a destiny," it said.

Wilhemina said, "Shit!", and rolled over across the bed to allow her gargantuan legs to spill off the mattress in wobbling folds of jello flesh, slightly grainy with yesterday's and the day before's dirt and smelling like old meat, sweet and dangerous.

She pulled on an old robe, tied the cord tight around her belly, and shuffled to the door. She leaned against the wood